W9-BYC-472

The Führer Seed

Other Works by Gus Weill

Novels

Paradiddle

A Woman's Eyes

The Bonnet Man

Biography

You Are My Sunshine

Plays

To Bury a Cousin

Geese

The November People

The Führer Seed

A Novel by Gus Weill

William Morrow and Company, Inc.
New York 1979

Library of Congress Cataloging in Publication Data

Weill, Gus.
The Führer seed.

I. Title.
PZ4.W42224Fu [PS3573.E388] 813'.5'4 79-385
ISBN 0-688-03452-7

BOOK DESIGN LESLEY ACHITOFF

Printed in the United States of America.

First Edition

1 2 3 4 5 6 7 8 9 10

This book is dedicated to Renni Browne.
Of course there is no way to really say thank you.

The last words anyone heard Adolf Hitler utter were to his valet, Heinz Linge. Hitler said:

"You must live for the sake of my successor."

Aftermath, by
Ladislas Farago

Part One

1

In his quarters in the Mishmar Elijah Kibbutz, off the road the Israelis called the Road of Courage, midway between Tel Aviv and Jerusalem, a man lay caught in the dream that always preceded his waking up.

There was the circus music, the tin horns and silly trumpets, coughing drum rolls, tremolos, clarinets, and then: the faces of clowns.

Red scars on white carmine, great black exclamation marks above and beneath the eyes, bulbous noses, cheeks like open wounds. Clowns, fleeing before the circus music.

And laughter. Where from? Not the clowns. The clowns had fled.

The man lay there smelling his own sweat, letting the dream subside, forcing his breathing to normalcy.

Outside he heard the sounds of farm machinery being started up and, farther off, a cow mooing.

He sat up and swung his legs over the side of his narrow bed. One foot touched the unopened suitcase that he had put down in the darkness only hours before. His clothes lay in a heap nearby.

He walked into the bathroom, where his eyes sought the small blue bar of soap lying on the washbasin. He swallowed rapidly, air gushing from his nostrils.

He saw himself in the mirror and thought nothing of the half smile that seemed imprinted on his face. The smile might have been a reaction to a minor pleasantry, a father looking down at a sleeping child, a beggar asking some small indulgence. He wore the smile like a birthmark.

The man, in his early forties, stood six feet tall, his body that of a laborer, his once-blond hair now a sandy color, burnt from the sun. There were old, faint scars on his cheeks, and his eyes were innocent and blue.

He relieved himself, then brushed his teeth with a battered yellow toothbrush. Next to it in a glass was a red one, new and unused. His eyes darted back to the blue bar of soap and blinked as though suddenly exposed to bright light.

He stepped into the shower, let the icy water pour over him, toweled himself dry. In the mirror he saw the deep scratches on his shoulders and the thumbmarks beneath his collarbone, already blue. The hands of Mahmoud Selah had fought desperately for their owner's life. He applied Mercurochrome to the scratches and left the bathroom.

He pulled a heavy wool shirt over his head and slipped into ancient corduroy trousers black at the knees from kneeling in the soil. Then he put on his socks and boots and, finally, a dark-blue jacket.

At 7 A.M. he joined the other ninety members of Mishmar Elijah Kibbutz in the dining hall, where he picked up a tray on which he put small portions of cheese and fruit. He carried it to an unoccupied Formica-topped table.

On the way he was greeted with nods and pleasantries—"Welcome home"—and no one seemed disturbed at his lack of response except for Yair Hacham, the bad little boy of the kibbutz, who stuck out his tongue before his ever-vigilant mother could box one of his big ears.

When the man carried his tray back to the counter he was joined by a friend, his only friend. It was Shemuel Reiter, secretary of the kibbutz, who had convinced the others to accept Max Levy for the one-year trial period.

It had taken but three months for the other kibbutzniks to acknowledge that Max was the hardest worker in Mishmar Elijah. His occasional absences went unquestioned—except by Yair Hacham, who was warned by the secretary, "If you ask that question again, you, your mother, your father and your sister Irma will be tied up and dropped by parachute at night into Damascus to be chopped up and stuffed into grape leaves!"

Max Levy crossed the graveled road and walked the half mile to the vineyards, where he would be the last to leave.

In West Berlin's exclusive Grünewald section the chestnut

and birch trees along Bismarckallee were bare. Beneath them, a chilling March wind tossed the drifting snow.

In the top-floor apartment once occupied by a cigarette manufacturer, a man awakened to Pavarotti singing "E lucevan le stelle"—and to Lise Straub's pink tongue making wet circles on his nipples.

He lay there letting the two sensations warm him inside, trying to push aside thoughts of the miserable day outside his window and the furious round of activities that would keep him out in that weather.

"Lise, for God's sake, stop. If I don't get at it the entire defeat will be blamed on me." She paid him no attention; her tongue was now traveling down his belly. He gripped her long chestnut hair in his fist and gave a gentle tug upward.

"Ouch!" She looked up at him, smiling out of her pink perfect face.

She pouted, and he pinched one of her nipples and said, "Must the daughter of a pig farmer act like a piglet?" A hurt look crossed her face; he pushed her over on her back and made soft oinking noises.

She felt herself grow soft inside as she watched his face. It was the face of a tragic actor, lean and somehow always in a shadow from which his green eyes seemed to burn. A shock of unmanageable brown hair fell across his forehead. She smoothed back the hair, reached between them and inserted him into her, and, when he made no movement, drove her hips upward until a rhythm was established. They came as Pavarotti hit a glorious B flat.

"That was the best ever," she said.

The man, still in her, said, "You say that every time."

Now he became conscious of the pain from the scratches in his back.

"Look what you've done!" he said.

"I've branded you. Now all the world will know Kurt Hauser belongs to me."

"My constituency won't be examining my back," said the man. "Keep in mind that I have to make seven speeches today, shake about a thousand hands, kiss at least a dozen babies, and drink two hundred cups of coffee with people who have no earthly idea why somebody is invading their homes and interrupting their favorite television programs!"

"But you love it. You know you do."

"I love you," he said as she kissed his scratches.

At 3 A.M. in a hacienda in the largely uninhabited Chubut Province, the heartland of Argentina's Patagonia coast, an old man sat upright in his bed. His first reaction, as always, was to marvel at the pain that demanded its fealty at this exact moment every morning. Even as he suffered he yearned for a time when proper, rigidly controlled experiments might have been conducted to find out why pain was so punctual.

On a dumpy green chair at the foot of the bed, the servant Agostino waited with the hypodermic needle. The two men did not speak as the old man held up his scarred arm and Agostino plunged the needle home. They remained silent as they waited for its contents to work their magic and make the pain go away for two more hours. Once the intervals had been four hours, then three. Increasing the dosage had no effect. This was a pain you learned to die with.

Agostino arranged the single pillow behind the old man's head. The old man pointed with a bony hand to the side of the bed, and Agostino handed him a white bowl in which to relieve himself. The old man tried never to look at the dead flesh in his hand, for this had once been a thing of beauty, a source of pride and joy to him. On this morning something in the sound of his urine hitting the basin made him look down, and he saw that the urine was mostly blood.

The sight brought the old man's narcotized eyes alive, and now they burned as though a lantern were held behind them.

"Well," he said, "so be it."

From a table by the side of the bed Agostino handed him a blue-lined tablet, a pen, a manila envelope.

The old man began to write, and the quickness of his hand suggested that it was a message he had written many times before within his head. When the message was finished he signed it with a flourish, but very carefully. The signature must be his as it was known to be.

He waited for the ink to dry, wondering if he again could be feeling the flickering pain in his gut. But no, not half an hour had passed.

He examined his message again, tore it from the tablet, folded it and put it into the manila envelope. Then, from the drawer in the table, he removed a celluloid folder, opening it once to stare at its contents, then closing it as though on life itself. This he also put into the envelope.

Now he addressed the envelope, printing the letters carefully: Reuters Limitada, Edificio Safico, Corrientes 456, Oficina 43, Buenos Aires.

He examined his completed work like a proud child. Agostino reached for it, and he caught the black arm in his bony fist.

"You will be certain to find this Reuters?"

Agostino nodded and only then did the old man release his arm.

"Must you do this thing?" said Agostino.

The old man's head flew backward, and from his sunken chest came a high screeching laughter like some kind of night bird at the moment of the kill.

Deep within the Sahara desert, six hundred miles south of the Mediterranean, the thousand inhabitants of Aubari, Libya, stood transfixed beneath a pounding sun as a man spoke to them from a makeshift platform.

He had been talking for more than four hours; his voice was hoarse with urgency. "Don't believe anything I don't tell you! I will tell you everything! We should have faith together!"

The crowd replied as if one, "With our spirit, our blood, our religion, we will fight at your side, O Qaddafi!"

A tall European, his hair silky white, wearing tailored khakis and oxhide jump boots, stood at the rear of the platform and watched quietly. He had been following the speaker for days in a journey that had taken him from Benghāzī to Surt to a dozen other cities and finally to this scruffy settlement where he had been assured he would at last "have his appointment."

An hour later the speaker, finally silent, went into a crumbling yellow sandstone building to which the European was directed.

The European said nothing as the man stared at him, then went to a cardboard box, took out a book and handed it over.

"The Koran. You cannot read this. You cannot comprehend it. But keep it by your side. It may help you to ask some questions."

The European nodded solemnly and then spoke, his voice as silky as his hair. "I bring a proposal."

The man laughed once. "I have all the proposals I need."

The European smiled. "My colleagues and I are experts—"

The man was no longer smiling. "I have all the experts I need."

"—in killing Jews," the European said.

The man caught his breath. His face relaxed. "Sit down, brother," he said.

The old and elegant Plaza Hotel, on the corner of Florida and Charcas streets in the European part of Buenos Aires, sees bombs go off, sirens wail, crowds disperse. It seems to proclaim in some bygone language, "I will sit here opposite the Plaza San Martín when all of your feverish footsteps have died."

In the Plaza's bar three newsmen sat killing a quiet afternoon, sipping their claritos and listening to one of them, Harry Sinclair of Reuters, theorize on what causes hair to go gray prematurely.

This subject of conversation was odd only in that all three of the men were bald, which, in addition to their profession, may have been a bond between them.

Sinclair had just finished explaining that "gray is the absence of pigment," when the three looked up to see a tall black man carrying a manila envelope.

"Reuters?" the black man asked.

The men from Associated Press and United Press International quickly identified their British colleague.

"That's him," they said.

The black man handed Sinclair the envelope and, while the three looked at it, disappeared from the bar.

"Be goddamn sure it's not ticking," said Ainsley, the AP man.

Sinclair obediently held the envelope to his ear. "Actually, it's not."

"All bombs don't tick," said Grisby, the UPI man. The three considered this for a moment.

"Let's see what we have here." Sinclair began gingerly to tear at the flap.

Ainsley contributed a loud noise—his imitation, presumably, of a letter bomb.

"Why are all Americans such idiots?" Sinclair asked, sipping generously from his clarito and removing a piece of blue paper from the envelope.

"Well?" said Grisby.

"You're not going to believe your eyes." Sinclair handed the page to Grisby.

"I'll be damned," Grisby said.

Ainsley motioned with his glass. "Read it aloud."

Grisby read it. "Reuters, you will kindly arrange a press conference for high noon at the Plaza Hotel exactly one week from today."

"Signed, Amy Carter," said Ainsley.

"No," said Grisby, "Martin Bormann."

"Are you serious?" Ainsley reached for the paper. "Never a dull moment."

"Look, it could have been Hitler," said Grisby. "Everybody knows he's living in Argentina too."

"Paraguay," said Sinclair. And then, "Hallo, there's more." He removed the celluloid folder. "Well, now, what do you make of this? A proper wedding certificate made out to Martin Bormann and Gerda Buch, 1929, and—look at this—witnessed by Adolf Hitler."

"Looks like an original," said Ainsley. "I mean, it isn't a photocopy. And get this membership card dated 1920, Martin Bormann, member of the Society Against the Supremacy of the Jews!"

Sinclair gulped down a last swallow of his drink. "Don't overlook the birth certificate. June 17, 1900, Halberstadt, Germany. Martin Bormann."

"Well," said Sinclair, taking up the envelope and its contents, "toodle-oo. Your turn, isn't it, Grisby?"

"Not my turn, my pleasure," said Grisby, who was a notorious tightwad.

When Sinclair was gone, Grisby asked Ainsley, "What do you think?"

"I'd say horse manure, just a whole pile of it. You know perfectly well there's a fake a month around here."

"Still . . ." muttered Grisby, paying the tab. "I'm going to send it out. You?"

"No choice, do we?"

"None."

2

West Berliners by the score watched the evening news on SFB, certain that anchorman Harald Karras would either put the story originating out of Buenos Aires to sleep or add to its weight. Karras did not let them down. He introduced his guest, Dr. Hugo Blaschke, whom he identified as Martin Bormann's former dentist.

The professional man was brusque and to the point. "In 1972 I made positive identification of Bormann's dental structure from the skull and bones accidentally discovered here in West Berlin. The dental structure is like fingerprints, there are no two alike. I again repeat that identification, Martin Bormann is dead!"

"Dr. Blaschke," Karras said very calmly, "all those documents, the birth certificate, the marriage license—"

"Obviously clever forgeries, or perhaps the originals themselves, stolen or found in the rubble right after the war. There was plenty of rubble, you may recall."

"But why would someone go to all that trouble to perpetrate a fraud?" Karras asked.

"Dear Mr. Karras, someone perpetrated an entire fraudulent memoir of the late American billionaire Mr. Hughes; why not a few simple documents?"

"But for what purpose?"

"For this," Dr. Blaschke said, "you will need a psychiatrist, not a dentist."

These remarks did not go unnoticed by the press, which was in any case inclined to treat the story very carefully.

Which did not mean, of course, that any of them were going to miss covering that press conference.

Sinclair shuddered at the sight of the Plaza San Martín well into the first stage of a monumental traffic jam. He tried and failed to take comfort from the sight of Buenos Aires police attempting to establish order under the command of a friend of his, Captain Luisito.

Sinclair greeted the captain with an apology "for all of this."

The young Argentinian touched his hand to his visor and said with a smile, "In order that I do not have to get the homicide squad down here, please avoid Señor Esteban."

"I'll do my best," Sinclair said, stepping over a thick television cable that extended from one of the large mobile units into the Plaza Hotel. He looked around him. Automobiles bearing press credentials abounded, most of them parked where they damned well pleased. There were motorcycles as well, ready to rush film to the airport or to television stations, the fastest means of transportation in this city of four million or so.

As he stepped into the lobby, Sinclair put his hand to the side of his face. The director general of the Plaza, Señor Esteban, blocked his way nonetheless.

"What have you done to the Plaza?" he demanded.

At that moment, Ainsley strode up and rescued his colleague. The AP man said in his best hot-off-the-wire manner, "Just got word from the airport, your man's on his way in."

Sinclair nodded and beckoned to Grisby, who joined the threesome. "Sinclair, I've done what you asked. Señor Esteban has opened the bar."

"You have?" said Sinclair. Esteban bowed, now the officious host.

"Only way I could keep the bastard from shutting us down," Grisby explained as the three newsmen moved into the press room, where Sinclair's appearance was greeted with a good-natured round of applause and lifting of glasses.

The back of the room was a solid wall of television cameras; the front contained three large tables where reporters had already staked out their territory. Technicians in white jump suits were still testing equipment; black electrical tape lay like funeral ribbons on the red carpet.

Among the reporters, and trying to look as if they belonged, were a seedy group whom everyone else knew to be low-level intelligence agents of this country or that. For the most part they were free-lancers who survived by selling bits and pieces of assorted rumor and occasional fact for whatever they could get. Watching them, Sinclair accepted a whiskey from Ainsley.

As the drink relaxed him, Sinclair thought he recognized an elderly man standing in the rear of the room. He was about to consult Ainsley when the bells of a neighboring church tolled the hour of noon and Sinclair suddenly experienced a feeling of fear: Suppose Bormann—genuine or not—doesn't show?

Ainsley looked sympathetically at his friend, wondering if the other man was aware that his bald head was covered with a thin layer of perspiration. Ainsley put his hand to his own bald head, relieved to find it quite dry.

Sinclair freshened his drink and moved among his fellow reporters. By one o'clock the television technicians were grumbling at the prospect of packing up their heavy equipment without a single frame of film or tape to show for their efforts.

At 1:30 Grisby sidled up to Sinclair. "I'm afraid it doesn't look too promising," he said.

In the rear of the room the elderly man looked at a pocket watch, his face impassive.

Sinclair spotted Señor Esteban, obviously looking for him, and shuddered. He was about to duck behind a television camera when someone shouted, "Fifteen to two!" and all eyes turned to Sinclair: "Patience gentlemen," he said. "Patience."

Sinclair's plea was met with silence as some technicians began the laborious task of disconnecting and packing up.

The church bell's announcement of two o'clock sounded like a death knell, and now Señor Esteban confronted Sinclair. His hands were positioned at his hips—a bad sign. Then sudden quiet fell over the room, and the drone of voices died away.

As though by command all eyes turned to the door through which a man in white peon's clothes, leaning on a black man, slowly entered the room.

He appeared to be in his middle or late seventies. His skin was gray, as though his blood was not making its way to where it should be, and there was little to his frame but bone, over which hung loose skin.

The black man led him to the front of the room, the reporters making a path for him. Someone got a chair for him but he refused it, standing instead behind it and using its back for support.

The old man cleared his throat and spat upon the floor. And now they all could see that his eyes had not yet joined the rest of him on his final journey. They burned, perhaps with fever, perhaps with passion or madness.

The old man stood patiently while the television and radio people dragged up a large table on which they could put their microphones.

The man from ARD, one of Germany's two national television networks, pointed to a microphone and said, "You'll have to sit."

"I will stand," said the old man.

A man from the *Los Angeles Times* decided to get the proceedings under way. "Who are you?" he shouted from the back of the room.

The old man's right hand jerked upward in a sign for silence as though pulled by a wire. The room fell quiet.

"The son of Adolf Hitler will make himself known." The voice then changed from a tone of announcement to that of a thinly veiled threat. "Or this service will be performed for him."

"By whom?" someone shouted.

"By the wind!" the old man cackled back, laughing now until he tottered back and forth as though he might fall.

Now the questions came fast and furious. "When was the child born?" "At the end." "The end? The end of what?" "The end of the world." "Before Hitler's death?" "Yes." "What name is this man using?" "That's for him to say."

A CBS correspondent demanded, "How do we know you're telling the truth?"

The old man shrugged.

"Isn't there anyone who can identify you?" the correspondent persisted.

Sinclair watched the old man's eyes sweep across the room. Finally they came to rest on the elderly man in the rear of the room.

"Perhaps," Bormann said with a smile, "my friend there can identify me."

Simon Weisenthal's voice rang out like a judgment.

"That's him all right. That's the slaughtering son of a bitch."

3

His colleagues referred to the Bormann revelation as "Sinclair's finest hour," and somehow, in the ensuing confusion, it became accepted fact that Sinclair had somehow "got hold of" the story.

"Lazy bastard," said Ainsley, downing his clarito. "It fell right into your lap."

Grisby advanced a meaner theory. "Admit it, Sinclair. You're an old Nazi and all your kind stick together."

Sinclair, with a tidy raise in pay and a couple of interesting job offers in his pocket, chose to refer to the event as "providential." He called on his colleagues to mend their ways—"And perhaps," he said, "Providence will befriend you as well."

"You damnable Englishman," said Ainsley, "have you seen what your press has done to the story? Good Lord, rewards for information on Bormann, stories on Bormann and that actress sweetheart whom they neglect to mention would be about seventy-five if she were still living!"

Sinclair's national honor was aroused. "What about your grubby Madison Avenue agencies looking for him to offer him deals like the ones your Presidents get? And let's not forget that bloody warfare going on between *The New York Times* and *The Washington Post*. Know what a chap from Geneva told me? The *Times* has a twelve-man team assembled with unlimited expense accounts to find him, and the *Post* has reunited its two superstars for the occasion."

"It is not," Grisby conceded, "the press's finest hour."

"Come, come, gentlemen, we're merely keeping the public's little habit supplied." Ainsley snapped his fingers for the check, but Señor Esteban had left instructions: "Mr. Sinclair drinks with the compliments of the house."

"You're our fucking celebrity," Ainsley said.

"And loving every minute of it," the Englishman admitted.

* * *

Chancellor Josef Haack did not care for Willi Fassmann, the leader of Haack's own Liberal Democrat party in Berlin. Nor did he try particularly hard to hide this fact.

The two had talked in Haack's office in Bonn some months before Martin Bormann's press conference. The Chancellor tried, not very successfully, to conceal his distaste for the man.

"So good of you to see me, Mr. Chancellor," said Willi Fassmann. "Things being as they are."

The Chancellor frowned. Fassmann's empathy translated into "You're in real trouble," and while this didn't bother the old man who knew that he would never seek public office again, the idea of a Willi Fassmann assessing his troubles was demeaning.

Haack nodded and took refuge in statistics. "Four percent of our people, that's close to a million who simply can't find work, and nothing we do seems to alter it."

Fassmann nodded gravely. He loved to hear about other people's problems. "Not to mention the possibility of national bankruptcy to our health insurance and pension system. Due, of course, to our inflation."

The Chancellor managed a smile. "You are an authority on our ills, Willi. You would make a good physician."

"Whatever troubles the Chancellor troubles me," said Fassmann.

Haack sighed. "No, it's true. Everything that was promising has, in the blink of an eye, become a problem. Only a few years ago Brezhnev said right here in Bonn that he had come here to overcome a history full of sorrows. Now, they've got at least ten thousand secret agents trying to infiltrate this government."

Fassmann was about to sympathize when he realized the Chancellor wasn't finished.

"We even find ourselves in sharp conflict with the Americans. Inevitable, I suppose, with our increasing economic power. It's difficult for rivals to remain friends."

"It's difficult for friends to remain friends," said Fassmann, who waited for a laugh that did not come. He smiled. He liked the Americans, whom he thought of as delightful fools. "Perhaps we should let the American President pray for us."

"I believe the American President is a sincere man," Haack said stiffly.

Fassmann immediately regretted his little jab, remembering how much the Chancellor loved sincerity. "A good man," he intoned, and started to launch into an account of how he, Willi Fassmann, spent many an hour "in prayerful contemplation." The Chancellor cut him short.

"What brings you to Bonn, Willi?"

Fassmann looked at the other man, wondering if he were, as some enemies said, senile. "Why, our elections in Berlin. What else?"

The Chancellor shrugged. "It seems only yesterday that the electorate gave us a good kick in the pants."

Fassmann sighed, the rolls of fat on his belly rippling beneath his pale-blue silk shirt. "The people, what do they know?"

Haack smiled. A question like that typified the difference between him and Willi Fassmann.

"The people know insincerity."

Fassmann took out a silk handkerchief and wiped his brow. The conversation was not going as he would have liked.

"I would put my compassion for my fellow man up against anyone's," he said, a tinge of anger creeping into his voice.

"I apologize, Willi, for whatever I said that offended you. The pressures of office just now—"

"I understand," said Fassmann. *Those five years he spent in a concentration camp softened his brain.*

The Chancellor changed the subject.

"Have we got a candidate for Governing Mayor?"

Fassmann smiled. "We do, we do. One who, I think, will meet with your approval."

"And who might that be?"

Fassmann said the name as if he were letting out a delightful secret. "Kurt Hauser."

The Chancellor was astonished. He had come to expect the worst from the party in Berlin, and they seldom surprised him.

"Bravo!" he said.

"I thought that would please you." Willi Fassmann nodded eagerly, like a child. "He's got it all. If he can't help us . . ." He left the sentence unfinished, not wanting to insult the old man, who still fancied himself a vote getter.

Josef Haack completed the statement: "Then no one can." He stood and walked to a window that looked out on Adenauerallee. "I've never known a young man like Kurt Hauser. First he was just another law student and I was president of Bonn University, teaching an occasional class, but it didn't take me long to know that Kurt was brilliant. More than brilliant, there was about him a sense of destiny, even as a young man."

Fassmann, more practical than Haack, said, "And he's certainly paid his dues to the party, gone right up the ladder with hard work, dedication. Overwhelmingly elected by his own constituency to Parliament, chairman of the Security Committee, vice-chairman of the parliamentary group—oh, he's done it all. And at age thirty-two!"

"A good man," the Chancellor said, turning to Fassmann. "A good man, Willi."

"I love the boy, everybody loves Kurt Hauser!"

Now it was the Chancellor's turn to be practical. "Any chance of his pulling it off?"

Fassmann sighed. "He'll help all of us, naturally; he should pull a few candidates into office with him. But enough for us to be in the majority and he to be Governing Mayor? No. No one could do that."

"What happened to our popularity, Willi? We started out so full of promise."

You happened to our popularity, thought Fassmann. With your old-world approach to everything in a world that changes by the second. He said nothing, which served perfectly well to get the message across.

"How does Kurt feel about all of this?" asked Haack.

"Who knows how Kurt Hauser feels about anything?" said Fassmann. "He keeps very much to himself, a strange quality in a young politician, but the voters don't seem to mind. It drives his colleagues in the party crazy."

"Tell him to come and see me."

Fassmann knew that this meant that their meeting was over. "Then you approve?" *We could give a shit less if you do or you don't.*

The Chancellor smiled as if he had read the other man's thoughts.

"Let me talk to Kurt first, I'll let you know."

Old fool, thought Willi, who was not far from the Chancellor's age. "Of course."

Now Haack was back in the past. "Do you know how he worked his way through law school?"

Fassmann, who knew perfectly well, said nothing.

"He was a guide on one of those tourist paddle steamers on the Rhine. His classmates told me no one could describe the Lorelei like Kurt. The steamer people wanted him to quit law school and go with them full time, and he actually considered it! Discussed it with me. I could hardly keep from laughing at him—that brilliant mind and golden tongue spending their life talking about a piece of rock! It amuses me even today. But Kurt was quite serious."

"I'm glad you dissuaded him," said Fassmann.

"But I didn't. I told him I thought he had no feel for the law, that another career might be just the thing. He looked at me incredulously—he knew he was the best student in the entire university. In fact he began to stammer. Finally I couldn't hold it in and I burst out laughing and sent him from my office with a warning for him not to bother me with such humbug again! He never did, but from then on I called him Mr. Tour Guide. He didn't seem to mind. What a splendid boy!"

"He's not a boy anymore," Fassmann said and immediately regretted it.

"When you're my age everyone is a boy," said the Chancellor. Willi Fassmann joined in with laughter that he didn't particularly feel.

A week later to the day Kurt Hauser sat in the Chancellor's office awaiting the old man's presence and staring at a bare desk, its top polished to a glasslike finish.

Willi Fassmann had returned from his trip with word that all was well, but Kurt still dreaded the meeting with his former mentor.

The door opened and Josef Haack slowly entered. Kurt was shocked at how much the other man had aged, at the slight tremor in his wrinkled hands. The Chancellor stared at him, and Kurt thought, He doesn't remember who I am or why I'm here!

Finally a smile broke across the Chancellor's face. He motioned for Kurt to be seated.

"Now you're the young man from the Rhine tour service," he said. "Here, I believe, to discuss a proposal for my club?"

"Yes, sir," said Kurt, without missing a beat. "We believe we have come up with the perfect tour for your distinguished group. Your ship the *Goethe* contains two decks and three dining rooms. It is, of course, a picturesque paddle steamer which your members should find suitably quaint. We have arranged for you the benefits of group fares, with all adults receiving a reduction of twenty percent off the normal fare. Now, as to the actual tour—"

The two men broke into laughter at the same time. Then the Chancellor leaned across the desk. "Any regrets?"

"Regrets?" Kurt was startled for a moment. "About not being a tour guide? Oh, hell yes!"

Josef Haack smiled. "I know how you feel," he said. "I should have remained a professor whose biggest problem was keeping the final examination from being pilfered. But that was many years ago."

"You look very well, sir," Kurt said dutifully.

The Chancellor rewarded him with a small bow of the head. "Yes, I think I may safely predict a bright future for you in politics." They laughed and then the Chancellor grew serious. "I look like what I am," he said in a voice that took Kurt back to hours spent listening to him lecture. "An old man filled with problems I'll never solve and regrets about all the things I didn't do."

"Regrets? You?"

"I forget your age, Kurt. Regrets are a territory exclusively occupied by the old."

Kurt sat silently, looking down at his folded hands. His narrow fingers resembled tapers in a box. There was a chilled feeling about his feet, as though he might be coming down with a cold, and he was already dreading the flight back to Berlin.

The Chancellor slowly shook his head as if he were brushing away cobwebs into which he had walked. "Have we any chance in Berlin at all?" he asked.

"The question is," Kurt said with a small smile, "has Berlin any chance?" He leaned forward and spoke very softly. "We are a dying city. Thirty thousand people will move away this year. A quarter of our population is over sixty-five, and demographic projections tell us that our population will shrink by twenty-five percent in the next fifteen years. Our isolation is more deadly than radiation. Eight hundred of us will commit suicide this year. In 1977, drug-related deaths rose to eighty-four from only nine in 1971. Germany needs jobs, and in Berlin jobs go begging. We've got one motorcycle plant that needs a thousand employees right now. We're trying to import them from England. I'm not certain that anyone can help Berlin, much less save her."

"I like your tone," said Haack. "You not only have your statistics well in hand, you sound angry about them. Are you? Angry, intelligent men are much needed in our times."

"Even if a miracle occurred and we won, and you and I know how slender are those chances, I'm not at all certain that anything can be done. But God knows I'd like to try my hand at it."

"Perhaps when I am no longer Chancellor, the Liberal party can be reborn. When fossils like Josef Haack and Willi

Fassmann have passed from the scene, men like you—"

"Please don't say that. You are what is good in Germany. It is men like you who have made it possible for men like me to hold our heads up."

The Chancellor smiled at the younger man's passionate outburst. "I see you have not lost your fire, Kurt. Well, don't. It's the only real weapon for fighting fire."

The two looked at each other as though they were sealing a compact. Haack broke the silence. "There is, of course, no doubt about your being reelected to Parliament. The question is, can you pull enough votes to carry in some of your less-desirable associates?"

Our associates, thought Kurt. He said, "That remains to be seen. But, yes, I'll be reelected. I've looked after the city and my constituency with equal—"

"Never mind that for now. I'd like to ask you what kind of man you are, Kurt."

"I beg your pardon?"

"I mean you say all the right things. But what kind of man are you? That's so strange for me. I consider myself an excellent reader of other men. But suddenly, as you sat there about to give me a political speech, the thought occurred to me, I do not really know him! Don't you find that extraordinary? I don't know you. Does anyone?"

"I suppose I . . . well, you know, you've always known I am a bit of a loner."

"Not all that strange in a politician. I am convinced we are all a little schizophrenic, part of us oh so public, part of us hidden, protectively. The public buys the part on display, but it's the hidden part that makes us what we are."

Kurt said nothing.

"Do you have a girl friend?"

"Yes, sir. A farm girl—a pig farm, forty kilometers from Hanover."

"I take it she is not now living on a pig farm?"

"Oh no, sir." Kurt seemed clearly embarrassed over the direction the conversation had taken. "She lives in Berlin, she's a publisher's representative."

"And will you marry this farmer's daughter?"

"Why . . . ah . . . I'd have to say, I've never really thought about it."

"No matter," said the Chancellor. "And it is with this young lady that you spend your spare time? Is she an opera lover too?"

Kurt was pleased. He hadn't thought the Chancellor would be aware of his passion. "No, I'm afraid not. She likes American rock music, as a matter of fact."

"At the proper time I will help reconcile the differences," said the Chancellor.

"Offer accepted," said Kurt, "though I can't imagine how you'd accomplish it."

The Chancellor stood. "I hope you do well, Kurt. I'll be keeping a close watch on you. I trust you."

"Your trust means a great deal to me," Kurt said simply.

"One thing more. Be careful of Fassmann."

"Of Willi?"

"You know his past."

"That was a long time ago, sir."

"The past dies hard. Sometimes we open a door and there it stands, waiting to be reentered. The past has a way of becoming the present without our being aware of the event that makes the change. Watch Fassmann!"

"God knows there is plenty of him to watch."

Chancellor Haack walked around his desk and took Kurt's hand between his hands.

"Yesterday," he said, "is the only thing on earth that frightens me. Not even death, with whom I have a rendezvous in the not-too-distant future. Good-bye for now, Mr. Tour Guide."

In a private dining room of the Kempinski Hotel, right off the Kurfürstendamm, which offers two miles of as gorgeous and expensive shopping as can be found in Europe, top leadership of the Liberal party gathered to assess their progress at this point in the campaign.

Senator and Party Chairman Willi Fassmann, cutting into

his roast goose and sipping from a glass of Rheingau, was the first to address himself to the business at hand.

"What I am about to say gives me no pleasure. Kurt Hauser's 'angel of death' telephoned me right before I came here and said it is imperative that he see us."

This announcement was first greeted with silence, then with muffled groans. Hauser's "angel of death" was Gunther Liedtke, the campaign publicist Kurt had forced them to retain before agreeing to be their candidate for Governing Mayor. They despised Liedtke, the constant bearer of ill tidings through the documents he shoved under their noses, documents he called "polls" and which did not paint a pretty picture of Liberal Democrat chances.

Hauser had defended Liedtke on a dozen occasions, explaining that the ill tidings were in fact reality, a commodity that the party, in his opinion, desperately needed.

"It will be either cancer or leukemia," predicted Hans Bachem, party tactician and a chess grand master.

"He was most insistent," Fassmann offered apologetically.

Emil Dahr, vice-chairman and an old acquaintance of the Chancellor, said, "Nothing he says will depress me; we are doing better than we ever have. Incidentally, the Bundeskanzler says he will do anything he can. He really believes in Hauser. He says all we have to do is give him a call on the telephone."

This offer was greeted with an embarrassed silence. All of the men fervently hoped that the unpopular old Chancellor would stay as far away from Berlin as possible.

"Let the Chancellor attend our inauguration," said Senator Fritz Imbach.

"The Chancellor, at least, is untouched by scandal, Herr Imbach," said Emil Dahr. Imbach's son had been recently exposed in an insurance scheme which would cost the party many votes.

The senator jumped to his feet. "Just what is that supposed to mean? I refuse to sit here and have my family tragedy discussed over roast goose!"

"Please, gentlemen," said Fassmann, rapping on the table

with his large pink knuckles, "let us reserve our anger for the opposition!"

"*We* are our opposition and always have been," Bachem said dourly, "which, I suppose, is all right. Good men can differ. But public awareness of our differences has crippled us. If we don't trust each other, why should they trust us?"

"That, too, is in the past," said Fassmann. "Gentlemen, the fact of the matter is that we have the most attractive and vibrant young, I repeat, young, candidate in the race. It's just possible that he can—well, help some of the rest of us."

Senator Rudi Rahms, a prominent lay leader of the Lutheran church, said, "My wife wishes he were married."

"What difference does that make?" Fassmann demanded.

"To women, a great deal of difference. It is my only criticism of Hauser."

"That he's not married?" Fassmann persisted.

Rahms sighed. "That he's practically living with that girl."

"Well at least no one can question his sexual preference," said Fassmann. "In any case, I have discussed the young lady with Hauser."

"Well?" someone asked.

"He says that it is his business, not ours."

"To the contrary," said Vice-Chairman Dahr, "it is the business of all of us. He is our hope."

"Anyone have a better suggestion for Governing Mayor?" asked Fassmann, his cheeks loaded with food.

"My wife says—" Rudi Rahms began.

"Let *her* run," said Dieter Jabusch, West Germany's wealthiest plumbing contractor.

Everyone, including Rahms, laughed. During a campaign no one irritated Jabusch.

"I suppose these days it really doesn't matter," said Hans Bachem. "People living out of marriage are quite the norm these days. It may even get us a few extra votes."

"For God's sake, don't say that to Liedtke, he'll want to put it in an advertisement."

"Where is the man?" someone asked. The question went unanswered, and the conversation turned to the many virtues of Kurt Hauser. A light rain began to slap against the window. As time passed and more fine bottles of Rheingau were emptied, the room became warm with stories of bygone elections. Fassmann dozed off a time or two, sitting up with a start at the crash of thunder and the simultaneous entrance, like a bad odor, of party publicist Gunther Liedtke.

"We are glad you didn't get wet, Mr. Liedtke," said Fassmann.

Liedtke began with "Gentlemen," to which no one responded. They eyed him warily, wondering what horror he had brought through the downpour. "I trust the goose was excellent," Liedtke said, offering his gloomy smile. "And the wine?" He picked up a bottle and examined the label.

No one offered him a glass. And then Liedtke did a thing that astonished them all: he lifted the bottle of Rheingau and took a healthy swallow—from the bottle.

"The man's gone mad," muttered Dahr, a wine connoisseur.

Liedtke wiped his sleeve across his mouth as though he had just taken a swig at a *Bierfest*. "Well," he said, looking at the others.

They stared at him. Then Fassmann blinked, ruminating about "the tragedy of Berlin youth."

Liedtke, in his early thirties, was one of those. Maybe the worst of those.

"If you have something to say, Herr Liedtke, kindly go ahead and say it," said Fassmann.

Liedtke made his little bow that somehow always seemed like an insult. "I take it you distinguished gentlemen haven't heard the news?"

"*Heard* the news, Herr Liedtke?" said Fritz Imbach. "We try to *make* the news."

"Our candidate has called a press conference for tomorrow at two," said Liedtke.

"What candidate? Come on, man, get on with it!"

"I'm referring to Mr. Kurt Hauser."

"So?" said Fassmann. "Let him. Press conferences are free, no cost at all, and he handles them beautifully."

"Mr. Hauser has an announcement to make," Liedtke said very softly.

"Oh?" said Fassmann.

Outside the rain fluttered against the window like birds seeking refuge. Liedtke waited patiently through a roar of thunder.

"Well?" demanded Emil Dahr.

Uninvited, Liedtke sank into a chair, his fingers rolling a bit of bread into an obscene ball. He now had the full attention of the others.

"Mr. Kurt Hauser," said Liedtke, "will announce that he is the subject of today's press conference in Argentina."

First there was silence. Even the rain stopped. Then all six men shouted at once, startling a headwaiter and two assistants who thought they had been providing the distinguished party with excellent service.

Fassmann's voice was the loudest: "We have been betrayed!"

4

Twenty-four hours earlier, Kurt Hauser, the subject of Fassmann's outburst, had been toweling his wet head, assessing the toll of the campaign in his bathroom mirror. There were circles under his eyes, and his right hand was sore and even slightly swollen from squeezing so many hands. He put the towel in the hamper, flexed his sore hand and considered the evening's activities that lay before him. In his bedroom the stereo (Pavarotti singing "Cielo e mare!" from *La Gioconda*) competed with the television set, which he had flicked on in order to hear the news.

First there would be a labor rally where he would try to explain for the thousandth time why filling Berlin's labor quota would not weaken but strengthen the labor movement through increased membership. There would be the usual skeptical hoots and boorish questions, all of which he would deflect with the puerile humor the workingmen seemed to love.

He would then attend a party of socialites who always made vague promises about contributions, large ones, contributions that seldom seemed to materialize. Still, he had no choice. This group did have influence with the press, and his attendance would earn him a few inches of complimentary news space.

Pavarotti was building to his high note, and Kurt stopped thinking about anything else. As he moved to turn off the television set he became aware that a special news bulletin was interrupting the scheduled newscast, was being handed to the reporter even as he began reading it.

"A man purporting to be a dying Martin Bormann today told a press conference in Buenos Aires that Adolf Hitler and Eva Braun . . ."

Kurt sank onto the bed, his eyes fixed on the nineteen-inch screen on which details of the Bormann conference were being supplied by a young newscaster.

". . . Bormann stated that Hitler would reveal himself or it would be done for him."

Kurt strode to the set and snapped it off. He stared at the screen, now dark.

Like words being typed across a page, thoughts floated to the surface of Kurt's mind. That the announcement would someday be made had been a certainty. That he, Kurt, would say "when" had been an absolute certainty. So much for absolutes.

The telephone rang.

"Yes, I just heard," he said, as calmly as he could. "He's dying, is he? Of course, cancer. Didn't anyone know? What'll I do? I'll do something. His threat was hardly subtle. Of course I'm angry! I was supposed to say when, remember? I know you're sorry, but it's *my life*. It is, you know. Foolish? I will forget you said that. No, I don't need to talk to anyone, I'll decide how to handle it. Perhaps I haven't made myself clear: *Do not do anything!* Pass that on. Do not embellish it, pass it on precisely as I said it. Forgive me if I find myself a bit weary of people who can't control a dying man. It was inexcusable, goddamnit! I do not accept excuses. From here on I'll make all the decisions concerning myself. The plans of other men—I only hope I haven't learned that lesson too late. Is he still alive? Only a week or two? You fool! What's to prevent him from calling another press conference? No. Absolutely not. His death would be investigated immediately. We don't need any more questions, can't you understand that? Keep him medicated. A dying man should get lots of rest."

He placed the receiver firmly in its cradle, poured himself a brandy and sat back on the bed. Leaning forward, sipping from the snifter, he stared straight ahead as though he were reading a book in the distance.

So the moment was at hand, no longer in the wings waiting for that just-right time to make its appearance and be judged. He had waited so long, catered to morons, laughed with bumpkins and bowed to inferiors.

"It's just as well," he said aloud. "I'm ready."

He found himself smiling. Being Kurt Hauser hadn't been all that bad, considering . . .

Of course there had been times—more and more frequent, he admitted—when he felt overwhelmed by the past that would inevitably dominate his future. These moments had been exciting, like playing a slightly dangerous game.

Now, at last, it was no longer a game.

It had been this knowledge, this secret, that had set him apart from others. That they liked and admired him was easily proved at the ballot box, yet even this triumph had been tempered by the thought, *They like and admire Kurt Hauser.*

His inner turmoil translated, in the public mind, into a kind of mystique; they said of him, "He's not like the others," and though they couldn't quite put their finger on why, the fact that he was different seemed to have great appeal.

Opponents saw him as "an independent son of a bitch" and loved to tease members of the Liberal party with this view of Hauser, referring to him as "Dr. Schopenhauer, Herr Nietzsche, Professor Kant."

On more than one occasion a fellow party member had hinted to Kurt that perhaps he should mix with the boys a little more. Kurt had given no promises, knowing that he would not "mix" because he could not.

I am who I am, he thought, then laughed at his silly simplification. "I am not who I am," he said aloud. "I am someone else!"

The telephone rang again. This time it was Liedtke telling him that they must not be late. "Or," he said, "our labor friends will tear down the hall and eat Willi Fassmann, who would make one hell of a rump roast."

"Liedtke," said Kurt, "I may be fifteen or twenty minutes late. Tell the band to play a few extra numbers. Oh, and Liedtke, don't make any plans for day after tomorrow, I shall need your help. No, I can't tell you now. God, what a pain in the ass you are!" Liedtke made no reply. "Your silence is ineffective," said Kurt. "I have just heard you call me a pig's head. Worse? Admit it, I was close! Good-bye."

He took a small sip of brandy. Now it was time to consider priorities. He pushed the brandy away. He needed no stimulant; the blood that flowed through his veins was quite sufficient, thank you. He found himself smiling: he was an accountant and they were figures in a ledger, to be erased, crossed out, changed, ignored. *Keep that in mind, that's all they are.*

First there would be the call to Josef Haack. The old man's face swam into his mind and he shuddered. A tough old nut to crack. *Weak, oh God, so weak!* But still the Chancellor and leader of the party. A public denouncement by Haack and the Berlin wing of the party would flee Kurt like pigeons before a hungry cat. But how to keep the old fool from making a statement? Not so easy, that. His silence was not for sale.

Goebbels had tried. The incident was legendary. The doctor himself had announced that Haack would receive a high honor for "scholarly achievements." It was an old Nazi trick, one that enjoyed a surprising success with most of Haack's peers in the universities.

Haack's refusal of the "honor" was made worse by his statement: "The only way that a pig can bestow an honor is by eating you, which makes you slop. I have no ambitions toward that end." He was arrested that evening as an enemy of the State, and only his worldwide reputation insured his imprisonment rather than his execution.

So. How did one "handle" such a man? One didn't. *Turn it around, turn it around! Let Josef Haack do the "handling." Lie back, supine. Be the victim—no, not the victim, the son! The* wayward *son.* Wasn't that their unspoken relationship, anyway? *Haack the father, I the son. Well, I've been a bad boy, a very bad boy.* There'd be punishment, of course. Wasn't it deserved?

Kurt began to laugh. "I've been a baddie boy!" he shouted to the empty room.

Still sitting on the edge of the bed, he pushed aside a pile of Lise's underthings, cream-colored satin trimmed in beige lace. Thinking of her, the laughter died in his throat.

He had met her two years before when he addressed a noontime meeting of Berlin Business and Professional Women, whom he found wanted to hear of nothing but Women's Liberation, about which he knew very little. He had tried to fake his way through the talk, it was one of four he would give that day, but the women were not so easily fooled. "Come, come, Herr Hauser, the question is, are you with us or against us?" one creature dressed like a parrot demanded.

Kurt smiled and said, "I don't suppose you'd buy neutrality?" It made his audience laugh, but only for a moment, the smiles quickly replaced by deadly earnest looks.

That was when the lovely young woman had said from the back of the room, "We are not Switzerland, we are Germany!" Now everyone laughed heartily and the tension was broken.

After the meeting, which had from then on gone surprisingly well, with Kurt working his way around to an eloquent declaration for women's rights, he sought out the young woman, whom he found to be even more lovely at close range.

"You saved me," he said. "I would have been drawn and quartered."

"You were quite good, actually." She lowered her voice and added, "Of course I don't believe a word you said!"

"Are you mocking me? Careful or I'll demand satisfaction!"

She looked at him for a long moment. "Yes, I'll bet you would," she said.

Kurt took her arm. "Just who are you?"

"Lise Straub."

"Well, I'm Kurt Hauser," he said unnecessarily.

"Yes, I know, and you're hurting my arm."

"I'm sorry!" He let her go as if his hand were burning; she laughed and said, "The pain wasn't that terrible."

"Can we have coffee?"

"Thanks, but I've a meeting to attend."

"Oh. Well, may I call you?"

"I suppose," she said, and when he looked crestfallen at her apparent lack of enthusiasm over that prospect, she added, "Of course you may."

She gave him her card with her office number and title, publisher's representative. On the back she wrote down her home number.

A day later he called her.

"My name is Karl Schmidt. We're getting a petition up to stop this silly women's rights movement in Berlin and your name has been furnished us as a possible protest marcher. We've a large sign that reads 'What in Creation is Women's Liberation?' and we need some sturdy person to carry it in our planned march this Sunday. Can we count on you?"

"Listen, Mr. Schmidt or whoever you are, you can—oh!" She started to giggle.

"*Fräulein*," said Kurt, "this is quite a serious matter. For example, did you know that half the married people in Berlin are women? As anyone can see, they're taking over!"

"Yes, I do see, and while I won't be able to carry your sign, I'll tell you what I will do with it . . ."

"I'm shocked, *Fräulein*," said Kurt. "I sense profanity about to be spoken." He burst out laughing, then he said, "I love you."

"What did you say?"

"I said, 'It's a beautiful Sunday and let's go for a drive.' "

She agreed and that was the start of them.

Now he contemplated losing her. It was a definite possibility. That he could do without her was not the point. He could do as he had always done—without anybody. Still . . . he shook his head. What a waste! It would be so unnecessary. She was more than an affair. In any case, he did not like affairs. Entanglements (Well, wasn't that what they were?) were inevitably messy. Someone was sad. Someone was let down. Lies had to be told. Stupid fabrications that weren't even worthy of brainpower. That's why he knew she was more. He did not want to be rid of her. The act of making love was followed neither by revulsion nor the wish that the other party would disappear.

He thought of her pig-farmer parents and even that had charm. Peasants. Good, hardworking people, she called them. Perfect. A man of the people, yet somehow not of the people. Definitely not. He shuddered as if he had stepped into oozing mud.

He wanted her with him. He liked her on his arm. He enjoyed the envious stares of other men.

He clapped his hands as though summoning a genie. A decision had been reached. He would not lose her. Until he was ready.

He would have to move quickly. In only a matter of hours the world would know. She would have to hear it from him.

How interesting. An old man and a farm girl were his immediate concerns. What more proof of one's humanity, the soul beneath one's hard exterior?

He threw back his head and laughed aloud. Then he

turned on the stereo and let Pavarotti soothe him as he dressed for the labor rally.

"Wonderful speech!" the workingmen had said, punctuating their praise with hearty claps on the back. His worst speech, thought Gunther Liedtke. I wonder what's on his mind?

The two stood outside the labor hall, where Liedtke dutifully mustered a weak compliment.

Kurt turned on him. "Don't patronize me."

"You were terrible," Liedtke acknowledged.

"That's more like it. Come on, Liedtke, I'll buy you a beer."

They entered a small bierstube and sat at a table for two so that they wouldn't be joined by anyone else. The waiter brought them each an enormous stein of dark beer, assuring Kurt that he was with the Liberal Democrats "all the way."

"Liedtke," Kurt said when he left the table, "listen to me very carefully. If you make an error with these instructions I shall see that the Liberal Democrat party fires you, which will not be at all difficult since I am the only one who wants to retain your dubious services anyway. Do we understand each other?"

Liedtke removed his glasses and polished them on a napkin.

"Now," said Kurt, "do you know who I am?"

Liedtke shrugged. "You're Kurt Hauser, you'll easily be reelected to Parliament, and if you weren't with those fossils who call themselves the Liberal Democrats, you'd be Governing Mayor of Berlin."

"Wrong," said Kurt.

"You have lost me, Mr. Hauser."

"The point is, I'm not Hauser."

At that moment Liedtke seriously thought that the election had "got" to Kurt. Many a candidate finished the campaign in a hospital under a doctor's care for "physical exhaustion," which was a way of not saying "nervous breakdown."

"Kindly refrain from looking at me that way. I am neither crazy nor drunk, though God knows these beer fumes could produce either effect. You see, Liedtke, I am not Hauser. I'm him. The son of Adolf Hitler."

Liedtke sagged in his chair, his eyes watery.

"Better drink your beer, you look like you need it."

Liedtke lifted the stein to his mouth and drained its contents. Kurt motioned to the waiter to refill the man's glass.

"You're not joking?"

"Please, Liedtke, don't be stupid."

Liedtke sighed. "So you're him."

"One does not choose one's parents," Kurt said. "And please don't look at me like that. Or, on second thought, do. I suppose it's something I'd better get used to."

"I'm sorry," Liedtke said, looking away.

"No, don't do that. That makes it even worse. Take a good look, Liedtke. Only the name is changed."

"You don't look—like him."

"That's all I would need. God!"

"My mother was Jewish."

"I didn't know that. It wouldn't have mattered."

"*I'm not!* I'm a Methodist. My mother became a Methodist."

"Then she was . . . all right?"

"No."

"I'm so sorry," Kurt said. "Can you still work for me? Knowing whose son I am?"

"I'm a professional."

"Which has nothing to do with it. Come on, Liedtke."

"I will work for you."

It was as if they'd just met for the first time, Kurt thought. Liedtke was examining Kurt even as he tried not to. Dear God, was he going to have to go through this with every single person?

"All right, Liedtke," he said. "Now here's what I want you to do, and none of it is going to be easy. Particularly telling my colleagues."

"Me!" squawked Liedtke, picturing Willi Fassmann's big pink face exploding with rage.

Kurt, knowing his man, laughed aloud. "I hope Willi doesn't eat you."

"Why me?" whispered Gunther Liedtke.

"Frankly, Liedtke, I need a punching bag. Someone they can take out their initial rage on."

"Do I get combat pay? You know, I don't earn all that much in this job."

"When I hired you, you were handling publicity for a dance studio and, as I recall, a used-car operation."

"I handled banks and other institutions."

"I tripled your income. True?"

"True," said Liedtke. "I was having a streak of bad luck, it can happen to anyone in my field."

"Obviously I believe in your talent, Liedtke. I hired you."

"That you did," said Liedtke. "All right, I'll do it. I owe you."

"And perhaps—just perhaps, mind you—you won't regret it."

How like a politician, thought Liedtke. He's hinting that he's a man with a future. Once the news breaks, his future is over.

"You have my complete confidence," Liedtke said.

Kurt nodded gravely and then gave Liedtke detailed instructions which the other man recorded on a small pad. Kurt, who had never seen Liedtke write anything down before, smiled.

Kurt had no difficulty getting Chancellor Josef Haack on the telephone.

"Hello, my dear boy. Tell me, how's our campaign? I get excellent reports. My spies say we'll do the best ever. If only you weren't carrying all that dead weight."

"Thank you for taking my call, sir. I know how busy you are."

"Never too busy for Kurt Hauser. You're our only bright penny, you know. And the campaign? Come, come, let me have an official report. How much goose has Willi Fassmann consumed?"

"He is contributing substantially to the economy of Berlin, sir."

The Chancellor laughed heartily. "I'm glad to see you haven't lost your sense of humor. In the heat of battle men often do. Well?"

"Actually, I've called on a very grave matter."

"I can't hear you, dear boy!"

"I have called a press conference. Naturally I wanted to report to you first."

Now the Chancellor's voice was cautious. "Oh?"

"I've called this conference because I had no choice."

"That's usually not a very good reason for anything," said Haack.

"Nevertheless, it's why I've called one."

A steely quality had slipped for a brief moment into Kurt's voice. The Chancellor did not miss it. What a disappointment, he thought, he's gotten himself involved in some kind of scandal. Money? Probably not. Sex? More likely. He sighed and looked out at the darkening Bonn clouds that would soon envelop the oak and pine trees. Finally he said, "What have you done?"

"I have done nothing."

"I don't understand."

"I am guilty of an error—only one. I did not tell you before. Why I didn't, I really can't say. Please understand, I never wanted to disappoint you. Do you believe that?"

"It might help if I knew what you are talking about," said Haack.

"At this press conference, I'll announce that I'm the son of Adolf Hitler."

"God in heaven!"

"My very thought," said Kurt dryly.

"Have you always known?"

"Since I was eighteen."

"Why didn't you—"

"Say so? Say that I was the son of a man forever acknowledged to be the Devil incarnate? What would that, what *does* that make me? As a younger man I could not have handled it."

"And now?"

"I can handle it."

"Perhaps you underestimated those of us who . . . who wished you well."

"I hope that I haven't hurt others too much. Of course I have hurt them. And that's something I never planned. I'm neither a sadist nor a masochist, and I find myself both."

"I'm an old man, my career is nearly finished, but the party . . . Lord!"

Kurt made no reply, and for a moment there was silence along the wires stretched from Berlin to Bonn.

"I guess that's it," Kurt said.

"May I offer a bit of advice?"

"It's what I had hoped for from you."

"Move out of your apartment, go someplace that no one else knows of. Notify my secretary where you'll be and I'll see to it that a security team from the Bundeskriminalamt guards you as long as it's needed."

"Do you really think that's necessary?"

"I do."

"But—"

"Your father came very close to murdering the earth," said the Chancellor. The line went dead.

5

Kurt held the buzzing telephone receiver in his hand and stared at it. His face was calm; his green eyes cloudy. He replaced the receiver slowly and lit a cigarette, sucking the smoke into his lungs and holding it there until it burned before expelling it through his nose. He loosened his necktie and unbuttoned the collar of his blue shirt, closed his eyes for a moment, then went into the bathroom where he washed his hands while staring at his face in the mirror.

There a newsreel montage in black and grays of another face, screaming and exhorting hundreds of thousands in one of Speer's settings, all torchlight and flags, unwound in his head as though it were at once projector and screen.

He opened his mouth and silently said, *Heil*, then laughed aloud and said, "Shit."

It all seems so insane, he thought. This schizophrenic existence, this being me and not being me, its being now and not being now. Yesterday laid atop today like some kind of sex act between periods of time. With me their issue.

Every time the baby sticks its head out of the womb something shoves it back in. It was a bloody cycle and it wearied him and he entertained the thought of saying, fuck it.

But fuck what? *It* was him. And *fuck* it meant *kill* it, and he had absolutely no desire to die.

He splashed cool water on his face, then took refuge in a towel in which he buried his head, his eyes clenched shut in the terrycloth darkness.

A few minutes later, another cigarette dangling from the corner of his mouth, he glanced at the steel watch on his wrist. He would have to wait an hour before calling her, time for her parents to be in bed.

Lise dried the supper dishes at the sink as her mother washed them, smiling gratefully at her daughter as she handed them over.

"Lower Saxony must seem terribly small after Berlin," she said.

"I didn't come to see Lower Saxony, I came to be with you and Father."

"We do appreciate it, Lise. I know your weekends are precious."

Through the kitchen door Lise saw her father sunk in his ancient chair, a pipe clenched between his teeth, his hands grasping a Lutheran publication as if it were a life preserver.

Lise sighed. "I wish he'd . . . well, at least adjust to it."

Her mother shook her head. "Shhh, please, don't bring it up—he'll leave the house."

"Greta hasn't murdered anyone," Lise said with as much of a defensive tone as she could muster.

Frau Straub looked quickly toward the living room to see if her husband had heard.

"To him, your sister's a common streetwalker."

"But that's unfair!"

"Is it? Is a kept woman better than a streetwalker? Or isn't that just another name for it?"

"But she loves him, he's married, and there's not a damned thing he can do about it. His wife has the money."

"Please be quiet! I couldn't bear a scene tonight. Oh, Lise, with what little we had we tried so hard for you girls—well, that's what our life's about. And for Greta to turn out to be some man's mistress—it's killed him more than the Russians did."

"He'll marry her eventually."

"Now, Lise," her mother said patiently, "I may not have your education, but you mustn't take me for a complete fool. He will never marry her. He'll use her up and then he'll leave her. She's not his first. He's notorious!"

Frau Straub handed Lise the last dish and squeezed her daughter's hand. "You're all we've got, really. You've made us so proud with your wonderful young man. So successful," she said, and Lise knew that what she really meant was *so single.*

"This must be his busy time," her mother went on. "We keep up as best we can, but what goes on in Berlin has very little to do with the production of pork."

"Oh, Mother," Lise said, "it's so exciting. If the Liberals win, he'll be Governing Mayor of Berlin. Think of it—my man running Berlin!"

"His picture makes him look very handsome, Lise. We thought you were crazy when you took your degree and moved to Berlin. Berlin! People move *from* Berlin and my daughter moved *to* it. Now it looks like we're the ones who were crazy!"

"I love Berlin, there's nothing like it."

"You're a fine, upstanding young lady, you've captured a prominent man who's single and who'll . . . he will, of course?"

"Will what, Mother?" *As if I didn't know.*

"Well, what I mean to say is, you two, some day, I mean at an appropriate time, you'll be married."

"We've never discussed it, Mother."

"Never?"

"Not once. We talk about politics, which is his life, or my work, which I have to admit I'm getting tired of. Or opera, which he's a fanatic about."

"I'm sure his intentions are the best," Frau Straub said, and there was a begging quality in her voice to which her daughter responded.

"When the time is right, Mother."

Frau Straub, overcome, hugged her daughter to her.

"Now go talk to your father, he's so lonely."

Hans Straub lay his magazine down and stared at his daughter, distantly, as though he were viewing her across a large field.

"You look well, Lise."

"I'm fine," she said, hating the distance he had put between himself and his family. Talking to him was like talking to a stranger, something she could tolerate only in small doses.

"Does your leg bother you much these days?" Her father's right leg had been amputated in a Russian prisoner-of-war camp after the battle of Stalingrad.

"No, no," he said. "It's amazing what you can get used to in this life. To me the wood is me, I mean it feels exactly like the other one. It's all a matter of adjusting."

She thought back to the time when they were growing up, when their mother as well as the two little girls had taken turns massaging his stump so he could hobble out to the barn on cold days.

"I wish you and Mother would come spend a weekend with me, Father. It would be so lovely!"

"Go to Berlin? We're the kind who'd wander into the Eastern Zone and be shot. Farm folk should stay on the farm. Sometimes I think it's where their children should stay too."

"I wish you would come, all the same. I'll show you everything, the botanical gardens, the Tiergarten, and we'll eat divinely. Please say you will . . ."

Herr Straub brightened—his daughter's enthusiasm was contagious. But even as she spoke she saw the smile die on his face as though he had gulped it down.

"We're not going anywhere."

"But you can't just sit here," Lise said, not realizing that her voice was growing louder. "You can't spend the rest of your life in—mourning!"

Her hand flew to her lips as if to pull her words from the air, but it was too late.

"We are not in mourning. One does not mourn a whore."

Lise's mother stood in the doorway, extending one hand in a helpless gesture.

Hans Straub stood up and the magazine fell to his feet.

"We worked among filthy pigs—it was like living with them, it was like being a pig yourself. And we worked in pain, pain so bad that I cried aloud every day certain that I couldn't go on. Why? For the lovely twin daughters God had somehow sent to humble people. Beautiful, perfect little girls who gave our lives a reason, who made the slops and the pain worthwhile. To do the best for them, send them to college, see that they were well dressed, piano lessons, ballet, all out of these few poor acres and our sweat and our tears. And for what?"

He shouted it again, "For what?"

He went to a nail on the door and removed his jacket and a cap. Putting them both on, he stormed from the house, slamming the door behind him.

Lise turned to her mother.

"I'm sorry, it was my fault and God knows you warned me."

"No it wasn't, every now and then he has to say it, sometimes he says it to himself sitting there in that chair."

"Is there coffee?" Lise asked. She was depressed, her father's malady was contagious.

"On the stove," her mother answered and kissed her daughter's cheek before going upstairs and to bed. Lise poured a cup and sat on the couch. Only a few minutes had ticked by when the harsh ring of the telephone startled her.

"Yes?"

"Lise? It's me."

"Oh, thank God you called!"

"Is anything wrong?"

"Kurt, do you love me?"

He laughed.

"Answer me, damnit, do you love me?"

"Of course I love you. Lise, what's wrong? Or is it just that same damned paranoia you get every time you go home?"

"This would be the place to get it."

"I'll cure you," he promised.

She smiled into the phone, and her voice softened. "You always make me feel better."

"Lise, I want you to do me a favor."

"Anything."

"I want you to come back."

"Tonight?"

"Yes."

"All right. May I ask why?"

"I've got something to tell you."

Kurt dialed Bonn and asked for Peter Salman, the Chancellor's confidential secretary, who could be counted on never—on any occasion—to have anything to say.

"Hello, Peter," said Kurt, amused at the silence that followed his greeting. "The Chancellor instructed me to tell you where I'll be." Just for the hell of it, Kurt waited for the other man to reply, which he finally did.

"Address?"

Kurt told him.

"TOA?"

"I beg your pardon?"

"Time of arrival."

"Oh," said Kurt, and told him.

There were no good-byes.

Kurt slipped into his dark leather overcoat and left his apartment, locking the door behind him and walking out through the frozen flowers to his silver Mercedes. He turned the key and listened with pleasure as the engine seemed to croon itself into life.

Lise was waiting for him out front of her apartment, shivering against the bitter cold that had come with night. He got out of the car and opened the door for her, leaning down for a kiss.

"Where are we off to?" she asked him.

"Luebars," said Kurt, naming the last of the old Berlin villages to retain its rural character.

"Is it our anniversary?" Luebars was the first place in which they had ever made love.

"Something like that," Kurt said vaguely, and she noticed his jaw clenching and unclenching, the only sign he ever gave of nervousness.

Lise reached over and turned on the car radio, looking for the American armed forces station out of Frankfurt.

"I wish you wouldn't," Kurt said irritably. She made no reply, but stared out the window. Kurt sighed and left the radio on.

For miles Kurt suffered through renditions of the American music Lise loved and he hated. Then came announcements, about a wine-tasting clinic and about certain Americans believed to be traveling in West Germany who should contact military authorities immediately.

A different announcer's voice broke in: "And now from the AFN, here is a special news bulletin."

Kurt's right hand moved to turn off the radio, then he thought better of it. Maybe it would be easier this way: cold and impersonal, coming from a stranger miles away.

The announcer continued: "Kurt Hauser, the Liberal

Democrat party's choice for Governing Mayor of Berlin in the elections now underway in that city, has called a press conference for tomorrow afternoon at which he will announce that he is the son of Adolf Hitler. Mr. Hauser—"

Kurt turned off the radio. He knew Lise was staring at him; he could not see her face. They rode in silence until they came to Luebars, where he registered under Lise's name.

They climbed the rickety stairs and entered their room, which was dominated by a bed covered with an enormous eiderdown. There was a roaring fire in an open fireplace with logs stacked neatly by its side. Before the fireplace stood an enormous misshapen chair of indeterminate age and origin.

Lise sat on the bed, her lightweight eyeglasses pushed back high atop her light-brown hair. She stared at the coverlet, tracing designs in it with a pink fingernail. Kurt stood before the fire, his back to her, his hands clasped behind him.

Over the sound of the rain and the popping logs there came, like a series of pistol shots, sharp raps on the door. Lise's hand flew to her throat; Kurt whirled about and looked at her. He stood that way for a moment, then went to the door.

"Who is it?" he asked softly.

"By orders of the Chancellor."

"Slide your credentials under the door, please."

Kurt bent down and picked up the celluloid card identifying its bearer as a special agent of the Bundeskriminalamt, then opened the door to a tall young man with blond hair.

"Mr. Hauser," he said, "we will be with you as long as you may need us."

Kurt nodded and the man turned away. Hearing other voices, Kurt closed the door.

"Armed guards?" said Lise.

Kurt shrugged. "It wasn't my idea."

Behind him Lise was crying softly. He held out a hand. "Come here, Lise."

She got up and stood before him like a child, refusing to come. He walked over to her and put her face against his shoulder; she neither resisted nor welcomed the embrace.

"You always smell like fresh flowers," he whispered. She didn't answer, and he gently led her to the chair. There was room for both of them.

"Lise," he said, "I'm the same man."

She met his eyes for the first time.

"No, you're not. And you never will be again. Not for me."

"Look at me, Lise. This is me—Kurt."

"I look at you and I see—oh, my God, dear God."

"If my love doesn't love me I'm alone," he said, so softly that he might have been speaking to himself. His hands gripped her shoulders more tightly. "Alone, Lise. Before you there was nothing else."

"You? Alone?"

"Who I was, the secret of it was what kept me apart from others. I knew they would despise me if they knew the truth. I've suffered, Lise—suffered for a truth that to me is meaningless. What do I care whose sperm started my life? It's *my* life! Mine, Lise. Not his, not anyone else's." Now she could barely hear him. "And then there was the little matter of shame. I am, you know. Ashamed. How can a man inherit another's guilt, and yet I have. I feel . . . guilty as hell."

She had stopped crying and was staring at him, angry now. "Couldn't you have trusted me?"

He looked down at her hands, which were clenched about a damp piece of tissue.

"You didn't. Me, who's given you whatever she has to give. You've owned me, you've been inside me by the hour and you've filled me, all of that, but you couldn't trust me. What does that make me? Another stereo record to ooh and ah over? Good for pleasure—'Faster Lise, put your lips there, Lise,' but not . . . not 'Trust me, Lise.' I wish I was dead. I feel like my sister. Used! Soiled!"

His hand swung down to crack her across the face. Just in time he got control of himself and touched her hair. "You're being hysterical," he said.

"Am I?" She was shouting now. "You didn't trust me, you don't love me, you've—"

He shook her, his hands gripping her shoulders. "Would you lower your goddamn voice? Those policemen outside the door, do you want them to report every word of this to Haack?"

"You're *hurting* me." She wrenched a hand loose and with her palm open struck him across the face.

For the briefest of moments a tiny smile surfaced at the corners of his mouth. He grabbed her wrist and pulled her toward him until their faces were inches apart.

"I didn't tell you because I was afraid to lose you, because I was afraid you'd hate me for who I was! Don't you understand that I *can't* lose you? You're what matters, do you hear me, you're what matters in my life!"

She sagged against him. He held her for a long moment, stroking her hair, then he shifted her weight back in the chair as one might move an invalid and stood before the fire.

"If you desert me, Lise—now, when I need you most . . ."

There was no mistaking the desperation in his voice. It occurred to her that he had never seemed so attractive to her as he did now, standing before the fire, the shadows dancing across his somber face.

"You look like Hamlet," she said.

Just before she came to him, he turned to face her.

"Hamlet? No. My father has killed me."

6

Reuters having informally designated Sinclair as "their Hitler man," the Buenos Aires bureau chief found himself assigned to the story full time. When the news of Kurt Hauser's press conference broke, he boarded a flight for Frankfurt and then Berlin.

Ainsley gave him a ride to the airport.

"You've got all the luck, Harry. Off to screw the *Fräuleins* and then come back with a hard-luck story to your wife about how depressing it is in Germany."

"Jealousy, jealousy," said Sinclair. "You're all jealous of me, in each of your miserable desk-bound souls there's a dream of being a hot-shot investigative reporter. . . . Harry Sinclair *is*—thanks to hours of toil unraveling complex schemes, frantic and dangerous night meetings in dim cafés."

"Harry, you couldn't investigate a pimple."

"I'll send you a postcard," the Englishman promised. "Who knows what I'll uncover next? The missing link, probably, or a young lady who has photographs of your President lusting after her, and not in his heart!"

Hours later Sinclair was in Deutschland Halle, where an unnaturally silent press corps was assembled. He sat with an old friend, Dan Rather, whom he had come to know in Dallas after the Kennedy assassination.

"Any politicos here?" Sinclair asked.

"I doubt it," said Rather. "They're avoiding him like the plague. Want to see how he goes over or under or whatever. No, he's a lonely one right about now, I should think."

"Who's the gentleman in red, white and blue? A flag salesman?"

"Gunther Liedtke, Liberal party publicist. After the conference I'll introduce you if you like."

At precisely 2 P.M. Kurt Hauser entered the room. He nodded to Liedtke; he hadn't been all that sure that the other man would show up.

To Sinclair, he looked unnaturally calm—considering the ordeal he was facing. Was he on tranquilizers? No, the green eyes were clear as the man began to speak.

"I want to apologize to all of you who spent so many hours and days seeking me out. Obviously I had hoped that my background would never come to light. When it did, the disclosure shocked me nearly as much as it shocked you. From that moment I had no choice but to come forward, though it took me some time to compose myself. I cannot tell you that I have dreaded this day, this moment, because quite frankly I saw no reason why it should ever come. I underestimated the past, something I will not do again."

Sounds like a professor, Sinclair thought. One well-prepared for what he has to say.

"With your indulgence I shall tell you what I know and then I will be happy—no, that's certainly not true, there is nothing happy about this moment. . . .

"I shall of course answer to the best of my ability whatever it is you want to know. As to the paucity of my information, I beg of you to bear with me. There is much that I don't know. Which, for the sake of my sanity, may be just as well."

A good intro, thought Sinclair: Give him high marks for that. One, no, *two* plays for sympathy.

The room was perfectly still. Hauser stood at its head, hands behind his back, and it came to Sinclair that he resembled a man standing before a firing squad. The red, white and blue fellow handed him a glass of water. Hauser took a sip and resumed speaking, this time in smooth, leisurely tones.

"On my eighteenth birthday, here in Berlin, a visitor knocked at the door of the house where I lived with Dr. Hauser, my adopted father. A servant answered and told me a man wanted to see me. I went down the stairs, very curious and even thinking that Bella had made a mistake and it was my father whom the man really wanted to see. He was a middle-aged man who carried a bulging briefcase—I remember wondering what could be making the bulge. His German was good, but with the slightest foreign accent.

"He began by saying that he hoped he wasn't disturbing me. I said he wasn't, but that I wished he would get on with it since I planned to meet friends for a game of soccer. In those years I dreamed of being a soccer star. Sometimes I wish I had pursued that dream."

"Like Kissinger," someone said in the back of the room.

Kurt smiled. "Yes, exactly like Kissinger. . . . This man, this stranger, said that he had come to see me with a specific mission. Those were his exact words, 'a specific mission.' He asked me to trust him, and this made me feel very uncomfortable. And then, when he opened that briefcase—well, you can imagine! I thought he must be deranged.

"He took out an ink pad, a small square of cardboard and a magnifying glass. I thought, 'My God, it's the Polizei,' and I frantically wondered what I had done wrong. He said, 'May I have your fingerprint?' and he said it so courteously that I went ahead and pressed a finger to the cardboard, on which I saw the photo of a fingerprint. He held the glass to his face and stared at my fingerprint. Then he said, 'It's you all right,' and took my hand and pressed it.

"By now I was sure I was in the company of a lunatic, and I started to edge toward the door. 'Do you know who you are?' he asked me. That stopped me cold—like every other orphan of the war I had wondered about my origins. I sat down and said, 'Yes, as much as possible.'

" 'Tell me,' he ordered, and I told him what I had been told by Dr. Hauser. On April 26, 1945, he and another gynecologist returned from delivering a baby. It was late at night and on his stoop Hauser found a bundle: me.

"Under ordinary circumstances he would have immediately turned me over to proper authorities, but this was Berlin in 1945, and what authorities there were, were busy taking cyanide capsules or trying to escape to the American forces.

"Hauser, a widower, took me in. He was too old to be a parent, but he raised me as his own son, told me this story when he felt the time was right. It was not an unusual story in Germany, we were a nation of widows and orphans. I thought of myself as just another victim of . . ."

Kurt stopped, his face no longer impassive. Liedtke attempted to give him more water but he waved the man away.

"Forgive me, I don't like or approve of public displays. In politicians such as myself it is most suspect. I'll go on—my visitor listened to this story without comment. When I was finished he sat there like a diner who expects another course. My silence informed him that this was all I knew.

" 'The story is not true,' the man said. 'Hauser's story is a sad one. The true story is also sad, but glorious too.'

"When he said this, I felt frightened. If not a madman, he

was a fanatic, and I have always hated and been frightened by fanatics.

" 'You were born in the spring of 1945,' he told me. 'Before your parents' marriage, which took place a few months before their deaths. Hauser was the attending gynecologist, and when he delivered you, two of your father's associates told him that he must take you with him.

" 'Hauser protested, but not too much, considering who your father's associates were and what they could have done to him had he refused.'

"He paused, and seemed to expect my question: Who *were* these associates?

" 'Joseph Goebbels and Martin Bormann.'

"I remember hearing the names and I remember the blood rushing from my head and the blue carpet coming up to meet my face. Then I was lying on a couch and the man was giving me brandy from a flask he must have taken out of that bottomless briefcase.

" 'Are you all right? Can you hear me?'

"I said I could hear him, and he went right on.

" 'Your mother was told you had been stillborn. When she began to protest she was given strong drugs on which she remained until she died. It was just as well. Believe me, it was for the best. She did not suffer.

" 'The handful of people who knew of your mother's pregnancy, including her personal physician and her servants, were executed. Only Hauser, Goebbels, Bormann and your father knew of your birth.'

" 'My . . . father?' I said.

" 'Of course,' the man said. 'Adolf Hitler.'

"I remember feeling dizzy again, I wanted to faint, but couldn't. 'Why have you done this to me?' I said.

" 'A man must know who he is,' he said, and then he took a camera with a flash attachment out of the briefcase. 'Sit up,' he told me, and I was too dazed to protest. He took two pictures of me, put the camera back into the case and went to the door.

" 'Why have you done this to me?' I cried out.

" 'A man must know who he is,' he said again, and then he was gone, and it might have been a dream except for the taste of brandy on my tongue.

"Later, Dr. Hauser came home and found me still sitting there.

" 'A man came today,' I said. He knew. He knew right away. He sat beside me on the couch and I cried as if I were eight and not eighteen. 'I'm so sorry,' was all he said, and we sat there for a long time, not talking.

"Then I asked him, 'Am I who the man said I am?' He nodded and said, 'I had hoped you would never find out. There was simply no reason for it.'

"In the weeks that followed I pressed him for more information, but by now he was quite old and I could get nothing from him that the man hadn't already told me.

"And now, ladies and gentlemen, you have been most patient and I will attempt to answer any questions you may have."

Sinclair's hand shot up. "Do you think Hauser knew more than he told you?"

Kurt's face clouded over. "I had no way of knowing. Perhaps he did, perhaps his memory had simply failed. He was a hell of a man, and when he died in my arms I called him 'Father.' "

There was a pause. Sinclair thought, Either we've just heard the truth or the bloke's the best actor since Sir Laurence. And then the questions came furiously, from all over the room.

"Did you later recognize this man from photos?"

"No. I examined photos of Bormann and several others. None of them resembled the man who visited me."

"Why do you think he wanted your photo?"

"Obviously to show to someone else."

"You never heard from him again?"

"Never."

"Have you discussed this matter with anyone else prior to this conference?"

"I telephoned the Chancellor."

"Why?"

"Because I was ashamed. That I had let him down. That all these years I had not been able to tell him."

"What was Chancellor Haack's reaction?"

"You will have to get that from the Chancellor."

"What do you see as your future with the Liberal Democrat party?"

"That is up to the Liberal Democrat party."

"Do you want to remain a candidate?"

"I have no comment at this time."

Dan Rather stood up. "No disrespect meant, but I for one find it rather hard to swallow that the man with the briefcase, who so obviously wanted to know if you were the son, *never* contacted you again."

"No disrespect meant either," said Kurt, "but you'll have to swallow it. That is precisely what happened."

Rather stared at him. "Why do you think he told you in the first place?"

Sinclair, sensing the gathering anger in Kurt, looked at Rather with admiration.

Kurt, to Sinclair's surprise, seemed to grow more calm.

"Mr. Rather," he said courteously, "if I knew that, I would share my knowledge, perhaps only with your network. Perhaps for a fee."

After the laughter had died down, Dan Rather said quietly, "Thank you, Mr. Hitler."

It's over, thought Sinclair. Not for the first time, he was wrong.

BERLIN (AP)—*At the close of the press conference during which Kurt Hauser, the Liberal Democrat candidate for Governing Mayor, gave reporters his version of how he learned that he was the son of Adolf Hitler, a 78-year-old Berlin pensioner, Horst Pahl, rushed Hauser screaming, "Murderer, son of a murderer!"*

The man leaped at Hauser and beat at him until agents of the Bundeskriminalamt surrounded the attacker and bodily removed him, still screaming "Murderer."

Hauser, who did not defend himself during the attack, said later that he would not press charges.

Horst Pahl sat on a bench and watched the prostitutes. Earlier he had watched the pigeons search for food. That was his schedule on days when his pension check had run out. When he had money, almost all of it went for whiskey, a little of it for food, a little for rent and some for Lili, his cat.

Lili had found him, come to his door starving and mangy. She would not go away and he took her in. Now, she fared as he did. When there was money she ate. When there wasn't . . . He didn't know what she did.

God knows there was no shortage of rats where he lived, but Horst Pahl could not remember ever seeing her make a kill.

He wore a ragged sweater through which his elbows stuck out where there had once been leather patches, a torn shirt, baggy corduroy pants, and shapeless slippers. He no longer walked, he shuffled.

Unnoticed in the grime of his sweater was a pin now covered with dirt. Once he had been a master carpenter.

Now his hands shook so badly that he held them together as though he were in constant prayer.

He saw a man stop and talk to a prostitute. There beneath a streetlight, for a moment only, he could have sworn that the man was his youngest son . . . Or his oldest son, or the middle one who played the piano. The man laughed. The girl laughed. The vision died in the streetlight.

He heard a church bell strike the hour and he counted slowly as though he were the starter for a race. Midnight.

He stood, was dizzy for a moment, held onto the bench and became aware that the girl and the man were watching him. He gave them a toothless grin.

"Give him a couple of marks," said the girl. "He's my good-luck charm."

The man said something and threw some coins at Horst Pahl's feet. He picked them up and touched his unkempt hair in a salute of thanks.

He shuffled slowly to an all-night grocery store where he bought a beer and a can of cat food. Even as he paid for it he tore the top from the can and drank until the beer trickled down his grimy face. Then, after saluting the grocery, he started home.

A police car slowed down; its occupants stared at him as if in warning, then drove away.

He climbed the stairs to his room and opened the door. He no longer locked it; his fingers couldn't manage the key.

He was opening the cat food under the light bulb that hung down over his bed when he realized that he wasn't alone. He turned slowly, holding out the can as if it were a weapon. A man sat in Horst Pahl's one chair, holding Lili, rubbing her fur with a black glove.

"Who?" asked Pahl.

"Don't you know me?" the man answered. Lili purred.

"Yes. Yes, I know you, Mr. Hitler."

"You were rude to me, Horst. Very rude. You struck me."

"Drunk."

Lili purred; the black glove tweaked her ear gently.

"You struck me—and in public. You humiliated me."

"Drunk."

"Do you know who I am, Horst?"

Lili purred. The man looked down at her and smiled.

"Does she have a name?"

"Lili."

"Do you love her?"

Horst Pahl shrugged.

Horst Pahl said, desperately, "You can't hurt me," holding on to his own trembling hands.

"I don't believe I can." Lili stirred, trying to get away from the black gloves that held her. The gloves tightened. Lili purred more loudly, began to struggle.

"Please," whispered Horst Pahl. "Please."

"You humiliated me." The gloved hand moved quickly; Lili yowled from the depths of her chest, then the sound died and her head hung at a grotesque angle, as though she were listening to her own heart.

The man stood. Lili's body fell to the floor. "You humiliated me," the man said again.

He went to the door, where he paused. "And now you must be a good boy, Horst, or believe me, you will join little Lili."

He smiled warmly and was gone.

7

In Jerusalem, in a small office in the Hadassah Medical Center located on Mount Scopus, Dr. Abraham Kadesh sat contemplating the closing moments of his professional career and awaiting Dr. Shelomo Pollak, his young successor.

The office floor was cluttered with cardboard boxes overflowing with scientific journals, newspaper clippings, even recipes.

Someplace in one of the boxes was a medal, Israel's highest military decoration, presented to Dr. Kadesh in secret ceremonies for his career as consulting psychiatrist to the Mossad, the Hebrew acronym for "Central Institute for Intelligence and Security."

On Dr. Kadesh's desk lay a large manila envelope. The psychiatrist was examining it when a polite rap on the door announced Dr. Pollak, who stuck his head in and asked, "May I come in?"

"May you? It's your office," said Dr. Kadesh, covering the tinge of regret that had colored his words with what he hoped was a big smile.

"Dr. Kadesh," said Pollak, "this will always be your office. Whenever you return to Jerusalem, you will—"

"I will never return to Jerusalem. When I get to that kibbutz on the Golan, dispensing aspirin and setting broken arms, I will not even think of Jerusalem. Not once!"

"Withdrawal symptoms, Doctor?" Pollak said gently.

A genuine smile broke across Abraham Kadesh's face and he threw back his head and laughed.

"Precisely, I'm having withdrawal symptoms!"

"Can I get you a cup of rotten coffee?" the young psychiatrist asked.

Kadesh stood up. "Goddamnit, man, don't treat me like an invalid."

Pollak bowed apologetically, and the two men went to the coffee machine in the hall, Kadesh carrying the manila envelope in his fist.

"It's a kind of distinction, you know." Pollak sipped the coffee and winced. "In all of Jerusalem we have the worst coffee."

"Dr. Shapiro told me his theory," Kadesh said as they carried their cups back to the office. "That we get our water from the sewer in the Arab section."

Dr. Pollak laughed, then put his cup down.

"Isn't our patient late, Doctor?"

"He'll be along, he's very dependable," said Kadesh. He then touched the envelope.

"It's all here," he said, indicating the envelope's contents, a fat dossier. He pushed it across the desk toward the younger man.

"He was on the first boatload of children brought here, smuggled here under the British, from the concentration camps. He had been in Majdanek, near Lublin, Poland, where some two hundred and fifty thousand Jews died. We waited for them like a farmer waits for seeds: this as yet unborn country needed them so badly and they needed . . . well, we needed each other.

"We had come to this desert to prepare it for them. It wasn't the most choice location—oh, my, all stone and sand, a few bushes, a handful of trees—but there was no other place!"

Dr. Kadesh did not realize that he was shouting.

"Isn't it strange, after all these years, I still can't get over it, no one wanted the victims? Not even in the United States, the United States! Did you know that an American senator, a Senator Wagner of New York State, in 1939 introduced a bill into the Congress to let ten thousand Jewish children into the United States, through their famous golden door. Such a door! The bill was defeated in committee, it never even got to the Congress for a vote. The door was slammed shut on all those victims."

Dr. Pollak was embarrassed, yet he did not turn from the other man.

"Do you read the Old Testament?" Kadesh asked. Dr. Pollak nodded.

"Lamentations four, verse four," began the old man, and Pollak continued: "The tongue of the sucking child cleaveth to the roof of his mouth for thirst; the young children ask bread, and none breaketh it unto them."

Dr. Kadesh nodded approvingly. "They were . . . well, you had to see them to understand, these little Jews. They had been deloused and given clothes. Some were sick. Some jabbered, couldn't stop talking, some were quiet. Some had nothing to say, for the rest of their lives they will have nothing to say. Some laughed hysterically. A few wept. And Max Levy smiled and held on for dear life to the hand of an older boy—they had been in Majdanek together. A boy named Shemuel Reiter. Time is something. I can close my eyes and still see them, eyes four times too large for their shrunken cranial structure, bellies bloated, skin the color of paste." Kadesh stopped; his eyes were closed, and Dr. Pollak sat waiting for the man's nightmare vision to pass.

Kadesh shook his head from side to side, opened his eyes and looked defiantly at the other psychiatrist, as if daring him to question his unprofessional behavior.

"I understand," Dr. Pollak said simply.

Dr. Kadesh smiled and said, "I'll bet you're a good doctor."

There was a gentle knock on the door. The two doctors stared at each other as though caught in an indiscretion, then Dr. Kadesh called out, "Come!"

A young man entered.

"Hello, Max," the older doctor said. "This is Dr. Shelomo Pollak, my replacement."

Max Levy looked at Dr. Pollak. Pollak smiled at Levy

as though they were being introduced on a golf course.

"Did the trip go as planned?" Kadesh asked.

Max Levy nodded. "I feel all right."

Kadesh stood up. "Good luck, Max. If you ever get up to the Golan, look me up. Maybe I'll cook you a fine meal." He made no motion to shake hands, nor did Levy, and in a moment the old physician was gone from the room and from Max Levy's life.

"I hope we will be friends," said Dr. Pollak. "I hope in time you may trust me and even like me, though that's not at all necessary. Will you miss Dr. Kadesh?"

Max Levy stared back and Pollak wondered if his silence meant that he was considering the question. He decided to remain silent and see. But Levy said nothing.

Seconds ticked by. From a nearby mosque a prayer wafted across the Jerusalem air like the cry of an exotic bird.

"Why did he go?" Levy asked softly.

"He got old. He got tired. No one asked him to. It was at his request. It happens, you know, men get tired. All men." Pollak smiled. "One day me."

Again, Pollak let time crawl by until it became obvious that Levy had no more to say on the subject. "You knew he was leaving?"

"He told me but he did not say it would be so soon. I thought perhaps in a year."

"He is a very wise man. He knew when it was time. Like an athlete—their legs give out, they're not so fast any more. Do you like sports?"

"I watch the basketball."

"Ever play?"

"No."

Dr. Pollak sighed. "I will give you the telephone number at my apartment. Please call me there if . . . if you like. During the day I'll usually be here or they'll know how to get me. Just like Dr. Kadesh." For a moment his eyes met Levy's, then Dr. Pollak lowered his to the envelope on the desk. Levy just sat there.

Dr. Pollak felt exhausted, as if he had spent too much

time in a steam room. He stood and did not realize that he was leaning on his desk for support.

"Thank you for coming," he said.

Levy nodded and was gone. Dr. Pollak waited until the other man had time to leave the building, then went into the hall for a fresh cup of coffee. With it he sat at his desk, the dossier before him, Max Levy's past written out in the old doctor's careful handwriting.

"Levy, Max. Born 1931, Alsace-Lorraine. Parents Julius and Celine Levy, internationally famous circus clowns under the professional name, The Merry Jesters. European favorites . . ."

Levy had traveled with his parents, who were stars of Circus Bakel. In the late 1930s Karl Bakel joined the Nazi party, which demanded identification of all Jewish employees. Bakel was among the first to submit his list, the Levys and a trapeze artist named Zeevi.

One night after a performance in Berlin, the Levys, still in their clown costumes, were arrested along with Zeevi and put aboard a train that, they were told, would take them to a work camp in Poland. They were packed 150 to a car, which was then sealed—sealed, that is, to everyone but the trapeze artist. Zeevi squeezed through a window of the train and escaped, only to be caught by villagers who beat him to death with stones.

Also in the same car with the Levys was sixteen-year-old Shemuel Reiter, now secretary of Mishmar Elijah Kibbutz and the source of an account of what happened at Majdanek.

Dr. Pollak's coffee had grown cold on the desk before him. He unbuttoned his collar and loosened his tie. By now it was growing dark in the room, and he switched on a small desk lamp which lit the pages before him like a spotlight.

Shemuel Reiter's statement was typed on a typewriter that badly needed a new ribbon. Already some of the words were beginning to fade on the page.

"I was separated from my parents at the railroad station in Berlin and I never saw them again. My mother asked them to let me go in the railcar with them, but a soldier punched her breasts and . . . I was sixteen, and my father shouted at me to be a man. I suppose I knew what he meant. I found myself squeezed next to this most strange couple and their child. At first their makeup and costumes frightened me. But their kid Max told me that they were clowns, and I honestly don't think we'd have made it in that car but for the Levys. They made us laugh with their absurd riddles and all sorts of imitations of farm animals. The father could bray just like a donkey—which, he said, was his imitation of the Führer. No one laughed harder at their antics than their kid; you could tell he was really proud, and I don't blame him, they were funny even in those awful conditions.

"It seemed we were in that car forever, and people slept standing against each other, though we managed to make room for one pregnant woman to lie down. She died, all the same.

"This kid Max slept up against my chest, and during the night, it must have been night, his father whispered to me to look after him if I could. It was so eerie there in the darkness, this white clown face whispering things in my ear.

"Finally the train came to a stop, and those goddamn doors were opened, and let me tell you it was one beautiful day. I've never seen the sky so blue or the sun so orange. It looked like we had stepped into a painting.

"We must have been some sight, fouled with our own urine and feces, the pregnant woman's body beginning to smell and the Levys, still in their costumes that weren't funny any more.

"The camp commandant was a jolly-looking man, almost a Saint Nicholas, not at all what you'd expect. He greeted us courteously and promised that those who did their fair share would get plenty enough to eat, while those who didn't—well, naturally it won't go too well for them, but what could you expect? He asked us that, 'What can you expect?'

"The secret of success, he told us, was simple: cooperation, immediate and unquestioning obeying of any order given by a German soldier.

" 'In a way,' he said, 'you will be good soldiers.'

"It must have been at that moment that his eyes hit upon the Levys, so strangely dressed, in spangles and sunbursts, in pompons and filthy white stockings. He ordered them politely enough to step forward. 'Clowns?' he asked good-naturedly, and the Levys smiled and said, 'Yes.'

"He addressed the rest of us. 'This is as good a time as any to teach you the golden rule of obeying. These clowns will perform for you, thus carrying out their function in life. As long as you laugh, they will live because they will be performing a useful function. When you stop laughing, they will be functionless.'

" 'Be funny,' he ordered the Levys. These people were not stupid, and as soon as attention was called to them they stepped away from their son. Levy's father threw me a look, well, I can't describe it but I took Max's hand.

"The Levys did begin to perform. Cartwheels, backflips, somersaults, loud noises and playful slaps at each other. At first, like a joke, 'I hear no laughter.'

"The laughter started though no face smiled. We must have stood that way for an hour until the Levys fell to the ground exhausted, and now we had stopped laughing except for the laughter out of Max's mouth. He tried to break loose from me but I held onto his hand while he laughed and howled until his voice was hoarse.

" 'What?' said the commandant. 'Are the clowns no longer funny? Not even worth a smile?'

"All of us were looking down at the ground except for Max. He was grinning insanely though he could no longer make a noise.

"The commandant smiled, then shrugged as though he couldn't help it. He said, 'You are now officially useless: kindly stand and march until I say stop.'

"The German soldiers were nudging each other in the ribs, some even laughing aloud at their commander's sense of humor.

"The Levys pushed themselves up from the ground, and I remember the husband took his wife's hand and they marched away like cartoon characters until they came to an open cesspool. They hesitated but they did not look back, and I pressed Max's face against my stomach.

" 'March!' shouted the commandant, and march they did, right into the muck and the slime. Until they were gone."

Dr. Pollak could not go on. He closed the dossier and slipped it back into its envelope. Carrying it under one arm, he turned off the desk lamp and went out into the Jerusalem night.

8

Senator Rudi Rahms answered the door himself. Nervously he looked up and down the street before stepping aside and letting the other man enter.

Without speaking he reached for his guest's coat and hung it in a hall closet. He remained silent as he ushered the man into his sitting room, which was dominated by a huge portrait of Martin Luther, flanked by two burning candles.

The room was stark, churchlike, and the chairs were as uncomfortable as pews. The curtains were drawn and even the fire in the open fireplace had been allowed to die down.

"You shouldn't be here," Rahms said, hysteria just beneath the surface of his flat tones.

"Believe me, there was no other way."

"Still, reporters—"

"No one saw me, Rudi."

Rahms looked unconvinced. He stood and went to the windows and peeped out. The other man could hear his breathing: shallow, as if he was fighting for air.

"What do you want?" Rahms whispered.

"I need your help. I really need it, Rudi."

"I *am* helping. I am praying for you continuously!"

"That gives me great comfort," the other man said warmly. "But I'm going to need a little more than prayers."

"I have no more to give," Rahms said, finality in his voice.

"Just a little more, Rudi, just a little more."

"No, I'm sorry. I'm a Christian and my heart is filled with compassion."

"That's true, Rudi. I know you to be a compassionate man."

"And fair! Very, very fair."

"You are certainly that, Rudi."

Rahms stood. "Then there's no more for us to talk about."

The other man remained seated. "I need your vote, Rudi. In fact, I've got to have it."

"I'm sorry, Kurt. I'll make up my mind when the leadership meets. I can promise you this, my mind is open."

"That just won't do, Rudi. You see, I've got to have that vote in my pocket going in."

"That's impossible. Because you know me you should know that. Frankly, I'm distressed that you would think that I—"

"It wasn't my fault that he was my father, Rudi, any more—"

"You must go!"

"Any more than it's your fault that Trudi is your daughter."

Rahms yelped like a puppy. "No!"

"I can just imagine the heartbreak for you and your wife. Believe me, Rudi, I, of all people, know about heartbreak for which there is no relief."

"We haven't seen Tru . . . her for ten years. She's dead."

"Theoretically, of course. In fact she's very much alive. And in Frankfurt, Rudi. Not so far away."

"I said she was dead. We never speak of her."

"Of course you don't. I can understand that. The wife—"

"My wife is not well."

Kurt reached into his jacket pocket and took out a photograph. He held it out. "Look at her, Rudi, go ahead, look at her." He stood and went to Rahms, holding the photograph before the man's horrified eyes. "At first I thought it was a man. But it isn't, is it? It's just little Trudi. I must say she looks exactly like a man, and I'm told the girls love her."

Rahms collapsed into his chair. "You are killing me."

"Why, no, Rudi, you are very much alive. As is your fine wife. I'm as concerned about her well-being as you are. Your wife must never see this picture, Rudi. You and I have a moral obligation to see to that. Don't we? Well, Rudi, don't we?"

"Yes."

"I thought as much. No, don't stand. I'll let myself out. Oh, and Rudi . . ."

"Yes?"

"Keep praying for me. Everything helps."

Willi Fassmann sat back in his chauffeur-driven Mercedes and considered that life "was actually pretty good at that." Just now there was a storm, but the storm would pass; it always did. Storms had certainly passed for Willi Fassmann.

Only a handful of years before: a prominent Nazi whose close friendship with Albert Speer helped him to build one of the most successful insurance agencies of that day. Now: a leading Liberal Democrat and still heading the biggest insurance agency in Berlin.

Fassmann smiled in the automobile's darkness. He had survived because he believed in what he sold. Insurance.

When the pogroms started against the Jews, Willi had gone along with his characteristic enthusiasm. "I am a team player," he assured Speer, who was, as usual, quiet on the subject. Besides, Willi's greatest competitor was the Jewish firm of Weiss/Goldschmidt. When those gentlemen were hauled off to their fate ("I had no idea what it might be") and when their main offices were burned to the ground by "God knows who, there were so many hooligans afoot," Willi Fassmann found himself in very good shape indeed.

Still, there was that gnawing doubt that, in "this most important matter," he had no insurance. He decided to take some out.

Willi's prewar tailor had been a Jew, a small man named Finkenstadt, whose wife and five children lived above his shop. Willi liked the man's work because Finkenstadt's tailoring managed to make Willi look at least twenty pounds lighter, especially in his rump.

Soon after the pogrom began, Willi bought his insurance. One night he awakened the dazed and frightened Finkenstadts, who assumed that "their time had come." Instead, Willi piled them into a truck and hauled them off to his farm, one of three he owned.

Throughout the war he hid them there and tended them, even remembering to bring the children little gifts at Hanukkah.

When the war ended and Willi was rounded up, he insisted that he had "in fact saved Jews, not slaughtered them."

His captors were nearly as skeptical as Albert Speer, also a prisoner. Whereupon Willi produced the Finkenstadt family, all seven of them, as happy and healthy as though there had been no war at all.

Once the Finkenstadts identified Willi as their guardian angel, he was begrudgingly released. The public prosecutor's protest that "a malicious confidence job has been perpetrated against humanity" was drowned out by the cries of joy from the embracing Finkenstadts and Willi.

After his trial, Speer had whispered to him, "You're a clever man, Willi." Fassmann replied with a deprecative shrug, "I am a human being."

He even took the Finkenstadts on a trip to Israel, where he and the family were photographed at the Western Wall, Willi wearing a yarmulke.

Willi did not see Speer again until 1976, when the two showed up at the same cocktail party. Both men turned away, having nothing to say.

Now the big car drew to a smooth stop in front of Liberal Democrat party headquarters. The chauffeur jumped out and opened the door for Willi, who suggested that he "go get something to eat, it'll be a long night."

He entered the room in which the executive committee, sixteen strong, was waiting. Newspapers were strewn over the table, each of them featuring front-page stories of Kurt Hitler.

Willi sank into his chair and rapped on the table.

"Let's get started, gentlemen. I have requested that certain of you prepare reports. Suppose we begin with you, Bachem."

Hans Bachem stood with a folder in his hands. A preacher, not a politician.

"I was given the assignment, the difficult assignment let me say, in the short span of time allotted to me, to try to project for us whether the name Hitler might not be an asset in Germany rather than a liability. To do this I have had to equate Hitler and Nazism. I believe this to be a safe equation, but I should note that—"

"Just get on with it," Willi said. "If you give us all sides of the issue we'll be sitting here for a week."

"As you wish," said Bachem. "I have asked myself this question: How have neo-Nazi groups fared in Germany in 1977? In last year's parliamentary election, the extreme right-wing National Democratic party got only three hundredths of a percent of the votes. It has no seats in Parliament. This very week I checked with the West German Interior Ministry in Bonn, with some help from Chancellor Haack.

"I am pleased to report that the Ministry informs me that Nazism is dead in West Germany today and forever. There are a few nuts—Roeder, a disbarred lawyer; Kühnen, a dishonorably discharged Bundeswehr lieutenant—and their followers, marching about Mannheim, desecrating a few synagogues and cemeteries, people living in their own madness and bitterness. Otherwise, nothing."

Willi motioned for the man to be seated. "Thank you, Hans."

At that moment Gunther Liedtke entered with a gracious bow to the group, which chose not to acknowledge it. He sat against a wall to Fassmann's rear.

"As agreed, I spoke with the Chancellor—" Willi stopped and peered down the table at Rudi Rahms, who seemed to be writing on a pad. "I thought we agreed that no records would be kept of this meeting," said Fassmann.

Rahms looked up, embarrassed. "I'm not keeping records, I'm doodling. I do it all the time." He held up the pad on which was a better than amateur drawing of Christ's face.

Fassmann quickly apologized, then complimented Rahms on the drawing: "I wouldn't mind having that." The pleased Rahms tore the page off and passed it to Fassmann, who handed it over his shoulder for Liedtke to hold. Liedtke stared at the face as if he knew it.

"As I was saying," Willi continued, "I spoke with Chancellor Haack on the telephone. I would have preferred to see him in person, but he did not seem to want this. I believe he said he had a cold or perhaps it was the gout."

The others laughed politely.

Willi smiled. "He said, not in these words, mind you, we're on our own. I gather he has taken Mr. Hitler's—may I call it deceit?—quite personally. He trusted Hauser, or whatever his name is now."

"It is Hitler," said Rudi Rahms, busy sketching again.

Gunther Liedtke cleared his throat.

"Yes?" said Fassmann, without turning around.

"I should like to comment," said the party publicist. "I believe you gentlemen may be missing an important factor, a factor that may work to the party's good."

"Do tell us what we have missed, Mr. Liedtke," said Fassmann.

"The publicity that has been engendered by Mr. Hitler's revelation has been—well, to put it mildly, immense."

"So was the bombing of Hiroshima," said Emil Dahr. Everyone laughed again.

"Publicity in our times, all publicity, good, bad, whatever, has some benefit. The Liberal Democrat party has had newspaper space and radio and television time that could not be purchased for ten million deutsche marks."

"All of it bad!" roared Fassmann, whirling about in his chair and shouting into Liedtke's face. The publicist shrugged.

Fassmann's voice was still uncustomarily loud.

"Gentlemen, as you know I am not one for crudity, I do not even like to hear it, but really there is only one word that I can think of that aptly sums up our situation and what has been perpetrated against us, all of us. We've been fucked!"

Fassmann did not get the reaction he expected. Judging

by the assembled expressions, he was getting no reaction at all. He did, however, have their attention.

"I apologize for my language," said the insurance magnate. "But how he could do this to us is inconceivable. We have honored him in every way that a political party can honor one of its own, sometimes to our disadvantage, and for him to—well, I think the Chancellor said it best—'for him to lead us on . . .' "

"In a word," said Emil Dahr, "we now face the most crushing defeat we or any other major party have ever faced. That's what it's really all about, isn't it? How many of us Mr. Hitler takes down with him, God only knows. I for one look for the people of Berlin to totally repudiate our unfortunate past, of which, like it or not, Kurt Hitler is a symbol."

"A symbol? He is the past," Rudi Rahms said quietly.

"What do you think, Bachem?" asked Fassmann. The party tactician lit his pipe and the others watched as the bowl slowly was puffed into life.

"One thing is certain," said Bachem. "The die is cast, there's not much we can do about it. As a courtesy we must hear Kurt—Mr. Hitler—out, but I can't imagine what he could say to us. There's no going back, is there?"

"It seems to me we've wasted years listening to him," said Fassmann, "and none of it was true."

"Granted," said Imbach. "But who would we put in his place before the electorate for Governing Mayor?"

Emil Dahr asked what was on all their minds: "Does it really matter, anyway? Is there any man in this room who has a single doubt that we will not be simply beaten but devastated at the polls? Come, come, gentlemen, there are no children in politics, certainly none in this room."

Fassmann turned to Liedtke and said, "Better check if he's out there yet; these walls are mighty thin."

Liedtke stood and went to the door, opened it and peered out while the others sat uncomfortably silent.

"He's not here," said Liedtke. "But twenty or so reporters are."

"Vultures," someone hissed.

"Shhh," cautioned Liedtke. "The vultures can hear you."

So stunned were the faces about the table that Liedtke said, "I'm only joking, no one heard."

"Gentlemen, gentlemen," said Willi Fassmann, rapping on the table with a big hand.

Now there was noise in the hall, loud voices. Liedtke peered out at the figure of Kurt Hitler making his way through a crowd of reporters who thrust microphones, cameras and legal tablets near his face.

"Later," said Kurt. Liedtke went into the hall and helped steer him into the now-quiet room.

"Gentlemen," Kurt said soberly. No one about the table offered him a chair, and Liedtke gave him his. Kurt sat in it, against the wall, like a student outside the principal's office.

Fassmann did not turn to acknowledge his presence. As if he were presiding over an ordinary meeting, he asked Dieter Jabusch for "his report." Jabusch, who seemed surprised to be called on, cleared his throat a great deal before getting to the point: "Two hundred and fifty thousand party posters are in place."

"And more to come?" asked tactician Bachem, a big believer in posters.

"Another two hundred and fifty thousand over the weekend. We have covered Berlin in posters."

"And in something else too," said Johann Geider. No one laughed.

"I don't know if we can afford another two hundred and fifty thousand posters," said Fritz Imbach. The others waited until the plumbing contractor came to the rescue.

"I will be happy to shoulder the cost of the additional posters," he said.

He was informed, predictably, that he was a good and noble fellow.

"We must all do our best," he said to no one in particular.

At the head of the room, Fassmann indulged himself in a sigh, one that clearly said, "This is it." He resembled a statue of Buddha; the face suddenly had no flexibility, the fat seemed to have turned to stone, the thick happy lips were stretched into a thin line. His voice was as cold as his features.

"And now there is the matter of Mr. Kurt Hitler. What we must decide here this evening is on the surface quite simple: whether Mr. Hitler will continue as our announced choice for Governing Mayor of Berlin or whether we will, by vote of this committee, require him to step down. Naturally, should that step be taken, Mr. Hitler will then have to decide for himself whether or not he desires to continue standing for his seat in Parliament. But that is no concern of ours. I am obligated to remind this committee that in a matter of days we have our precious television time, exactly five minutes, in which Mr. Hitler was to sum up our party platform to the electorate."

Fassmann turned to Kurt for the first time. "Mr. Hitler," he said coldly, "you may speak."

Kurt sat still for a moment almost as if he had not heard the other man's words. *He's got nothing to say,* thought Liedtke. Then, with the slightest shake of his head, like a man awakening from a daytime dream, he began to speak, so softly that someone at the opposite end of the room shouted, "Louder!" Kurt nodded but was silent.

He's in shock, thought Liedtke.

"I've let you down terribly," he said in his quiet voice, "and the animosity that I feel in this room is totally justified. In your shoes, I would feel the same. We've all been through so much together, most of it bad. Defeat after defeat. Election nights that were nightmares. Suffering the smug smiles of our political enemies. Taking it and trying to come back another day. Losing. That's what most of our efforts really came to, and nothing, *nothing* hurts like defeat. We smiled while we were dying inside. Every one of us.

"Sharing one terrible experience after another does something to people. It brings them closer together. It's as though they huddle together for warmth, for comfort, to make their pain less. And somehow, in that process of surviving, they become brothers. A family.

"I see some of you smiling and I don't blame you, but do believe me, you are—were—my family."

The smiles died.

"Now, my family must sit in judgment over me and I've lost the right to ask for mercy. I imagine I lost that right a long time ago, at the beginning, when I didn't come clean, tell you who I really was and that there wasn't a damned thing that I or anyone else could do about it.

"But I didn't. My secret was so terrible I could barely whisper it to myself, much less proclaim it aloud. So, I've betrayed you. That also is difficult to say aloud. Perhaps it's time that I start saying the things that hurt and learn to accept the consequences. I know I will never be silent again about—about things that can hurt innocent people. If I've learned nothing else, at least I've learned that lesson."

Rudi Rahms had put down his doodling pen. His eyes were closed and his hands were clasped before him. Willi Fassmann stared stonily ahead. Dieter Jabusch nervously pulled at an ear.

"I am prepared to accept the consequences of my actions," Kurt said. "Or should I say, my lack of action? No matter, it's the same. If you throw me out of the party, be assured that I will go quietly and will have nothing to say to the press against your actions. Nor will I bother you again."

He stood up and took a step forward. His hands were clasped behind his back. "Should you, on the other hand, allow me to continue as your choice for Governing Mayor, I'll give you the best that's in me. I'll represent you with my heart and my soul. Surprisingly, considering my heritage, I do have both: a heart and a soul. These possessions desire to serve you, this party and this city.

"Regardless of your decision, you've given me much more consideration than I deserved. Whatever your judgment, believe me, it will never be as harsh as the judgment which I've made upon myself.

"If you cast me from you, I wish you well. I truly mean that. Still . . . still I hope that once again you'll let me be your brother. For that is what we who are in this room really are: brothers."

He looked at Willi Fassmann and said, "Thank you, Mr. Chairman."

He had ended so softly that few of them knew he had finished. He stood there, unmoving, until his hands finally moved from behind his back and rested by his side.

"Do any of you want to say anything in Mr. Hitler's presence?" Fassmann asked into total silence. Fassmann shrugged. "Then, Mr. Hitler, I shall ask you to step into the other room while we vote. Mr. Liedtke, I would like you also to leave."

Kurt Hitler and Gunther Liedtke stepped into a small room which contained a bench, a table and a flag of Berlin too big for the room. Liedtke slumped onto the bench, where the end of the flag enveloped him as if he were a coffin at a military funeral.

"That was some speech," said Liedtke. Kurt stood there, not answering him. "What do you think your chances are?" Liedtke insisted.

Kurt stared at the other man. "I don't know; I do know how I'd vote if I was in that room and someone named Hitler was in here."

"And that is?"

"Against."

"Are you quite serious?" Liedtke asked, his glasses shooting off tiny beams of light in all directions.

"I'm serious."

Liedtke shook his head, then asked, "Where are your security men?"

"I released them."

"Was that wise?"

"No," said Kurt, smiling for the first time that evening. "Policemen make me nervous."

"There may be more incidents," said Liedtke. "Like that maniac."

"That was not a maniac. He was an old man who had lost seven children and his wife in the war. All good Germans. He had every right to feel the way he did."

"You *spoke* to him?"

"Yes, I went to his apartment when he had gotten control of himself. His name was Horst Pahl, he's become an alcoholic. He never stopped weeping, but this time on my shoulder. I'm going to have a lot of experiences like that. I do not intend to avoid them."

Inside the larger room Willi Fassmann was speaking.

"Now, gentlemen, it is time to vote. We may do so in one of two ways. Openly or secretly."

"Secretly," said Rudi Rahms.

Emil Dahr turned to the chairman. "What do you think, Willi?"

"I do not feel that I should give an opinion, as I will not be voting. Unless, of course, there is a tie."

"I say vote in the open," said Werner Mader. "I can tell you I am not embarrassed of my vote."

"It's not a matter of embarrassment," said Fritz Imbach. "It's a matter of, well, privacy."

"Shall we first vote on how we'll vote?" said Fassmann with a smile. "Very well, all in favor of voting in secret say 'Aye,' those opposed, 'No.' Gentlemen?"

By a wide margin the vote was for a secret ballot, and the pieces of paper were quietly handed down the table. Some voted immediately, then folded their ballots and held onto them tightly. Some of them whispered quietly together.

"Are we all done?" Fassmann asked, and there were replies of "No!" Fassmann waited patiently as the minutes ticked by. Finally he said, "And now, gentlemen, if you please, your ballots."

The ballots were poured out from a large box onto the table where everyone could watch Hans Bachem tally them. He did this meticulously, then announced, "That's it."

Bachem looked at the sheet of paper on which he had recorded the votes and read aloud. "For . . . for . . . for . . . for . . . against . . . against . . . against . . . for . . . for . . . against . . . for . . . against . . . against . . . against . . . for . . . . against. Eight to eight, a tie."

Chairman Willi Fassmann sat feeling his jowls with a pudgy forefinger, all eyes on him. No one said a word.

He stared at Bachem, as though for counsel; the other man lowered his eyes.

"Well, Willi?" Johann Geider said.

Willi Fassmann said, "For."

9

For Kurt's dreaded trip to see the Chancellor in Bonn, Dieter Jabusch had loaned Kurt his private Lear jet.

Kurt sat back in a blue chair with the plumbing contractor's initials on it and sipped a glass of cool white Riesling. They were flying at thirty thousand feet and would be at the airport in Cologne in a matter of minutes.

The captain's voice came on the intercom: "Will you need transportation in Cologne, sir?" Kurt thanked the man but declined.

At the airport he jumped into a taxi for the twenty-five minute ride to Bonn.

The Chancellor's official residence, Adenauerallee 139-141, was a starkly modern two-story house of glass and concrete that sat incongruously among old oak and pine trees. The living room where Kurt waited was decorated in severe Scandinavian steel and wood modern.

Frau Gerda Umbreit, the Chancellor's housekeeper—the Chancellor's wife had been dead for many years—asked Kurt if he'd care for coffee. In the past she would have automatically brought out sugar cookies or even puffs filled with fresh whipped cream. He thanked her but said no, thinking that what he'd really like was a good jigger of schnapps.

Frau Umbreit, who must have been as old as the Chancellor, attempted to make small talk. Neither she nor Kurt was able to pull it off. She simply could not stop staring at him as though he were a freak in a sideshow, then flushing whenever he seemed to catch her at it. She finally solved her problem by removing her gold-rimmed glasses and holding them primly in her lap. Now, he knew, she was practically blind.

As a law student Kurt had on at least two occasions borrowed twenty marks from her to tide him over until his check came from his tour guide job. The transaction had always been very formal, with Kurt insisting on drawing up an I.O.U. Haack, then a professor, had even caught them at it once and had agreed to sign the document as a witness.

Kurt had promised Frau Umbreit repeatedly that after graduation he would marry her. Her reply was always the same: "You are too old for me!"

Now they sat like strangers and Kurt was relieved when she left as Josef Haack made his entrance. As always, he carried himself perfectly erect. As always, Kurt thought, how like a Chancellor he looked.

The two men shook hands—the Chancellor's touch was cold and dry—and settled into two chairs facing each other.

"Congratulations on your, ah, victory," said Haack.

"Thank you, sir. They didn't boot me out, which I suppose makes it a victory."

"I was surprised that you got Willi Fassmann's vote," said the Chancellor. "Especially in view of our telephone conversation earlier in the day."

"He's a strange one," Kurt said vaguely.

"No," said the Chancellor, "Willi Fassmann is a totally predictable man. That's what makes his vote so surprising."

Kurt did not comment.

"And now the campaign," said the Chancellor. "I know you will give it your best—that was always your way."

A note of warmth had crept into his voice, and Kurt responded eagerly.

"I'll work like a field animal."

"Like you did in law school," said the Chancellor.

"I had inspiration in law school," Kurt said, looking straight into the old man's eyes.

"You were a good student," the Chancellor said, "not the brightest, but you had more . . . promise."

"Have I lost that?"

The Chancellor did not immediately answer. Finally he said, "Only you can say. And not with your tongue, which we all know to be golden, but with your actions. You will be minutely scrutinized, Kurt, your every move in the campaign, your every appeal. I would be less than honest if I did not tell you that I also will be looking."

"But that's so unfair," Kurt said softly. "I'm the same man."

"No," said Haack, "not the *same* man, and you never will be again. You are your father's son."

"What a cross," Kurt said, his voice tired.

The Chancellor nodded. "Isn't it?"

"May I make a request of you?" Kurt asked him.

"It depends," said the Chancellor. "That may sound harsh, coming from me to you, but I'm an old man and we do not give our trust easily to those whom we doubt."

"You doubt me, then."

"It's something you'll have to get used to," said the Chancellor. He went to a huge glass window, viewing the fir trees that stood like sentinels. Then he turned and faced Kurt.

"I look at you and try not to see him," he said quietly. "But I do see him. And God help us all if we ever stop seeing him, if we ever forget him. He robbed us of everything, but worst of all, he robbed us of our vision. We are without vision. Guilt stands in our way. Shakespeare speaks of being 'naked to mine enemies.' We are naked to ourselves. And I see no end in sight."

Kurt slumped in the chair like a dog that had been whipped. The Chancellor stood before him.

"Now what was that request?"

Kurt spoke without lifting his head, the old man leaning forward on the balls of his feet in order to hear him.

"Give me a chance. Do not judge me until you have seen my actions."

Joseph Haack said, "Look at me." Kurt slowly lifted his head. "I will do what you ask."

In the door Frau Umbreit coughed softly, her signal to the Chancellor that he was not to tire himself. Kurt stood and the two men shook hands formally. Haack offered transportation; Kurt said no, he would rather walk "and do some thinking."

When he was at the door and Frau Umbreit was about to let him out, the Chancellor called out to him. "Remember, Kurt. I will be watching."

10

The antique store of Yosef Rabinadav, on Hayarkon Street in Tel Aviv, was an obligatory stop for any lover of antiques and good conversation. Not that Yosef Rabinadav was easy to deal with—oh, no! He would show you much more that "he would not part with for any price," then he would show you merchandise actually for sale. Some suspected that the man took a kind of perverse pleasure in letting you look at something you would never own.

If he felt that he could trust you—a judgment immediately made and never changed—he could tell you sad stories about new immigrants to Israel who had smuggled family treasures past Communist border guards and customs agents, treasures they brought to the house on Hayarkon Street for a sale to Yosef Rabinadav and a start in their new homeland.

"They open false-bottom boxes, even kerchiefs, and I take a look and they look at me, and a good part of the time I see that their treasure is worthless, that they have risked their lives and pinned their dreams on dust. Well, what should I do? Tell them? Say, 'That's of no value or worth a few hundred lira'? Well, I can't do it; of course I can't do it! 'I'm sorry,' I say, 'that's not the kind of thing I deal in, perhaps someone else.' "

Yosef Rabinadav and his wife Rivka kept a guest book, which they freely showed, with names like Isaac Stern, Wolfson, Rothschild and Sinatra. Rabinadav would read the few words that went along with the signature out loud, often producing a story about the signer's wanting something that he, Yosef Rabinadav, would not sell.

"This rich gentleman from England—look, here's his name, see the nice things he said about me, that was before I told him no. Would you believe he called me a bastard—here, in my own shop? Such a man thought he could purchase anything. He offered me a million pounds!"

"I almost fainted," Rivka said, delighted.

Yosef Rabinadav would shrug at his guest's expression of horror.

"The things that happen here, I couldn't begin to tell you!"

This was true in more ways than one. The antique shop contained two rooms, actually three if you counted the big walk-in safe secured with the finest Swiss time mechanism. First, there was a small waiting room in which Rivka brought you coffee, always served in fine bone china cups. In the next room was an old American rolltop desk, an antique captain's chair, a couch with its stuffing beginning to emerge, and of course the safe from which the dealer took his treasure.

In this safe, to the right of the time mechanism, was an air-filter gauge that worked like a combination lock. The right series of turns would cause the rear wall of the safe to slide open hydraulically, revealing a rectangular office that resembled the city room of a modest newspaper.

This housed the branch of the Mossad so secret that it had no name and had never in its history been referred to in any document, public or governmental. The typewriters atop each desk in the room were connected to a machine that automatically turned whatever was typed into code. The system, which represented an improvement over the German coding machine the British had broken in World War II in the famous Ultra-Secret escapade, had been developed by the Weismann Institute for the Mossad.

The branch was assembled so that it could be disassembled in minutes. Among its handful of operatives, no man knew what the man at the next desk was engaged in. The computer allowed each man to work in a different code which changed daily, insuring total secrecy.

Only one man had access to the central decoding machine. His name was Baruch Eliat; as a branch chief he occupied the lone small office in the otherwise open room.

Eliat was a stocky, red-haired man who had once been likened to a raging bull who has had a bad day in the fights. Running perpendicular to his eyebrows were two long, thin white scars; running horizontal to his cheeks were two more. It appeared that someone had played ticktacktoe with a very pointed object on the face of Baruch Eliat. Sometimes, when he road a bus home to Ramat Gan, a town right outside Tel Aviv, and saw children staring at him, he would take out a pencil and pretend he was going to have a game on his face.

Now Eliat, scratching the red hairs on one thick arm, called through his open door to Samir Abramovitz, his specialist on Germany.

"Samir, come *sprechen*!"

Abramovitz, who had been anticipating this summons, closed a folder on his desk and took it into Baruch Eliat's small office. He sat opposite Eliat, awaiting the other man's questions.

They came, as always, from an unexpected point. "All I hear about is you and those El Al stewardesses. It's the scandal of all Israel. Well? Does your friend have a friend? A sister? A mother would do."

"Yes," admitted Samir Abramovitz, "she does have a young sister, in fact a twin, a perfect duplicate, but she is taken."

"By whom?" demanded his chief.

"By me!" Laughter rang out in the small cubicle beneath the street, and then Baruch Eliat got serious.

"Now, then. What's new with our friend?"

"He talked his way out of his difficulty," said Abramovitz. "It was a tie vote—a tie broken by Willi Fassmann, who did a complete about-face. Before the vote, as you know, he had been the most vocal injured party."

"That really is interesting," said Eliat. "The humanitarian Jew-saver saved our Hitler's ass."

"Later, Mr. Hitler—"

"You're so formal. Mister?"

"The name takes some getting used to," Abramovitz said. "Well, Hitler visited the Chancellor. We don't know what went on there."

"I'll bet old Haack was as curious about the Fassmann vote as we are. Fassmann's too old to change and Haack's too old to be bullshitted. Damn, I wish we could have had access to that conversation."

"I'm sorry I wasn't able to bribe the Bundeskanzler for information," Abramovitz said.

"It's a weakness that we'll have to correct. In this matter we damned well do need to know what's going on in Bonn."

"So far, Hitler's done all the right things—wouldn't you say?"

"I'd say he's a virgin bride."

"Except for Fassmann. Believe me, Fassmann and virgins are against the laws of nature. Which, we are taught, are irrefutable."

"What can we do?" asked Abramovitz.

"Dig and wait, dig and wait."

Eliat turned in his chair, which meant dismissal. Abramovitz picked up the folder and went back to his desk, closing the door behind him.

Eliat turned over a photograph that had been facedown on his desk. Then he reached over and switched on a small desk fan and sat like a man in a hypnotic trance, staring at the face of Willi Fassmann.

Dr. Shelomo Pollak and his wife Leah stood on their tiny balcony, still enchanted by the sight of Jerusalem by night. They could see in the distance the floodlit Damascus Gate, and the walls of the Old City were ablaze with lights that gave a mystical quality to the crenellated ramparts, the spires, minarets, domes and steeples. The city itself seemed to be rising from a pink-orange fire.

"I'd better get back to work," said Pollak. "And you," he slapped her rump gently, "had better get back to your Hebrew. The Shema just won't get it when you want to buy cake mix at the supermarket."

Leah settled onto a couch with a book of Hebrew grammar. Her husband went into their bedroom, where his locked briefcase lay on a chair. He unlocked it, took out the envelope marked "Recipes" and removed several pages, then returned the envelope to the briefcase.

Back in the living room, he sank into a chair and began to read. Leah looked up at him for a moment, then lowered her head. She never asked him about his work. Once she had asked him about a case and he had told her: all of it. She hadn't been able to sleep for a week.

Kadesh's notes were in black ink, the penmanship a series of straight lines and almost no curves—as if the writer had sought to hide any clues to his identity or, for that matter, his feelings. It was strange, the passionate old man writing in such a dispassionate hand. Pollak began with a page headed, General Observation of Children from the Concentration Camps.

"Some knew little about themselves, their origins, their families, and so were reluctant to talk. Experience outside the death camps baffled them. Others, who had responded to internment with an upsurge of strength and stamina, experienced a sharp depression into grief, anguish and guilt over having survived while their families perished.

"There were three basic responses: 1) blind anger at parents who had abandoned them; 2) a feeling that they were bad—otherwise the kind of punishment they had experienced would never have been visited upon them; and 3) self torture (a survivor complex).

"At an age when most children believe that their parents are all-powerful, these children had not only watched their parents die, but had first seen them helpless and weak in the face of nameless terror.

"Once in Palestine, the children displayed a curious mixture of practical precocity and emotional immaturity. They wanted to remain children, with no responsibilities. They distrusted all externally imposed discipline and controls.

"How interesting, how strange, that these battered bits of humanity were the most precious asset we in this new land possessed. All these cripples were to be our future."

Now there was a black ink splotch on the page, marking a spot where Abraham Kadesh had let his pen rest before going on. Next to the black splotch he had written, "None of this applies to Max Levy."

"He is quiet but not, I think, angry. He is totally docile, unnaturally so, yet his intelligence quotient is near genius! If I told Max Levy to jump from the top of the Western Wall I believe he would do so. I have not seen him laugh. Certainly I have not seen him cry. Sometimes I have the feeling that he is a time bomb, ticking away inside, while I with my childish practices attempt to understand him. Yet there is no menace about Max Levy. Still, the bigger boys, even the bully, leave him alone. He has one friend, Shemuel Reiter, who can perhaps throw light on the subject. In the concentration camp Levy was like any other inmate, hanging on from day to day. Shemuel Reiter told me one camp incident that I will return to at a later point. It seems that for several days before the Russian liberation, when papers were being furiously burned and when the camp was beginning to fall into disarray, eight German soldiers (guards) were found stabbed to death over several evenings. Some had suffered a single wound, some two or three, just enough to kill. Had the Germans time, obviously they would have executed everyone in the camp, but there was time only to try to get rid of the evidence of their horror and, if possible, escape, which many of them did. More on this tomorrow."

Dr. Pollak put the papers down and rubbed his eyes. Across the room, Leah stood and said, in near-perfect Hebrew, "I'll never learn it!" Her husband laughed and blew her a kiss. She walked to the doorway of their bedroom, then turned to face him.

"Coming?"

"Later," he said, and returned to Max Levy.

The page, dated July 26, 1946, was headed, "Conversation with Subject in Nonclinical Surroundings." Let's see, thought Pollak, Dr. Kadesh must have been about thirty-nine and Levy was eleven or twelve and Israel was Palestine and . . .

"Come on, Levy, let's walk to the water, bathe our feet. Oh my, that's good! God bless the Mediterranean. God bless all oceans that separate us from . . . except those inside us. Yes, look at me. Look at me, Levy! Men. That's me, and that's you in a short time, we build walls like the Wailing Wall and oceans like that one. Now the question is, why? Why would a man construct such things within himself? An ocean in our head? A wall up here right between the eyes? To keep the enemy out, of course! That's reasonable. Next question, who is this enemy? Memory. That's the bastard and he's a tough one. Worse than a stomachache. Surgery is required to remove him. And there's a catch. Always one of those, huh? We've got to operate on ourselves. Oh, someone like me can stand by and assist, like the nurse in the operating room. But each man must perform his own operation. He's got to tear down those walls he's so carefully constructed, he's got to destroy that ocean that he needed so badly, and he's got to look at his enemy, identify him and worse . . . worse, he's got to reach down into that murky darkness and drag memory out. Confront him! Look him in the eye! Spit in his eye. Shake him good, handle him, see that he's nothing but a fraud! He's dead, he's the past, he's yesterday and he's toothless. He can't hurt us anymore. Think we can do it? What happened in that camp, Max Levy?"

The ocean lapped about them, the sun beat down, and the child stared back at him.

"Your friend Shemuel Reiter told me some German soldiers were killed there at the end, not in battle—stabbed. Murdered. Were you aware of this? Eight German soldiers?"

Levy made no response and Dr. Kadesh stood up, hands on his hips, looking down at him.

"I can't do the surgery for you, Max."

Levy looked out across the water and Dr. Kadesh turned to begin the walk back.

"Thirteen!" called Levy.

Now Kadesh got down on his haunches. "Tell me, Max," he said, his face only inches away.

"Doub Doub," said Levy.

And it occurred to Dr. Kadesh that despite all tests to the contrary, Max Levy was quite mad.

Again he stood up. "Come, enough water for the day, maybe tomorrow, huh?"

Max Levy followed him through the sand.

Dr. Pollak put the file down for a moment and then went on to an interview with Shemuel Reiter, "who has become a leader of the other children and who, in some inexplicable way, seems less scarred, more adjusted than any of the others . . ."

Q. How many German soldiers died under mysterious circumstances in the camp?

A. Eight.

Q. You're quite certain of that number?

A. It was all we talked about. It made us feel good—and scared. You must understand that we were glad that some of them were getting their just deserts, but at the same time we were frightened about who might be doing it. Someone crawling about at night with a knife, even when the knife is meant for your enemy, does not give you the best dreams. Doctor, may I ask you a question? When we leave this place, let him go where I go. I will look after Max Levy. Thank you.

Q. What does Doub Doub mean to you?

A. Say again.

Q. Doub Doub?

A. My God, I had already forgotten him! I wonder how many I have forgotten. Doub Doub was not his real name; we called him that and I can't give you a reason why. He was a gypsy boy, the olive skin and black hair. He was—well, with a little imagination . . .

Q. Please go on.

A. Well, he, Doub Doub, resembled a girl, a gypsy girl, and this kept him alive.

Q. Do you mean that he serviced the German soldiers?

A. Yes. We all knew it but we weren't making judgments on anyone. A person stayed alive the best way he could. The Russians came, and I never saw him again—oh, yes I did! I forgot. He was talking to Max Levy, or at least they were talking together, standing by an abandoned truck. And that was that. I never saw him after that. Perhaps he's telling fortunes someplace, I hope so. Doub Doub, can you imagine? That wasn't even his name!

The question-and-answer narrative ended. Below it, Dr. Kadesh had written, "Tomorrow I will know about Max Levy."

Dr. Pollak looked at his wristwatch. It was 2 A.M., and his eyes burned. He closed the folder and went into the kitchen, where he opened the icebox and drank orange juice from the bottle, a habit his wife detested. Then he went into the bedroom where his daughter slept, holding tightly to her teddy bear. He bent down and kissed her nose. And then, suddenly, tears began to stream down his face. Leah called from their bedroom—"Are you all right?"—and when he didn't answer she came to him and led him to bed, where he slept until the sun roused him. While his wife and daughter slept, Dr. Pollak moved a web-bottomed chair out onto the balcony and settled down to the next entry in the Levy dossier.

It began as if Dr. Kadesh were describing a picnic.

"We again went to the Mediterranean, and I detected a reluctance on the part of Max to accompany me. Not that he said anything. No, I would have liked that or any reaction, rather it was his manner, his slight hanging back while we walked, his sitting a little away from me when we bathed our feet.

" 'Shemuel Reiter has told me about Doub Doub,' I began. Max just looked at me. 'Is Doub Doub alive?' I asked him.

" 'Doub Doub did not want to be alive.'

" 'Did you kill those soldiers?' No answer. 'Did you kill them while Doub Doub serviced them?' He stared out at the ocean. 'Did you continue killing them after the Russians took over the camp?' I watched his face and saw only that infernal smile of his.

" 'How did you accomplish it with Russian soldiers all over the place?' I asked him. His hands were outstretched behind him in the sand, like a bather trying to get a good tan.

" 'They kept the Germans within a fence,' he said finally, 'and Doub Doub went to the fence at night. While they used him . . .' Max shrugged.

" 'And Doub Doub?'

" 'Doub Doub said to me, "Max Levy, I, Doub Doub, now like this thing I was forced to do. If I live it is what I will do. This is not enough for a man to live for."

" 'Doub Doub . . . ' I whispered to Max Levy.

"He smiled back at me. And I felt the rage—at this thing, these things that twisted people, gouged them and pummeled them.

" 'And what about you, Max Levy?'

"I will until I die remember his answer, spoken so unemotionally from the mask that was his face.

" 'I am like Doub Doub,' he said, 'I too like this thing I was forced to do.' "

11

Kurt Hitler arrived at the SFB television facility exactly ten minutes before air time.

There was a studied attempt by all parties to act as if

this were just another speech of summation on behalf of a political party. Clearly, this was not the case. Eurovision would carry the speech live; Telestar would beam it to the world outside Europe. It seemed that everybody on earth wanted to have a look at this young candidate for reelection to Berlin's Parliament.

Kurt ran out of cigarettes five minutes before air time, a crisis solved by Gunther Liedtke, who tossed him an unopened pack.

Kurt nodded his thanks, as grateful for Liedtke's company as he was for the cigarettes. No member of his party had shown up for this, their last important crack at the Berlin voting electorate.

"They're waiting to see which way the wind blows," said Liedtke.

Kurt nodded, almost absentmindedly. "Can't say that I blame them."

A man stuck his head in the door. "About five minutes, sir!"

Kurt nodded.

"Where's your speech?" said Liedtke.

Kurt pointed to his chest and his head.

"Isn't that . . . dangerous?" said Liedtke.

"Very," admitted Kurt.

A few minutes later, Kurt was seated in a comfortable chair before a plain, blue-curtained backdrop. Over his protestations, a thin coat of powder had been put on his face.

The camera opened on a wide shot—the figure in gray might have been anybody—then zoomed in for a close-up of Kurt's face: Well, here he is, get a good look at him.

Kurt did not begin well. His nervousness caused a frog in his throat, which he cleared with an uncomfortable look on his face. His long fingers gripped his chair.

"I'm nervous," he announced.

Oh, Jesus, thought Liedtke.

Kurt smiled self-consciously, like a boy caught in some mild indiscretion, and then continued.

"But who wouldn't be nervous in my place?"

The smile died on his face.

"My father, Adolf Hitler, was the most evil man who ever lived. There is no life, no family, no individual, whose existence either at that time or for all times was not in some way touched for the worse by my father. To you the name Adolf Hitler conjures up horrors. To me the name Adolf Hitler conjures up a special horror, for I feel not like the son but in some strange way like the father—and I feel that the guilt of this man whom I never knew is particularly my guilt."

He paused and seemed to have turned his green eyes inward, to be looking into some private hell accessible only to him.

"Sometimes that guilt overwhelms me," he said. "Some evenings when I walk in the Tiergarten I could scream aloud and never stop screaming, there comes over me a sense of drowning and I do not call out because I do not feel that I have that right!"

Now his body relaxed; his fingers loosened their grip on the chair.

"I, of course, do not scream aloud. But I think—my God in heaven, how I think! And always it is the same. I ask myself, how can I make amends? That is what I think about."

The camera came in for a tight shot of Kurt's face, of the sweat beneath his nose and the beads of perspiration dotting his forehead.

"It's madness," he said, "of course it is, that I, one man, should even ask such a question. For I cannot go to every orphan, I cannot go to every widow and say to them, 'Look at me and who I am, strike me, humiliate me, kill me.' The world is too large and time is too short and any man can be killed but once."

He leaned forward, his hands clasped before him.

"I am therefore left with a single choice. I must, every day of my life, in every moment that is allotted to me, try with whatever abilities I possess to make amends, to heal wounds. As a private citizen I can do so little. As a public servant, I have a chance.

"That is why I, Kurt Hitler, son of Adolf Hitler, dare to come before you tonight to ask that you give me the right to be your servant, to spend my days in the service of that which is good in man.

"I will never be guiltless. The crime is too great. I will never be whole. The crime is too great. But I will be your servant. If you let me."

The floor man made a "cut" sign, the red lights on the studio cameras died; the program was over. Kurt sat exhausted, not even aware that someone was removing the microphone from beneath his necktie.

Liedtke handed him a cigarette, already lit, from which Kurt gratefully took a long puff.

"Well?" he asked Liedtke.

"That's the goddamnedest political speech anyone ever gave," said the publicist.

"But was it any good?"

"I'll tell you election night," said Liedtke.

In the Bad Godesberg section of Bonn, on an acre of heavily wooded grounds behind a high fence with huge iron gates, stood a stucco mansion built in 1894. The drive leading to the house was extraordinarily well lit, almost like a parade route, and off among the birch trees flanking the driveway men with large Alsatian dogs could be seen.

The mansion's library—high-ceilinged and with giant, naked wooden beams—was its showpiece, containing some fifty thousand volumes on every side, most of them rare, many of them priceless. At one end of the room there was a great open fireplace in which, on this particular evening, logs crackled and hissed, sending sparks upward like tiny Roman candles.

Dominating the room was a massive oaken table, its top so highly polished that even in the shadowy atmosphere one could still see one's own reflection. At one end of this very old table there sat, incongruously, a color television set with the image of Kurt Hitler coming to the end of his speech.

About the table, drinking red or white wine, were six men who appeared to have two things in common: each of them seemed affluent and all but one of them was old.

Charftag, the ancient butler (did he have a first name?), waited patiently against the wall, statuelike. Some said Charftag had been conceived the year the house was constructed. Actually, he was not quite that old; he had served on the Russian front in World War II. If anybody asked him about it, which hardly anyone ever did, he liked to nod stoically and say, "Yes, yes, but I remember Stalingrad." He did not remember, except in nightmares, having stayed alive by eating a newly frozen comrade.

Amgard Vieten, the master of the house, sighed and lifted a finger; the gesture was Charftag's signal to turn off the television. The image disappeared into darkness. Vieten tottered to his feet, one hand leaning on the table for support. The other held his wine glass, which he lifted.

The other five men got to their feet, holding their glasses high.

"First," said Vieten, "a toast to those no longer with us but whom we remember." All of them drank their wine in the respectful silence that followed.

Ludwig Zimmer, the oldest man in the room, cleared his ancient throat, and the silence deepened. Zimmer, whose forefathers had financially backed both the Krupps and Farben, was one of the five wealthiest men on earth.

"Yes, yes, Amgard, to the past, of course—but to *now*. A toast to now!" On "now" his voice broke, as though his vocal chords had constricted into a tight fist.

The others downed their wine with fervor, and Charftag refilled each glass.

Now Rainer Terbach, the most powerful trade-union figure in Germany—his umbrella organization numbered some six million members—proposed a toast. "To the workingman, who must never again in our times be dishonored by unemployment."

The others drank again, somewhat less enthusiastically.

The youngest man in the room, whose steel-gray cropped hair and perfect bearing marked him as a soldier, lifted his glass. He was General Hermann Wahlen, number-two Commander in Chief of the North Atlantic Treaty Organization forces.

"To the United States of America . . ."

The others stared at him.

". . . Who have armed NATO with nuclear weapons. Under my command."

There was a collective sigh of relief, and then the others responded.

Now it was the turn of Heinz Oestreich, a tall man with a mane of beautiful white hair, who had been first deputy to Admiral Wilhelm Canaris, wartime chief of the Abwehr. Some said that it was Oestreich who had turned his chief into the Gestapo, bringing about his execution.

"To the future generosity of Colonel Muammar el-Qaddafi," Oestreich said simply.

The others drank and were getting back into their chairs when Amgard Vieten turned to the sixth man in the room.

"What? No toast from you?"

The sixth man got back to his feet and beamed at the others.

"To the glory of the Fatherland," said Willi Fassmann.

In the clubroom of Mishmar Elijah Kibbutz a handful of people watched Kurt's speech on an old and oft-repaired television set. The club contained two levels: the first was dominated by the TV set, a bar and a small oven in which the kibbutzniks could make pizza pie should the spirit move them. The chairs were orange plastic and uncomfortable; their only virtue was that they had been cheap.

The second level of the club was an area for reading, for being away from the others but at not too great a distance. It offered more orange chairs, magazines, a card table for chess, a small shelf filled with the books of half a dozen different nations, and a view of the television set below.

On the ground level Shemuel Reiter watched Kurt Hitler intently while his wife Alisa knitted an item for their expected fourth child.

"He's a convincing devil," Reiter admitted—to which someone said, "Make that devil."

"Think they'll buy it?" asked Daniel Palmon, who was from the United States. The others looked at him, perplexed. "You know, do you think they'll believe him?"

"They believed his father," one man said. A young woman added, "The Germans love to believe in anything—myths, gods and heroes, especially heroes!"

"He seemed genuinely penitent," Shemuel Reiter persisted. The lighting in the room was poor, and the others could not see the mischief in his face. His words inspired a storm of protest. "They're all penitent."

"Like Eichmann. Now *he* was especially penitent." The argument went on, the prevailing sentiment being "not trusting anything German."

Not joining in this lively discussion was Max Levy, who sat on the upper level looking down at the television screen. His face showed no emotion; the screen might as well have been blank.

Shemuel Reiter looked up and caught his friend's eye and smiled at him. Max Levy stared back, his eyes unblinking.

In Tel Aviv, beneath Hayarkon Street and Yosef Rabinadav's antique shop, Baruch Eliat and Samir Abramovitz sat before a television set. Slightly behind them, nervous in these strange surroundings, was Dr. Shelomo Pollak. Only one hour before he had received a telephone call asking him to wait outside his apartment. Samir, driving a battered Volkswagen, had picked him up. The two men, who had never met, said nothing until they arrived at their destination in Tel Aviv. There, Baruch Eliat offered a single word: "Watch."

When Kurt's speech ended, Baruch turned to the other two. "Well?"

Abramovitz stirred in his chair and cast a sidelong glance

at Dr. Pollak, who sat hunched forward, his hands clasped in front of him as if he had just finished wringing them in anguish.

"Come, come, Doctor," said Baruch.

"I don't understand," said Pollak. "What is it you would like to know?"

"I would like to know just how big a liar he is."

Dr. Pollak closed his eyes for a moment and then began to speak as though he were reading from notes.

"He is a remarkably assured young man. There was no script in his hand, nor was he looking at a TelePrompTer. His eyes were totally free and he utilized them in a highly professional manner. Nor did he falter, not once—except, of course, when overcome by emotion."

Baruch pounced. "And that? The emotion?"

"It seemed genuine enough, but all good actors can call up emotion when they need it. It has nothing to do with reality, only the need of the moment."

Baruch smiled. "So what you're saying is—"

Dr. Pollak also smiled. "I really don't know."

"But if you had to make a bet?"

Dr. Pollak shook his head, "I wouldn't do it. I'm a psychiatrist, not a gambler."

"I never met a doctor who was worth a shit," Baruch said to Abramovitz, who threw back his head and roared with laughter.

Baruch turned to Abramovitz. "And you, Samir? What did you think of young Mr. Hitler?"

"Most believable. That is, if I didn't know who he was I would hire him tomorrow."

"For what job?" Baruch wanted to know.

"What job? Any job at all! Face it, Baruch, he makes a hell of an impression."

"Would you hire him for Governing Mayor?"

Abramovitz made a small bow. "Gladly."

"Now just one more question: Would you hire him for your Chancellor?"

The smile died on Abramovitz's face.

"Well? Well? Would you?"

"I would," said Abramovitz.

Later, Dr. Pollak sat beside him in the battered Volkswagen.

"Your boss is quite a man," ventured Pollak.

Abramovitz's face was blank. "Yes, isn't he."

"Strange business."

"Oh, not that much different from yours," said Abramovitz.

"I'm afraid the likenesses escape me," Dr. Pollak said.

"Well, you try to get *in* people's heads, right?"

Dr. Pollak nodded.

"We, on the other hand, try to knock off their heads."

Dr. Pollak turned in the darkness to see if the other man was smiling. He wasn't, and they finished the drive to Jerusalem in silence.

A videotape of Kurt's speech was shown the next day in the Oval Office to the President of the United States and to his Secretary of State, who had already seen the program live along with a number of undersecretaries and assistants in the State Department's German Section.

The President walked to the television and snapped it off. The Secretary of State smiled. The President took so much pleasure in doing common chores, including opening the door for others, that those around him had learned to expect them from him. It was the Secretary's secret opinion that the President spent a fair amount of time thinking up gestures like that.

The President refilled their coffee cups from a silver pitcher. The Secretary was relieved that he didn't put in the sugar and cream.

"Well?" asked the President, his blue eyes wide, their expression candid if not innocent.

The Secretary tried the same look, but couldn't quite pull it off. He seemed merely to be opening his eyes wide to rid them of a minor irritation.

"Mr. President," began the Secretary, who hadn't decided

whether he would tell the President what he really felt. "I think we may safely assume—"

"I don't want any of that 'make the President feel good' bullshit. I want to know what you think of young Adolf's speech."

"He's smooth," said the Secretary. "Very smooth."

"Kind of fellow you'd buy a used car from," said the President. "Think he meant a word of it?" Now he was grinning: he was the man who suspected the rest of the earth to be in on a con job.

The Secretary sighed, then reached into his briefcase for a folder marked TOP SECRET. "So far, he checks out, he's the real thing. His story about Hauser, the visit from the guy who told him who he was—as much as it can be checked out, it's true."

"So much for that," said the President. "Now that leaves us with this one little problem. Suppose the guy wins?"

"According to the latest information out of Germany, the Liberals will, at best, run a good solid third. But not better. Third."

"German poll or ours?"

"Ours. The Princeton Center. Of course we had a German cover group do the legwork, but the statistical part is good old U.S. of A."

"You know, your belief in those computers is something. About like folks back home believe in the Lord. But I have to admit, I'm relieved about that poll. I keep having this horrible thought, suppose Hitler wins and wants to see me, I mean officially. Lord!"

"Our Jewish friends wouldn't let up much of a howl," the Secretary said somberly.

"One of those howls to a term is about as much as I can handle," said the President, and the two men went on to other topics.

12

The William Hill Organization, Britain's largest bookmakers with more than a thousand cash shops, saw the Berlin election's outcome at three to two against Kurt Hitler's Liberal party. From Las Vegas, Nevada, came word that Jimmy the Greek called it five to one against.

In Berlin itself, most experts admitted that, thanks to Kurt's appearance and oratorical ability, "the Liberals will do better than they have in years: they will run a strong third."

If Kurt heard these dire predictions he kept his thoughts to himself. Harry Sinclair had summed up the young candidate best in a story filed from Berlin:

Following his now-legendary television speech, Kurt Hitler hit the ground like an escaping convict and has never stopped running. His schedule includes as many as twenty speeches a day, and some of these to only four or five people. It doesn't seem to bother the candidate. In the few days remaining it is doubtful that there will be many hands in Berlin that he has not shaken. The candidate is, quite obviously, a man possessed.

It was a typical campaign day, with one exception. Harry Sinclair had asked to accompany the candidate, and now he sat in the back of the car driven by Liedtke as Kurt poured coffee from a thermos into a cup and handed it over the seat to him.

"Liedtke tells me you're my discoverer," Kurt said to the Englishman.

"Quite by accident, I assure you."

Kurt, who had heard the truth, appreciated the other man's honesty. "And your assignment now?"

"You. Full time."

Kurt shook his head slowly. "God, what a waste."

"May I quote you on that?"

"You may quote me on anything I say, though I expect

you will understand that I won't say very much!"

The three men laughed, and Liedtke looked at Kurt in the car's darkness. Sinclair thought, He likes his boss.

"Where are we off to?" Kurt asked Liedtke.

"Schiller Motorcycle Works. We want to hit the 4 A.M. shift. Just coming to work."

They drove in the predawn silence to the gates of the huge plant enclosed by a cyclone fence. A security guard looked into the car, stepped back and saluted Kurt smartly. He was an old man and it was not a civilian salute, Sinclair thought as he heard Kurt sigh.

Liedtke carried a bundle of blue-and-white cards that carried Kurt's photograph on one side, the Liberal party platform on the other. As the workers began to stream in, Kurt handed each a card and offered his hand, asking them to "please consider my candidacy."

Sinclair noticed that Kurt never introduced himself. He wondered if the candidate assumed that everyone knew who he was or whether there was another reason.

Things were going routinely when one man drew back and said, without emotion, "No, I do not wish to shake your hand."

Kurt recoiled as if he had been struck, and Sinclair saw his face go pale. By now the next worker was before him, taking a card and shaking his hand.

Finally Liedtke said, "We'd better go." As they got into the car, Kurt said, "Only nineteen stops to go!"

"Did that bother you back there?" Sinclair asked.

Kurt did not turn around. "Yes. It bothered me."

They were approaching a street corner in downtown Berlin, filled with children on their way to school and people on their way to work. A portable platform had been set up and they could hear Willi Fassmann winding up his speech.

"A man told another man, 'I want to sell my car.' 'How many miles does it have?' asked the other man. 'Eighty-nine thousand,' said the car's owner. 'What?' said the other man. 'No one'll buy it unless you turn the odometer back.' The next day the man saw the car's owner and asked him, 'Did you sell that car?' The owner said, 'With only six hundred miles on it? Do you think I'm crazy?' "

The crowd laughed good-naturedly. They had heard Willi Fassmann many times before, and no one really expected him to say anything.

Willi stated the predictable: "And that's what the opposition is trying to sell you, the same old government with the mileage turned back!"

A few Liberal party hacks, most of them retired pensioners, clapped to get something going in the audience, but with little success.

Willi saw Kurt approaching and went into his introduction.

"And now, a young man who represents the best that is in all of us, a true German, the kind of brother you'd like to court your daughter. The next Governing Mayor of Berlin, Kurt Hitler!"

Sinclair saw Kurt wince at Fassmann's corny introduction, but he bounded right up the short flight of steps to the platform, which had been hastily decorated with posters and colored bunting.

The good-natured smiles that had greeted Fassmann died at Kurt's appearance. Sinclair also noticed that the school children had pressed closer to the platform, their upturned young faces reflecting curiosity as if they were watching—Sinclair searched his mind for the right comparison—a circus act.

Had Kurt picked up on this? His remarks were quite obviously directed only at the children in the crowd.

"I remember when I was your age and on my way to school too. I can tell you I wasn't all that excited about it. First of all I wasn't too good in math and had to get a friend's help at school. For an entire semester he helped me before I realized that he wasn't any better than me. Can you imagine being that dumb? *A whole semester*!"

The children laughed, and as Kurt continued speaking, Sinclair thought, he wants them to like him, he doesn't want to be a freak or a curiosity.

"And so if you'll tell your mothers and fathers and your uncles and aunts that you heard us and we weren't all that bad, Chairman Fassmann and I will appreciate it. But if you decide to tell them to vote for us, we'll do even better than that. Every schoolchild in Berlin will be invited to our inauguration."

"Don't hold your breath for that, kids," a skeptic in the crowd cackled and the meeting broke up.

"Well?" Kurt asked Liedtke when the three of them were back in the car.

Sinclair knew exactly what he meant by the question. "The children."

"Yes," Kurt said soberly, "the children. They make me most uncomfortable of all. It's the way they look at me. They expect horns, a tail . . . Well, Herr Doctor-Professor-General Liedtke, where to next?"

"Noontime, the beer hall, where else?"

Kurt groaned. "I hate to speak to people who have been drinking. I always expect a belch in response. Or worse."

"Nothing to it," said Liedtke. "Most of these people are pensioners, your kind of crowd."

"Meaning?" asked Sinclair.

"Liedtke means I do better with old people. They too are captives of the past. It's a connecting link between us."

"And while I hate to be a crass politician, in Berlin there are more of those than any other kind," Liedtke said with a wide grin.

Once inside the beer hall, they were surrounded by old men who patted Kurt's back and advised him cheerfully to "stick the bastards where it hurts." One senior citizen requested Kurt's autograph for his grandson; when Kurt signed the card, Sinclair heard the old man say, "Got his daddy's handwriting too!" If Kurt heard this he gave no sign, and soon they were on a small stage.

Willi Fassmann was winding up, a half-filled stein in his pudgy hand.

"I'm not here to demean the opposition, thieves though they may be. That will be taken care of by their Maker and their consciences. But decency commands me to point out that they, every one of them, have gotten mysteriously rich. No Volkswagens for them—oh no, not like old Willi who still drives a three-year-old model—no, they need big, fancy American cars, Cadillacs . . . Oh? You didn't know? You didn't know that the present Governing Mayor of Berlin has a Cadillac? A golden one with three aerials, God knows what he does with three aerials! Maybe on Election Day we'll tell him what to do with them!"

The pensioners, who loved this sort of thing, shouted their encouragement.

"As many times as I've heard this speech," Kurt told Sinclair, "I detest it more each time."

"We call it Willi's Cadillac speech," Liedtke chimed in.

Now Fassmann was introducing Kurt.

"God didn't bless old Willi with a son. I've got three fine daughters, all married to good boys. But let's face it, there's something about a son, a son is the future . . ."

Kurt's face was ashen. "He's going too far."

"A son is the past and a son is tomorrow. If I had been blessed with a son, I'd want him to be like this young man, this fine, moral, clean-cut young man. Make no mistake, my beloved friends, he is our future. Yes, you heard me right. All our futures. Today Berlin's—tomorrow—I give you the next Governing Mayor of Berlin, Mr. Hitler!"

"That son of a bitch!" Kurt muttered.

The crowd had grown quiet; the milling about had stopped and not one stein of beer was slammed down on a tabletop as Kurt made his way through the crowd as if through a vacuum created by Willi's words.

A smiling Willi adjusted the microphone for him; Kurt did not smile back. Willi, his eyes dancing with some secret amusement, mopped his brow with a large blue handkerchief.

Kurt forced a smile and was about to begin when from the back of the room there came a buzzing sound, a disjointed humming.

Kurt smiled foolishly like someone who wants to be in on a joke; the sound got louder.

Kurt threw a glance at Liedtke, who shrugged his shoulders. The humming had become singing from a group of men sitting together in the middle of the hall. Now the singers were standing and singing at the tops of their voices, and Sinclair saw tears on the face of some as they sang.

> Raise high the flags! Stand rank and rank together,
> Storm troopers march with steady quiet tread . . .

The "*Horst Wessel* Song," favorite of the Nazis.

Kurt stared at the singing men, his face expressionless. This served only to make them sing with more fervor, louder, as if to coax him into a sign of recognition.

He stared at them for a moment longer, then slowly left the stage and walked through them until he was out the door, where the singing could still be heard.

The three men got into the car.

"Let's get the hell out of here," said Kurt.

They rode in silence, until Kurt finally turned to Sinclair. "I guess you'll have to write about that."

"Yes, I will."

"What could I do? They were old. And Willi incited them. Willi's old too."

"It certainly wasn't your fault," Liedtke said, feeling guilty himself for having advised Sinclair's tagging along for the day.

"Were you tempted to speak to that crowd back there?" Sinclair asked.

"No," said Kurt, "I wasn't tempted. And what about your day, Mr. Sinclair? Will you stay with us, or are you off to write your story?"

"As a matter of fact I have an appointment with an old friend of yours. Do you remember Herr Horst Pahl?"

"Who?" asked Liedtke.

"The old man who struck me."

"What could you possibly want with him?" Liedtke asked.

"Oh, how he feels," said Sinclair.

"He feels drunk," Liedtke said.

"His feelings about—well, not you, but the past—that

was in the beginning. I want to see how he feels now that he knows more about you, has had more access to you."

"But he's a goddamn drunk," said Liedtke. "Why not question a sober man—or is that against Reuters' rules?"

"I think the idea is a good one, Mr. Sinclair," Kurt said. "I'm sure you'll have no difficulty with Horst Pahl. As for me, I will read your story avidly."

Late that night a weary Kurt bid Liedtke a faint "good-night," and trudged into his apartment, his teeth chattering against the freezing night air. Lise lay in his bed, a curved ball, fast asleep beneath the covers.

Kurt dropped his clothes to the floor and quickly showered, then put on blue pajamas and got into bed. He was exhausted but not yet unwound, and he lay back in the darkness, a cigarette in his mouth, and tried to give the day some kind of perspective, hoping that out of order would come peace and sleep.

The telephone rang.

He felt Lise stir awake as he reached for it.

"Yes. Inspector who? Oh? I see. Yes, I understand. Thank you very much, Inspector. Good night."

He returned the telephone to its cradle and sighed.

Now Lise was sitting up. He kissed her nose and whispered, "Go to sleep, little girl."

"Who was that?"

"Politics. Just politics."

"No!" she said. "You mustn't do this to me!"

"Mustn't do what?"

"You're locking me out and I won't have it! I know what happened at the bierstube today, everybody knows, it's the talk of Berlin."

Bravo, Mr. Sinclair, thought Kurt. He said, "Some relics singing about the past."

"And what about that telephone call you just got."

"Politics."

Suddenly she was out of bed and reaching for her clothes. He leaped after her and dragged her back.

"I'm sorry," he said.

"I simply won't be treated like everyone else! I'm either your—whatever it is I am or—let me go!"

"Calm down," he said. "It's just that I don't want you to have to go through all the unpleasantness."

"Don't protect me. I'm not a flower. I'm a grown woman."

"All right. The telephone call was from an Inspector Mueller. The police have received a threat on my life that they consider quite serious. Well? Satisfied? Now you know."

"Oh, my God." She stared at him, her eyes filled with fright.

He patted her shoulder. "Shhh," he whispered, "a hazard of the trade."

"What will we do?"

"The police are already guarding me. It's really not worth getting upset over."

"Who would want to kill you?"

"Are you serious? Half the world obviously consider themselves my victims. *Mine*. That's why security is so ridiculous. The number of people who feel they owe me my death couldn't be controlled by NATO, much less a handful of policemen."

"I'm so afraid," said Lise.

"Which is why I didn't want to tell you."

"I wouldn't want to live without you, Kurt."

"*I* wouldn't want to live without me," he said lightly. "Now kiss me and let me sleep. Tomorrow's another day, and God only knows what it will bring."

He listened in the darkness until he heard the rhythmic breathing that meant that she was again asleep.

His father had robbed them. It was just that simple. He hadn't given the crowd the good time in the arena for which they, in all their hypocritical piety, so desperately thirsted.

How they would have loved a trial! A long trial, time to draw out with delicious delight every act of genius (Well, wasn't that what it really was?) that had comprised his time upon his earth.

His earth.

Would they have executed him? Would they have taken

him from village to village, country to country, like some caged beast, to be reviled by his enemies?

Would he have been tried with that pack of deviates and incompetents at Nuremberg? His face among those faces? No! It was too terrible to even speculate about.

He had, after all, defeated them. A pistol shot, a can of petrol, and a god had left an anthill.

The bunker: the twilight of a god.

Now: "Behold, I am among you again."

The final rally would be held in a soccer stadium. Some party members grumbled about "additional expenditure." But Willi Fassmann won the day: the rally would be held "at all costs."

Kurt and Liedtke sat in Kurt's apartment drinking beer. Liedtke was grumbling too. "When Willi said 'at all costs,' he meant it. He's spending money on this one like he's got a printing press turning it out in his basement."

"You don't approve of old Willi," Kurt said innocently.

"One shouldn't take such a man lightly," said Liedtke, not realizing the humor of his remark until Kurt laughed. "I'm serious. When I first met Willi I found him to be a pompous old windbag. Then I realized that's how Willi wants to be taken. Then I got to thinking: pompous old windbags don't survive the way Willi Fassmann has. No, it takes a lot more than that. I guess you could call Willi the king of the survivors."

"Liedtke, if you give your survivor speech one more time I shall either toss you through that window or jump myself. You try very hard to make survival a crime. It is not. Survival is the primary obligation of the species, any species!"

"Some species shouldn't survive."

"Why, Liedtke, you sound positively murderous."

"That's precisely the species I'm talking about. Murderers."

Kurt sighed loudly, a signal that he no longer wished to pursue that line of conversation. "Exactly what is it you object to in Willi's rally plans?"

"Searchlights. Willi's rounded up every searchlight in Berlin."

"I fail to see the criminality in that. Besides, I wasn't aware there *were* any searchlights in Berlin."

"Oh yes. War surplus. Now they use them to open shopping centers and trade shows. People follow the lights. I've used them myself."

"So? Why not use them for a political rally? Is it all that different from the opening of a shopping center, or a carnival with freaks on display?"

"There'll be a crowd, a big one. Hell, he'll pack the stadium."

"I doubt that," said Kurt. "No one's going to leave their television sets in this bitter weather, not to hear the same speeches they've heard a dozen times before."

"You underestimate Willi."

"Oh? What has our robust compatriot done now?"

"Willi's giving away a Volkswagen. Everyone who attends gets a ticket and at the end of the rally there'll be a drawing."

"Sounds like good public relations to me. Know what I think, Liedtke? I think you're jealous that you didn't come up with those gimmicks."

Liedtke laughed. "You may be right at that. Still—"

"Come on, Liedtke, what exactly do you object to? Don't we want a crowd? Wouldn't it be nice for some poor devil to win a Volkswagen? Surely the searchlights don't injure your sense of aesthetics?"

"I don't like it when Willi Fassmann does something on his own, in secret. Willi Fassmann and secrets are old chemistry, bad chemistry. God knows what those fat lips have whispered in their times. I don't like it when he locks everyone else out of his plans. I don't like—"

"Willi Fassmann. Well, you're in good company," said Kurt. "Neither does our Chancellor."

"God bless him."

"Why, Liedtke, I wasn't aware that you were an admirer of Josef Haack."

"I am grateful for men like him who keep men like Fassmann from ever getting in power again," said Liedtke.

"And me, Liedtke? How do you feel about men like me?"

"Only time will tell."

For a moment there was silence between the two. Kurt broke it, standing and putting on his overcoat. "Well, let's go have a look at Willi's searchlights. And maybe, just maybe, Liedtke . . ."

"Yes?"

"You'll win."

"Win what?"

"The Volkswagen!" said Kurt.

The two rode in silence. The going was slow. There was a traffic jam for miles around the stadium. Policemen directed traffic as best they could, frost from their mouths punctuating their words.

The temperature hovered at below freezing, and high above the stadium a full moon burned away in the winter darkness.

"Park back here," said Kurt.

"There is a space reserved for you at the stadium entrance," Liedtke said.

"Park here, the walk will do us good." Kurt sat so low in the seat that no one could recognize him.

"Well, Willi got his crowd," said Liedtke.

"Shhhh," Kurt said softly, and the two sat in silence and studied the eerie effect of Willi Fassmann's searchlights.

The sharply defined beams had been placed around the field at intervals of forty feet and were visible to a height of twenty to twenty-five thousand feet, after which they merged into a general glow. The effect was that of a large room with the beams serving as great pillars of infinitely high outer walls. Now and then a cloud moved through the beams and across the face of the moon, giving the heavens a peculiarly surrealistic landscape.

"Well, he's done it," said Liedtke softly, unable to see

Kurt smiling in the darkness. "He's recreated one of Speer's old tricks, 'the cathedral of light' they used for the Nazi party rallies at Nuremberg."

"The effect is astonishing," said Kurt.

"It was then, too."

"A little theatrics never hurt anyone," said Kurt.

"Didn't it?"

Kurt got out of his overcoat. "Lock the car, Liedtke."

"You'll freeze."

"I'm quite comfortable," Kurt said as the two began the walk to the stadium.

"Well," said Liedtke, "you've drawn quite a crowd."

"Me or the Volkswagen?"

"Do I have to answer that?"

"I'll fire you if you do," said Kurt.

A policeman snapped to attention and smartly saluted Kurt, who stopped. "What's your name, officer?" The policeman told him and Kurt said, "I'll remember that."

The stands were completely filled, as were several thousand chairs set up on the field. At its north end stood a speaker's platform, a huge blow-up of Kurt Hitler behind it. Otherwise the decorations were subdued, without bunting or flags.

"Listen," Kurt told Liedtke.

"To what?"

"The quiet. Have you ever heard a crowd so quiet?"

"I wonder why he didn't use a photo of you smiling?" said Liedtke.

"There's not much to smile about in Berlin."

Kurt mounted the platform, shaking hands with party members. He stopped at Rudi Rahms and whispered, "You add a touch of dignity with your presence, Rudi."

The other man did not reply.

Willi, going to the microphone, had the look about him of a magician about to produce a rabbit. Kurt avoided looking at him as he took his seat. He was the only person on the stage not wearing an overcoat, and self-consciously other party leaders began to remove theirs.

Now Willi was introducing him—and to Kurt's surprise, in an uncharacteristically low-keyed manner. He spoke of Kurt's working his way through law school and even of his service as a tour guide. He closed: "And now, our good friend, Kurt Hitler."

Kurt stood and went to the microphone, where he and Willi shook hands. There was a strange silence, none of the applause or shouting to which Kurt had become accustomed. It was almost as if they had not heard him introduced or were even unaware of who he was.

He talked softly, never raising his voice. "Thank you for leaving your homes this evening. It's very good of you, and I'm told that at least two interesting television programs are scheduled. Your presence is truly appreciated."

As he droned on there was movement in the stands. At first a few people in various parts of the stadium stood, watched for a moment; then, as though responding to some secret signal, began to move down the aisles.

"We are a hundred and ten miles within East Germany, surrounded on all sides. We are an island. Wherever we stretch our arms there is an impediment blocking us. More cruelly, many of us are separated from our loved ones by a man-made barrier. Germany lost the war. Somehow, Berliners lost even more . . ."

At first the rest of the crowd did not notice the others, and then they did, and this seemed to set off a chain reaction as more people stood, watched, then began moving from the stadium onto the field.

"The English poet John Donne has observed that no man is an island unto himself, each is a part of the whole. To me this makes sense, and I see its wisdom proven every day of my life here in Berlin. Human beings are not an island unto themselves—as long as they have each other. And that is what we have in Berlin, and that is what we have in this election: each other."

They were very quiet, no one speaking to anyone else. They were simply moving, coming closer . . .

"If we stay apart in this city, if each of us lives his or her own life to the exclusion of others, then we have suffered the ultimate defeat that humans can suffer: isolation. But if we not only *acknowledge* each other's existence, but work toward . . ."

The heads of the people in the chairs on the field turned and saw entire sections standing, moving down, and they too began to stand and move closer to the platform.

"If we stand together, we cannot be defeated. There is no barrier that can be created by any man or any ideology that can wall in a brave and true heart. . . ."

Now the field was jammed with thousands of silent people who pressed even closer to the speaker's platform and to the man who spoke so softly to them.

It was as though he was only at that moment conscious of them, the thousands of faces pressing about him, inching closer by the moment. For the first time that evening Kurt's arms moved upward and out from his sides. Liedtke saw it as a gesture of protest, stopping them.

The crowd saw it as an embrace: Come to me.

And then—as one, from twenty-five thousand throats, as if by signal—the name poured forth in a mighty roar: HITLER! HITLER! HITLER!

13

The next morning's newspapers featured Sinclair's interview with Horst Pahl. Under the photograph of Pahl striking Kurt ran the caption: "HE'LL VOTE FOR HITLER!"

Sinclair quoted Pahl as saying that Kurt Hitler would definitely get his vote, "because I believe him."

The afternoon newspaper pointed out that Pahl was not, and had never been, a registered voter.

Sinclair felt foolish. Why hadn't the old sod told him that?

The opposition made what it could of the Horst Pahl

business, but no one could predict exactly what effect, if any, it would have on the election.

Liberal Party Chairman Willi Fassmann was quoted as saying that a stunning upset might be in the works. The prediction did not exactly electrify Berliners, but it was good for a laugh.

In Bonn, the Chancellor uncharacteristically refused all comment on the elections in Berlin.

As campaign intensity reached a fever pitch Lise saw increasingly less of Kurt, though they managed to talk on the telephone nightly.

"For God's sake be sure and vote," he told her.

"Mr. Pahl and I solemnly promise it." Then she said, "Is it going to be that close?"

"If we lose by one vote I'll hold you personally responsible."

"And will you punish me?"

"Most certainly."

"How?" she wanted to know, and he told her.

She went to sleep while he went off to address one last group—telephone operators on a 2 A.M. coffee break.

The night's work finally ended, and Liedtke dropped him off at his apartment.

"Good luck tomorrow," said Liedtke.

"What do you think?" Kurt asked him.

"Easy victory."

"Come on, man, what do you really think?"

"I think you almost caught the bastards," Liedtke said with a sigh. "I think you needed another week. We simply ran out of time."

Liedtke was about to ask Kurt for *his* prediction, but the candidate was gone. Liedtke took off with a roar of the engine, hurrying to his late date with someone else's wife. "My only weakness," he was fond of saying to himself.

Though this was not true, it always made him feel better.

It rained all Election Day, which pleased the Liberal party

greatly. Over the years they had become true believers in the theory that the fewer people who voted, the better for them. The rain turned to sleet at midmorning, and weeds froze on vacant lots.

Kurt was photographed at his polling place but refused the photographer a victory sign. "Time for that later," he said lamely, before hurrying off for a tour of some of the city's other polling places. At noon he ate a veal steak and drank some dark beer with Liedtke. The two plainclothesmen assigned to protect him following the death threat sat at a nearby table, eyeing him and the door.

Two bearded men entered. The security men went quietly to them and examined their identification papers. Kurt doubted that anyone else in the restaurant even noticed.

"I wonder how they really feel about protecting someone like me," said Kurt. "Has it ever occurred to you that they may both detest me?"

"Maybe we ought to get them drunk and ask them," said Liedtke.

"Always count on you for ingenious solutions, Mr. Liedtke."

"It's just that you're so calm. My God, if someone said they were going to kill me—"

"Perhaps I'm simply out of adrenaline. No, that's not true. The truth is, I understand them."

"Them?"

"These would-be assassins. I'm not at all convinced that hatred is all that unhealthy an emotion," said Kurt.

"Perhaps you should shoot yourself and satisfy them and you," the publicist replied.

"Perhaps we should go and check some more polls. Unless there's an extremely late surge of voters, the turnout will be the lightest ever."

At one precinct they ran into a smiling Willi Fassmann, who pointed to his chest and said, "I've got a good feeling inside about what's going on today."

"Willi," said Kurt, "the only good feeling you've got inside is that goose you just consumed."

Fassmann laughed. "As a matter of fact, roast duckling with a near-perfect orange sauce."

They left him in front of a crowd of people who had already voted and were now being assured that "Willi Fassmann's heart always beats in concert with the people."

Liedtke grinned at Kurt. "What's he wasting that speech for, can't he see they've already voted?"

"Come on," said Kurt. "He's working on the next election!"

Politicians, actors and actresses, society figures, call girls, the press and hangers-on who were attracted to drama like moths to light, mingled at Schoenberg Hall amidst the shrieking of music, a sea of beer and the heady taste of sausage by the hundreds of pounds.

By 8:01 P.M., based on the returns from a handful of precincts, computers were calling the results. Between 10 and 10:30 P.M., when most of the votes had been counted, the computers' superiority had once again been clearly demonstrated.

That Kurt Hitler was reelected a member of Parliament came as no surprise. He had, however, carried in with him a majority of the Liberal Democrat party, which meant that he would be Governing Mayor of Berlin.

The Liberal party had garnered 76.8 percent of the popular vote, a new record that no one else had ever come close to.

There was one other surprise. The vote had been heavy. The rain hadn't stopped anyone that day.

14

Chancellor Haack and Minister of the Interior Dr. Alfred Nauman were sharing a glass of sherry in Haack's office.

"Come now, Nauman, admit it, it was a fantastic victory," Haack said.

"Numerically, it was that."

"Perhaps the Liberal party is making a comeback," prodded the Chancellor.

"You don't believe that," said Nauman.

"No, I don't." Haack sipped his sherry and made a face. He drank anything other than tea only to be sociable. "It is, quite simply, a mystery."

"Is it?"

"My Minister is suspicious."

"Frightened," said Nauman, staring into his sherry.

"Please be specific."

"Why did this man win? Why did he win by such an astonishing vote? Why did Germans vote for him?"

"He's an attractive candidate," said Haack. "A young, attractive candidate."

"Must I be the devil's advocate?" Nauman said, smiling.

Haack nodded.

Nauman sighed. "We have had other young, attractive candidates. A few have won, but just barely. Most have lost. To put it bluntly, most have been soundly defeated. But not our Mr. Hitler. They loved him."

"Is that bad?"

"They loved the son of Adolf Hitler, and—"

"That's bad," said the Chancellor. "What are your most recent statistics on neo-Nazism today?"

"The National Democratic party has only 9,000 registered adherents. In the 1976 general election, the party received only 122,000 votes out of 37.8 million cast. There are 126 illegal neo-Nazi groups in West Germany. None of them has more than 300 members. In 1976 there were 330 incidents attributed to the Far Right. In 1977 the figure rose to 613."

"So?"

"So up until Mr. Hitler's triumph, statistics indicate that everything was under control. But when they had a chance to vote for—for that name—well, how shall I say it?"

"The control disappeared," said Josef Haack.

The Minister of the Interior nodded. "They voted for Hitler."

"That," said Nauman, "is exactly who they voted for."

"In the name of God, I wonder why?" said Haack. "He destroyed their land, their honor and many of their loved ones. They should despise him."

"Yes, shouldn't they," Nauman said. "Particularly in Berlin, with that reminder of defeat staring them in the eyes every day of their lives."

"Perhaps that's it. Maybe they were voting not *for* him but *against* defeat."

"You don't believe that and neither do I," said the Minister.

The conversation was beginning to depress him, and the Chancellor changed the subject. "Come to the bungalow tomorrow night. I'm anxious to hear your plans for the trials."

The forthcoming terrorist trials were in the public mind second only to Kurt Hitler's astounding victory.

"Fine," Nauman said, standing. "I'll have the complete report."

"Come early, we can listen to Kurt—to Hitler's inaugural address," said Haack. "Perhaps he'll change your mind."

"Perhaps I've been a prosecutor for too long. It may be all right."

"You are my advocate," Haack said. "I need you!"

"Your devil's advocate."

"You fill the role to perfection," Josef Haack said.

"Did you know my boyhood dream was to be a defender, not a prosecutor? So much for boyhood dreams."

"I'm so old I've forgotten mine," the Chancellor said.

"Come now, Mr. Chancellor. You are one of those unique people whose dream has come true."

"Oh? And what might that have been?"

"To serve your fellow men."

"That didn't sound at all like a prosecutor."

"I have my weak moments," said Dr. Alfred Nauman, and he and the Chancellor laughed.

* * *

The atmosphere in the library of the house in Bad Godesberg was as jovial as its stark decor permitted.

A merry fire crackled and hissed in the great open fireplace, in front of which Charftag dispensed vintage French champagne to the six men assembled there.

"You're keeping an eye on the time?" asked Amgard Vieten, now occupying the foot of the table in deference to the large television sitting in front of his usual chair.

"Fanatically," said Charftag.

Amgard wondered if Charftag hadn't perhaps tested the champagne before the arrival of the guests. The rest of the group broke into laughter, and old Ludwig Zimmer's bony back had to be slapped, though gently, to help him regain his valuable breath.

"You know, Ludwig," Willi Fassmann said to the billionaire, his small eyes aglitter with good friendship, "I like your sense of humor."

"Is that all you like about me?" Zimmer gasped, which again broke up the room. Zimmer liked to joke about how rich he was, but the figures were no joke.

Fassmann, who handled some of his insurance, was wondering even at this moment how to get his thick pink fingers on still more. "You're a national treasure," he whispered to the old tycoon, who shrugged modestly.

Charftag leaned down to Amgard Vieten and whispered, "It's two minutes till, sir."

"Turn it on, then," said Vieten, rapping on the table for attention.

"Gentlemen, the moment has arrived. Suddenly, we who have worked and lived for a new day are confronted with just that. We—"

His words were interrupted by an announcer: "We now bring you the inaugural address of Mr. Kurt Hitler, the newly elected Chief Governing Mayor of Berlin."

"Doesn't he wear anything but gray?" Vieten asked crossly.

General Hermann Wahlen, also wearing a gray suit, said,

"Gray is perfect for a serious occasion—or for that matter, any occasion."

Rainer Terbach, the union leader and by far the best-attired man in the room ("My members want me to look good"), said, "That collar, it looks like the kind my father wore. Too high."

"But the hair is just right," observed Heinz Oestreich, the intelligence chief. The others smiled in agreement about Kurt's hair—which, as always, seemed uncombed in a perfectly neat way. A woman might have called it tousled.

Kurt's speech was short, notably lacking in passion or even many adjectives. He sounded more like an accountant than a politician. He made no wild promises, he never raised his voice, his eyes looked directly into the camera, and even when camera positions were changed he easily followed them so that his contact with the audience was never lost.

His speech was also notable for the absence of the usual not-so-subtle blasts at the East Germans right across the wall. Instead he spoke of brotherhood, and when he said the word, its overused syllables somehow translated into simple truth.

Vieten said, "There, when he tilts his head; there, just so, see it? See it?"

Willi Fassmann nodded enthusiastically. "It's *him* all right. They may not like it and they may be too polite to say it aloud, but he's back. And by their vote. *And* as the new prince of peace!"

Ludwig Zimmer coughed for attention. The room grew very still.

"I am reminded of August 19, 1934, when the plebiscite was organized to confirm power in his father's hands. Do you remember that vote, gentlemen? Four million against—thirty-eight million for! Who says that history does not repeat itself? Though I would be the first to admit, sometimes history needs a little shove in the right direction."

"To that little shove," said Heinz Oestreich, who lifted his glass in a toast.

The others lifted their glasses, but uneasily. It was said

that Oestreich had toasted Canaris right before betraying him.

The union leader Terbach proposed a toast: "To what the world needs most—practical men. That's us. Isn't it, gentlemen? Practical men."

"We are certainly that," said Ludwig Zimmer, looking directly at Willi Fassmann's smiling face.

Terbach was not finished. "As practical men, we know that nothing can be gained without something being sacrificed."

"Or someone," Heinz Oestreich said. "Or many."

Terbach still was not finished. "And we have conceived of a painless way of accomplishing that change."

"Not so painless," General Wahlen said.

"Something up?" asked Amgard Vieten, swallowing nervously.

Wahlen stood up, a remarkably handsome man in superb physical condition. He looked to be thirty and was in fact fifty.

"Charftag! More wine," called Vieten, and the old butler puttered about the table doing as he was bid.

Wahlen waited until every glass was filled. The others watched with expectancy. Wahlen could always be counted on for high drama. "As you may know, the United States has created the neutron bomb."

"But what in hell *is* it?" asked Vieten.

"It's a kind of micromini-hydrogen bomb," said Wahlen. "It exploits fusion reaction. The explosive release is one-thousandth of an old-fashioned hydrogen bomb. The old bomb did its damage with a blast. The neutron bomb minimizes blast, some eighty percent of its energy being released in the form of neutrons, radiation."

"All very interesting, to be sure," said Zimmer. "But what does this have to—"

"A short time ago the American President had not yet decided on deployment of this weapon. My superior, General Haig, has been one of its great advocates. Naturally, I have said nothing. We learned this week that deployment has been agreed upon. NATO will get the bombs. They will be under my direct control."

There was silence around the table except for Zimmer's breathing.

"With these bombs," said Wahlen, "Germany could take Russia in a week."

"That sounds terribly familiar," said Willi Fassmann.

The general made a short bow in his direction. "I am not talking about horses that can starve or tanks that can freeze, sir. I'm talking about burning a population to cinders in minutes."

"And under your control, General?" said Zimmer. He began to laugh, and Fassmann couldn't decide whether to slap his back or let him choke. He slapped his back.

Zimmer said, "You're always around when I need you, Willi."

"Like any good insurance man, Ludwig," said Fassmann.

Amgard Vieten stroked his pointed chin, on which a bit of beard was making an appearance. "A vigorous Chancellor will, thanks to NATO, have at his fingertips the capability of destroying . . . whatever requires that unique form of purification. But even without this—correct me if I'm wrong, General—our own small West German Army could take Europe itself in a week."

General Wahlen nodded. "First, Russia—"

"And just what will the Russians be doing while the rest of Europe goes under?" asked Vieten.

"I don't believe you understand," said Wahlen. "The Russians will be counting their casualties, lining up for blood counts, mobbing whichever of their burn centers remain standing. In short, with the neutron bomb, the Russians will be doing exactly what the people of Hiroshima and Nagasaki did. They will be dying.

"China? They'll be happiest of all. Stupid peasants. The United States? Pious statements, along with the Pope's protests through proper channels—but we are speaking of armed conflict not on their shores. Who doesn't want Russia to go under?

The eastern bloc? Nonsense! Slaves desire the deaths of their masters."

"You have not misplaced our trust, General," said Vieten. "So! We have all the ingredients, don't we? A young leader who needs a bit of time to mature is our base. We build on him."

Ludwig Zimmer was suddenly laughing again. He stopped long enough to wipe his watery eyes on a silk handkerchief.

"How we've had to kiss their asses, the whole world's asses: those silly Frenchmen we defeat every time by shouting 'boo'; those Englishmen, now in hot pursuit of national suicide; those Yanks—how I hate that word. Those nigger Yanks with their boogie-woogie and their coffee-colored bastards putrifying the strains of the only pure race the world has ever known. In only a few years we've become everybody's friend, no man's enemy. Germany, the good Samaritan. Even Israel loves us. With suspicion, but love is in the air. I donate a million marks a year to them. They've got a hospital in Jerusalem named for me. For me! Eichmann must be turning over in his grave or wherever it was they dropped his ashes. Very well, love us—fuck us if that's your pleasure. We will still own the earth!"

Again he was laughing, this time in the face of the others' nervousness. This was no time to have Ludwig Zimmer and Ludwig Zimmer's resources lost to madness. Amgard Vieten cleared his throat. "None has contributed more than you," he said.

The old tycoon's eyes now retreated into craftiness. "Don't attempt subtlety with me, Amgard. How much is it this time?"

Vieten turned to Heinz Oestreich. The intelligence chief removed a blue-bound folder from a briefcase.

"Spare me the details," said Zimmer. "I'm beyond being read to."

Willi Fassmann had retreated from this low talk of finance and was busy examining some of the library's treasures.

"Setting up an intelligence network worldwide is a ferocious undertaking," said Oestreich. "What it's costing us alone to vet—"

"To what?" asked Zimmer.

"To, ah, buy an informant right out of the Chancellor's ass, that alone—"

"Well? Well? How much?"

Oestreich ran a well-manicured hand through his luxuriant head of white hair. "The next nine days should cost us between four and six million marks." He said it sadly, as if he were announcing the passing of an old friend.

Ludwig Zimmer did not hesitate. "Six million marks will be deposited tomorrow to the account in the Swiss Bank Leu in Lucerne."

Willi Fassmann turned from the library shelves. "You are a great man," he said to Zimmer.

General Wahlen clicked to attention; his heels actually popped together as he held his glass aloft and said, "To Ludwig Zimmer, a great German."

The others downed their wine as though it were water. Amgard Vieten pointed to the now-dead television set. "They worshipped his father, they will worship him."

Willi Fassmann turned to Oestreich. "And what of our missing ingredient? Have we no word?"

For a moment Oestreich blinked in reply, not understanding the other man. "Oh! You mean the good colonel."

Willi nodded. "That's precisely who I mean. The good Libyan colonel without whose billions our plans are somewhat unrealistic."

Oestreich smiled. "Patience, Willi, have you no patience?"

"Oh, I've got plenty of that," Fassmann said.

Frau Gerda Umbreit sat in the chrome and aluminum kitchen of the Chancellor's bungalow. The chefs and waiters had gone home for the day, and Josef Haack was having one final meeting.

She watched the lone flame under a pot of boiling water. They would end the day with tea, and that was her favorite time. Nervously her eyes darted about the kitchen, inspecting it for flaws; as usual, there were none. The chef was even more fanatical than she.

She looked her age under the harsh fluorescent lights.

She had never been a pretty woman. Attractive. Solid. She felt the lines that crisscrossed her face and remembered when her skin had been smooth and her cheeks rosy. Now, sometimes she used rouge. Sometimes she didn't bother.

She had started as his housekeeper. His wife, Flora Haack, had been a sickly woman, but very beautiful. Never had she been more beautiful than during the year it took her to die from a malignancy that strangely tore at her insides, leaving the lovely surface untouched.

Frau Umbreit had fallen in love with Josef Haack in his time of greatest suffering. Nor had her feelings for him started as pity. One day she knew she loved him, and she suffered when he did and comforted him when he let her.

She would have shared his bed had he ever given the slightest sign. He never did, and she remained a virgin. It would be he or no one.

That he loved her like a sister was obvious, and for a time she took pleasure in it. But as her youth faded, the pleasure diminished—and finally, like her youth, it faded too.

Now, on some days, she actually had to hide the hostility that she felt toward him. And herself.

Then she felt ashamed.

She went to the door and listened to the men's voices. Frustrated, she picked up a cloth and began to polish the already-gleaming kitchen counter.

Josef Haack and Dr. Alfred Nauman had taken time out from their discussion of the terrorist trials to watch Kurt's inaugural address.

Off in the corner, clutching his steno pad and pen, sat Peter Salman. The Chancellor's confidential secretary, said his enemies, "knew too damn much for a civil servant."

Over the years the Chancellor had lost confidence in his memory, thus the importance of Peter Salman, who could take perfect dictation faster than anyone in Europe.

"He makes no errors," the Chancellor often boasted.

When people complained that it was impossible to get the most perfunctory answers out of Salman, the Chancellor would say, "Peter Salman is not paid to talk."

At a nod from Haack, the secretary clicked the television set off and resumed his seat in the corner, pen at the ready. The Chancellor motioned for him to put the pen down.

"Well," said Haack, "did Mayor Hitler change your mind?"

The Minister of the Interior smiled apologetically. "He's too good to be true."

The Chancellor said, "That also occurred to me. And then I asked myself, 'Why not? Why not a good man?' There is no law of nature that denies the possibility that one does exist. Is there?"

"Yes, there is: the law that men are men, thus flawed. Only young Mr. Hitler seems to have escaped that frailty. It frightens me, makes me realize my own frailties."

"Come, come, Nauman, what harm can the Mayor of Berlin do? If a miracle should occur and our party be returned to power, you will be Chancellor, my chosen successor."

"I promise to keep an open mind," Alfred Nauman said.

Haack motioned to Salman to resume his note-taking, and Nauman went into a detailed explanation of the trials.

When they were finished, Haack walked his Minister to the door, where Nauman's four security men waited with his Mercedes.

"Please don't come outside," said the Minister. "It's much too cold."

Josef Haack gripped his arm. "For God's sake be careful," he said, almost in a whisper. "We are dealing with the most murderous men in the world."

Nauman squeezed the old man's hand and thought how easy it was to love Josef Haack.

The Chancellor returned to his sitting room, where Peter Salman waited like a statue. "Good night, Peter," said Haack, dismissing him. In his place was Frau Gerda Umbreit, who carried a steaming mug of tea laced with lemon and honey. She arranged the bun on the back of her neck and sat staring at him.

He liked to tease this prim and proper woman. "What are you staring at, Frau Umbreit?"

"There is a spot on your collar."

"Lipstick," Haack said.

"Not likely," said the woman.

"Oh? Don't you think the Chancellor might be able to get an occasional kiss should he desire it?"

Frau Umbreit covered her mouth with her hand and began to giggle.

"What are you laughing about?"

The woman shook her head.

"I order you to tell me in the name of the Federal Republic!"

"Have me shot," Gerda Umbreit said. *The blind old fool,* she was thinking. *Don't you know what's in my heart, what's always been there?*

At the chateau in Bad Godesberg, Amgard Vieten stared at Heinz Oestreich and wondered at the secret of the man's youthful looks.

"The problem," said Vieten, "is how to elevate Kurt Hitler the next step up the ladder? How do we get him in position?"

Oestreich replied in his silkiest voice, "The problem is, the old Chancellor simply does not trust him."

"Are you quite certain of that?"

"My operative is all but sleeping with Haack. We know these things."

Vieten frowned. "Surely he still has affection for his former protégé."

Oestreich smiled. "Perhaps. But he still resents Kurt's not coming clean with him. Nor is Dr. Nauman helping things. The Minister of the Interior believes Kurt to be a fraud."

"We need a break," said Vieten.

"Yes, a break."

"Come, come, Oestreich, men don't wait for breaks. They make them!"

The intelligence chief teased him. "I'm not sure I follow you, Amgard."

"Our seed money has been unlimited," said Vieten. "Though how long we have it I can't say. Zimmer, for one, seems to be laughing more and more."

"He's a most generous patriot."

"He wants results for his money. His patience seems to be wearing thin."

Oestreich ran a beautifully shaped bronze hand through his hair. "What he wants, what we all want, takes time."

"That's the catch! None of us has time. Damn! Time, eh?"

"And money," said Oestreich. "Murder is not free as it was in the good days."

"In other words we can't do without Tripoli! What do you think, Heinz, what do you really think? Will Qaddafi join us?"

"Of course he will. His goal is exactly as our own. But he's no fool. A fanatic, yes, but no fool."

"Then what's he waiting on?" Vieten asked.

"Tangible evidence of our—he called it 'ingenuity'—then he'll pick up the tab for everything. No limit."

Vieten whistled softly. "We must get Kurt out of Berlin politics and into position."

"Position?"

"For Haack's retirement."

"But he's chosen Dr. Nauman as his successor," Oestreich said innocently.

Vieten stared at him. "Yes. Nauman."

"It will be very dangerous," Oestreich said softly.

Amgard Vieten smiled. "What we are doing is very dangerous."

15

Willi Fassmann had called the meeting. "It is time," he said, "to take stock." The Liberal party had now been in office for eighteen months.

Kurt, seated at one end of a long table, tried to hide a smile as Fassmann, at the other end, called on Liedtke, now Kurt's executive assistant, for a report on press evaluation.

"The BZ News 'heartily approves of his efforts to inject new blood into a tired city. We need a tonic desperately, and he just may be what the doctor ordered,' " read Liedtke.

"Not bad," someone muttered.

Hack writing, thought Liedtke. "The *Bild* says, 'Governing Mayor Hitler has done more in eighteen months to defuse the inflammatory emotions that his name conjures up than one could have imagined possible.' "

Fassmann said, "True enough."

Liedtke read from another clipping. "*Tagesspiegel* sees him as 'an enigma, young and handsome, compassionate and earnest, and yet one cannot help but wonder, what is going on inside Kurt Hitler? Of course he dreams, all men do. But what is his dream?' "

"I do dream," said Kurt. "Of never having to read the *Tagesspiegel*!"

Everyone laughed.

"One more," said Liedtke. "The Englishman, Mr. Sinclair. He writes, 'What Mr. Hitler is doing is diffusing Mr. Hitler. So loaded is the name with emotional dynamite that the young Mayor has obviously made banking all the fires that automatically accompany what he has said and what he will do in the future, his number-one priority. Perhaps he feels that only then can he really get down to the job of accomplishing anything. In the meantime he is not your neighborhood politico, he is the son of Adolf Hitler.' "

"Manure," someone called out.

"There's a little more," said Liedtke. He read, "The question in this reporter's mind: Is that good? Should the name Hitler and all that it conjures up ever lose its force? Or, better, should we ever forget the past?"

There was silence.

"Frankly," said Fassmann, "it's not the past that concerns me. It's right now. If I hear Kurt give that 'Berlin Needs Tourists' speech one more time, I may vote against him. Kurt, surely you know the people expect something more meaningful, more meaty. More provocative."

"But Willi," said Kurt, "I'm not President of the United States or even Secretary General of the United Nations. I'm the Mayor of one city."

"You are you!" said Fassmann, his small eyes darting about the table to find a reaction. He liked what he saw in their eyes. "They expect more from you."

Kurt smiled. "Perhaps there isn't any more."

The other politicians laughed; Willi Fassmann stared at Kurt, as if to ask, "Are you crazy?"

Kurt Hitler winked.

Twenty-eight thousand feet above Germany and still climbing, Lufthansa's flight 604 began a journey that would culminate at Tel Aviv's Ben-Gurion Airport that afternoon at 2:55.

August Acht, a young tour guide who made an excellent living showing people the Wall and East Berlin, lit a cigarette and congratulated himself on having the good fortune to be assigned a seat next to a bearded Jew wearing a yarmulke and already deep into a Hebrew manuscript.

He, August, would start a conversation with this holy man and try out some of the Hebrew he had learned in his night classes at the Jewish Community Center and on his past four trips to Israel. He truly loved the young country; what had begun as discovery of an interesting place to spend one's holiday had turned into something quite different. On this trip he would actually live in a kibbutz with friends he had made on his other journeys.

August leaned over ever so slightly toward his seat companion and said in Hebrew, "I hope this cigarette smoke isn't disturbing—"

He stopped—understandably—at the sight of a small pistol in the "holy man's" fist. Now the man stood up, as did three other bearded men, each of them wearing yarmulkes and holding weapons.

The man spoke in perfect German: "Attention! You are now military prisoners of Black September!"

A woman screamed; from the back of the plane a child laughed at what he knew must be a joke. The speaker gave no sign that he heard either sound.

"My associate is in full control of your pilot's cabin. He will fly to a location where certain of you will be removed, after which this flight will be allowed to continue or return to Frankfurt, as your captain wishes."

Young August Acht felt his heart fly into his throat.

"Certain of you—"

An elderly man raised a hand, and the terrorist motioned with his weapon for the man to speak.

"Would you mind telling us who will be removed? And why?"

The terrorist took off his yarmulke and tossed it in the old man's direction. "Try that on, if it fits you'll be removed. You see, on our recent, highly successful incursion into Tel Aviv, two of our brothers were captured. We want them back. We will trade you for them."

Reaction to the hijacking was immediate. The Pope expressed "Christ's sorrow," the U.S. State Department condemned terrorism for the thousandth time; in France the Quai d'Orsay refused comment until "full facts can be ascertained," and Chancellor Josef Haack ordered Minister of the Interior Dr. Alfred Nauman to personally undertake an investigation.

In Kampala, Uganda, the leader of that nation said, "The entire thing is a British-Zionist plot to personally hurt the stature which I enjoy in the world." Secretly, he sent a plea to Black September friends to refrain, "in the name of love, friendship and fraternity, from landing in Uganda."

In Libya, Muammar el-Qaddafi issued a statement: He "knew nothing of the matter," and felt obligated to warn one and all "that Libya is not Entebbe." Whether this warning was intended for the terrorists or the Israelis, no one was certain.

Gunther Liedtke, entering Kurt's office, found his boss reading a newspaper. From behind the paper Kurt asked a question. "Who is this Associated Press man, Eric Vogel?"

"Just another reporter. Breezy, nice enough, but he'd misquote you without batting an eye. Why, if I may ask?"

Kurt put the newspaper down. "He seems to be asking everyone in Europe how they feel about the hijacking."

Liedtke remained silent.

"Why doesn't he ask me?"

"He's probably afraid you'll talk about tourism," said Liedtke.

"Tell him to be here at two o'clock. Tell him I will not talk about tourism."

Liedtke paused. "Are you quite certain?"

"No, I'm not," said Kurt.

Liedtke nodded.

At precisely 2 P.M. he brought the Associated Press man in, made the introductions and departed. Eric Vogel resembled a rabbit, right down to sharp front teeth and a bouncy walk that, with a little imagination, could be seen as a hop. He bowed very formally as he and Kurt shook hands. Kurt motioned him to a comfortable seat opposite his desk and, while the reporter took out his pen and notebook, lit a cigarette.

"Do you smoke a lot?" asked Vogel with a toothy smile.

"Too much."

"Ever try to quit?"

Kurt nodded as if Vogel had asked a profound question.

"Hijacking is something," Vogel said, almost as an afterthought.

"It's an abomination."

Vogel wrote the word on his pad, looked up and smiled at Kurt.

"Come now, Mr. Mayor, does anybody really give a good fuck about a handful of Jews?"

Vogel could hear Kurt catch his breath; he seemed engaged in fighting some personal battle, perhaps to get hold of his temper. Whatever it was, the effort showed clearly on his handsome face.

"Mr. Vogel," he said softly, "I very much, to use your words, 'give a fuck' about a handful of Jews. If someone, anyone, had 'given a fuck' about a handful of Jews in the thirties, the handful would not have become six million."

"Your father," Vogel said, just as softly, and Kurt wondered why no one had ever knocked the man's two protruding teeth down his throat.

"You mean my father, Adolf Hitler," Kurt said without hesitating. "And the people who followed my father, the whole murderous pack of them."

"May I quote you on that?" Vogel asked easily.

"You may quote me on anything that I say," said Kurt. "Just kindly refrain from quoting me on what I do *not* say."

"Do you think there's much anti-Semitism today?"

"I do think there is anti-Semitism today, how much I can't say."

"In Germany?" Vogel shot back.

"In Germany."

"Wouldn't you say that most anti-Semitism today originates from the oil crisis—I mean, the Arabs have the oil. Certainly no one can deny the importance of oil."

Kurt nodded. "Oil is arguably the second most important fluid on the earth today. The most important fluid remains the blood from human beings. If we ever forget that . . ."

His voice trailed off, but Eric Vogel would not let him off the hook.

"If we forget that, Mr. Mayor?"

Kurt looked straight into his eyes. "If we ever forget that we will invite the past to join our future, and we will create on earth a hell worse than the one we created before."

Vogel was writing furiously.

"Now as to the hijacking of the German airliner," said Kurt. "I would gladly trade places with the hostages, become a hostage myself to insure their release."

Vogel got up. "Is that a serious offer?"

Kurt nodded, and with a wave of his arm Vogel was gone. Kurt sank back into his chair, a hand pressed to his forehead, his heart pounding with relief.

Eric Vogel had his story.

In a gray castle topped with black turrets near St. Guarshausen on the Rhine, three men sat at a breakfast table eating seabird eggs and drinking dark Brazilian coffee. The castle's master, Ludwig Zimmer, sat at the table's head. On his right was Amgard Vieten, under whose elbow rested a thick manila envelope; on his left was Heinz Oestreich. The face beneath the intelligence chief's silky white hair fairly glowed; Oestreich looked as if he had just had a facial massage.

Zimmer, who was interested in such matters, suspected that the youthful glow was inspired by the two teen-age sisters Oestreich was rumored to keep. His thought was interrupted by Vieten, now removing a gray folder from the envelope.

"For a change, something good," he said, Father Christmas bestowing fruits and sweets on the assembled children. Ceremoniously he opened the folder, clucking softly to himself.

Zimmer said, "Come on, man, get on with it! If you've got something, please be so good as to give it to us, that clucking is quite disconcerting while I try to eat seabird eggs."

The other two men studied Zimmer to see if he hoped for a laugh in response. His face gave no clue, and they laughed, but mildly. Zimmer nodded. They had read him right.

"Following the Governing Mayor's statement on the Jewish hostages," said Vieten, "we immediately commissioned a nationwide poll. I now have the results."

"Degree of accuracy?" Zimmer was suspicious of polls.

"Three percent either way," said Vieten. "That's the best anyone can do."

"Well?" asked Zimmer.

Vieten smiled. "He is easily the most popular public figure in Germany today, leading Chancellor Josef Haack by twenty-three points. More amazing still is his negative, which is three. *Three*! He has no negative!"

"So?" Zimmer persisted. "Where are we?"

Vieten squirmed noticeably in his chair. "We are in what the air-traffic controllers call a holding pattern."

"Which means we are not going forward."

"These things take time," Vieten said uneasily.

By now Zimmer was drumming his ancient fingers on the tabletop. "I'm afraid, Amgard, you've named the one element that none of us at this table possesses."

Vieten glanced down at his plate.

"Amgard, be so kind as to look up, look around you. Yes, look at me and at Commander Oestreich, and pray remember your own countenance. Has it occurred to you that you and I are in our eighties, and the Commander here is—"

"Seventy-one," said Oestreich, who had seen that birthday come and go five years before.

"*We are running out of time*!" Zimmer shouted.

"Now, Ludwig . . ." Vieten was afraid the other man would start laughing or choking to death.

"I have paid a fortune for results. Goddamnit, I want results!"

"We have made a great deal of progress," Oestreich interjected smoothly.

"We have?" said Zimmer.

"The Chancellor now has complete confidence in Kurt Hitler."

"Are you certain of that?" Vieten wanted to know. "I hope you're not basing it on what Willi Fassmann says. Willi makes up most of those conversations with the Chancellor, who detests him."

Oestreich smiled. "I assure you, Senator Fassmann is not

my source for the Chancellor's likes and dislikes. With all due modesty, I have had a bit of experience in these matters."

Vieten nodded, remembering certain of Oestreich's exploits that had caused him the nickname "Cobra." Zimmer also nodded, recalling Goebbels' once telling him that he was certain Heinz Oestreich carried poison in his ring. The ancient tycoon studied the red ruby on the man's little finger and suddenly felt uncomfortable.

Oestreich went on. "The Chancellor is calling him 'dear boy' again. The freeze is over, all is forgiven, the past is never mentioned."

"So?" said Zimmer. "And what good does this do us? That the Chancellor calls our Mr. Hitler 'dear boy' does not strike me as a bargain, particularly at a cost of forty million marks. In the old days that wouldn't have been worth a good piss!"

"But it is not the old days," Vieten said patiently. "We cannot round people up and shoot them, however much we might like to. Step one was to get Kurt back in old Haack's good graces, to make Kurt the logical heir apparent without the slightest bit of manipulation showing. We've done that. And now, if opportunity knocks—"

Ludwig Zimmer hit the table so hard that his coffee spilled. "Goddamnit, I want opportunity to knock now! *Now*, do you hear me? This plan's succeeding when I am in my grave will give me no satisfaction whatsoever!"

"In addition to which, Qaddafi is pressuring us for proof of our intentions," said Vieten.

"Well," said Zimmer, "what will it take?"

Amgard Vieten told him.

Dusk fell in the austere room on the figure in the white prayer robe. Youseff Raji, a burly, distinguished-looking Arab in a beautifully tailored suit, watched quietly. He had waited many times for the other man to finish praying. Sometimes he had prayed beside him.

A light misting rain fell outside, and once lightning flashed across a window, giving the figure in white a ghostlike appearance. Raji studied the praying figure, wondering what would come from his lips when he finally spoke.

A decree to have adulterers stoned to death? Last time it had been a new way of meting out punishment to embezzlers. Now their heads rather than hands would be chopped off—embezzlement was, after all, a crime committed with the head.

Raji, a Ph.D. from Harvard, was a student in survival. Since returning to his native land and entering government service, he had come to know that survival was the most important art of all. He had applied himself to the Koran and especially the Shari'a, the ancient Islamic legal code, with all of the passion that he had once given his economic textbooks. It was as if his life depended on it. In fact, it did.

The figure in white turned.

The voice was soft. It was always soft at the beginning. "I have prayed for two days and two nights."

Raji said nothing, but lowered his eyes before such piety.

"The pan-Arabic, Islamic federation, my dream, has failed. It has failed for two reasons: the Jews and the Egyptians. One, an eternal enemy. The other, a brother. I have tried everything. Millions to Egypt. Millions to Syria. Millions to the Palestine guerrilla movement and to Mali, and to Chad and to Uganda and to Niger and to Congo. And always I have asked only two things: Will this money help Islam? Will this money hurt Israel? It has done neither. The children of Islam fight like carrion over a carcass. Israel grows stronger."

Raji nervously swallowed.

"Well?" said the other man. "Well?"

Raji said, "It is so."

"Yes," said Muammar el-Qaddafi. "Yes, yes, yes."

"What are the Colonel's wishes?"

"Go to Germany. Look at this group. Look at this Hitler. Then tell me. Come here to me and tell me. Then—then, if I say yes—I will ask two things of them. Two holy objectives. The death of Israel and the return of our territory."

Raji, face impassive, wondered to what territory his leader referred.

As though reading the other man's mind, the figure in the white prayer robe replied, "Spain, Portugal and Sicily."

"Of course," said Raji. "Spain, Portugal and Sicily."

"Lost to Islam five centuries ago."

"I will go. I will report to you."

"Hitler," said Qaddafi, "Hitler."

16

As suddenly as he had dropped from sight, Max Levy was back among them, carrying his breakfast tray in the dining hall. Shemuel Reiter saw him first, left his wife and their new baby, and joined Levy.

"Welcome home," he said.

"Thank you."

Shemuel noticed Max's hand carrying food to his mouth. Inside the wrist were blue circular bruises.

"How's the new doctor?"

"He's young," said Max.

"Do you miss the old one?"

"No," said Max, standing with the tray.

"Max . . ." Shemuel began, then considered the other man's clouded gaze and decided not to say what was on his mind. "Have a good day, Max."

He rejoined his wife, and they made small talk about the baby. Then she said, "You seem upset." He looked at her quickly. Her ability to read his mind at times amused him. At other times—like now—he found it disconcerting.

"I don't know what to do," he said.

"Is it about Max?"

He nodded, wanting to say more. He knew he would not.

She turned back to the baby. What could she say? What did she know? She only suspected.

"Excuse me," said Shemuel. He gave the baby a quick kiss, walked down the cobbled walkway to Max's house and tapped on the door.

"Come," called Max.

He sat on the bed, a blue floppy hat on his head. He was lacing up his old shoes. He looked at Shemuel.

"Max," said his friend, "are you all right?"

"Yes."

"Israel is a democracy, and—my God, I sound like a high school civics teacher—what I'm trying to say is that you're a free man, a free man like any other man. You don't have to go on—you may do as you please!"

"It's all right," Max said and stood up. Shemuel nodded and felt foolish, and there were even the edges of a gnawing thought, that he had been slightly traitorous. Still, he also was a free man!

Outside, Shemuel headed back toward the dining hall while Max walked to the vineyards.

The vines were in full flower and the weather was calm and warm as good wine-growing weather should be. Now would come the task of thinning the shoots, tying the best ones to the slender wires.

Bending over, Max took pleasure in the loose grainy dirt between his fingers and the sun's warmth on the back of his neck. He worked for hours that way, not thinking of where he had been or what he had done. The face of Shemuel Reiter came into his mind, but before it could speak he blotted it out. Then came the face of the man whose fingertips had closed about his wrists as though the two were locked in a kind of sexual combat. Max tossed a pebble behind him onto the road. He remembered now; someplace there had been guitar music. Something Spanish, slow. Methodically, with great care, he turned the wire about the slender vine. The other man's eyes, doing all the communicating. The man had been intelligent and had not wasted energy on sounds. The sounds were those of hands clapping, of words being called out, yet still musical. A rhythm.

Shemuel Reiter saying, "You don't have to . . ."

He dug with his hands into the loose earth and let his hands rest there as if seeking refuge from the sun. Clapping in time to the music. *Olé*! *Olé*! Someone was dancing. Someone was dancing while— A ruined plant, trapped in the shade, starved for sunlight. Would never make wine. He removed it. The wine, the wine, he repeated it to himself; it was a litany. Like arms wrestling in a pub, but no laughter, no jolly bets. Winner takes all and loser . . . loses. Lost. Hands letting go and doing their own dance in the Madrid air. Behind him. Forget, forget. Wine.

Until the next time.

His enemies said that the Israeli Prime Minister was schizophrenic. His friends defended him as best they could. In public he was kind, affable. It was in private that the real man emerged. His wife told him that he had a basic mistrust of people. He was in fact capable of cutting off human relationships with the simple throwing of some internal switch.

He was a young man, he was neither a war hero nor a "founding father" of the nation. Immigrating from Lithuania as a penniless youth, he had become one of the country's first self-made millionaires.

In public he was never seen with a necktie and was perceived to be a casual man. In private he never appeared without a tie and usually wore expensive London-tailored suits.

He had promised the people prosperity and had defeated a war hero who reminded the people of many things they preferred to forget.

Now he sat in his home in Jerusalem drinking a gin and tonic and reading a copy of *The Wall Street Journal*, with which he kept up as to how his fortune, now in a blind trust, was doing.

His wife, a tall, handsome, blond woman of French-Jewish stock, said, "That man is here."

"Send him in," he said in perfect French. It amused him that he had mastered the language as a hobby, and now spoke it as well as she.

His wife asked him in Hebrew, "May I sit in?"

"*Non, chérie.*"

She left the room.

Baruch Eliat entered, the remarkable scars on his face resembling threads taut white against his tan. The Prime Minister put his drink and newspaper down and motioned the bull-like man to a seat.

"Well?"

"Those people in Bonn are ready to make their move," said Eliat.

"And that is?"

"We don't really know," said Eliat. "Something violent, murder I should think."

"Why don't you know?"

"Our agent was not present at the meeting where the exact act was decided upon. He knows only that it was. My best guess is murder."

"Of old Chancellor Haack?" asked the Prime Minister. "I rather like the man."

"I think not. They need Haack, he's the key to getting their man promoted."

The Prime Minister took another sip of his drink, and Baruch wondered if it ever occurred to the man that he too might like a cool drink.

"You think that's their goal, getting young Hitler promoted?"

Eliat nodded. "Haack is old and tired. We are told this is his last year."

The Prime Minister nodded also. "How nice. And in would step young Hitler, not only leading Germany, but sitting in the councils of NATO and God knows what else."

"I believe their ambitions extend beyond the Fatherland."

"Are we certain of this?" asked the Prime Minister.

"Absolutely. They've put together a group that includes military and labor power, plus the millions of that maniac Zimmer. Anybody who takes that group lightly—"

The Prime Minister smiled for the first time. "We can't let that happen, can we?"

Baruch Eliat made no reply. The Prime Minister was talking to himself.

"Would you like a gin and tonic?"

"No," said Baruch Eliat, who knew what was coming.

"We have two choices. Wait and see, or stop it now. If we wait and see . . . well, history does not deal well with Jews who wait to see. If, on the other hand, we act now, if we act intelligently where no possible blame can befall us, the operation could be a simple one. Any ideas?"

Eliat was silent.

"Come, come, man, I do not want your silence."

"I am not the Prime Minister," said Baruch Eliat.

The Prime Minister leaned forward and spoke very softly. "Do we have the right people?"

"We have the same one."

"Oh, yes, our Mr. Levy."

Eliat could not contain a smile. It sounded so strange to hear Max Levy called "Mister."

He came in from the fields at lunchtime and slowly walked past the roses that bordered the walkway to his quarters. There was one huge yellow one, standing there like some kind of glorious mistake. He removed his cap and ran his hand through his wet hair. He was covered with perspiration, and there were wet rings staining his khaki shirt beneath his arms. He went into the bathroom, staring at himself in the mirror while he reached down for the small bar of soap on the basin.

As he touched it, without looking, he knew that the soap was not blue but yellow. He let it lie in his palm for a moment, now examining it as if it were some kind of archaeological find. "It" had come so quickly on the heels of the other one: he would have preferred more time to work the grapes.

He washed his hands and went into the dining room. His eyes met those of Shemuel Reiter, who brought his own tray over. Reiter sat beside him and the two men ate quietly. When they were finished, Max said, "I will need an automobile this evening."

Shemuel Reiter nodded, his eyes not meeting Max's.

Max returned to the vineyards, where he worked until suppertime, and then to his quarters, where the soap was, once again, blue. He showered, dressed in a white sport shirt and a suit that had never known good days. He took a cheap suitcase from an open closet and laid it across the bed. Into it went a few items of clothing and some catalogs on Israel's fledgling furniture industry. The last thing he put into the suitcase was the unused red toothbrush, which he laid atop his underwear and alongside a cheap camera.

The kibbutz owned three vehicles: a Peugeot 504, a white Ford station wagon and a Citroen station wagon, which Max climbed into, throwing his suitcase on the backseat. He was soon on the road to Jerusalem.

The sun had not set when he reached the city, and he drove directly to a small controlled parking area before the Wailing Wall. He got out, locked the automobile behind him and walked through the military control point that led to the wall, where the usual group of worshippers and tourists was assembled. Someone handed him a black cardboard yarmulke. He walked across the limestone blocks and sat on a small bench. The cries of prayer rang out like strange birdcalls as a few people wept or kissed the ancient stone.

Some of them scribbled messages on tiny pieces of paper that they shoved into chinks in the wall; others chanted almost frantically, as though there would not be enough time to finish. A few old men in black offered to say kaddish for one's dead for a small fee that "would go to orphans." Some seemed quite mad, talking to themselves and to disinterested or frightened passersby.

Max Levy waited patiently. A lean, wiry man stood some distance from him, snapping pictures. He appeared to be an American. He wore a green leisure suit, a green shirt with a white floral pattern, a slightly dirty summer hat. On his feet were loafers and over his shoulders he carried a leather bag. His ears were large, as was the Adam's apple that bobbed in synchronization with the finger snapping away at the cheap camera's shutter release.

He sauntered over to Max's bench and collapsed onto it with a sigh.

"Hot one today," he announced to no one in particular as he removed the film from his camera and inserted a new roll. While he worked, his eyes swept the area behind Max. "You're okay," he said.

Max nodded.

He took out a disreputable-looking handkerchief with which he mopped his face, then wrung the cloth out and stuck it into his back pocket, where it dangled from the bench like a flag of surrender.

Lou Seegal, a genuine American gangster off the streets of Brooklyn, had specialized in a rather precise occupation that easily carved him a place in a basically Italian Mafia. Seegal had been one of the best spotters in the business. His job was learning the habits of a victim: where he kept his clothes, his car, his family and his woman; where he worked, where he slept, where he played. He knew the routes men unconsciously follow day after day to and from the various destinations that make up their existence.

Then Seegal had made an error, an unforgivable one: he made a deal with a mob victim who also happened to be a millionaire. He tipped the man off that he was being set up. His fee for the tip was two hundred thousand dollars. The man paid Seegal and then dropped from sight. At first no one was suspicious; he wasn't the first target to disappear at an appropriate moment. But the word got around—at first a joke, then a whisper, then an enraged accusation—and it was time for Lou Seegal to do a disappearing act. He flew to Israel where, as a Jew, he sought refuge.

Israeli immigration officials checked him out with their American counterparts, who said that Seegal was not a desirable character by any stretch of the imagination. They weren't, however, looking for him on any charge at the moment, though they understood that "others" were.

A bright young Israeli immigration officer tipped off the

Mossad about their would-be immigrant. The outcome of a chat with Seegal, along with a complete check on him since his birth, motivated the Mossad to make him a proposition. He could, indeed, become an Israeli citizen—with one catch. Lou Seegal would continue in his chosen profession as a spotter, the Mossad replacing the Mafia as his employer.

Seegal hesitated for only a moment, thought with a shudder of what awaited him back in the States, and accepted the offer on the understanding that he would never again set foot in the United States, where he calculated that his life expectancy would fall between twenty-four and forty-eight hours. The deal was made, and Seegal now operated worldwide.

His expertise had resulted in the deaths of thirty-three men and two women.

"The Brazil thing was something," Seegal said admiringly, thereby breaking a cardinal rule: never refer to past exploits. Max made no reply, nor did Seegal expect one.

Max was watching two boys bring an old man on a stretcher and lay him before the wall, where he stared as though watching a sunset.

Seegal opened his bag, took out a fat envelope, and he put it on the bench between them. Max's hand covered it, took possession of it.

"Money, credit cards, airplane tickets, passwords, contacts, telephone numbers and photos, front and side . . ."

One of the boys was holding the old man at the wall in a sitting position. The man reached out with a thin arm.

"Plane'll leave from Ben-Gurion tonight, midnight, take you to Frankfurt, change to Lufthansa on into Berlin."

The old man was crying aloud; the other boy was holding his head against his chest.

Seegal laughed. "If my old man could see me at the Wailing Wall. Me!" He stood and stared down at Max. "In the United States you could be a millionaire, Max," he said and walked on.

Now they were carrying away the man on the stretcher. When they were almost at the police control point the two boys again stopped and the man took one final, long look backward at the wall. Then he dropped his head to the stretcher and they disappeared from sight.

Max Levy opened the envelope and stared at the glossy photos. They were excellent, the face slender and handsome. There was DM50,000; they always gave him too much money. It cost him little to live, and his work cost nothing at all. In the beginning he had returned whatever money was left. They told him that wasn't necessary, so now he left it in Shemuel Reiter's house. Which might have explained why Mishmar Elijah Kibbutz had a nursery for the children that was the envy of other, larger kibbutzes. When questioned, Reiter explained that the money came from a wealthy American who wished to remain anonymous. One man demanded the American's name so they could rename the kibbutz after him, but Reiter said the man insisted on anonymity.

"He may even take the nursery back," Reiter warned, and the matter was dropped.

Max folded the envelope and shoved it into his coat pocket, took off the cardboard yarmulke and returned it at the control point. Then he went back to his automobile and began the drive to Ben-Gurion Airport outside Tel Aviv. In his rearview mirror the lights of Jerusalem blazed behind him. Max thought of Seegal: *If my old man could see me at the Wailing Wall!*

For a moment he knew a feeling of panic, a fear that he never felt when "doing his job," a formless fluttering within his chest. Then he blotted the American and the wall from his mind and found refuge from himself in the long lines waiting for the airport security check, the most stringent of any airport in the world.

Fifteen minutes later he stood before a security agent, a young woman who looked to be about sixteen. She examined his passport and asked the usual questions: Had anyone given him a package to take on board the airplane? Would he please open the suitcase and see if anything had been tampered with? Max opened it, and the girl's hands made a thorough, professional search.

And what was the purpose of his trip? He told her he was

introducing some new lines of furniture into Berlin. The quietness of his demeanor seemed to disturb her, and she walked over to an older man. The two whispered for a moment, looking in Max's direction.

The man returned with the young woman, asked virtually the same questions she had asked, went through the suitcase once more. He was about to pick up the red toothbrush when his hands instead casually took up the old camera. "Loaded?" he asked pleasantly, his eyes never leaving Max. Max shook his head. The man smiled and with a finger clicked the camera open.

Empty.

He shrugged to the girl, who motioned for Max to close his suitcase. He did so and they took it from him. He would not see it again until he reached Berlin.

After a personal search in a blue-curtained cubicle, Max was finally ushered through a door where an armed policeman motioned him aboard a bus with the other cleared passengers. It soon began its short journey to the blue-and-white El Al Boeing 707 that waited, guarded by soldiers carrying submachine guns. Max sat in the rear section of the airplane, next to an empty seat. He opened the envelope and now began to study its contents seriously, a labor that occupied him until the plane landed in Frankfurt. As the airplane touched down he took one final look at the photograph: he would recognize the face under any conditions, at any time of day or night, standing still or on the run. A relationship had begun.

In the huge Frankfurt air terminal he went into the men's room, where he entered a toilet cubicle. There he tore the photograph into tiny jagged squares which he flushed down the toilet. He washed his hands and went to the Lufthansa area to await the plane to Berlin.

On this flight he sat next to a man whose small firm had failed in Bremerhaven and who was going to Berlin to "make a new start." They make it awfully attractive, the man explained. If things "went well," he would be joined by his wife and two children later, although they "weren't all that anxious" to make the move.

Only when he was collecting his suitcase did Max become aware that he was being observed. He did not see the other person; it was a matter of pure instinct and it never failed him. He turned casually, suitcase in hand, and swept the area with his eyes. He neither saw nor heard anything out of the ordinary, but he knew.

He had two choices: he could locate it and deal with it or— He chose the second alternative, which was to do nothing. He went out of the terminal and into a taxi for the ride into Berlin.

17

In the offices of the United States Army Intelligence and Security Command right outside Berlin, Major Dan Frazier, chief of the Informants Section, called to his new assistant.

"Hey, Train, c'mere a second!"

Captain Albert Train, a blond-haired Texan with a degree in criminology, closed the file he was examining, put it back into the filing cabinet, which he padlocked, and went into his chief's office.

Frazier—who, like Train, wore civilian clothes—was a dapper little man with carefully combed jet-black hair. "Just got a tip from a friend of ours at the airport. Max Levy's in town."

"Max who?"

"Damnit," Frazier said, "that's the third time this week I forgot you're new here. Think I'm getting senile?"

The Texan grinned. "Will it affect my efficiency report if I answer that?"

"Yes, it will," Frazier said with a smile. His eyes were small and mean.

"No, sir," said Captain Train, "I don't think you're senile at all."

Frazier gave a short laugh. Everything about the man was compact.

"Should I know this fellow Max Levy?" asked Train.

"In a way, yes, in a way I hope you never do. Max Levy's a Mossad boy. I'd say he's one of the best hit men in our business."

"Bad ass, huh?"

"The baddest. We know he's done jobs in Paris on a PLO guy, in Nicosia on a rep of Al Fatah, Athens on a Jordanian agent, Vienna on an Algerian, New York on a Syrian diplomat—and God knows how many others."

"So," said Train, "he's a member of a hit team?"

"No. He always acted alone after the hit team botched that job in 1973 in Norway. Recall the case?"

"Oh yeah, they killed the wrong man. A Moroccan waiter, wasn't it?"

Frazier nodded. "That was the end of the hit teams. From then on they went to a single operative. As for Levy . . . style, Train, Max Levy's got style."

Train smiled. "Style" was one of the major's favorite words.

Frazier laughed once, knowing what the younger officer was thinking. "Well, what would *you* call it? Listen, one victim choked to death on the cap from a catsup bottle. Now what would anybody be doing chewing on that? Another one died with a freshly laundered shirt half on, the cellophane bag that the shirt had come in around his head, smothering him. Style?"

"I see your point," said the Texan.

"So what is Max Levy doing in Berlin?"

"We gonna do anything?" asked Train.

"Yes. We'll talk to him. Our friend at the airport followed him to a pension. He'll be there."

Train's open face grew serious. "We gonna tell anybody?"

The major studied him. "How long have you been in Berlin, Captain, a month?"

The Texan nodded.

"Have you ever seen anyone rush to tell *us* anything?"

Captain Train shook his head.

"Fuck them," Major Frazier said precisely, and seemed to expect a reply from his assistant.

The Texan was a practical man. "Fuck 'em!" he said.

The moment she entered his office, Lise could see that Kurt was in a terrible mood. She felt relieved that it was Liedtke and not she who was "catching it." Both men acknowledged her presence perfunctorily, then Kurt continued his diatribe.

Liedtke interrupted him by speaking to Lise. "No one would believe this."

"The trouble with you," said Kurt, "is that you think like a whore!"

Lise could not resist. "What is it? Sounds like World War Three."

"It's this job, the frustration builds all day long. There's just so much I can do, and by the end of each day there's little real evidence to show that I've been here at all. Let me stop this moaning, I'm even beginning to bore myself."

"Kurt—" she began.

He recognized the tone of her voice. "Please," he gestured, holding up a hand, "nothing heavy today."

"I take it the rest of us aren't entitled to problems. They're the special preserve of politicians."

He threw back his head and laughed. "You're right! Okay, tell me what's wrong."

"My mother called. My sister isn't well."

"Oh, I'm sorry. Is there anything I can do?"

"It appears that she's having problems. A nervous breakdown."

"Damn!"

Lise looked at him coolly. "Damn *him*! Her boyfriend, he's gone off and deserted her. A younger woman, he's found himself a younger woman."

"These things happen," he said lamely.

"Yes, to people who let them happen," she said, suddenly angry.

"My God, you're being defensive," he said.

"Defensive? No, I don't think so at all. I'm being . . . realistic. The question is—"

"The question *is*," he interrupted, "you're confusing your sister and you."

"Maybe so. I hope so. I tell myself so, but—"

A cleaning woman opened the office door, picked up on their intensity and left hurriedly.

Outside, the sun had set and the first stars of evening were coming out over Berlin.

Max had registered at an inexpensive but respectable pension, the Kaiser, on Meinekestrasse right off the Kurfürstendamm. It was the kind of place where a not-too-successful salesman might stay, someone short of operating capital or trying to make a few marks on an expense account. He opened his suitcase and laid it across a chair. He seldom unpacked. He removed the furniture catalogs and placed them on the bed with a pencil and tablet. That would be the extent of his cover. He went down the short flight of stairs to the tiny lobby, passed the desk clerk who bid him a good day, then walked down the great avenue until he came to the Bristol outdoor café, where he sat and drank a cup of coffee and watched. He was definite about the feeling now and knew that it was only a matter of time before he would spot whoever was following him. Then he would deal with it.

Seeing nothing in the passing crowds, he paid the check and started walking, stopping occasionally to stare in the display windows of the stores that lined the street. He entered a department store, where he purchased a pair of thick cotton workman's gloves. He crossed the street to a tobacconist's, bought a cigarette lighter, tried it, asked the clerk to fill it with lighter fluid. Then he bought a single cigar.

He carried a paper sack containing these purchases back to the Kaiser, where the desk clerk told him with a smile, "Your friends are waiting."

"My friends?"

The clerk seemed perplexed. "The two Americans. They said you were expecting them."

Max nodded to put the man at ease and went up the steps. He paused for a moment in front of his door, then opened it.

Major Dan Frazier sat on his bed, onto which the contents of the suitcase had been dumped. A younger, blond-haired man sat in a chair tilted back against the wall. In his fist was a .38, pointed at Max.

"Hello, Levy," the major said. Max nodded.

"Search him?" Train asked, standing.

"Yes, but you won't find anything. Levy is against weapons, legitimate ones." While he talked Max turned and, his legs and arms outspread, faced the wall. Train expertly patted him down.

"Levy here is—well, you might say the kind for accidents," said Frazier. "Remember the last time we met?" Max turned and lowered his arms. The major continued. "Military attaché to the Syrian U.N. delegation. Died. Sawed his own throat with a kitchen knife. Surprising for a newlywed. The jokesters said 'bad pussy,' but we all knew. It was in September 1973, not quite two months after the Israeli military attaché was shot to death outside his home in D.C. An eye for an eye, and Levy here was the collector for the eye that was owed."

Max was staring at Train's .38. There had already been three occasions since entering the room in which he could have killed the two Americans. He wondered why such a sophisticated country sent children to do this kind of work.

It was as if Frazier could read his mind. "Put the piece away," he told Train. Then he asked Max, "What's in the paper bag?"

Max turned the bag over, spilling its contents on the bed.

"The gloves?" Frazier asked.

"To unload new furniture," said Max.

"I didn't know you smoked," Frazier said, examining the lighter. Max pointed to the cigar. Frazier nodded. "No film in your camera, none in your suitcase."

"I will buy some," Max said.

"What brings you to Berlin?" the major's voice was cold. They were down to business.

Max reached for something on the bed and Train shouted, "Freeze!" Max looked at the tall blond with new respect. The .38 had come out of the shoulder holster quickly and smoothly. Max picked up the furniture catalog and handed it to Frazier.

"So you're in the furniture business. Oh yes, with your gift for gab no doubt you're a natural."

"I am," Max said gravely, "a salesman."

"I'll bet no customer has ever complained," Frazier said.

Train wondered why he felt cold. He tried to examine his fear; it was ridiculous, standing there holding a gun on an unarmed man and feeling afraid. The .38 felt small in his fist, and his hand was sweaty. What was it? That insane smile imprinted on the other man's face? Or the eyes, the blue eyes that neither reflected nor questioned; they could have been glass eyes in a doll's face. He hoped that Frazier would end the conversation soon.

"Let's understand each other," said Frazier. "If you and the Arabs want to play cops and robbers, we could care less. We'll furnish the artillery for both sides and even act as referee. Just don't bother good old Uncle Sam. We'd come down hard, Levy; we'd come after your Jew ass and we'd get you. You understand me, Levy?"

Max stared at the major. Frazier sighed. Then Max said, "I have one question." Frazier waited for him to ask it.

"Are you having me followed?"

Frazier stared hard at him. "Why in hell should I answer that? Or anything? Besides, why should a furniture salesman give a damn? Could be a customer, someone tracking you down to buy a convertible sofa."

Max said nothing.

"Let's go," Frazier said to Train, and the two men backed out of the room, closing the door behind them.

"Major, I need a drink," Train said as they went down the stairs. "A double."

Major Frazier nodded. "He does seem to have that effect on people, doesn't he?"

18

When the two Americans had left, Max carefully rearranged the contents of his suitcase. Then he walked down the stairs and out onto the Kurfürstendamm. At the corner was an American Burger King. He entered it, bought a Whopper and a Coke, sat at a small table that looked out on the street and ate, watching the faces passing the window. Three G.I.'s, a woman walking two black poodles on a leash, some girls in blue jeans, a middle-aged couple embracing at the corner. Nothing. He went back out onto the street and returned to his pension. It was time to get down to work.

He propped a chair beneath the handle of his door, then opened a window through which he could throw what he would be working on should he be suddenly disturbed. He took off his shirt and put on the cotton gloves.

Returning to the window, he looked out. There. Quickly looking away. Now staring straight ahead. A man waiting for a friend, a wife, an associate? Glancing at his wristwatch, then toward the Kaiser. Now looking up. The window. Max stared down. Something attracted the man's attention; he moved his head to the left, a quick glance, then straight ahead. Leaning against a building. Feet spread. Ready for a long night. Hoping for no rain. Max knew: he also had waited many times. It created a kind of bond between them.

Max turned from the window to the open suitcase on the bed. He picked up the camera and stared at it, then replaced it and removed the red toothbrush. He sat on the bed; holding the brush in one hand, he lit the cigarette lighter with the other and put the toothbrush handle to the flame until the red plastic began to soften, change shape, melt until it was almost liquid. Now Max let the flame die, dropped the lighter to the bed, and began to peel the soft plastic back from the toothbrush.

Out of the red material emerged a seven-inch needle, thinner than a darning needle, its sides flanged into tiny points, two and one-half inches from a perfectly honed steel tip.

Because of the flanged sides it was an instrument that once smoothly plunged in would be impossible to remove, except surgically. Any attempt to pull or jerk it out would only tear more of the flesh. Its minute circumference would ensure a minimum of external bleeding. All of the damage would be taken by the organ into which it had been shoved. Its victim, aware only of a sharp pinprick sensation, would be dead within two and a half minutes.

Max Levy had used it twice before, once highly successfully: for at least fifteen minutes the victim was thought to have expired from a heart attack. The other time had been a bit messy, as the instrument had hit a rib before reaching its mark. Still, it had worked, and Max believed in it. He preferred a less exotic weapon, something that didn't have to be brought in, something lying about the victim's own surroundings. But you couldn't always count on that; sometimes the victim was surrounded by nothing that would hurry him to his death.

Max removed the cellophane from the cigar, plunged the needle down into the cigar, replaced the cellophane and put the cigar into his top pocket. He put the gloves, the lighter and the again-hardened red plastic into the bag, crumpled it up and shoved it into his coat pocket. Then he put on his shirt and coat, turned out the light and sat on the bed for twenty minutes, watching the man on the corner decide what to do. The man looked at his wristwatch twice, rubbed his sleeve across his mouth, flexed his knees and, with an almost imperceptible gesture of the head, walked to the corner and disappeared.

Max watched for another five minutes. Nothing. He removed the chair from the door, closed the window, went down the stairs past the desk clerk, who wished him a good evening without looking up from the figures he was working on.

Max continued along Meinekestrasse, avoiding the brilliantly lit Kurfürstendamm. From time to time he stopped and listened, but there were no footsteps behind him. He deposited the bag in a trash can, shoving it down under a pile of magazines and egg cartons, then walked to the corner and headed back in the direction of the Kurfürstendamm, on which he was soon lost in the crowds.

Now he walked with a kind of purpose. His mouth was dry, his breathing heavy like that of a man anticipating a sexual experience; though he was not aware of it his hands were clenching, then opening and clenching again.

His destination lay within an enclosure, decorated with the timeless circus colors of red and yellow and blue. The evening's show was over, and the performers and workers of Circus Busch had gone to bed, were relaxing or doing chores. At first glance the enclosure contained only inanimate things: brightly painted wagons; huge trailers that knew and would know thousands of Europe's miles; campers containing sleeping people who could leap from trapeze to trapeze or put their heads into the mouths of lions; diesel trucks with names lettered on their sides that gave each of them a kind of independent life; and, finally, the great tent, a miraculous thing that went up in moments and disappeared while people slept, only to reappear in some other place, five hundred kilometers away.

Outside their trailer, on a barrel top, two midgets were playing a game of cards. One of them slapped down the cards and proclaimed his triumph—"Ah, ha!"—as though a world had been won.

A huge woman fanned herself with a folded newspaper, put it down, poured a drink from a pink pitcher. Off in a corner a lion roared, and from across the lot an elephant answered with a surprisingly gentle sound.

A young man and woman walked about the enclosure, holding hands and talking. When they stepped beneath a lamp-post, they looked unnaturally handsome, more cardboard cut-outs than human beings.

Now came the sound of a wooden mallet striking wood, pegs being driven more firmly into the earth, soon to be pulled up, boxed, transported, pounded again into other earth.

Male laughter. A joke. Told? Played? Funny? Painful? It died in the throat as quickly as it was born, leaving the silence more acute. No, wait—there was music. A radio playing soft dream music.

Another time: Being a damn fool is no fun, but it's lucrative. Fools, my son, great fools—not your ordinary, everyday, common about-the-house-or-office fools, but professional fools, respected if you will—well, such fools make us feel better about ourselves, about this suspicion we have that this is us, but it isn't! How could it be? There we are laughing, the audience! We're not them! Hurrah, we're not what we think we are. We're better. Still . . .

Another voice: Let the boy do his homework. Theorize tomorrow.

Smaller voice: Zeevi wants to teach me to be a holder! He says there are very few—

First voice: And what's the matter with clowning?

Question never answered; voices receding. Max Levy standing there, this man with the soft smile on his face, watching silently.

A real voice: Hey, you!

Max's eyes moved to a thin man chomping on a cigar, his suspenders hanging about his sunken stomach.

"Want a job? We need some labor. Exciting work, a circus. Girls. Lots of girls. Travel. See the world, next week we'll be in Zurich. Oh, those Swiss girls."

Max turned his head and the man turned away.

He heard the music within his head, the tin trumpets and the growling bass. He smelled the animals he could not see and thought, for a moment, that he heard crowds laughing. He stood there, bent forward like a sailor leaning into the wind, then turned quickly and lost himself in nighttime people losing themselves.

* * *

At Fasanenstrasse 79, opposite the Kempinski Hotel, stands the Jewish Community Center, built after the war on the site of a synagogue destroyed by the Nazis.

The building, which incorporates some of the remnants of the old structure, has a library, meeting rooms, a kosher restaurant and an adult education center where interested Germans can learn about Jewish psychology or sports in Israel or can even study Hebrew.

The Germans are proud of this building, heralded in travel brochures as though it were a museum housing archaeological treasures.

Before the war, Berlin's Jewish population numbered some 175,000. Now there are about 5,500 Jews in a city that treats them very carefully, like an endangered species.

The courses offered in Hebrew are well attended: many Berliners, fascinated by Israel, have used their precious vacations to visit the country three or four times. They enjoy discussing their trips, including the friendships they have struck up with Israelis.

It is difficult to find a Berliner who knows "what was going on with the Jews." Many are too young to understand, and the old can offer only a failing memory. About one in three has a relative who helped Jews escape or hide, and some even tell proudly of their own parents who were sent to camps for such efforts.

The Jewish Community Center is one of the more heavily policed buildings in Berlin, a city in which "there is no anti-Semitism."

No one wants anything bad to happen to the Jews.

At one minute before noon, Max Levy entered the Jewish Community Center. A man seated behind a reception desk was eating his lunch, a sandwich on a long loaf of bread. Max walked around and looked at the relics of Berlin's Jewry before the war, then returned to the desk and said, "I would like to see the memorial."

"It will be open in an hour," said the man, his mouth full of food.

"I have only fifty minutes," said Max.

The man swallowed, put his sandwich down and came around the desk, removing a key chain from his belt. He led Max to a glass door, which he unlocked and then locked again as soon as Max went through the door.

He was in a walled-in courtyard where brown flower boxes were filled with red geraniums. There was a bricked pond which was empty, its spigot capped off. On a stone wall was a large Star of David surrounded by plaques containing the names of concentration camps and ghettos in which Jews had been murdered.

In front of the wall there stood a bronze memorial from which a flame should have been burning. The flame was out.

Off to the side an old man with white hair and a fine white moustache sat on a wooden bench. Before him he held a walking cane, black ebony with a gold handle.

The man did not look at Max as he walked about the courtyard. There was a gentle breeze, a bird sang, and within the building a woman laughed. Otherwise there was silence, as though the two men were the earth's last inhabitants.

The old man finally turned toward Max, who now stood before the dead memorial. Pointing his cane at him like a rifle, he said in a hoarse voice, "Well, come on, get on with it, say the goddamn password and I'll give the goddamn answer!"

His voice sounded unnaturally loud in the empty courtyard, the birdsong had stopped, and whoever had been laughing was no longer amused.

Max turned to face the older man. "Why does the flame not burn from this memorial?" he said.

The man sighed. "Because the flame only burns on special days."

Max sat down on the wooden bench.

"I'm a religious man," said the man. "What I am doing makes me ill."

Max said nothing.

"Oh, I've dealt with your kind before. Gestapo, S.S., all of them—what's the difference what the name is, the result is always the same." He rocked back and forth, using his cane as a fulcrum. "What's a life? Hell, a dozen lives? Easy come, easy go, and the deceased is forgotten soon enough. Mourned for a generation, forgotten a generation later. So what's the difference anyway, eh?"

Nothing the man said made the slightest impression on Max Levy. All of the people in his business were madmen. It was a business for madmen, for people who had crossed over some invisible line that rendered one's own eternity meaningless.

The man could not stop. "It doesn't matter to me a damn that you don't reply! What can you say? The best answer is silence, all of us know that."

Max turned to look at the man, whose next sentence seemed to die in his throat. Finally he said, "You needn't smile—it's not funny, you know!"

No response.

"We couldn't put you on his lap, sorry about that, we're not professionals here. You'll have to lean over some, hope that doesn't trouble you, eh?"

He took from his pocket a small gray square. On one side of it was a telephone number written in pencil. Max turned it over; the other side was printed. It was a ticket.

DEUTSCHE
OPER
BERLIN

Reihe 1. RANG Sitz Nr.

---

3 Rechts 19

"You'll be exactly two rows behind him. Seated directly behind him or his companion. He has two seats."

Max nodded. He would have time to study his victim's back, to consider carefully the exact point of insertion.

"When you're finished, call the telephone number. Say yes or say no. Nothing more. If you say yes, you may leave whenever you like. If you say no, go to the Kempinski's outdoor café the following day at two P.M. Someone will join you with further instructions. He'll be wearing a red necktie."

Max slipped the ticket in his pocket next to the needle. They nestled there like two old friends.

"Oh yes, go to the opera by subway. Under no circumstances take a taxi, all of them report regularly to the police. Now, when you come out of the subway station and onto the street, there will be a pay telephone on your left. Use that telephone to make your report."

Max nodded; the man stood and went to the wall bearing the death plaques. The old man lifted his cane and pointed to one of them: TREBLINKA.

"I was a guard there," he said.

Max stared at him, then turned and went to the glass door and waited until the man from the desk came to unlock it.

As Max left the courtyard, the old man was still standing before the dead memorial. The birds were singing, and the woman within the building had begun to laugh again.

The music was screaming in his ears, the calliope had gone crazy and there was no melody, only a mad, dissonant assault on its keyboard, penetrated now by a tin horn bleating a single note over and over. The clowns ran before the music, each in black, only their faces white masks with red slashes across them. They flailed their scarecrow arms every which way; they were like windmills, each arm going in a different direction, and suddenly a figure all in red stood before them and shouted: "March!"

The dream ended.

The lids of Max's eyes sprang open and he caught himself just in time before he screamed, "Noooo!" Now he was staring, wide awake, into the darkness of his room. He blinked several times as though clearing his eyes; his pupils were dilated and he knew that his heart was beating more rapidly than it normally did. He felt a chill that would stay with him until he was finished: it was as if he were encased in ice.

It was always that way before a kill.

He thought of the first time. He remembered Doub Doub.

The gypsy was applying a bit of soot over his eyelids and biting down on his full lips to make them more red. They were friends who had never really talked together. Doub Doub had spoken, he loved to chatter on, and the fact that Max Levy hardly said a word never seemed to bother him.

Perhaps that was why they got along. Expecting no response from Max, he went on with the conversation as though Max were giving all the right answers. Max alone did not avoid him. That mattered too.

Not that Shemuel Reiter hadn't half warned Max: "Don't let Doub Doub do anything to you. You know what he is, don't you?"

Max knew.

"If I could have anything on earth I wanted, Max, I mean anything at all, bet you'll never guess what it'd be. Give up? A purple silk shirt. Full, great sleeves, finally closing here at the wrist, maybe big purple buttons! Does this look all right? If I had a bit of rouge, just a touch, but—" Doub Doub shrugged, then suddenly stopped. Max's face, usually impassive—except for that smile—seemed constrained, as though its owner had something on his mind.

"Well, what is it?" Doub Doub asked, his eyes huge beneath their silken lashes.

"Where do you go tonight?"

"Oh, Max," Doub Doub sighed. He did not want to talk about it. He hoped this would not mean the end of their friendship.

"Who will you be with?"

"How come you want to know?" Doub Doub asked petulantly.

"Why?"

"Oh, very well," the gypsy boy said. "Corporal Roem.

He's on guard duty at the motor pool. He got a package from home today. Smoked fish and sausage. Perhaps I'll share with you, if he's generous. Would you like some smoked—"

"Don't let him turn around."

"Don't what? Max—" Panic was beginning to edge Doub Doub's soft voice.

"Don't let him turn around. And when I say 'Now,' leave quickly."

"I don't want to get in any kind of trouble, I just want to get by, to go home, to—"

Max was gone and Doub Doub felt the sudden urge to relieve himself.

Later. Corporal Roem's tongue was between Doub Doub's lips and he was whispering feverishly, "Little baby girl, little baby girl." Doub Doub pushed himself away from the corporal and fell to his knees before him. Roem spread his legs as Doub Doub's hands found him.

Doub Doub heard nothing but the corporal's harsh breathing as he sagged forward, his hands tightening on Doub Doub's shoulders. He heard Max Levy say, "Now," and he had the insane desire to answer, "Now, what?" but he quickly stood, and as he did the corporal was falling backward, slowly, and Doub Doub had to fight the urge to scream. He raced away without looking back.

The next day nothing was said between the two friends; Doub Doub spent his energy not listening to the furor over Corporal Roem's death. By nightfall he had convinced himself that "it" had never happened, and the following morning he came to hate Max Levy who told him that "it" would happen again that very night.

"I can't go on like this!" Doub Doub cried—until he saw the look on Max Levy's face. "I'm just a gypsy boy," he said weakly.

Memory died, and now Max's mind was totally free of anything but the job to be done.

He went down the hall to the bathroom, where he showered, doused his hair with water, dried it off and combed it with a small red plastic comb. He returned to his room, took a fresh suit, shirt and necktie from his suitcase, and put them on. Removing the needle from the cigar, he polished it with the bed sheet until it glistened in the light. He inserted the needle into the material of his inner coat pocket, slipped the coat on, turned off the light and left the room.

The desk clerk looked up from his evening newspaper. "Mr. Levy," he said, "you never did say how long you'd be with us." Max Levy did not answer the man because he did not hear him. Nothing superfluous would enter his consciousness for the next four hours.

The man at the corner wasn't there, but it didn't matter.

He walked to the subway station. It was bright and clean. The yellow subway cars looked new. He got aboard one and sat among a group of people. From here on he would try not to be a lonely figure who could be recognized, perhaps even described.

Those who took notice of him at all would have thought he was a man remembering a joke.

19

He had picked up Lise at the airport. It was a hysterical Lise who had flown to Frankfurt to visit her sister in a psychiatric hospital. Now, in her apartment, he was still trying to calm her, all the while glancing at his watch, realizing that he had missed an important meeting.

"These things happen, Lise."

"Somehow that gives me no comfort, and would you please stop looking at your goddamn watch. If you've got to go—go!"

"You yourself say she has the finest doctors."

"Hurrah! Those 'finest doctors' were discussing shock treatments for her when I left."

"She's not a child. She's a woman."

"She's *my* sister!"

"All I meant was—"

"All you meant was that when he had gotten his dirty rocks off, she should have disappeared like any cooperative piece of ass does!"

"For God's sake! I never said—"

"Oh, Kurt, don't you understand? We're twins. That makes it all different. When I look at her I see me. It was me sitting there with bandages on the wrist. It was me those discussions about shock treatments were about. It was me, used up and tossed away like a condom."

"Please, I understand."

"I doubt it. Men have a resiliency, they bounce back. They're even admired for it. But women? Slightly damaged, bargain-counter stuff."

"Not you, Lise, you're—"

"Yes? You were saying?"

"You're mine."

"Your what, Kurt? Your woman? Your mistress? Your convenience? So I am, and I'm certain that suits you just fine."

"I love you," Kurt said.

"If I hadn't just seen my sister in the hospital, those words might comfort me no end. But—"

"Tonight, after the opera, we'll talk."

"We do a lot of that."

"About us. About the future."

"Do we have one? Of course we do, I've just finished pressuring you into saying so. God, what a fool I am!"

"You've pressured me into nothing. I had intended speaking to you about . . . us."

"Oh, Kurt, do you really mean that?"

"I mean it. After the opera."

Finally he had been able to leave and catch the tail end of the meeting. Now he was back, nervously looking at his wristwatch as she made her entrance and stood, posed, in the doorway.

She was indeed more beautiful than he had ever seen her. She wore a long, black silk dress and there was a white flower in her hair, which she wore up, displaying a lovely, perfect neck.

"You're very beautiful," he said and kissed the tip of her nose.

"We'd better go."

He took her arm and they went down the stairs to his silver Mercedes and into the Berlin night.

Max Levy climbed the stairs out of the subway station and faced the German opera house on the corner of Bismarckstrasse and Richard Wagner Strasse. On his left was the telephone booth. He was soon immersed in the crowds of handsome men and women going into the handsome modern building.

Among them were older people recalling names that meant nothing to him: Caruso, Gigli, Martinelli, Björling, Melchoir.

"Don't forget Placido Domingo," one enthusiast insisted. "Pavarotti's got the high notes, but Domingo's voice has the balls!" The man's wife quickly shushed "that kind of language."

To the casual onlooker, Max Levy was a man enjoying the conversation going on about him. He seemed pleasant if a bit shy.

Finally people began to move to their seats and Max went to his, still part of a crowd, softly excusing himself to the people whose knees he brushed against as he made his way down the narrow aisle between the rows.

He was surprised to see that the two seats he had been assured Kurt Hitler would occupy were empty! Only five minutes remained before the announced curtain time. Then, behind him, he heard admiring murmurs and even a smattering of applause. He did not turn around as the Governing Mayor of Berlin entered, Lise Straub at his side.

Kurt acknowledged the applause with a wave of his hand to the people below, who were turning in their seats and looking up to see what was causing the stir. A murmur ran through the house as Kurt was recognized, and now the whole audience began to applaud. The noise built to a soft roar; some men and women were standing as they clapped.

"This is embarrassing," Kurt said to Lise. "Why don't they stop?"

"I don't think they will until you acknowledge them," she said.

Some members of the audience were now shouting, "Hitler! Hitler!" nearly drowning out the faithful diehards calling out "Pavarotti! Pavarotti!" There were sounds of laughter and affection from the crowd, who finally sat down and settled into silence.

The houselights dimmed and then there was darkness. The remaining light from the orchestra pit struck the conductor's silvery hair as he approached the podium, and there was more applause, then silence, and then Puccini's glorious music, *La Bohème*.

Kurt seemed enraptured, his chin resting on the top of his hands as he leaned forward on a railing.

Max watched his back. The needle would be plunged one and a half to two inches lateral to the spinal column, preferably from the left side. The object was to miss the scapula and go exactly between two ribs, just a bit below the arm pit and into the heart.

As Pavarotti finished the aria "Che gelida manina," Kurt was applauding wildly. He turned to Lise; there were tears in his eyes and he was shaking his head. "He's unbelievable," he whispered as the applause continued to thunder across the opera house.

At the end of the first act Max remained in his seat when Kurt and Lise went out. He stood only when his row of seats was nearly empty, not wanting to sit alone where he might be remembered.

He followed a group out and into a small restaurant, one of the many close to every seating area. People were drinking beer or coffee, and some were eating small sandwiches.

He saw them. The man's eyes were bright with excitement. The woman watched him, her face tender. Max felt disquieted, suddenly overtaken by an unnameable discomfort. It had nothing to do with the job he would do tonight. That was . . . what he did. It was the relationship between the man and his woman. He had never known such a relationship and he felt awkward, even a little embarrassed that this man and this woman, of all the people in his life, had made him feel this way.

He went into the rest room and washed his face. His smile was what he saw, and he scrubbed at it as a woman might apply a paper towel to lipstick she wanted removed. But when he was finished, when the paper towel was dropped beneath the basin, the smile was there and he experienced a feeling of panic in his gut, like the fear of a sharp pain in the heart.

As he stared at himself there came over him the need to cry, to have tears pour from him, old tears, tears he had never shed, sorrow that was attached to him like his smile.

The face of his parents flashed through his mind, the sound of laughter and weeping intermingled, and his own boy's cries.

He was brought back to reality by an attendant who said, "The second act is about to begin." Max looked around him —the rest room had emptied out except for him and the attendant—and hurried back to his seat.

He tried to concentrate on the man in front of him, the man for whom he had come this great distance with this thing that had to be done. But his own face intruded and he shuddered at the picture of himself smiling there in the darkness.

Musetta was singing her waltz and Kurt's hand squeezed Lise's. She looked at him, he was like a child. She felt a mixture of embarrassment over what had transpired between them earlier and a feeling that had of late asserted itself more and more frequently: their relationship must culminate one way or the other.

The thought suddenly came to her that this evening might be their last together. If he would not marry her, that would be "it." "It" would be painful, but . . .

She considered her possibilities should he tell her there

was nothing that he could do. It all came down to getting away from him, as far away as possible. Definitely, she would leave Berlin and Germany. There would be no way to escape Kurt and memory there. The response of the opera crowd to him that very night was just another indication of his ever-increasing domination, his influence in the world in which she was living.

Like most Germans, her English was excellent—she might go to London and try to build a life there. She had made several good contacts at the Frankfurt Book Fair, and there were people on whom she could call. She could write to them, the very next morning.

If, on the other hand—and here she paused to say, "Please, dear God, let it be!"—he would marry her, she would be the happiest woman on earth. "I'll never ask another favor," she informed God, with whom she found herself speaking more and more of late.

Kurt liked to tease her about her "newfound religiosity," calling her his "little nun." That he invariably did this while inside her body, she found deliciously wicked.

He was the only man to ever possess her, and she could not imagine letting anyone else touch her again.

She would have been surprised to know that Kurt, sitting there beside her, seemingly enchanted by the music, was in fact thinking of her and not in a kind way. He did not fault her for bringing up their future or even her sister, she had every right to do that, but he was angry that she had chosen this of all evenings to do so.

He was finding it difficult to concentrate on the music in which he had planned to lose himself. For a moment he had the urge to hurt her in some small way and he stole a glance at her from the corner of his eyes. She was staring back at him, love in her face, full of hope, blind trust. She reminded him of the animals he had once seen in a slaughterhouse. Mooing contentedly. Quickly he smiled at her and squeezed her hand.

Suddenly the music on the stage seemed somehow pallid,

and he yearned for Wagner, and he thought of his father and said the words aloud in his head: my father. If he could have known him, if he *could have only known him*! The memories, the scholarly research of other men, even the cold statistical record told him so little. All of it colored by hatred or hysterical devotion. Yet someplace in all those words, there was a man. And such a man. His heart filled with joy.

How he had searched. He had poured through Toland and Fest, Bullock and Trevor-Roper. He had read Speer's two books and Goebbels' diaries and even the record of the Nuremberg trials. But he had not read them like other men. He wasn't other men.

To him they were family scrapbooks—kept by strangers, yet all he had to go on. That the photographs within were yellowed with age, their sharpness diffused, that in some cases the wrong photographs were included, the important ones left out or lost, he had no doubts. But they were all he had.

And then one day he had stopped his search. He no longer needed deductions and clues, fragments of truth bearing the coloration of passion. He no longer needed the past to guide him, nor did he require some kind of tangible link between yesterday and the present.

The past was dead but his father was not. It was that simple.

He did not doubt this even for one moment. Neither did he doubt whose world it would be.

On the stage Musetta was finishing her aria, and Kurt felt his eyes tearing. Beauty always affected him that way.

He would be a benevolent father, quick to forgive, admonishing gently. A slap on the hand. A stern admonition. Except, of course, for the Jews.

They did not have a role in the scheme of things. This time they would all die: every one of them.

Would there be an outcry? That was the secret. There never really had been. From the Pope on down, the world had shared the unspoken agreement that *they did not belong*.

Israel. Already in its brief span of days an outlaw among

nations. They had even lost their only ally, America. The public opinion polls said so. Vietnam hadn't hurt any, either. America and noninvolvement were synonymous.

All that fine German know-how and all that Arab money.

Kurt found himself excited. He stirred in his seat.

Max saw him sit up and, for the first time that evening, had a perfect opportunity to examine the black-clad target area. The Governing Mayor was slight enough so that the needle would easily reach the heart. Max was glad that his target was not the fat man on the stage.

The curtain came down and the artists took their bows. The Musetta received an ovation and, in keeping with her character, threw kisses to the audience. Finally the performers disappeared behind the curtain and Max watched Kurt and his woman leave their seats. He waited for only a moment before following them into the small refreshment area where they were drinking glasses of champagne. They were not saying much; they seemed to be staring at each other. Max sipped a glass of wine, not even tasting it. He had managed to block out the troublesome thoughts of the previous intermission. Now he concentrated on Kurt Hitler's musculature.

Lise said to Kurt, "Your fans are something."

"My fans are above all else a mystery," said Kurt. "I've done nothing to earn them. It makes me feel like a confidence man. Perhaps that's what we politicians are meant to be."

"That one over there," Lise said. "He's been smiling at you since you sat down. Like a proud parent."

"Which one?" asked Kurt, warmed by her description.

"Right over there. Oh, damnit, he's gone."

Kurt laughed. "Oh well, there's always more where he came from."

The lights flickered to announce the final act.

"Don't be embarrassed if I cry," Kurt warned as they took their seats. "Mimi's death always gets to me."

"Just don't cry on my new dress," she said. "It cost a fortune."

Mimi's death was, as ever, eloquent, with her friends

covering her last moments in clouds of tenderness. Pavarotti's final "Mimi!" at the realization that she was dead made Kurt's throat hurt, and he joined the rest of the audience in loud fealty to the artists who had given them so much joy.

Finally the big tenor joined the others, his face open and beaming. The audience went wild; they had come to hear the best, and the best had been delivered.

Max hurried from his seat while the audience was still standing and shouting its bravos. He waited in the aisle, his back to the wall. It was imperative from here on that he be directly behind his target.

Kurt, smiling and holding Lise by the arm, finally came down the aisle; Max fell into step behind them.

They went out a door and toward the staircase for the walk down to ground level. Max had decided to insert the needle four steps from the bottom. They were surrounded by people shaking hands with Kurt, who even stopped to sign two autographs and pose for snapshots. Whenever a flashbulb went off, Max's hand was before his face as though he were removing something from his eye.

Max looked down; there were only three steps remaining before the final four. His hand slipped into his inner coat pocket and he removed the needle from the material. He gripped it tightly—though the insertion, if done properly, would penetrate to the heart with only a small amount of force.

Kurt was waving to someone and still another person called out for an opinion on the tenor. "Wonderful!" Kurt shouted.

There were two steps to go. Now Kurt paused to speak to a reporter, the critic for one of the newspapers. Kurt was very animated; the reporter couldn't remember seeing the young politician quite so lively.

One step to go and a group of people, none of them sober, applauded Kurt, who seemed embarrassed. One man held out a silver flask; Kurt thanked him, shook his head, and said, "I'm drunk on Pavarotti!" This delighted his would-be benefactor, who shouted, "Hitler for Chancellor!"

Kurt laughed, "God forbid!"

And now it was time. Max's eyes were focused exactly on the target area. As he drew his arm back, elbow high, suddenly there was another highly animated body between him and Kurt, a man tugging at Kurt's arm. Max was barely able to stop the momentum of his thrust—the point of the needle actually penetrated the other man's coat.

The man, so near death, seemed deliriously happy.

"Mr. Mayor, Mr. Mayor, the Deutsche Oper has a surprise for its number-one fan! Signor Pavarotti will be happy to greet the Mayor in his dressing room!"

"Are you serious?" said Kurt, his face alight as though he were standing in a spotlight. "Lise! Did you hear that?"

"Come," said the other man.

"Hurry!" Kurt said to Lise.

"No," she said, "I'll let you worship in private."

He seemed exasperated. "Wait right here!" he called, already on his way with the other man.

Max watched, the needle cupped in his palm by his side. Suddenly his eyes met Lise's, and she remembered him.

"It's the only thing on earth he goes quite crazy over," she said to the friendly stranger, who nodded.

Max left the opera house and walked to the telephone booth on the corner, where he deposited his twenty pfennigs. On the second ring a voice answered.

"Yes?"

"No," said Max.

He hung up, then went down the subway stairs for the ride back to his pension. The car roared through a tunnel, and he dropped the needle through a window behind him. He felt nothing, neither disappointment nor dismay at the missed opportunity. Nor did he feel anticipation as to his next instructions, which he had no interest in guessing in advance.

20

Samir Abramovitz knew from the brevity of the telephone call and the way that Baruch Eliat's scars seemed to jump from his face that the news was not good.

Baruch stared at Samir, shook his head and said, "Shit."

"Wonder what happened?" Samir mused, wishing that he could look away from his chief's face.

Baruch shrugged. The muscles in his shoulders rippled beneath his khaki shirt, unbuttoned all the way down his chest to expose red hair blossoming like an exotic weed.

"Now I've got to call that bastard who fancies himself Wolfson or Rothschild. God, I wish he were my enemy instead of my leader."

Samir smiled, though he would have liked to laugh. He had voted for the Prime Minister, and everything that irritated Baruch about the man was, for him, an attraction. We cancelled each other's vote, he thought.

"Next?" he asked Baruch, immediately regretting his question. "Next" was none of his business.

Baruch neither looked at him nor made a reply. He stared at the telephone, sighed, dialed a number in Jerusalem.

"Yes?" The Prime Minister answered in a voice that Baruch assumed was intended to make underlings piss in their pants.

"No go," Baruch said, his voice expressionless, certainly offering neither regret nor apology.

"Oh? And why not?"

"We don't know."

"I expected more . . . information."

"We are not an information-gathering agency," Baruch said.

"One of these days you and I must chat about your manners, Mr. Eliat," the Prime Minister said.

"I will know more in the morning," Baruch conceded.

"I expected it now." Baruch made no answer. He could

hear the Prime Minister swallow. Then, in a much softer voice, he said, "I trust that nothing transpired that would embarrass . . . anyone?"

"No. That much is certain. We'd have heard about it by now."

"I also trust that the operation didn't fail because of some failure on *our* part. Planning, perhaps?"

"That was not an inanimate object we went after. People do things that necessitate a change in plans, a decision made on the spot, it's that kind of *business.* Charts and forecasts are of no value at all."

For a moment the nation's leader yearned for the not-so-recent past when one could hire or fire a man without thoughts of consequences. Then, with effort, his voice became warmer.

"I'm satisfied that you did your best; I'm not questioning that in the least."

Baruch knew that this was, in fact, precisely what the Prime Minister was doing.

He looks just like he's swallowed the telephone, thought Samir Abramovitz. Baruch's scars stood out like tiny pipes running through his face and carrying a fiery white liquid.

"I'm quite aware of your competency," the Prime Minister continued. Eliat made no reply. "Now, what's next?" The Prime Minister might have been inquiring about the next course in a meal.

"That," said Baruch Eliat with pleasure, "is your decision."

"Get him," the Prime Minister said, then hung up without waiting for a reply.

Baruch's scars calmed down; he smiled and pushed the telephone across the desk to Samir.

"Get your contact."

Samir placed the call, then handed the phone to Baruch.

"Continue until it's done," said Baruch.

"Yes," said the toneless voice from the other end, and the call was ended.

Baruch stood and stretched. "My God, I'm famished."

"Me, too," said Samir.

"Know what I'm in the mood for? Some good Lebanese food."

"That's treasonous, you know."

"Then let's go get some treason," said Baruch Eliat.

Kurt stood over the stereo in his apartment in the Grünewald, about to put a record on. Lise sat on a couch.

"Kurt, please don't."

"Of course." He returned the album to its jacket, then walked to the couch where he sat on the ottoman at her feet.

"Now." He reached for her hand, which she drew back.

"Let's just talk, Kurt."

"But I only want to hold your hand—"

"Just talk!" Lise said.

"All right," said Kurt. "Can we begin with my surprise?"

"Oh, Kurt, you make it sound like we're starting a footrace, and that's not it at all. I feel like a bitch even starting this conversation, I know I've ruined your evening, but, well, I've got to be just a little selfish. I've got to look after me, Kurt; I have this feeling no one else will."

"That doesn't make me sound like much of a man. As for our past together, it's as though it meant nothing."

"That's the trouble," she said, "I don't want to be a part of your past or anyone else's."

"Lise, will you just stop talking for one minute and listen to me?"

"All right, but no speeches, I'm not your constituency."

"You're my love," he said softly.

"You say it well, Kurt, but I don't know. Anyway, I'll listen to you."

"The International Congress of Mayors is meeting next week in New York at the Plaza Hotel, and I've been asked to deliver an address."

"Good for you," she said tonelessly.

"No, good for us. Us!"

"I'm happy for you, Kurt, but what does it have to do with me? Lord, I don't like having to talk this way, but it's time I did."

"I want you to go with me."

"That's impossible. You—"

"No, it's marvelous! We'll have a wonderful time."

"And me? Will I go as your secretary? As your nurse? As your whore?"

"Lise, for God's sake, stop it!"

"But that's what I'm slowly becoming."

"You make it sound as if I hide you. Actually, you go everywhere with me. Like this evening."

"Yes, the Mayor's mistress was, as always, by his side. That's simply not my role in life, Kurt. I will not be your woman or any other man's woman. My mother before me wasn't and by God, I'll not be either!"

"Shhh, calm down, calm down."

She began to cry. "I want to be calm, but I won't, I can't. And I can't be the secret part of your life; I'd rather not be in your life at all than be that."

"Please don't cry," he begged her. "You know that I love you. Look at me, Lise. Don't you? Don't you know that I care as much for you as you do for me?"

"No," she said, "I don't really know that."

"Come with me to New York. I'm taking Liedtke—you'll never be alone and he certainly won't bother you, you're not a married woman."

As soon as Kurt had said the words he realized his mistake.

"That's right," said Lise, "I'm not a married woman and from the looks of things never will be. Not to you, at any rate."

He smiled. "Do you know you're very tough, Lise? You'd make one hell of a politician yourself. No, don't hide your smile, you're smiling—yes, you are!"

"I love you," she said.

Now he was shouting, "Goddamnit, I love you!"

"How dare you curse at me!" she shouted back.

"I am not cursing at you!" he shouted, and suddenly they were both laughing.

"We sound like old married people," he said wryly. She

made no reply, and he studied her carefully. "Have I ever lied to you?"

"How would I know? You're so clever."

"Now you're being bad, Lise. I've a good mind to turn you over my knee, lift up your dress and spank all that wonderful pink flesh."

"Stop that! This is one discussion that's not going to end up in your bed."

"Can't blame a man for trying. Besides which, you really are very pink. Okay, I'll stop. It's just that, well, all of a sudden, I'm hot."

"Stop it, Kurt. Stop it this instant!"

"But look at me, right here, see what you've done to me."

She stood. "I'll call a taxi."

"Sit down," he said, his arms raised in surrender. She sat. "Life and politics are one and the same," he began, ignoring her theatrical yawn. "Both run on compromise. That's what I'm going to ask you to do, Lise. Compromise."

"I won't, you know."

"Will you at least listen? Will you?"

"Yes."

"Come with me to New York, your room will be right down the hall from mine. No one will know. You won't even be there. Except for me."

"Is that it?" Her voice was filled with hurt.

"No, little child, that is not 'it.' When we return from the conference, we'll make our announcement to the press!"

"Frankly, Kurt, I could care less about your announcement."

He took her by the shoulders. "You're turning me down?"

"I don't give a damn if I ever see New York. What's New York to me?"

Kurt burst out laughing.

"Tell me the joke too," said Lise.

"You didn't hear me! Your mind is so closed you didn't hear me."

"Hear what?"

"Our announcement . . . *our* announcement. You adorable little fool, I'm proposing, goddamnit. Proposing, do you hear?"

"Proposing?"

"When we return, we'll announce our engagement. A short time later you'll be my wife."

"Do you mean it?"

"Lise," he said with exasperation, "why should I lie to you?"

"Well, I am the only other person here," she said.

He laughed again. "You already sound like a politician's wife. Very knowledgeable."

She looked at him.

"Well? Do you accept?"

"I'll have to think about it," said Lise.

He put his hand to his forehead. "Women."

"First things first," said Lise.

"Something else is first?" said Kurt with disbelief.

Her voice was very soft. "All of a sudden, I'm very wet."

"We'll have to do something about that," said Kurt.

"Yes," Lise said, "do something. Now."

Kurt looked across the desk at Gunther Liedtke.

"Have you ever been to New York?"

"Practically my second home."

"Yes, but have you ever been there?"

"Twice," said Liedtke. "I have friends there."

Kurt sighed. "I was afraid of that."

"The cultural attaché at our U.N. mission is an old friend. Well, actually he's not, but other family members are."

"One of these days . . ." Kurt began.

"It *is* my only weakness. In some cultures it is not even looked upon as a weakness."

"The Eskimos."

"A great and misunderstood people," said Liedtke.

Kurt sighed again. "Look here, I've decided to accept that speaking invitation. Well? Give me that alleged expertise the good people of Berlin are paying you for."

"You'll have one hell of a press."

"Meaning?"

"Everyone will be there."

"Yes, to see the freak."

"You are hardly that anymore, Mr. Governing Mayor."

"Come on, Liedtke, what do you really think?"

"I don't know what it is you want, but I expect you'll get it. That's what I really think."

"Want? I want to be a good mayor."

"Of course, of course."

"At any rate, I should like you to accompany me."

Liedtke's eyebrows shot up above his glasses. "Me?"

"Yes, I need an assistant. A trusted one. A highly trusted one."

Liedtke, who knew what was coming, said nothing.

"Lise will accompany us, unofficially of course. I'll want you to entertain her when I'm not available. I take it that I do not have to define 'entertainment?' "

"I shall treat her like a sister."

"A single one," said Kurt, now amused.

Gunther Liedtke smiled and bowed his head.

"Oh, and call Bonn and make sure the Foreign Office secures me some tickets for the Metropolitan Opera."

"Any particular ones?"

"Anything will be fine—no, wait, there is one. See that I get to hear the Spanish tenor Placido Domingo while I'm there. Even Signor Pavarotti touted him to me. After I hear him I shall announce my decision to the world. It will be quite historic."

"Your decision?"

Kurt grinned. "Of course. Who is the greatest—Pavarotti or Domingo."

Liedtke, who had been making notes, put his pad and pencil away and waited to be dismissed.

"Will you forgive a personal observation, Liedtke?"

"Have I a choice?"

"Of course not."

"Yes, I'll forgive a personal observation."

"If it will not damage any of your highly developed aesthetic values . . ."

"Yes?"

"Will you, in the name of God or Germany or whatever you hold dear, please buy some conservative neckties? That one looks like you've bled all over the front of your shirt."

"I'll follow the Governing Mayor's recommendation, although, I must say—"

"Yes?"

"Red neckties are quite in this year."

Max stood across from the Kempinski's outdoor café. It had opened for business only moments before, and he watched waitresses prepare tables for the day's business until, finally, a few customers straggled in off the Kurfürstendamm.

He stood there for half an hour, then crossed the wide street and sat at a small table, where a waitress took his order for a cup of coffee. His furniture brochures lay out on the table in plain sight. He resembled a down-at-the-heels traveling salesman. A friendly one.

As he sipped his coffee his eyes watched the street. He saw his man briskly approaching, seeming to pay no mind to the already heavy traffic. The man sat at an adjoining table, his back almost pressed against Max's.

"So you're him," the man said. He sounded excited.

"We are being watched," said Max.

"Oh," said the man and Max heard him gulp his coffee down.

They sat silently, Max studying his brochures, the man nervously stealing glances at him.

"You don't look menacing," said the man. "Are you as good as they say?"

The man did not wait for a reply. "He's going to New York, the International Congress of Mayors. He flies by Lufthansa a week from today. He will be at the Plaza Hotel."

"Any security?" asked Max.

"What for? Everyone seems to love him."

Max nodded and turned the page of a brochure.

The man smiled broadly. "He will be accompanied by his trusty aide and his girl friend, though she will not occupy his suite."

Max waited for the man to say more. When he did not, Max asked, "My instructions?"

"The same." The man stood, leaving an envelope next to his cup. *"Bon voyage."*

Max slipped the envelope into his pocket and watched the man disappear down the street. In a moment, he too was lost in the crowd.

In Hardtke's, a restaurant on Meinekestrasse, Kurt Hitler and Willi Fassmann sat eating lunch surrounded by prosperous-looking Berlin businessmen.

Willi was attacking his beloved sauerbraten; Kurt was having grilled liver. As both men drank from large beer steins, Willi waved across the room to a potential insurance customer, making sure that the man saw him in the company of Berlin's youthful Governing Mayor.

"Do you know," Willi said, "you're the only man I ever met whom I genuinely envied."

"Get off it, Willi, I'll vote for you."

"No, no, I'm quite serious. Do you realize that it took you ten minutes just to make your way through the handshakers to this table? You're a phenomenon!"

"Is that what I am? Sometimes I wonder, Willi."

With an expansive wave of his fleshy hand, Willi pushed aside this piece of introspection. "You're one of destiny's blessed children, that's what you are. She's chosen you for big things. The biggest. All you've got to do is—"

"Yes?" asked Kurt, smiling in anticipation of the familiar spiel.

"Be you."

"I assume you mean *Kurt* Hitler."

"But who else?" asked Willi, his face all innocence.

"I don't know about you, Willi. I really don't."

"You haven't let old Haack brainwash you against Willi, have you?"

"It's true, Willi, you're not his favorite."

"And have no wish to be. We're too different, he and I. He's all steadfast, rooted in place. I, on the other hand, am . . . well, pliable, bending if you will. Life's that way. But come now, we didn't meet to hear my philosophy, though God knows it's simple enough. You have big news?"

"Nothing monumental. I'm going to the United States, the conference of mayors. Can you think of any reason why I shouldn't?"

"On the contrary, I can think of many reasons why you should. So? The United States. New York, no less. Yes, I'd say that's most interesting."

"Do you think New York will give me . . . difficulties?"

"I can't imagine why."

"For God's sake, Willi, drop the bullshit. New York's population is heavily ethnic."

"You're referring to our Jewish friends?"

"Yes, I am. I have to face them, Willi. There's no reason to put it off. I guess I'd rather get it behind me, if it'll *get* behind me. I'm under no illusions."

"The press will certainly be watching."

"And the Jews? How will they treat me, Willi?"

"They remind me of a diamond. An almost priceless one. Almost, because of a near-imperceptible flaw. They are most compassionate, forgiving. They love to forgive."

"You manage to make the Golden Rule sound erroneous."

"Just don't forget what happened to its originator."

"You know, Willi, you just may be a bad man."

The party leader threw back his head and laughed so loudly that people throughout the restaurant turned to look. "We are all bad men," said Willi Fassmann. "Didn't you know?"

Kurt shook his head. They called for the check, but Willi's potential customer had already picked up their tab. Willi stood and bowed to the man, who smiled proudly.

"Rather nice, don't you think?" said Willi, now waving to a group of businessmen occupying a corner table. "See?

They're motioning us to join them for an after-dinner drink."

"Give my apologies; I'm late now for a meeting on next year's budget."

"I don't believe I'd overly concern myself with next year's budget," Willi said. "I assure you, you'll be dealing with much bigger things."

Kurt caught hold of the other man's arm and pulled him closer. "One more little secret, Willi," he said. "I'm ready for bigger things."

21

Major Dan Frazier wanted one more look. He held the magnifying glass over the blowup of the photo and, as he studied it, spoke to Schacke, the small neat man seated across the desk from him. "You don't know the guy at the other table?"

The German shook his head. "No, I've never seen him."

Frazier put the glass down. "And that's been his only contact?"

"The only one. He speaks to no one. He walks, he eats your American hamburgers, he sleeps. He has been to only one other place, the opera."

"That's a new one—I've never known that son of a bitch to be a music lover. Did he do anything inside?"

Schacke sighed. "I don't know. The performance was sold out and naturally I had no ticket. I left him there."

Frazier shrugged. "What the hell, maybe he likes opera."

"Beyond that, nothing, until this morning. He and the other man were definitely engaged in some kind of conversation, though back to back. They can't fool old Schacke."

"How long did they talk?"

"Their meeting did not last five minutes."

"If we knew this other man we'd know what Levy is doing in Berlin," said the major.

"Shall I continue the surveillance?"

"No," said Frazier, "I can't afford it. What do I owe you, anyway?"

"Two thousand would do it."

"Mind if I pay you in greenbacks?"

"No, thank you, Major; if you don't mind I'll take it in deutsche marks."

Frazier sighed, took an envelope from his desk and shoved it across the desk.

"You will call me if there is anything else?" said Schacke.

"You bet I will. Oh, and Schacke, I would be very disappointed if you peddled that photo anyplace else. I mean really disappointed."

"Please, Major, I am a professional."

"You're certain he didn't see you?" Frazier asked when the German was at the door.

"I am a professional," Schacke repeated.

"Because he's a bad boy, but really bad, and there wouldn't be a thing I could do about it. Christ, I don't even know you."

"Let Schacke worry about Schacke," the man said, and with a small bow was gone.

Frazier called out, "Train!"

The Texan entered and examined the photograph. "Your little German really delivered. Who's the other guy?"

"I don't know, but we'll find out."

"I've never seen the face in our files. Gonna let the chickenshits have a look?" "Chickenshits" was what the counterintelligence agents called the Central Intelligence Agency."

"No, I'm not. Believe we might be able to do a little trading with the Gestapo," which was what the Intelligence and Security Command called the Bundesnachrichtendienst, the West German Federal Intelligence Service.

"Guy looks like a pimp," Train said, pointing to the photo. "In Texas we used to call classes like that 'bebops.' "

"The Gestapo'll know him," promised Frazier.

Max Levy, having spotted the other man while seated

at the Kempinski's café, had made his decision. He could have done the job at any time, but there had been that unspoken rule: Perform the primary mission first, invite no complications before that. But now his primary mission would be days away and in another country.

The decision-making process was now his. Losing the other man had been nothing. Getting behind him, following him, took years of experience. A minor annoyance was going to be taken care of.

Cleanly.

Schacke felt very good indeed. His deutsche marks had joined an ever-increasing stack in a safety deposit box, and he was enjoying the prospect of a lovely weekend in the forests with his wife and his son, who showed every indication of wanting to study medicine.

Schacke had good reason to feel proud. Left an orphan by the Allied bombing, he had been forced for a year to take to the streets in order to stay alive. There was nothing he had not done toward that end, from black-marketing to pimping for a pair of orphan sisters who also preferred to stay alive.

"Hey, G.I., two for the price of one, yes?"

The move from petty crime to detective work had not been all that big a step. He was, in fact, a very respectable private detective, specializing in delicate matters, often providing evidence in divorce cases where great compassion and understanding were called for, almost like an undertaker.

The next step was working for the various intelligence agencies that abound in Berlin. Schacke loved that kind of work. All cash. No records. No taxes.

Schacke, an avid anti-Communist, worked only for the Americans, British and French. As he thought of certain fine contacts, he promised himself that bright and early morning that he would sell the photo to his other friends. It was absolutely safe: considering the lack of cooperation between the three, there was not the slightest possibility that one of them would share the photo with another.

He mentally banked six thousand deutsche marks, then sighed, not all that certain that the British would come through for two thousand. He might have to come down as much as five hundred deutsche marks for them.

Whistling "The Lorelei," he walked down to the subway station for the twenty-five-minute ride home. After changing trains once, he would be two blocks from his apartment. The station was jammed with people who had finished a good week's work and would now escape their claustrophobic life in Berlin for the weekend. On Monday they would return refreshed and energetic—like me, thought Schacke, who had worked his way forward so that he stood along the track and could hop aboard and get a seat as soon as the train pulled in.

As the train approached he leaned forward for the sight of its head lamps approaching in the darkness.

"Watch it," Schacke turned to tell the people pressing behind him. The two words never quite left his throat; he felt himself pushed forward and, as he fell, heard what he thought was the scream of subway brakes but was actually the scream of a woman who saw him pitch forward onto the tracks, where the yellow train cancelled his dreams.

22

In West Berlin there is a lonely neighborhood bordered by the fringes of the downtown city, the Tiergarten Park and the Berlin Wall. In the evening prostitutes work the fringes; during the day, most of the few people still living in the area bring their dogs to an exercise yard tucked away in a scruffy woods.

The streets in this abandoned world are of cobblestone, and the gas streetlights stand along untraveled sidewalks surrounded by weeds. Dominating one street is the mammoth red stucco embassy of Mussolini's Italy, its main doors sealed, its courtyard in ruins.

Across the street, in the hulk of the Japanese embassy,

huge reception rooms stand decaying and empty. Lion dogs and elegant brass gratings still guard uncarpeted marble steps and hallways leading into the dark interior.

Among the buildings in this burial ground is a small one once used by Nazi Foreign Minister Joachim von Ribbentrop as a mini-headquarters where he could meet with other foreign ministers in their own neighborhood. This building, too, appears to be abandoned. But on this night it was not. Nor was its interior what might have been expected: the main meeting room had been restored to its former glory, including a huge oil portrait of the Führer, in which he looked down on a globe of the earth that his shy, confident smile pronounced would soon be his.

Electricity in the building having long ago been discontinued, thin white tapers burned in gold candelabra, sending wraithlike shadows up red-brocaded walls. The boarded-up windows were covered inside with thick silk draperies.

From the street there would be no light; the building would seem as dead as all the buildings about it, a ghostly reminder of yesterday's terrible nightmare.

The six men inside stood chatting in small groups of two, their voices hushed and nervous.

General Hermann Wahlen, in full uniform, was talking with Rainer Terbach, the union leader, their light conversation strangely at odds with their demeanor. Heinz Oestreich and Willi Fassmann stood close together, Oestreich wetting his upper lip with a dry tongue. Willi's hands were held behind his back, the fingers opening and closing as if engaged in a child's game.

Amgard Vieten stood by a chair in which Ludwig Zimmer was seated, a robe thrown over his legs. Both men were looking up at the Führer's portrait.

"Such a man," Zimmer said.

Vieten shook his head. The two were, after all these years, still in awe, still transfixed. For them, the man had never died.

General Wahlen looked at the steel wristwatch on his wrist. Zimmer saw him and called across the room, "Patience, General, patience."

The general gave a small bow in response.

"This could be dangerous, Senator," Oestreich said. "We should have met in Bad Godesberg."

"There was nothing we could do about it," said Fassmann. "Zimmer insisted. This night, this room."

"Of course, of course," said the intelligence chief, his tone implying, "if Zimmer wants it, fine with me."

"Are we late?" Rainer Terbach wanted to know.

"Still a minute to go," said Vieten, watching Zimmer's fingers beat a silent tatoo on the robe covering his bony knees.

And now the tension succeeded in stopping all conversation: the six stood rooted as in a wax museum tableau.

More seconds ticked by; Oestreich wondered if there was any drinking water to be found in this accursed building. He did not have the courage to ask.

For a long moment only the breathing in the room could be heard. Then, finally, came a sharp rap on the door.

"Come!" called Zimmer, his ancient voice trembling.

The door slowly swung open with a creak, and the man they had been waiting for entered the room.

The other six raised their right hands in salute and in one voice shouted, "*Heil*, Hitler!"

Kurt looked back at them, his eyes glassy.

Part Two

23

At 2:52 P.M. on a cold November afternoon, the lieutenant in charge of security at John F. Kennedy Airport averted a minor disaster when with his walkie-talkie he called in a detail of tactical police to augment his force.

The expertly trained riot squad moved quickly between brown-shirted members of the American Nazi party and members of the Jewish Defense League, who were beginning to swing their signs: DER FÜHRER GO HOME!

A pink-faced Nazi officer explained to a television interviewer, "We are here to greet our leader." A bearded Jew in a yarmulke told the same interviewer, "Let him stay there in his Third Reich—we don't need him in New York!"

The police, some of whom were privately wishing that the two groups would go for each other, ordered each to a different sidewalk where they could march and shout to their heart's content.

JDL and Nazi spokesmen alike claimed that their rights were being trampled. A handful of snowflakes began to fall.

Inside, the V.I.P. lounge blazed with television lights as reporters exchanged shoptalk and cursed the traffic leaving the city and the snow predicted for that evening. Their eyes kept darting to the door through which Kurt Hitler would enter. There was a great stir when the door opened—only to admit Deputy Mayor Francis Arizzio, representing Mayor Morris Hirsch in greeting the distinguished visitor.

Arizzio was immediately surrounded.

"Where's His Honor?"

"Important meeting."

"There was no meeting on his schedule."

"Emergency meeting."

Derisive laughter.

"The Mayor have any real reason for not personally greeting Adolf Hitler?"

Arizzio smiled. "I believe our visitor's name is *Kurt* Hitler."

"Whatever."

"I just told you, the Mayor is in an important meeting."

"An important meeting or an important election?"

Laughter. Arizzio winked. More laughter. The door opened, and suddenly the room was quiet.

Kurt entered alone, blinking in the light. His hair was, as usual, untidy; the knot of his dark-gray tie was slightly askew. There was a shy smile on his face as the Deputy Mayor shook his hand and welcomed him "to the greatest city in the world."

"But I just left there," said Kurt. The reporters laughed and Kurt stepped up to the battery of microphones. "Thank you for greeting me, Mr. Deputy Mayor—and you, ladies and gentlemen of the news media. In my own country the news media is not normally an official member of the greeting party, so I am doubly appreciative. And now, if you'll excuse me . . ."

The chorus of groans was followed by a wave of laughter when the grin broke out across Kurt's face.

"In all seriousness, I am happy to be here. This is my first visit to the States and I look forward not only to the conference, but to seeing this city. And now I'll try to answer any questions you might have."

Q. Do you wish your name was still Hauser?

A. Or Jones, or Doe or Smith.

Laughter.

Q. Have you gotten used to your real name?

A. (Pause.) No, I haven't. I preferred my old one. I had no choice in the matter.

Q. Was life better as Hauser?

A. Certainly it was more simple; I was accepted for myself as myself. Now . . . (A slight shrug.)

Q. What is your future?

A. I can't yet conceive of one. So much of my time is spent coping with my past. Because I had nothing to do with that, I waste a lot of time battling abstracts. It's a bit disconcerting. Hopefully, after a time I'll learn to handle it. I had hoped you would ask me about my present, because I would like to tell you about the beautiful and friendly city which I am honored to govern. Any questions about Berlin?

(Silence.)

Not even one? Ladies and gentlemen, you're making it difficult for me to earn my salary, much less my travel expenses!

(Laughter.)

Dan Rather lifted a hand. "Mr. Mayor, do you find it interesting that Mayor Hirsch did not personally greet you?"

"The Deputy Mayor will do just fine, though I certainly look forward to getting to know Mayor Hirsch. He is, after all, Mayor of the greatest city on this earth. I hope to learn from him. It seems to me that he's doing a fine job in what has to be a task of unbelievable magnitude. I am told he does so with great humor. If I could just learn *that* from him . . ."

Rather thought: Whenever the questioning is going in a direction he doesn't like, his answers get longer.

"Mr. Mayor," he said, "do you believe Mayor Hirsch's absence might portend a protest of your visit by leaders of the Jewish community?"

Kurt's face was serious. "No, I don't think so. And I certainly hope not."

Rather: Would you like to meet with Jewish leaders?

Kurt (almost shyly): Yes, I would like that.

Rather: What will you tell them?

Kurt: If you don't mind, Mr. Rather, I believe I'll tell them.

Rather sprang like a cat. "May we take that to mean that such a meeting is on your agenda?"

Kurt: No.

Rather: But you would like it?

Kurt (somewhat harried): Yes, I would.

Rather had one further question, saved for last like mints after a meal. He began with a compliment. "Mr. Mayor, you've been most patient, but—"

"I thought you'd never say it, Mr. Rather."

The reporters laughed; Rather smiled. "How do you assess your father?"

Kurt shook his head slowly, as if responding not to the newspeople but to a dialogue going on within his head. "I never knew him," he began, "so you must not expect any more insight from me than from anyone in this room. From what I know of him I would certainly say that he was a madman, but again, I am not a psychiatrist and somehow madness is an excuse that I really don't know is justified. He was an extraordinarily destructive man; they seem to crop up every century or so and act as a kind of magnet for the uglier parts of human nature that we normally keep under better control."

He said this so solemnly that there was a brief silence before the questions began again.

Q. Do you hope to accomplish anything specific on this trip?

A. Yes. I want to get to know Americans.

The next question was greeted with laughter. "Why?"

A. Why? It was this country that saved the world.

The laughter stopped.

That night, Kurt, Lise and Liedtke met in Kurt's suite at the Plaza. Kurt stood at the window looking out at the heavy snow filling Central Park.

"Looks like home."

Lise joined him. "It's very beautiful, Kurt. The park is like a world caught inside one of those glass balls."

Liedtke, who had been on the telephone, replaced the receiver and turned to Kurt. "You did it," he said.

"Did what?" Kurt asked.

"Press officer at the mission just called. Your conference got good reviews."

Kurt smiled wryly. "You make it sound like a theatrical performance."

"Isn't that what a press conference is?"

"I suppose so. With Mr. Rather the Grand Guignol, wouldn't you say?"

Liedtke nodded. "He's tough."

"In addition to which, he doesn't trust me."

"You don't know that."

"Oh, but I do. Lise has taught me how to spot it."

"Me?" said Lise.

"Of course. You don't trust me either."

"On that note," said Liedtke, "I shall bid you both good evening. Or, as the Americans say, 'G'bye.' "

Kurt bowed. "Good night, Mr. Liedtke."

His assistant turned from the door. "We can discuss this tomorrow, but I thought you should know—mission said speaking invitations are pouring in."

Kurt grimaced. "Thank all of them for me and give them my regrets."

"Even Barbara Walters," said Liedtke. "She wants to do a ninety-minute interview with you."

Kurt's grimace was replaced with a look of curiosity. "What do we know about her?"

"We know ABC pays her a million dollars a year."

"Would you be dumbstruck to learn that I am not interested in her salary?"

Quickly Liedtke said, "We know that she's tough."

"Oh? How tough?"

"Her technique is to start out asking innocent questions. How's the weather in Berlin, that sort of thing. Then, bang!"

"Bang?"

"Yes, bang!"

"Please be specific, your sound effects are less than precise."

"She asked one former First Lady if she had a drinking problem. She asked a President of the United States if he and his wife slept in double or twin beds."

"And?"

Liedtke blinked, not understanding the question.

"What did the President say?" said Kurt.

"I don't remember," Liedtke admitted.

"Well, what else?"

"It's not so much the questions you worry about, it's her

follow-ups. She pushes for explanations to simple answers."

"I see," said Kurt. "Her bangs."

"Exactly."

"You're certain about all of this?"

"The mission's press officer has given me a full briefing of the American press," said Liedtke.

"German diligence."

"Yes, we are a diligent people."

"Accept the Walters interview."

Liedtke stared at him, considered saying something, changed his mind and left.

Now Lise stared at him. Kurt smiled.

"What a strange man you are," said Lise.

"Oh?"

"That interview. You *want* confrontation?"

"No, but it's inevitable in my case. I might as well choose the battlefield and the time. Mr. Rather gave me the first taste of it. I dreaded the question but once it was spoken, well, somehow it wasn't so bad. I might as well get used to it. It's obviously going to be a way of life. On the other hand I realize how childish I'm being."

"Childish?"

"As long as I live there'll be those questions. Trying to put them behind me in one great leap is a fantasy. I guess I'm entitled to one or two."

"The other?"

"Actually it's rather personal."

"Don't tease," said Lise.

Kurt sighed. "Well . . . while we were standing here, it suddenly occurred to me . . ."

"Yes? Go on!"

"I've never made love to you in the United States of America."

"No, you haven't," Lise said, and began to remove her clothes.

Max walked slowly along West Forty-seventh Street, from

Fifth Avenue toward Avenue of the Americas. He was early. His instructions had been explicit, and over the years he had learned to follow them to the letter. Doing this relieved him of making decisions about details that should not concern him.

What did concern him was two questions: how and when?

The diamond district should have reminded him of home, Hebrew being a common language on this street. The old man had once pointed that out to him, awaiting a reaction that never came. He had then tried to impress Max. "This isn't just any street, Levy. In this street millions of dollars in diamond transactions are carried on every day. The diamond inventory on this block can't even be estimated!"

Finally the old one had hit upon a subject that seemed to get a reaction.

"And such security! You, even *you* couldn't . . . look, Levy, our safes are among the most sophisticated known to man. Would you believe that we've got burglar alarms so sophisticated that if one goes off by accident the police are sometimes denied access to the office for fear they'll learn how it works?"

Max was looking at him, he had to be listening.

"We've got burglar alarms that use infrared or ultrasonic rays, we've got alarms set off by the heat of the hand. See that office—four doors, Levy, each of them stays closed until the one beyond it has closed and the person going through has been seen inside by a television camera.

"Maybe, Levy, you're thinking no one can be trusted on this street. Not so! This is a street of trust. I, myself, and I'm not unusual, have carried millions of dollars worth of gems, stopped in the middle of the block, taken them out of my pocket, opened the tissue paper and examined them out here in broad daylight and never, never once have I carried arms!

"Deals, Levy? Sealed with a handshake. Nothing more. Of course there are safeguards. Anyone who reneges on a transaction is blacklisted all over the world through the diamond dealers' clubs on this block, and in the diamond centers of Antwerp and Tel Aviv. Just pray you're never blacklisted, Levy; you won't be able to work in your industry again. . . ."

Max reached his destination sixty seconds early: a supermarket for precious stones. He entered the large building that had been divided into booths and soon found his way to a moderate-sized area that bore a sign: YOEL FRIEDMAN, IMPORTER & WHOLESALER, Member N.Y. Diamond Dealers Club.

Max's eyes wandered about the huge room and the signs that proclaimed all it had to offer: Diamond Setting. Loose Diamonds. Expert Watchmaker. Expert Setting, 10,001 Castings Always in Stock. Original Designs. We Assay-Sweeps-Solutions. Expert Pearl Stringer. $5 Charge for Weighing and Testing. Polisher-Plater. Old Jewelry Remodeled. Gemmological Appraisals. Baguettes, Tapers and Marquises. His eyes came back to Yoel Friedman, who was finishing a transaction with a handshake and a *"Mazel un Broche"*—good luck and blessing.

Yoel Friedman was almost eighty and he looked like God. His beard was full, white streaked with steel-gray, the color of the eyeglasses he wore just above the tip of his nose. It was the position of these glasses and of his eternally quizzical right eyebrow that gave him the appearance of always looking down on things. A black yarmulke sat on his now-thinning white hair, it too streaked with gray.

Behind him, at a bench, his twenty-year-old grandson Naftali sat examining a stone through a jeweler's loop he carried on a chain about his neck. Naftali had taken his grandfather's expression one step further: beneath a mop of red hair his face reflected that *he knew*.

The old man stared at Max Levy. Without turning to his grandson, he said to Naftali, "Now winter is truly here."

Naftali winked at Max over the old man's shoulder. Max had aged since the last time, and Naftali felt a chill go up his back. His grandfather had told him Max was coming but that was all. He knew better than to ask for explanations.

Yoel Friedman put on his overcoat and, with a nod to Naftali, motioned Max to follow him.

The street seemed filled with Hasidim, "pious ones," in their broad beaver-cloth hats, frock coats, black shoes and stockings. Some wore trousers, some knickers; all were bearded and with *payess*, the dangling, curled sideburns.

They climbed the stairs to a kosher dairy luncheonette over a small street synagogue, choosing a booth in the rear. Yoel recommended the gelfilte fish, which Max ordered. They ate quietly.

"I'm getting too old for your kind of business, Max Levy," said Yoel Friedman. "I say to me I am doing God's will. But as that moment approaches when I will have the opportunity to find out firsthand if indeed I have done his will, I must tell you, I'm not so sure."

Max Levy swallowed his food.

"You obviously do not share my doubts, neither does Naftali, but you're not at eighty. I feel bad about that boy, God bless him, if my son had lived he would not be . . . he would not be a part of this business you and I transact."

Max drank from his bottle of cream soda.

"What we must do won't be all that easy, but you know that. I saw him on the news last night. I'm told he made quite an impression. Seemed a nice enough boy to plenty of people, not to Naftali. Naftali said he reminded him of a Hollywood actor. On the other hand Naftali once said David Berkowitz seemed like a nice boy. So much for Naftali's judgments—oh, and you remember that, *he's* just a boy. Naftali's all I've got so you remember that please."

Levy stared at him. "Why?"

Yoel stared back. "Why? Oh! Why do I let Naftali . . . oh my, I understand that perfectly. There's no doubt in me, none at all. I am a victim of that ethnic disease, you hear it called the 'holocaust mentality.' I believe with all of my heart and everything in me that if we do not kill them first, they will kill us. That's not normal, of course not, but—*but*—history has not been kind to Jews who waited."

For a moment he stared at Max as if he expected a reply, some kind of verbal reassurance. Then he said, "You'll have to move quickly. Tonight. Is tonight too quick?"

"No," said Max.

"Tonight he tapes a television interview at the ABC studios. After that he attends a party at the Windows on the World restaurant, on top of the World Trade Center. It's being given in his honor by a socialite who likes to do these things, a Mr. Breckenridge. This Breckenridge offered to have his limousine pick Mr. Hitler up, but the offer was politely declined. He will arrive at the Trade Center at about ten o'clock in a 1977 dark-blue Buick Electra, license number 384-TCB."

"How do you know all of this?"

The old man dabbed at his beard with a napkin. "Breckenridge is ours."

"I'll need a twenty-two with a silencer," said Max.

"Like the Mafia. They seem to set the trend in everything."

"And I will need Naftali and his taxi. He should pick me up in front of the Wayne Hotel at nine P.M."

"Will that be time enough?"

Max Levy looked at him, turned and left.

Friedman watched the other man disappear down the stairs. "He'll freeze to death without a coat," the old man said aloud.

The Wayne, a hotel frequented largely by salesmen, was situated across the street from Madison Square Garden. Max looked up at the skies that threatened more snow. Later, visibility would be poor.

He needed some hot liquid to warm him. He entered the hotel's Plymouth Rock Coffee Shop. It was nearly empty, but there was a loud, highly dramatic fracas under way. A fat man, obviously the manager, was chewing on a cigar while he argued with a young waitress.

"Now, I'm not kidding you, Cassie, the next time you

show late, I'm gonna have to fire you! Do I wanna? No, I don't wanna. Will I? I'll have to."

The girl, who appeared to be about twenty, held her breath for a moment and then began to let out an ungodly scream: "Eeeeeeeeee!"

"Aw, come on, Cassie, now cut that out!"

There was something ridiculous about her in her pink waitress outfit, a tiny pink cap perched atop her chestnut hair. Suddenly she was on her knees, her arms wrapped about the man's thighs.

"Gimme a break, mister, a break's all I need. I don't wanna follow my dad into the mine because the mine's cold and dark and—"

The man tugged at her arm—"Come on, Cassie, cut out that crap—" but he was laughing too. Then the two became aware of Max sitting in a booth. "Miss Roberts," said the man, "I believe the gentleman there wants to be waited on."

She stood with a great show of dignity, gave a small bow to the man and joined Max. Her eyes were big and brown, almost too large for her round face. Her nose was small, her lips thin and in need of makeup.

"Good day, sir," she said, one hand pushing the bangs back from her forehead.

"Coffee," said Max.

"Are you sure that's all?" she asked him. "Because we also feature the finest ice water in New York. But you hafta ask."

From behind the cash register came the man's voice: "Cassie!"

She stuck her tongue out in the voice's direction and winked at Max, looking directly at him for the first time.

"Here for the franchise show?" she asked.

"No," said Max.

"Well, then, lemme guess—automobiles!"

Max shook his head and said, "Furniture."

"You don't look like furniture, I'd figure you for compact cars. We get mostly salesmen in here and I hit it about ninety-three point seven percent of the time. Furniture, huh? Compact furniture?" She tilted her head back and laughed, all the while studying him beneath long eyelashes. She stopped mid-laugh. "Now what was it, iced tea?"

The voice from behind the register: "Coffee!"

She hunched up her shoulders and put her fingers across her mouth like a child with a secret, and hurried away.

The man waddled over to Max's booth. His cigar was down to a nub, and the part that was in his mouth was wet and chewed.

"She's something else, huh? Screwy, I say, but all right, but not as a waitress. Actually she's an actress. Least, that's what she says. Some say, 'Ernie you ought to fire that nutty dame,' but I say, what the hell, she's a good kid and it's a free show. Still, I'm apologizing. I find myself doing that all the time for Cassie."

She was back with the coffee. The man looked at the saucer, into which some of the liquid had spilled, and moved away. His big buttocks shifted from side to side as he walked, and Max found himself watching the girl whose head had taken up the rhythm and was moving from side to side like a metronome.

"Would you believe that in the '73 Olympics in Arizona he was a high jumper and just missed the bronze?" Max looked at her and she said, "You smile plenty but when do you laugh?"

He sipped at his coffee and she sat opposite him, not heeding a "Cassie!" sent their way from the rear of the coffee shop. She picked up the menu and hid behind it, whispering to Max, "We're not supposed to mix with the customers; they're afraid we'll turn this place into a B-joint, you know, hustling iced tea and scrambled eggs." She waited for his laugh. "You smile a lot, but—" Something in him stopped her and she looked straight into his eyes. "This your first trip to New York?"

"I've been here before."

"Ever been sightseeing?"

"No."

"Strictly business, huh?"

He nodded.

"Do you like the theater?"

He shook his head.

" 'Cause I could have recommended some shows you might enjoy."

"Thank you," he said.

She waited for him to say more, to take her up on her hints, and when he didn't she stood. "I'm not sure I completely like you," she said seriously. He wondered what he should say. "Later," she said, putting his check on the table with a flourish and joining the man at the register.

Max finished the coffee, left a tip and paid the check.

"If he's a salesman, I'm Billy Graham," she informed her boss as Max went out the door.

24

Kurt felt extremely conscious of the makeup the man applied to his face with such gusto, punctuating each application with a "There" or an "Um hum," and finally, "Bye-bye bags!"

"The makeup is perfect," said Liedtke, turning his attention from the buttocks of a young lady who was picking up a piece of paper lying on the floor. "Does wonders for you."

Kurt managed to remain quiet.

The young woman led them to a small green-carpeted room where "Mayor Hitler could relax," then offered them coffee, which they declined. As she left them, Liedtke's eyes followed her out the door.

"I feel like a painted whore," said Kurt.

"At least a very expensive one," said Liedtke. He was rewarded with a small smile.

"Is Lise having a good time?" asked Kurt.

"We went to the Metropolitan Museum."

"How was it?" Now Kurt grinned, picturing Liedtke among the paintings.

"Very big."

"It's important that she enjoy herself while I'm at these damned sessions," said Kurt. "If she has a good trip there is the vaguest possibility of a pay raise when we get back to Berlin."

"That's not at all necessary," said Liedtke. "But I accept."

Suddenly Kurt began to laugh. "Oh, Liedtke, I can just hear the first question! Mr. Mayor, is it true that you're living at the Plaza with a girl friend you've imported from Germany?"

"What would you reply?"

"Why, Liedtke, I'm surprised you ask. Of course you know what my answer would be."

"I do?"

They were interrupted by the young woman, who peeped in the door and said, "Mr. Mayor, they're ready for you in the studio."

"That's odd," said Liedtke when the door had again closed.

"What's odd?"

"I was told that Miss Walters has a little chat with her guest before the interview."

"Maybe in the studio?"

"Hardly."

Kurt's face was glum. "Probably a very bad sign."

"I'm sure it doesn't mean anything."

"Well, *I'm* sure it means that she has nothing to say to me at a personal level and is waiting with bared fangs to have at me before the camera." Both men laughed.

"We'd best go in," said Kurt.

The two men entered a small studio. Its ceiling seemed made up entirely of lights. Kurt counted four cameras and at least ten people. A man approached, introduced himself as the director, and immediately pronounced himself dissatisfied with Kurt's makeup. "Billy, there's gonna be a shine on the Mayor's forehead!" More makeup was quickly applied while an assistant dabbed at the sweat forming under Kurt's nose. Kurt was seated and still another person straightened his necktie and pulled his suit jacket downward. Only then did Barbara Walters make her appearance.

Why, she's lovely, thought Kurt. They shook hands, and he felt the first tremors of nervousness. He smiled. "I trust you'll not be too hard on a stranger to your shores?" Her response was a warm smile, and he realized that he hadn't let go of her hand. Quickly, he stepped back. "I've gone and let myself become nervous," he said, smiling.

"Me, too," she said. "I'd be suspicious of anyone who wasn't."

From the control booth, the director called, "Places!"

They sat in easy chairs. Kurt asked for an ashtray and one was put on a small table near him. He arranged his cigarettes and lighter at the corner closest to him. The voice from the booth called, "Tape rolling," and the camera's red eye lit up as the lens focused on Barbara Walters.

"Mayors from most of the major cities of the world are now in attendance at a conference being held here in New York City. This conference is not unlike a dozen or so other conferences held every day in Manhattan. Not unlike others, except in one respect: the presence of the Chief Governing Mayor of Berlin, Kurt Hitler."

As she gave his title the camera pointed at Kurt and zoomed in. His face now filled the monitor, which both he and his hostess could see.

"Kurt Hitler is not just another mayor. Nor is he just another man. He is the admitted son of Adolf Hitler and Eva Braun, a fact that became known at a press conference called in Buenos Aires by a man now dead who has been positively identified as Martin Bormann.

"Martin Bormann's identification was followed by Kurt Hitler's election as Chief Governing Mayor. As many of you know, Kurt Hitler received an unprecedented seventy-six point eight percent of the popular vote. No one in Berlin's history has even come close to that figure." She paused as though she were talking to another person and awaiting their reaction.

A third camera established a wide shot of the two as she

said, "In just a moment we'll talk to Kurt Hitler."

The red eyes atop the cameras shut down, the voice from the booth said, "Thirty seconds," and someone dabbed at Kurt's upper lip. Again the voice called, "Tape rolling," and again the red lights came alive like the tiny eyes of an animal waking from sleep.

"Mr. Hitler, I believe this is your first trip to the United States?"

Easy enough, Kurt thought. "Yes, Miss Walters."

"Any first impressions?"

"I'm afraid not, I've just arrived."

"Did the fracas outside Kennedy Airport at your arrival disturb you?"

"The life of a politician in our times is filled with such things. The lunatic fringe holds no terror for me as long as there are competent police nearby, and I understand that yours are among the world's finest."

She sprang. "Lunatic fringe? Are you referring to the—"

"I am referring to the American Nazi party."

"Actually there were two groups, weren't there?"

He gave her nothing. "That's also what I understand."

"Does it disturb you to have the American Nazi party greet you as their spiritual leader?"

"Yes, it disturbs me. Deviant mentality is distressing, and as I am not a psychiatrist or a psychologist, there is nothing I can do about it."

"The other group was the Jewish Defense League." She waited; he made no response. "Also a 'radical fringe group,' " she said. "What would be your feelings toward them?"

He lit a cigarette, took the first puff and smiled across the short space between them. She seemed in no hurry.

His face was serious for the first time. "In light of the past, the terrible past, I believe I can understand this particular group. Perhaps if there had been such a group in the thirties, what happened might not have happened. On the other hand, extremism is always a bit frightening—and difficult to manage." As soon as he had spoken the last word, he regretted it.

"Manage?" she asked sweetly.

He smiled back at her. "Yes, manage, in the sense of giving people with strong views an outlet for those views so that tension and stress do not build up and become acts of violence against people and property."

She inclined her head toward him and said, "Now, let's move on to Germany."

Kurt laughed. "That's the most attractive offer I've had thus far!"

She laughed and said, "West German Chancellor Josef Haack is now eighty-one years old. The two of you are friends, are you not?"

"I would hardly call us friends," said Kurt. "We hold office in the same political party, which makes us colleagues. He was my teacher when I was a law student at Bonn University, and so I believe it's fair to call me a disciple of his philosophy of government. But 'friends' is a bit more than the relationship deserves—though it would please me immensely for him to consider me in that way."

"Rumor has it that you may one day be a member of the Chancellor's cabinet."

"Yes, rumor. I am quite satisfied with my present employment. The people of West Berlin are kind to their mayor and I have much to do in repayment of that kindness."

"So you would not accept a cabinet position?"

"None has been offered, Miss Walters!"

"But suppose one was, Mr. Hitler?"

"I promise you, should this unlikely event occur, I will telephone you and we will discuss the matter fully, and only then will I make a decision."

He smiled. She didn't.

"Surely you have political ambitions."

"I am a politician," he said. "Ambitions are symptomatic to politicians."

"Chancellor?"

"This may strike you as double-talk, but I have never considered it."

"Well, then, let's consider it."

"There are many men more qualified to hold the job than I."

"Name one," she said.

He smiled broadly. "The Minister of the Interior, Dr. Alfred Nauman, who is personally prosecuting the terrorists that have infested Germany like the plague."

"What is your relationship with the Chancellor now?"

"Good, I think. At least I certainly hope so! I genuinely respect the man."

"We understand that there was a period of coolness between you two, a period following your now-famous press conference in which you acknowledged who you really are."

"That is absolutely true—and absolutely understandable. The Chancellor resented my not coming to him with the truth much earlier and under different circumstances."

"Why didn't you?"

"That might take all evening."

"Please go ahead. We're not pressed for time."

"Very well. I was completely satisfied with life the way it was. I had worked my way through law school, I had worked long and hard to be elected senator and then to gain a position of leadership within my party. The culmination of those years of work, *as Kurt Hauser*, would have their moment of truth when my party announced that if it was successful, I would be Governing Mayor. I very much wanted that moment of truth. One works for a goal. Mine seemed quite near."

"You sound as if you lost when in fact you won."

"But did Kurt *Hauser* win?"

His simple question struck her as sincere and for a moment she found herself feeling sympathetic to him. "*Would* Kurt Hauser have won that election?" she asked.

"Only the good citizens of Berlin could possibly answer that question."

"Nonetheless, I'd be interested in your opinion. As I'm sure our listening audience would."

"I would prefer not to speculate."

"What did the polls say?"

"Polling is an imprecise science, to say the least."

"But what did they say?"

Kurt lit a cigarette. Out of camera range Liedtke held his breath.

"They said that we would lose."

"Of course you didn't lose. Your margin was, in fact, extraordinary. To what do you attribute this?"

Kurt grinned. "An extraordinarily bright electorate."

"Do you think the name Hitler was a factor?"

"Surely this is a question better put to a political scientist."

"But you must have an opinion."

"*Must* I?"

"Don't you?"

Kurt sighed. "Yes, I believe that the name Hitler, my name, was a factor, but not for the reasons you think."

"Please go on."

"This will sound self-congratulatory, but I was well known in Berlin, it's probably fair to say well liked. When I finally came forward and told my story, it's just possible that a wave of sympathy came forth from the people. After all, Miss Walters, I did not choose my parents. I never even knew them. Suddenly I was a victim. Germans may be like Americans, always cheering the underdog."

"That's an interesting theory. Could we explore another?"

Kurt laughed. "Not only could we, but by the look in your eyes I have every reason to believe that we *shall*!"

"Could your vote be attributed to the German people still harboring some positive feelings about your father?"

He lit a cigarette, the camera on his face, which filled the monitor. "Here again you are pressing me into performing the services of a political scientist or historian, neither of which I am qualified in the slightest to be."

"Surely Kurt Hitler has thought about this factor."

Kurt's sigh was audible. He seemed locked into his own thoughts and Liedtke said to himself, For God's sake, why doesn't he say something?

Barbara Walters' expression was one of great kindness, as if she wished him well before he jumped. Kurt exhaled smoke through his nostrils.

"No person known to have Adolf Hitler's political leanings has been elected to public office in West Germany since the fall of the Third Reich. Our internal security people have issued report after report, and I might add that they are most efficient, stating that fewer than one thousand people are known to harbor sympathies for the causes espoused by Hitler. So there is really no evidence . . ."

She stepped into his pause. "None except for your amazing numerical victory, wouldn't you say?"

"You have, of course, a perfect right to view that victory as evidence for whatever you like."

She waited for him to say more; he waited for her to move on to the next question.

"Let's take a break," came the director's voice, and the red lights blinked shut.

"May I stand?" asked Kurt.

The director's voice said, "Of course."

Kurt looked around for his hostess, who was already off the set. "How do you think it's going?" he asked Liedtke.

"I think Torquemada has been reincarnated in our times."

"She's had me on the defensive all evening," said Kurt. "I'm worn out."

"Not much longer."

"I wonder if I dare cancel out on that damn party?"

"It's in your honor," said Liedtke.

"I'm not in a festive mood."

"After you have a drink—"

"I wonder what in the name of God she'll want to know next—goddamnit, here comes that creature with the powder puff."

The makeup man offered "just a bit of freshening up," which Kurt accepted in silence. "Places!" called the director, and Kurt sat again in his chair looking at Barbara Walters, who was studying some notes. "Tape rolling." The red light came to life.

"Mr. Hitler, many thought it most unusual that the Mayor of this city was not at Kennedy Airport to greet you."

"I am not among the 'many.' The Mayor of this or any other major city has a lot more to do than be an official greeter."

"Some felt that the Mayor's absence might be an indication that the Jewish community in this country may be protesting your visit."

"I have heard nothing that would lead me to make such an assumption—which, I might add, I certainly hope is not so. In Berlin I am on excellent terms with our very active Jewish citizenry."

Again, he regretted his words the moment they were spoken. He knew exactly what was coming next and she did not disappoint him.

"How large is Berlin's Jewish population?"

"It numbers about fifty-five hundred," he said, then decided to answer her next question before she asked it. "That's down from a population of about one hundred seventy-five thousand before the war."

To his surprise she did not pursue the matter.

"Will you see the President while you're in this country?"

"I would of course be honored to, in many ways we admire your President—especially his stand on human rights—but there would be no official justification for my having a meeting with him."

"Mr. Hitler, is it a great burden to be who you are?"

"Yes. That's exactly what it is."

"Could you tell us about how you manage it?"

"Sometimes I do. Sometimes *it* manages me."

"I don't think I understand."

"Nor am I anxious to explain. None of us likes to admit, much less on national television, that we have problems that sometimes overwhelm us. On the other hand it would be an untruth if I did not acknowledge that this particular problem sometimes seems overwhelming."

"Guilt?"

"That's as good a word as any. Yes, guilt, but guilt of an

unusual kind for it is not my own. Genetic guilt, if you will."

"And when you feel overwhelmed?"

"I try to back off, get at a distance from myself, gain some kind of less emotional perspective of who and what I am. Sometimes I succeed.

"Sometimes I dream of going into some other field, of doing some work that is less trying, more gentle, perhaps even being a television interviewer."

She laughed and moved on to West Berlin's peculiar problems: the Wall, the jobs going begging, the aging population. He answered these in a professorial manner, citing statistics, giving examples.

She listened patiently, then interrupted his recitation. "Are you comfortable with Jews?"

He reached for a cigarette; his pack was empty, and he seemed clumsy and vulnerable as he crushed it in his hand.

"Your question has for some reason stunned me," he said. "I guess because I've simply never thought about it. Let me say, Barbara"—he noticed no reaction to the use of her first name—"some people make me comfortable, some make me uncomfortable. But I must say, I feel very comfortable with you."

The camera zoomed in for a tight shot of her face, relaxed and smiling. "Mr. Mayor, I want to thank you for being my guest—on behalf of ABC, our viewing audience and myself."

"And I'd like to thank you for having me, Barbara. Though I can't say the evening has been an easy one. It's been anything but easy—because I find much of what you've asked me, even after almost two years, almost impossible to articulate."

"I believe that," she said evenly. "It would be difficult for anyone."

The floor director held up a card: 30 seconds.

"May I also note," Kurt said with a small smile, "that your reputation as the toughest interviewer on American television doesn't do you justice. I herewith award you the European title also."

"Remember, Mr. Mayor, I can't vote in West Berlin."

They both laughed. "I see that we have less than half a minute," said Kurt. "May I ask *you* a question?"

Barbara Walters, secure in the knowledge that the tape would be edited, said, "Go ahead."

"What are you doing for dinner this evening?"

She flushed and rearranged her sheaf of notes. Finally she said, "Thank you, Mr. Mayor, but I have other plans."

The red light atop the camera went dark and the director called out, "Great show! Great show!"

Kurt stood up and stretched, then followed her off the set. She was warm in her thanks; he was equally warm in complimenting her on her skill as an interviewer. Then, with a wave of the arm, she was gone.

He looked after her, smiling, then said softly, "Jewish cunt!"

25

Max Levy awakened from a short nap, showered and dressed. It was almost five P.M. as he went to the lobby in an elevator where other occupants were discussing the "Knicks." He was the last to leave the elevator.

In the lobby he stepped around a large registration desk where people were being handed identification badges and packets. At the cashier's desk a crowd of men and women—still another convention—was checking out.

The world Max stepped out into was already dark, the skies still threatening snow. The girl from the hotel coffee shop was leaving; when Max reached the corner she caught up with him. "Remember me?"

Her face was so serious that he stopped.

"Cassie Roberts," he said.

"And you're Mr.—" she snapped a finger—"furniture! Compact furniture, wasn't it?"

"Max Levy," he said and didn't know why. He was not a man who introduced himself. "Where are you going?" he asked her. Her coat was thin and worn, and she had tied an absurd kerchief about her hair.

"Home," she said. "How about you?"

"Just walking."

"Great!" she said, clapping her mittened hands. "So am I."

They were at West Thirty-fifth Street and Herald Square. A bronze figure carrying a mallet stood poised to strike a bell. She began to sing: "Oh, give my regards to old Broadway and tell 'em, yes tell 'em, that Cassie, I said Cassie, will soon be there!"

About the bronze statue people on broken benches sat staring into the cold, some nodding, some talking to each other or to the first snowflakes that fell from a small tear in the sky. Max wondered if Cassie saw them. She had finished her song and was bowing.

One block south a black man sat by a fence, shouting into a bullhorn, "You don't know who you is!"

"Oh, yes, I do!" Cassie shouted back to the man, who plunged into a recitation of human ills.

The sour-sweet smell of food engulfed them. Pizza, sausage, falafel, Greek heroes, souvlaki gyros, lamb shish kebab, barbecue chicken and spareribs.

"Anything you want to eat," Cassie shouted to Max like a sideshow barker. "Anything at all!"

Some of the food was like some of the people: it had waited on Broadway too long.

They passed a gay theater which offered *Heavy Equipment*, starring Jack Wrangler.

"They say he used to be a girl," Cassie announced, and a young man standing out front called back, "Don't you believe it, sweetie!"

They waved to each other. Some kind of spasmodic contact had been made. Someone had acknowledged someone.

A black whore with blood atop the whites of her eyes offered to show them something "you ain't never seen."

"Not me," said Cassie. "I've seen it all."

"You too skinny!" the whore called back and then turned

her attention to a Puerto Rican youngster on his way home from work who had been stopped cold: his mother had promised him that in New York he would see things he had never seen.

For Cassie the difficult part of the walk had begun. On the side streets, lights from the Broadway theaters sent their kilowatts out in search of her, found her and pinned her to dreams not coming true.

"I don't know," she said to this strange, silent man with whom she walked. "Sometimes I just don't know."

He looked down at her. The simple sentence was like an echo, like words *he'd* said and then left, only to have them catch up with him later at some vulnerable moment. A thought hit him like a hammer: it was good not to be alone. He deflected it, turning in to Cassie's plaintive conversation.

"I love this place. The trouble is, I'm not sure it's a two-way romance."

He seemed to want to say something; she looked up at him, waiting, then filled the silence. "Not a day, a single day, goes by that I don't regret I came here, but not a day goes by that I'm not glad I did it. It's so awful—and so wonderful."

A small demonstration was in progress. Mostly women carried pickets: WORKING WOMEN UNITE! BOYCOTT J. P. STEVENS TEXTILE PRODUCTS. "And the Wayne Coffee Shop too!" she shouted, stealing a glance to see if he would laugh.

She clutched at his arm and pointed, "Oooo look!" He stared at her and she said, "A penny arcade, I love 'em! Come on, come on." She tugged at his sleeve.

There was the electronic palm reading; NUTS FOR SALE: mixed, cashews, smoked almonds, walnuts, Brazil, pecans, filberts, Indian, sunflower seeds, pistachios, pumpkinseeds and macadamia; Pepsi; COLOR PHOTOS: 2 poses in 4½ minutes; hockey, unscramble, SHOOT GAMES: 1 million BBs, Junglejims, flying saucers.

And fortunes told by Zoltan the Arab, who had a crystal ball that lit up, or by Esmeralda the fortune-teller, whose withered hand pointed to the three of spades and whose other hand rested on a skull with boxcar eyes. And more! A biorhythm to tell you your cycles and a disposition register to tell you "How you really are!"

And Gun-Duck-Hunt, Ski Ball, TV Pinball, Demolition Derby, Duck Shooting, Night Driver, Breakout, Roadrunner, Sea Wolf, Sprint, Tornado Baseball.

PINBALLS: Base Hit, Upper Deck, Big Hit, Aladdin's Castle, Super-Ship Ahoy, Team One, Times Square, Royal Flush, Little Chief Cinema, Stampede and Cannes.

Max felt a band of sweat forming across his forehead. It was the sounds, like a zoo full of animals being tortured. Things were falling, metal crashing, cars screaming about a curve, roaring, screeching, hooting, clicks, whirrs and the incessant bells.

His hands shook; he shoved a quarter into a machine, picked up a rifle. Ducks fell: bang, bang, bang, bang, bang, bang, bang bang, *bang*! Another quarter into another machine. He couldn't stop, rifle in hand, bang, bang, *bang*, and his rifle toppled rag dolls as if they were exhausted; and then a hand was tugging at his arm again and her eyes were big and not understanding, and she was saying, "Take it easy, take it easy!"

He put the rifle down, and now she was in focus and he was standing in a dirty arcade filled with noisy games. Who was this looking at him as if she knew him, in whose face were those frightened brown eyes?

He asked her, "Who are you?"

"Cassie," she said, frantically, throwing her name at him above the noise. "I'm Cassie Roberts from the hotel!"

His shoulders sagged, and he wiped at his brow with his palm. She opened the brown bag on her shoulder and began dabbing at his forehead with a crumpled piece of Kleenex.

He grabbed her hand in his and stared at it; his fingers opened one by one, but she left her wrist in his open hand where it lay like something in need of mercy.

"I want to go home," she said.

She lived in a room reached by dark stairs.

"Want to come up?"

He shook his head; neither of them said good-bye. Quickly he turned his back, like a man fleeing.

At five of nine he went out to the street and climbed into the backseat of a taxi. Naftali Friedman, his red hair showing beneath a cap, grinned at him in the rearview mirror. "*Shalom*, Max," he said, and laughed when Max Levy made no reply. "Grandpa sent you an overcoat." Naftali pointed to a dark bundle on the seat. Max reached beneath the coat.

There was a new .22 caliber automatic rifle that had been sawed off and equipped to reduce the shots to a soft *pffsst.* Tubing had been cut and machined to fit the end of the sawed-off barrel; rubber rings had been arranged inside to act as baffling, a clamp was attached. The only technical requirement was that the silencer bore line up with the trajectory of the bullets leaving the muzzle.

Max slipped into the overcoat, which hung loose on him.

"Where to?" Naftali asked.

"Show me where he will enter."

"Coffee?" Naftali handed a thermos over the seat; Max poured some into the plastic top and drank. And thought of dark stairs. He patted the .22 nervously and asked himself for the first time: How long can I go on?

He was not an introspective man; he did not want to know more about himself than he already did. Naftali was asking him a question. He hadn't heard it.

"What?"

"You've been pretty busy, huh, Max?"

"You've been in college . . . Naftali."

"I'll be a great doctor, Max. Maybe you can send me some business, huh?"

Max Levy made no reply.

The 107 floors of the World Trade Center's twin towers were before them. Limousines were emitting handsomely dressed people. Taxis were letting passengers out, picking them up. In the center of the line of limousines was an empty space for the guest of honor. The snow seemed to be falling with serious intent, and the drivers of both private and public cars stayed in their vehicles.

Naftali pulled into the back of the line of taxis. "When?" he asked Max, who replied, "Shhh." Naftali grinned as if Max had delivered the punch line of a joke, but Max neither saw nor heard him. His face was pressed against the taxi window like a child looking at a toy display.

He opened the car door. "Go around the block a couple of times," he instructed Naftali as he stepped from the taxi. His hands were empty, and Naftali almost found himself calling, "Max, you forgot!" Instead he leaned back over the seat and locked the door. The .22 lay on the floor of the taxi like a parcel forgotten by its most recent occupant.

Naftali pulled out of the taxi line and started around the block.

Max crossed Liberty Street and stood in the shadows against the building. The snow had let up a little, but the temperature had dropped. A uniformed chauffeur stepped from a dark-blue Cadillac for a quick smoke and, when he had finished, ground the butt beneath his foot. A taxi driver left his cab to join another driver; Max could see the two men eating sandwiches.

Icy rain was now mixed with the snow, and Max clenched and unclenched his hands against the cold. He had waited so many times in so many places this way. Now he remembered the first time, the simplicity of extinguishing the German's life. Doub Doub gagging, a girlish yelp, a finger to the lips from Max, the gypsy boy scurrying off like a rabbit from hiding . . . .

As he remembered turning the soldier over to look at his face, he saw a dark-blue Electra pull into the spot reserved for it.

Kurt Hitler got out of the car with three other men, all in dinner jackets. The four of them entered the building like dancers in a silent ballet. When they were gone, Max went back to Naftali's car.

"What now?" the boy wanted to know.

"We wait."
"After, huh? On a full stomach."
"Be quiet, Naftali," he said gently.
The rain turned to sleet.

26

The elevator containing Kurt and his companions made its silent ascent in fifty-eight seconds. The doors opened and Kurt's group stepped into a tawny world of beige and white and gold, a world inhabited by an army of waiters, bartenders, hostesses and a concierge who could have been the general director of a very expensive mental institution.

Kurt had the feeling that he was above the earth in some not-yet-designed jumbo airplane, sailing through black heavens over an earth sprinkled recklessly with diamonds.

His host, Arles Breckenridge, the supermarket heir, the dilettante of pop, op and his most recent passion, "behind the canvas" art, wore a black velvet blouson set off with a red silk handkerchief and classic tuxedo pants.

He offered Kurt a weak handclasp and an immediate discourse on "the Berlin I remember," including one rather long story about those "mad Mitford girls."

"Mr. Breckenridge," said Kurt, "you're a legend." His host nodded. It was true.

He had produced Yuri Gagarin soon after *the* flight, Sir Edmund Hillary after *the* climb, and Clifford Irving after incarceration! Tonight, he had produced Kurt Hitler.

Breckenridge steered his guest into a private room that was all silk and gold leaf, brass and pink marble.

The food seemed to be awaiting a camera to give it reality. There were sesame-dressed Japanese noodles, clams in aspic, soused shrimp, Madagascar lemon relish, turkey-apple salad, apple-wood-smoked chicken, bay scallops en seviche, sea bass salad, lentil salad, country paté, stuffed baby zucchini, fresh ham with cream and cider, chicken curry, trays of cold meats and sausages, braised breast of lamb, veal stuffed with spinach, and pork loins stuffed with prunes.

Kurt felt a bad taste rising in his throat when someone mercifully handed him a scotch and water. Quickly he turned from the table after complimenting his host, who lowered his head in humility.

Suddenly Kurt became aware of icy blue eyes studying him. He recognized Otto Preminger and approached the producer-director with hand extended.

"I'm Kurt Hitler, Mr. Preminger. I'm an admirer of your films, particularly *The Cardinal.*"

"I wish you were a critic instead of a politician," Preminger said in German, his frosty eyes warm for a moment.

"I know what you mean," said Kurt. "Politicians also have critics."

"Politicians need critics," Preminger said.

There was a moment of embarrassed silence. Preminger seemed to be studying him. Kurt could not resist. "Do I remind you of someone?"

"I hope not, for all our sakes," Preminger replied, then made a curt bow and moved on.

"I do hope Otto was kind." Breckenridge again.

"He was charming," said Kurt.

"Otto? Charming?"

Breckenridge gently but firmly steered Kurt to a window where a man stood looking out. He turned for Breckenridge's introduction: "Kurt Hitler, Bill Buckley." The two guests shook hands, then stood together in silence. The view, snow falling on diamonds, seemed to leave very little to say.

"Whenever I'm here I try to articulate it," Buckley said finally. "It's a compulsion, I suppose. The closest I've come is pilfering someone else's words: *A View from the Bridge.* Surely this is it." He paused, then asked, "How do you feel about high places, Mr. Mayor?"

Kurt smiled. "They don't make me dizzy," he admitted.

"I should think not," Buckley said. "Symptomatic of your profession, wouldn't you say?"

"I beg your pardon?"

"High places," said Buckley.

Kurt waited for a moment to reply. "Forgive me for aspiring quietly, Mr. Buckley," he said finally.

"Oh? Is aspiring a bad word?"

"Not when it produces penicillin or the Sistine Chapel."

"And the Third Reich, that too came out of singular aspiration, wouldn't you say?"

"Precisely," said Kurt. "I'm afraid aspirations frighten some men."

"The majority," Buckley said.

"Amen," said Kurt Hitler as Buckley excused himself "to sample some of Arles's ceraceous-looking food."

Breckenridge was back with the announcement that Bill Buckley was one of his favorite people, though he had never agreed with him on a single subject.

Now the introductions came fast and furious. Some of the names meant something to Kurt, most did not.

By now, with the aid of two drinks, Kurt's tension had abated. Still, he stole a glance at his wristwatch. He would stay for another thirty minutes.

Then he saw her.

She stood alone, watching him. Even across the room her shoulder-length hair was the blackest he had ever seen and her skin the fairest. She wore a wine moiré evening dress with a velvet jacket trimmed in sable, and her violet eyes never left his as he approached her.

"I'm—" he began and faltered.

"I know who you are." He waited for her to introduce herself and she seemed amused at the silence. Finally she said, "I'm—"

"The most beautiful woman I've ever seen."

"Diane Abramson," she said, as if she hadn't heard the compliment.

"You really are," said Kurt.

"I really are what?" She was laughing now, not stopping when he answered the question.

"The most beautiful woman I've ever seen."

"German women are fat."

He thought of Lise and said lightly, "Not all of them."

"Do they still wrestle in the mud in Hamburg?"

"Is the Bronx still burning?"

"I loved it," she said.

"The Bronx burning?"

"Those naked women wrestling in all that gooey mud. My late husband took me—we didn't stay till the end because I told him I had the urge to take off my clothes and get down in the mud with them. Would you like that?" she asked into his shocked face, an expression that he was barely able to hide. "To see me wrestle in the mud?"

"Perhaps with me," he managed, and she laughed again.

"You're like a little boy. I've shocked you. Are you a little boy?"

He felt life stir between his legs. "No, I'm afraid not."

"Wonderful!" she said. "I am so tired of little boys."

He had no idea what to reply.

"My late husband was one. I seem to attract them. There may just be something of the mommy about me. Do you think so?"

"No, I don't think so. I don't think you're a 'mommy' and I'm quite certain that I'm not a little boy. I'm a man, and—lest I forget—a politician. A tired one at that. I want to see you. Tonight, if that's possible."

"I'm afraid I have other plans."

"A man?" he asked her.

"A boy."

"Do you have to see him tonight?"

"I don't have to do anything," she said. She seemed to consider his invitation for a moment, and he found himself holding his breath. "A drink," she said. "One. Maybe two."

"Two will be fine."

"My house," she said and gave him the address.

They were joined by Arles Breckenridge, who pecked Diane on the lips. "I'm angry with you, Diane. Actually not angry, shocked."

"Oh?"

"My lawyer said you were richer than I am."

"But I am. Didn't you know?"

"I suspected. Still, it's very bad for my insecurity."

"You?"

"It's one of my secrets," Arles said. "I have several."

"I'll bet you do," Diane said and left them.

"Who is she?" Kurt asked. Breckenridge smiled nastily. "Our most glamorous widow—well, all right, our second-most-glamorous widow."

Kurt waited.

Arles shrugged. "He was very rich. He died. He was Jewish. She's not."

"I don't care about that," Kurt said quickly.

"Of course you don't," Breckenridge said smoothly. "In any case, she's quite successful as a private dealer."

"A widow."

Arles covered his mouth with a hand and muffled a giggle. "The medical report said a heart attack. Gossips say otherwise."

"Yes?"

"Some say she fucked him to death. But you know people."

"I really don't," said Kurt aloud.

Arles smiled wickedly. "What's to know?"

"What time is it, Naftali?"

The young man told him. Max opened the taxi door and, with the .22 by his side under his coat, got out of the car.

"Good hunting," Naftali whispered.

He made no reply, but he heard Naftali and caught his excitement. He felt something else as well. Something he couldn't identify but which nonetheless occupied a place deep in his mind and seemed to be trying to surface.

The defense mechanisms of his brain were worn down; with the slightest push they might crumble entirely, and it occurred to him that exposed, truly himself, he might be a raving maniac. He could see bits and pieces of his fortress suddenly flawed, attacked by a virus or the weather or time. He heard the soft sound of male voices, and his trigger finger tightened ever so slightly.

From the cab, Naftali watched and wondered. It was one thing to help Max, but could he himself do it? Trying to imagine the feeling of pulling the trigger on something alive, something human, he shuddered.

Max saw them then, a man on either side of Kurt Hitler, one in advance of the other two. All walking close together like good friends.

Security.

Why hadn't he spotted it when they entered the building? Where was his mind? It was so simple. Taking a piss. Drinking a glass of water. *That* simple. But now it wasn't.

Now they were at the Electra, and one of the men went around to the driver's side to start the engine while the other opened a rear door for Kurt. There was some discussion, the second man nodded and opened the front door opposite the driver. As Max heard the big engine come to life, he could see Kurt clearly. There would be no clean shot until he was seated; then his profile would be a giant target, impossible to miss. Kurt entered the car, the door was closed and the man went around to get in on the other side. Now.

Max advanced from the shadows, the .22 out of his coat and level with his belt, pointed through the glass at Kurt's head. Kurt was lighting a cigarette when Max pulled the trigger.

Pffsst. It made no noise, no one looked until the cartridge hit the window.

It shattered but held. A hand from the backseat shoved Kurt's head down and the car roared away. Everything else was quiet.

Max, the .22 held limply at his side, got into Naftali's cab and said, "Let's go, but slow."

"Did you get him? Did you get him?"

Max was looking through the cab's rear window.

"No, I didn't."

"But—"

"He is guarded, the window is bulletproof."

"Oh, shit."

"Take me to the hotel, Naftali, then go home."

He lay his head back against the seat and closed his eyes, unaware that his finger was still on the trigger and that he was crying quietly.

Inside the Electra, Kurt, a handkerchief pressed to his cheek where the shattered glass had opened up a small cut, was instructing his security men: "I want nothing said about this, neither to German nor American authorities."

"We have certain obligations," one began.

"Your obligation is to do precisely what I say. Do we all understand each other? Now, find someplace to buy some adhesive bandages."

"Who do you think—"

"I don't," said Kurt. "In my case the better question might be, who didn't? The inevitable holds no fears for me. It happened, it will happen again. If you prevent it, you have my congratulations. If you don't . . . is that a pharmacy there?"

27

Max tried to sleep but couldn't. He had lain there for barely half an hour and it felt like a week. He did not think he could just lie there any longer, nor did he think that he would eventually be able to sleep. He got up and dressed, and went down in the elevator and out in front of the Wayne, where he hailed a taxi.

The streets were like a frozen marketplace, a neon setting for whispered commerce. Those buying and those selling made compromises, hurried their dealings, anxious to get in out of the cold.

He had failed. Again. That had never happened before. In Berlin something had happened, something that he could not have planned for. Those things were to be expected. But here, this night, that was not the case. That his target would have security was a certainty. That the vehicle that transported him would be armored was a probability. That he had taken neither possibility into consideration was— He would not live very long that way. And the fact that he thought *this* thought surprised him. The consideration had never been a factor before. The taxi had stopped, the driver waited for his money.

The stairs were almost dark as Max climbed them, barely lit by lights from the street below. There were three doors and a small bathroom at the top, and he stared at the names scotch-taped to them.

She had drawn two big stars on either side of hers. Max knocked.

"Who is it?" came a small frightened voice. " 'Cause I'm heavily armed. I've got a baseball bat and a Swiss Army knife!"

Silence was met with silence, then sounds of bolts being thrown, then the rusty noise of the door as it swung open. The room was small and dark, lit only by a battery-operated hunter's lantern tied to the head of an old iron bed. The cold inside shocked him; it was not much warmer than on the street, and for the first time he asked himself what he was doing in this small cave.

She wore a long, thick, pink cotton nightgown that was tattered and showed many coffee stains. Holding the baseball bat in her fist, she seemed childishly small.

"It's you," she said. "The weirdo." But then she said, "Well, come on in."

There was a bed, a battered chest, a hot plate, some dishes, some books, a closet and nothing else.

She saw him studying the room. "Well," she said, "what did you expect?" Now, she studied *him*. "Where'd you get that coat? Harpo, Chico or Groucho?" He took it off. "You'll freeze to death," she said, and motioned him to sit down on the bed where she sat too. "I'm studying." She held up a script. "An audition in the morning. Want a drink?" Without waiting for a reply, she reached under the bed and took out a half-filled jug of red wine and a glass. "We'll have to share, my good crystal is put away for the winter."

Max nodded.

"Look," she said, perturbed by his silence, "I've got to study this script. It's a Broadway show—it's a long shot, but you just don't get many long shots like that. Make yourself at home."

She got under the covers and began to read. He sat there, drinking his wine and putting the glass in her hand when she reached for it.

"Want to help?" she asked. He nodded. "Okay, you come read the guy's part. He's in one of those way-high-up offices and he's called in this young woman, this secretary who's putting her husband through law school. Now he's going to ask her to go make love to this guy he's trying to get to be his client. He's a bastard. They all are. But sad, ya know?"

There was a single pillow; he propped his head up on it, next to hers, and she began to read aloud. "Well?" she asked when it was time for his line. He was asleep. "A lot of help you are," she said, then got up and tugged off his shoes and worked him under the blankets. She read until her eyes were exhausted, then reached up and switched off the hunting lamp. She turned her back to him, but her curiosity got the best of her and she rolled over and faced him.

Trying to study Max Levy's face in the darkness, she fell asleep.

Looking at the building, Kurt fought the feeling that he had been there before. His head was pressed against the car seat as his security men checked the street, then, upon his orders, returned to the car. They did not look happy.

How strange, he thought, this street and this house. Where? Set back on a quiet street in the East Eighties, it was four stories high. He stood before the ornate oaken door, wondering . . . A butler answered his knock, his face impassive. It was— The man, who seemed to be expecting him, said, "This way, sir."

It was the same inside, this feeling of familiarity. The furnishings had been selected without pedantic consistency in source or period; most of them came from France or England, but other countries were represented as well, and they ranged in date from the sixteenth to the nineteenth centuries. They were carved, lacquered and gilded.

But it was the walls that made him realize where he had seen such a house before. They were unpatterned and covered in fabric, along with expanses of mirrors. Like the walls in the house Willi Fassmann lived in on an acre of land in the Grünewald. Willi, thought Kurt, a tiny smile playing about his lips. He shook his head.

The butler had disappeared, leaving Kurt standing before a white door. He raised a hand to knock, decided not to, and opened the door.

He was in a bedroom, all blues and greens and beige, furnished in Louis XV. On the bed a white Persian cat stared at him with topaz eyes. Diane Abramson was in the bed, the covers pulled up to her chin, her black hair startling against an enormous pillow.

She's appraising me, he thought. He stared back. Her eyes closed.

"I was so tired," she said.

"Perhaps I shouldn't have—"

The violet eyes opened. "Oh no! I'm counting on you to rejuvenate me. Can you?" Her expression was quite serious, her question sounded like one posed to a physician.

"I don't know. I'm afraid rejuvenation was what I was looking for from you."

"Was Arles's party that trying?"

"No, Barbara Walters was."

"Oh? Were you interviewed?"

"Yes, before the party."

"Was she trying? Of course she was. Poor dear. She is what she is."

Kurt decided not to press that. For the first time that evening he wondered what he was getting into. There was something unsettling here, something not quite the norm, beyond his experience.

"*They're* all trying," she said. "*They* and art are two of the three subjects I qualify as an expert on."

He decided to change the subject. "The third subject?" he asked.

"Come here," she said, and with a hand motioned him to stand by the bed. He did as she asked. The white Persian studied him gravely, its topaz eyes huge.

"I have to know," she said, "it's as simple as that. I simply won't waste a second on a boy." While she spoke her hand found its way from under the covers and was on his zipper. With an expert tug it was undone and her fingers were around him like a tape measure. She looked up at him petulantly. "I can't tell!"

He wanted to leave. She wasn't playing a game. Her hands held his testicles as if she were weighing them. "Better," she said, squeezing just hard enough to give pleasure, not quite enough to cause pain. He was getting hard; she smiled and took his sex from his pants, watching its progress of growth with deep interest.

She tugged at his pants and shorts. "Get out of them, get out of everything."

He did and she pointed to her red mouth. "Get over me, get over me here." He straddled her head; she tickled the underside of his balls with a long fingernail. "Gimme," she hissed, and he plunged into her mouth.

She took all of him, his pubic hair brushed against her face, and when he was about to find release the hand squeezed his balls, causing him a flash of pain and killing his orgasm.

"Don't be selfish," she said, pushing him off her body. Then she got from under the covers and stood by his side so that he could look at her.

She was not slender. All of her was ripe; her belly had a slight curvature and her buttocks were at the same time firm and jutting and dimpled. Her breasts were large, the nipples light brown and surprisingly small.

She handed him four small, white silk handkerchiefs which he held, not knowing what to do. She lay atop the covers spread-eagle: "Tie me," she said. Kurt shook his head, and she said, "Or get out!"

As he tied her, she nibbled at her bottom lip with anticipation. "Well?" she asked when he was finished and she was his prisoner.

"Well?" What did she want?

She told him. "Fuck the shit out of me!"

He got on top of her, entered her wet body and beat into her with a fury. He began to groan, it wouldn't be long and she was strangely silent; if she felt anything at all she gave no sign.

"Get off," she said. "Get off!" He looked at her calm face. "Untie me." He did.

"What's going on?" he asked. She turned over and her buttocks thrust out at him. "Now," she said, turning her head to look back at him. "Do it!" she ordered and he entered her.

She started to groan and cry and curse, her buttocks moving frantically, and then she began to scream. The sound seemed to start in the pit of her stomach and work its way up and out through her contorted mouth.

They came together and he collapsed over her back, his face buried in that coal-black hair. She looked over her shoulder at him, the hair covering most of her face, the violet eyes peeping out like exotic flowers. She smiled.

"You'll do just fine," she announced.

She got up and brought them snifters of brandy. Now, passion spent, there was something almost shocking about her nakedness, something strident, lewd.

She looks like the cover of a fuck book, he thought. He said, "I've never known anyone like you."

"Known? In the Biblical sense? Am I your first Jewess?"

He went along with her. "Yes, you were."

"Well? Do we feel different inside?"

"Less inhibited, I should say."

She leaned forward and let brandy trickle inside his

mouth from hers. "The joke's on you, I'm not!"

"The joke's on you, I knew you weren't."

"Damn Arles, spoils everything."

"I suppose it's amusing," he said. "People keep handing me their prejudices."

"If you'd been married to Isadore Abramson, you'd be prejudiced too."

"But I'm not," he said, watching her expression carefully. "Does that disappoint you?"

"No. Because I don't believe you. We all are. 'The chosen people,' do you know they actually believe that crap? Take it from me, they love it. My little Yid gave Israel over twenty-five million dollars, a hospital named in honor of his mother who when she died performed the only decent act of her life."

"You hate them."

"Yes, wouldn't your father and I have gotten on famously!"

He was stunned. No one, *no one* had ever spoken this way to him. She's saying things the rest of us think and can't say, he thought. Still, he was careful.

"Had my father not been an anti-Semite he might have owned the earth. He lost Einstein, the atom bomb—all those brains. They were irreplaceable."

"Well, now, you *are* practical. I like that. And on the outside, a visionary, peering into the future for the common good. Inside, in the real you—that's something else, isn't it? As a matter of fact anti-Semitism was the major contributing factor to your father's climb up. People needed a villain, and that's what the chosen people have been chosen for. Funny, the Jews never seem to learn that. With all those brains, they've got a blind spot or two."

"You're a lot deeper than I thought."

"In the Biblical sense?" she asked, reaching for him.

The lights in his suite were on and a frantic Lise flung open the door.

"Just where in hell have you been? I called Liedtke, naturally his phone doesn't answer. I've been worried out of my mind. It's four o'clock—I didn't know what to do, I don't know anybody in this lousy city! Well? Well?"

"Somebody tried to kill me," he said.

"Oh, my God!" She saw the Band-Aid on his face and rushed into his arms, all her other questions forgotten.

He smiled over her shoulder and patted her back.

He slept for ten hours and awakened to her breath tickling his face. He opened his eyes, ran his hand through her hair and kissed her gently.

"I would die without you," she said.

"Lise, you wouldn't do any such thing. You—"

"Yes, I would. You're my life, Kurt. It would stop for me if anything happened to you."

He rubbed his face against hers. "Nothing's going to happen."

"Last night happened."

"They missed. Probably never try again."

"You don't know that."

"No, I don't," he said, avoiding her eyes.

"Please look at me!"

"All right. I'm looking at you."

"I'll always love you."

"I know you will."

"Kurt, is anything wrong?"

"Wrong?"

"You're acting . . . I don't know."

"Poor little bunny rabbit. I've upset you. I shouldn't have even told you. Risk of the trade."

"God, what a trade!"

"Isn't it."

"Say that you love me. Say it, Kurt; I need to hear you say it."

"I love you."

"And you won't stop?"

"Yes."

"Say that too."

"I won't stop. Loving you."

"Now, Kurt," she said and turned over on her back. "But gently, I need you in me ever so gently."

"Gently," he whispered, entering her. In his mind he saw Diane's face.

Mocking him.

Max sat up with a start, not knowing where he was. He was alone. But why was that different? He was always alone. Then he remembered her and in the early morning darkness became aware that someone's absence meant something in his life. He reached out and touched the part of the bed where her body had lain, his fingertips feeling for clues about another human being. Outside he heard the rumbling of trucks. Somebody was already playing loud music on a radio.

As he got out of bed he heard a key turning in the door. He stood awkwardly as she entered, carrying a paper sack.

"Hiya," she said and took off her overcoat. She was wearing jeans and a man's blue shirt. "You really slept."

He nodded. She sat on the bed and handed him a plastic cup of coffee, another of orange juice. She removed a Danish roll, which she carefully cut in half, handing him his portion.

"You owe me sixty-five cents," she said gravely. "I remembered what you take in your coffee—sugar, a lot of sugar." She had on mascara but no other makeup. She looked about fifteen years old.

They drank their coffee silently; he watched her chew the roll and gave her his half. "Make that fifty cents," she said. He gave her fifty cents with mock solemnity.

"Say, look, I don't mind you flopping here, just for one night you understand. And I'm not one for prying, but are you who you say you are?"

"I am Max Levy."

"You on the run?" she asked, her tongue licking at a crumb of Danish at the corner of her mouth.

"Not yet," he said truthfully.

"Are you a crime figure?"

He didn't know what to reply. He didn't know what he was.

"Afraid I'll turn state's evidence—go after the reward? Is it a big one? Wish I had the guts to collect it. How much? Come on, tell, how much?"

"How much would you like it to be?" he asked her.

She had to consider that one. "One eighty-five," she said. "Now finish your orange juice."

He drank it down. "One eighty-five?"

"A hundred for the rent, eighty-five for Con Ed to get the electricity back on."

"I'll give it to you."

"You mean that? And what's my end of the deal, me being reasonably sure there is one."

"There is," he said.

"I'm not gonna let you touch me, so you can forget that right off."

He nodded and said, "Let me stay here."

"That's all?"

"Yes."

"For how long?"

He gave her the best answer he could. "A few days, not a week."

She chewed on her bottom lip, her brow furrowed. "No sex?" He didn't answer, and she felt foolish. "You're a strange one," she said, immediately regretting the words. Not that his expression changed, it didn't. But she had this feeling . . .

"One condition," she said. "You gotta tell me who you are and what's the deal."

"I'll tell you."

"Then shake, roomie," she said, extending a small hand. They shook hands solemnly. "Now, I don't wanna be greedy, but I could use that money now."

He gave her three 100-dollar bills. Her hands crumpled them, they had given away her desperation, and she looked at her clenched fist and without looking up asked in a small voice, "What's the other hundred and fifteen for?"

He had no idea what to answer. "Food," he said finally.

"You like anything in particular? I'm the best in the American theater at heating canned soup."

"No."

"Well," she said nervously, "I better go take care of those bills and then I've got my audition."

He nodded.

"How about you?" she asked him. "Wanna come to the audition? It's a small part, but . . ."

"I'll come."

She told him where to meet her, then left with her script and an envelope full of unpaid bills in her hand.

28

Max stood before Yoel Friedman's booth in the diamond center now filled with people.

The old man—a worried God, now—would not meet his gaze. On the counter, laid out on a black velvet cloth, were many diamonds. Friedman pointed to them while he softly spoke. "They want you to come home."

Max had been expecting that. He said nothing.

Friedman examined a stone in his loop. "No reflection on you, but two failures, they've decided to wait."

"No."

"It's an order, Max."

Circus music in his head. The diamonds twinkling in his eyes. And the face of a girl.

The old man watched him, frightened. "What is it? What's wrong?"

He made the music stop. Now the diamonds were just shiny stones. Only the girl's face remained. He wanted it to.

"What will I tell them?" asked Yoel.

He didn't know the answer to that.

"They won't like it, Max."

"What's his schedule?"

"You're out of it. Haven't you heard anything I've said?"

"I heard you. Now tell me what his schedule is?"

"I don't know what to do!" the old man said frantically,

his hand shaking as he held a diamond. "I'm old," he pleaded and then, stopped by Levy's unchanging expression, he sighed and laid the stone atop the velvet and took the loop from his eye. "He goes to the meeting sessions in the hotel. Nothing else. In three days he goes back to Germany."

Max knew the old man was lying. Casually, he laid a hand on the velvet, uncaring of the stones beneath it, and wrapped his fingers about Yoel Friedman's bony wrist. The fingers closed and the old man thought his wrist would snap in two.

"Max, for God's sake, Max . . . I'll tell you, please!" The fingers opened. Yoel massaged his wrist with the other hand. "I'll report this," he promised. Max looked at him.

"That you would hurt *me*," the old man said, near tears. "But what do you care? Very well. The night before he returns to Berlin he goes to the opera. He's crazy to hear some singer. He will be the guest of the general manager."

"You must do something," Max said. It was an order.

"Do what? Do what?"

"Get someone for me. Someone who knows the opera."

"The opera? Max, that doesn't make any sense, what do you mean?"

"The house. How it works. Who goes behind the curtains."

"Oh, a stagehand," Yoel said, relieved. "Yes, I can do that."

"What is the opera?"

"I Pagliacci."

Max Levy stared so hard at him that the old man found himself shaking again. "What is it, Max? What is it?"

"I Pagliacci," Max said softly to himself and turned.

"I am not your friend," Yoel Friedman called after the other man's back. But he was gone.

The small off-Broadway theater was in the Village at the end of a dead-end street. It was a popular place for auditions.

Max got there before Cassie and waited out front as a parade of young women passed by him and into the theater. All of them were friendly: he could be a derelict—or, God forbid, the director. No one was taking any chances.

Finally he saw her getting off a bus on Sixth Avenue. The wind whipped her coat about her as she raced across the street, narrowly missing being run over by a Macy's delivery van. Even at that distance he could tell something was wrong. He said nothing, simply followed her into the theater, where a single light lit the stage.

He sat in the last row. A big woman who spoke in a strong English accent introduced herself as the stage manager and said that she would now "introduce the dignitaries." The girls scattered about the theater laughed dutifully into the tension, which hung like a curtain.

The director was a small curly-haired man who looked like a boy. The playwright, a bearded man with a red nose, sat alone in a cloud of foul cigar smoke.

An assistant stage manager went up the stairs to the stage and pulled two rickety chairs from the wings. Holding a script, he sat down, crossed his legs and called the first actress.

The actress climbed the stairs and curtsied cutely. The others laughed until the director said in a soft, playful voice, "For God's sake, Beth!"

The two of them began the scene. The stage manager read in a dry monotone as if he were ordering breakfast; the actress gave her all. After ten minutes the director called out, "Thank you." He then joined the girl in front of the stage, talked softly with her and shook her hand. She left the theater with a wave to everybody.

The process continued with other young actresses and finally the stage manager called, "Cassie Roberts."

She looked small and frail from where Max sat, and when she began he couldn't hear all of her lines. It became obvious that she had really studied the script, which she held to her side at one point, not referring to it.

The assistant stage manager picked up on her intensity and for the first time began to read with some expression.

It was a kind of miracle: the scene was coming to life.

Max saw the director look over his shoulder at the playwright who nodded, spilling ashes across his gray coat.

"Thank you," the director called and joined Cassie. He

held her résumé and questioned her about it, then returned to his seat. As Cassie walked down the theater aisle the playwright called, "Good reading."

"Thank you!" she called back.

She seemed to have forgotten about Max's existence when he joined her in the small lobby. Her eyes blazed with excitement, and when they were outside she gave a scream like the one she'd given the first time he saw her.

"Eeeeeeeeeeeeeee!"

She took his arm and they went out into the cold. "Come on, come on." She tugged at him; she wanted to skip, and he let her go and watched her. She leaped into the air and shouted, *"Olé!"* and when people stared at her, covered her mouth with a hand and stared back at Max with her "little girl caught" look.

He followed her into a small shop that featured mugs of hot chocolate topped with big gobs of whipped cream. She ordered for them and asked him, "Well? Don't just sit there, Mr. Bump-on-a-Log, did I or didn't I? You better believe I did! A star is born!"

She stood up and began to sing, "Somewhere over the rainbow . . ." No one looked, though one man clapped. She sat back down and lifted her face from the cup of hot chocolate, emerging with a drop of whipped cream on her button nose.

" 'Call me tomorrow at two,' he says. I've got it—oh, I know I've got it! Wanna know why? I was prepared. Better believe it. Do you realize some of those girls had never looked at the script? We've all had it for a week, and some of them never looked at it, and then they wonder why nothing happens! You gotta be ready. . . . So how was your day, Mr. Strong-and-Silent?"

"Good," he lied.

"You sure don't say much. Any reason? Aw, I take that back; if there's a reason it's your business. Oh, hey, I forgot to tell you, I got fired. He didn't wanna do it, he's my friend, but . . . what the hell, huh? I should worry, I should care."

She began to snap her fingers and sing, "I should care, I should go on loving—"

"What will you do?" he asked her.

She reached across the table and gently pinched his nose. "Where have you been? Didn't you hear what I said? You were there! It feels like I've got that part! What'll I do? I'll act, that's what! I'll do what I came to this bleepity-bleep city to do."

"Good."

She covered his hand with hers. "Just good? Not hurrah! Not great! Not super! All right, I accept. Good'll do just fine." She turned his hand over and looked in his palm. "You don't have a mobster's hand. This is a workingman's hand. What do you do?"

"I work in a vineyard."

"You don't sound like a Frenchman to me."

"Israel."

"I never met an Israelite before; is that what they call them?"

"Israeli."

"What kind of place is it?"

He wanted to tell her. "You would like it."

"Oh, yeah? Why?"

"It's like you."

"You do have a line after all. Hey, I'm just kidding! How's it like me?"

"Full of life."

"What happened to you?" she asked him, thinking that she had never met a man so sad.

"Nothing."

"You're right, it's none of my business. After all, we're just sharing a bed. Mine!"

He had the need to reach out for her, to pull her close to him, to feel warmth against him. His hands clenched and unclenched. She saw them.

"You working a vineyard in Manhattan?"

"Yes."

"When's the harvest?" she asked softly.

"Three days."

"Then?"

"I go home."

"I wanna ask you this but you don't have to answer. I mean you do owe me an answer because you're using my place. Is there any danger? To you?"

He nodded.

She sighed, not surprised. "I don't think it's grapes you harvest," she said.

29

"Do your men have to sit so close?" Diane asked him. She and Kurt were in the Russian Tea Room at her usual table, in the first alcove on the left.

She was in white pajamas, the top loose, the pants narrow.

"I'm afraid so," he said. His security team had been augmented by two, which meant that five men were virtually on top of them.

Kurt had never seen anything like the Russian Tea Room. He looked around him at Christmas decorations—rows of gold tinsel and little red balls hung next to murals of the ballet, at a collection of samovars, at photographs of famous customers and flocks of oil paintings in Barbizon frames.

Somehow the dark-green walls made it all look right. He studied Diane's enormous emerald-cut sapphire with diamonds on her right hand. Her drop earrings, also sapphires, hung by diamond links.

"Your ring is startling," he said.

"So's your thing."

"My what?" he asked, looking around him self-consciously.

She laughed. "That'll teach you not to bring chaperones!"

The security men sat stoically, each of them staring at a different section of the room.

"I've never known a woman like you," Kurt admitted.

"Nobody's ever known a woman like me."

"Modest, too."

"I believe I'm wet," she said.

"For God's sake, Diane!" Kurt said, barely managing to keep his voice down.

"I can't help it, you excite me. Potential excites me. The more potential, the more excited I get. I've always been that way. No one waited for Christmas like I did. For vacations. For a man's dick. For money. Now . . ."

"Yes?"

She changed the subject. "Do you like vodka?"

"It tastes like—"

"Me. That's why I order it."

He looked at her with astonishment.

"My late husband told me so; his activities were limited to tasting, but you know, I've got to admit he did that very well. Oh, he aspired to do more, but the specialists told him sex was out. He kept changing specialists until he found one who told him *all* sex wasn't out. He was okay as long as he stuck to his . . . prescription. Then one night he decided he had to have more. Well, a wife can't deny her husband, can she? Cause of many a divorce and all that. He should have followed his doctor's instructions."

Kurt drank.

"I trust I've made you curious," she said, the sapphires flashing through her jet-black hair.

"Everything about you makes me curious. When I know you better, maybe I'll know why."

"Maybe," she said, and then she added, "I know all about you."

"Oh?"

"My late husband said that I could read people better than anyone he'd ever known."

"Tell me about me," he said, smiling.

She tasted her caviar, wrinkled her nose. "I hate the stuff. You. Hmm. Well, now, let me see. Oh yes, yes of course! I know you. You're the one who'd like to run the earth." The smile died on his face. She reached out, patted his hand. "You can't help it, it's in your blood."

"I wasn't aware that you were also an authority on the genetic composition of human blood."

She laughed. "Is the little boy angry? Has Mommy made him angry?"

"Mommy is a bitch."

"*Your* bitch. Do you like that?"

"Yes, I'm afraid so," he said, taking a sip of vodka. "I do like it."

"Of course, I was right. No wait, don't protest. Modesty doesn't become you. You've nothing to be modest about. I know. The question is, can you do it?"

"What are you talking about?" he asked, but he knew. He pushed his vodka glass away.

"Do not, repeat, do not, treat me like a member of the press—or, worse, a constituent."

"And you, what do you want?"

"Actually, my shopping list is not all that long, thanks to my genius for inheriting four hundred million dollars."

"Are you that rich?" he asked. He kept the excitement out of his voice as he asked the question, but not before her violet eyes had seen the tremor in his hand.

She seemed amused. "Steady," she said wickedly.

As if they were transacting business, he asked, "What do you want?"

She leaned forward; he could feel the breath from her nostrils tickle his face. "To come, but I mean really come. To come like you made me come last night. I want to drown in it."

"Funny, being a stud doesn't exactly set me on fire."

"Oh, but you don't mind. And it's no insult, you know."

He toasted her.

"It's not your cock," she said, "I've had bigger. In Côte d'Azur I had a man who could stay hard for seven hours. I timed him."

"I never had illusions that I was the sexual champion of the universe."

"It's who you are, that's what it is. Oh, God, but that turns me on!"

"I believe you're confusing me with someone who's been dead for thirty-two years. I'm not him."

"Aren't you? Wouldn't you like to be? Is there a living son of a bitch with balls between his legs who wouldn't like to run the earth? We settle for less because we have to. Even people like me have to compromise. But you . . . hmmmm."

He responded with a broad grin, as if he were making a silly joke. "Will you be my Rothschild? Will you finance my takeover?"

"Won't I!" she said, and she wasn't smiling.

"You know," he said, "people get put away for talking like this."

"The question really is, are your balls big enough?"

"Well, you've seen them," he said. "You ought to know."

"They're big enough."

"The question is, how to begin?" Even as he posed the question, he answered it in his mind: money. That's what it always came to. Dreams, visions, ambitions, all demanded the same currency. He thought of Zimmer's ancient face and the fanatic face of the Libyan, and he shuddered inwardly. Then he looked at Diane's face. Suddenly he felt better.

"Careful, you're thinking and it shows. But good thoughts. I can tell."

"You're a very dangerous woman."

She laughed and people turned to look. "Do you know, those are the last words my late husband uttered?"

He shook his head as if he were shocked, but he was beyond shock with this woman who had suddenly become more than an erotic experience. All that money . . .

"It is a lot of money, isn't it?" she said, startling him. "Does it turn you on?"

"You turn me on."

"Come, now, I'm it and it's me, the same way he's you and you're him."

"I need to make love to you," he whispered.

"That's not how I want you to say it."

"What do you want me to say?"

"Say you want to fuck me, you want to suck me, you want to bury yourself in all my juicy places."

Instead he said, "You'd better watch out, or I'll come."

"Don't you dare!" she hissed. "It's *mine*. I won't have you waste a drop of it."

"Then we'd better get out of here. I've reached the limits of human endurance."

They rode in her limousine, Kurt's chief security man seated next to her chauffeur. The rest of the men rode in cars before and after them.

She pressed a button, and the window separating the front from the rear seats went up smoothly. "Now," she whispered. "Privacy."

He pulled her to him and kissed her. Her lips opened for his tongue while her hand expertly unzipped him. "Excuse me," she said, as if she were leaving him. She settled her head in his lap and fed on him feverishly.

They spread out a newspaper on Cassie's bed and opened a huge pizza from a take-out stand down the block. The battery lamp gave off its feeble light. Con Ed promised "electricity tomorrow."

She ate as if she were starving. When she saw him watching her, she rubbed her hand across her belly and said, "More, more, I can never get enough."

He could not stop looking at her, and she knew it and liked it, though sometimes when she found his stare too intense she crossed her eyes and stuck out her tongue at him.

His suitcase sat in the corner.

Finally she pushed the pizza box away and said, "Oooo, I'm full!" He nodded, and she took his hand and said, "Feel my stomach." It was flat, and the top of his hand felt her rib cage. "Would you like to watch TV?" she offered, then said, "Me too." There was no television set.

"I'm so excited!" she told him. "Oh, Jesus God, but I'm excited. Today, Miss Nobody. Tomorrow—" She began to sing, "Hey, look me over—" then, quite suddenly, she stopped.

"Max, I don't wanna press you, but really I think it would be best if you go ahead and tell me."

"Why?" he asked her. He was happy and he didn't want that to end.

"It's the way I find myself feeling," she said. "You understand?"

He didn't. And he didn't want her to go on. Now he was afraid. Something had begun in him, some tiny, slumbering part of him had imperceptibly clicked into life and he dreaded its dying half born.

"Look, fella, I . . . well, hell, Max, I like you."

He looked at her and only his eyes showed his pain.

"I really like you," she said, and it sounded like an admission of defeat. "Do you care?" She stood up. "I'm going to bed because tomorrow's gonna be the best day in my life."

She took her nightgown, a washcloth, her toothbrush and some toothpaste and left the room.

When she returned he was under the covers in his shorts and T-shirt. She clicked off the lamp and got into bed. She lay in a ball, her back to him; he lay on his back, an arm held behind his head.

"Actually," she said, "I don't care who you are or what you do. What's it to me?"

He thought: What is it to me?

"I mean, we'll never even see each other again, with my theater work and all."

The need in him to reach out and touch her was so great that he bit down on his lips. His eyes were closed, his hand knotted behind his head.

"And you'll be going home anyway."

His lips tried to form the words; instead, he swallowed down the taste of defeat. Longing overwhelmed him, sought out every place in him like water bursting from a dam.

Now she was silent and it was the quiet, the overwhelming crushing quiet that forced the words from the dark places in him where they had hidden.

"I should not tell you," he said into the darkness.

"I said I didn't care. Okay?"

"I kill people."

He heard her sharp intake of breath. "For money?"

"No. When they need killing."

"Is that what you're doing in New York?"

"Yes."

She got up with a start and switched the light on. She was on her haunches, looking down at him. "I've never known anybody that did that," she said. "I wonder if I should be afraid."

He had closed his eyes; her face was inches from his as she studied him. He could smell her toothpaste. "You don't look dangerous," she said. "You look . . ." She sought for a word and, when she found it, turned the lamp off.

When the room was dark, she said the word: "Alone."

30

The eighteenth floor of the Steigenberger Hotel in Bonn was ablaze with lights as West German Minister of the Interior Dr. Alfred Nauman entertained his counterpart from India.

Security was tight, a subject that Dr. Nauman was discussing when he saw a waiter approaching with a silver bread dish full of the hot rolls for which the Ambassador was noted.

When the black-coated waiter was three paces from the head table, the door to the restaurant was rocked with an explosion. It produced more noise and smoke than danger, but it did cause all heads, particularly those of the security men, to turn in its direction.

As they turned, the waiter dropped the bread tray and the royal-blue cloth holding it, exposing his hand, which held the magnum revolver that he fired twice into the Minister of the Interior's face, blowing his head away.

At that moment, the screams and curses and smoke-producing grenades exploded like popping champagne corks. In the confusion of the moment, the waiter and his accomplices escaped.

* * *

Chancellor Josef Haack was in a state of despair and exhaustion. He had just flown back from Dr. Nauman's funeral in Stuttgart, where he and the Bundespräsident had escorted Nauman's widow to the great cathedral.

The funeral had seen the tightest security measures that modern Germany had ever witnessed. It was as though the entire republic had mounted an offensive to apprehend the terrorists whom everyone felt certain had murdered the Minister of the Interior.

Bonn itself looked as though it were under siege. There were sandbagged gun emplacements, miles of barbed wire and heavily armed police patrols surrounding the offices and residences of West Germany's leaders.

At airports, train stations and street corners, police distributed thousands of handbills reproducing a composite drawing of the killer, along with his description.

The picture was also carried in newspapers and on television. Special telephone lines were set up to receive information from the public. Police roadblocks were set up on major roads. A large reward was offered for information leading to the capture of the killer.

On Haack himself the pressure was unmerciful, as his government bore the editorial and public condemnation for "its seeming inability and downright failure to control urban guerrillas embarked on a campaign of terror against the people of West Germany."

Haack was under no illusions: Unless he did something quickly, something that restored public confidence, his already-shaky government stood a good chance of falling.

The "beloved, venerable statesman" had suddenly become "a tired, old man, perhaps too tired and too old to meet the challenge to us all."

Peter Salman took his usual seat in the corner, and for once the Chancellor wished he would either say something or leave the room.

"There's no perfection," Haack informed him. "I've got the experience, but the juices no longer flow. On the other hand, if I were young I would not have the experience."

Salman stared at him, and Haack wondered if the man's eyes ever blinked.

At that moment, Frau Umbreit entered carrying hot tea which she had laced with brandy.

"Sit down, Gerda," the old man said. She sat primly and he found himself smiling. "You've got that look," he said.

"I'm certain I don't know what look the Chancellor is referring to."

"Now, now, Frau Umbreit, you and I know the precise meaning of that look. You have something to say." He sighed. "Must we play this senile game?"

She "hmphed."

"Frau Gerda Umbreit, in the name of the republic, I order you to say what it is you so obviously have on your mind. Let me remind you, these are extraordinary times, thus giving me extraordinary powers. I can have you shot—or worse, banished from the kitchen!"

She looked at Peter Salman, willing him to leave the room. Instead he stared back at her.

"You need help," she said. Haack nodded. "Someone who can take your wisdom and add his energy to it. Someone whom the people trust."

"Do you have such a person in mind, Frau Umbreit?"

"Kurt Hitler."

"In what capacity? You obviously have thought it out."

"Minister of the Interior."

He stood up. His head was down, his chin almost resting on his chest, and he paced the room, stopping for a moment to stir the logs in the open fireplace. He spoke aloud, but it was to himself.

"Kurt Hitler as the top policeman of this country? Head of all internal security, the border guards, the federal police? If he was anybody but who he is, yes, without hesitation, in a moment, but . . ."

He sat down. He had never felt so tired in his life. Frau Umbreit was on her knees before him, removing his shoes and rubbing his feet.

* * *

As he grew older, Chancellor Josef Haack had limited the number of press conferences he held to three or four a year, a practice that had drawn considerable criticism from the German press.

Now, the modern, gray press center was jammed with reporters and security men who had taken cameras apart, had bodily searched and double-checked the credentials of every person in the room. There was much grumbling. The press preferred reporting such practices to participating in them.

The Chancellor entered the room accompanied by the Minister of Press and Information, who informed the reporters that the Chancellor would make a statement, after which he would answer questions for fifteen minutes. Questions would be restricted to the Chancellor's statement.

More grumbling: they would have liked to question him for at least an hour. The Chancellor gave no sign that he heard them. He looked frail and weary, which did not pass unnoticed by veteran reporters.

His voice, however, was surprisingly strong. "Dr. Alfred Nauman was my friend and now he is dead. Such a man is irreplaceable."

The reporters looked at each other and wondered if they were in for another long eulogy. They wanted more than that.

"Obviously I have a problem: to find a man who can in time and with work and luck, do the job, the job of protecting the people of this republic from those who would send us back into the Dark Ages.

"He must be a very special man, one who can handle power and not let power handle him. He must always, I repeat *always*, use his power *within the law*.

"I believe I have such a man and I shall this day ask him to join my cabinet as Minister of the Interior. I do not think he will deny me because I do not think he will deny his country. I refer to the Governing Mayor of Berlin, Kurt Hitler."

They eyed him warily, this beautifully dressed, swarthy stranger in their midst. Heinz Oestreich stood over him like a mother hen. General Wahlen smiled a tight little smile that could have just as well been a grimace. Willi Fassmann grinned broadly, but it was an empty grin that betrayed itself.

Outside, wind howled about the dark turrets of the castle near St. Guarshausen on the Rhine.

Amgard Vieten tried to ease the room's tension. "Our distinguished guest must forgive us if we seem . . . not ourselves . . . but I'm certain that he will understand that he is the first outsider ever to join our little group."

The Arab nodded, understanding.

Oestreich, dressed in a dark leather hunting jacket that set off his luxuriant white hair, cleared his throat. "Our guest has traveled a great distance to be with us."

"He comes at a moment of triumph," said Ludwig Zimmer. "Your operation succeeded brilliantly, Heinz."

Rainer Terbach said cautiously, "Shouldn't we hear from our guest first?"

Oestreich nodded. "Gentlemen, it is my honor and our good fortune to present Youseff Raji, the most private emissary of Colonel Muammar el-Qaddafi."

Youseff Raji stood quietly, like a concert artist waiting for his audience's absolute attention. "My leader is a pious man. In another age he would be a mystic, in the Christian religion he would be a saint."

"A great man," Willi Fassmann whispered, just loud enough to be heard.

"I am an economist," Raji said, almost apologetically. "For me, numbers tell all. One person in six is a Moslem, and Islam is the dominant religion in dozens of countries from Africa to the Pacific. There are a hundred sixteen million of us in Indonesia, sixty million of us in India, twenty-three million of us in the Soviet Union, twenty-five million of us in China, two point two million of us in the Philippines. South of the Sahara in mid-Africa, we number seventy million.

"We have the bodies and I know that I do not have to tell you that we now have the financial resources. What we have not had is a leader, a man behind whom we can commit those bodies, regardless of the country in which he may dwell, for the belief in our faith transcends nationalism. Indeed, we know that both nationalism and socialism have failed.

"We had hoped that man would come from Egypt. Alas, the Egyptian is an old woman, while we need a warrior—one to whom the death of one's enemies is a matter of honor! We believe that your own Kurt Hitler is such a man.

"I am therefore authorized to inform you that Colonel Qaddafi is prepared to offer you unlimited support. Let me repeat: unlimited support. He will begin by depositing into your accounts one hundred million dollars."

There was absolute silence. Then, the men in the room, one by one, stood and embraced Youseff Raji.

Willi Fassmann squeezed his arm. "I have long been a great admirer of Colonel Qaddafi!"

Amgard Vieten brought the group back to reality. "There'll be no trouble with your . . . operatives, Heinz?"

Oestreich smiled. "At this moment my men are back home in Argentina, ten witnesses prepared to swear they were never gone."

Ludwig Zimmer rapped on the table. Tonight, in the lapel of his dark-blue pinstripe double-breasted suit, he wore the Iron Cross personally presented to him by the Führer many years before.

"Our own Heinz Oestreich has redeemed my faith in mankind," said Zimmer. "I thought that men with vision, with, of course, the exception of Colonel Muammar el-Qaddafi, were a dead species. The genius of Oestreich's plan—its boldness, most important, its total success—tells me otherwise. With such vision, along with the help from our brothers in Libya, I now *know* what I had only hoped: The Third Reich may slumber, but believe me, gentlemen, it will never die.

"Now, with the marriage of our own plans, our own expertise and the remarkable resources of Colonel Qaddafi and the prolific multitudes of Islam, *we shall not fail*!"

"*Heil*, Hitler!" shouted Youseff Raji.

"*Heil*, Qaddafi!" answered the group.

"By the way, what do we hear from our Mr. Hitler?" asked Vieten.

Oestreich laughed. "Nothing. But we know. That young bull has found a new piece of ass."

Everyone laughed.

"A very rich one!" Oestreich shouted, and everyone laughed again except Willi Fassmann.

31

At the Plaza a waiter had just rolled in a breakfast cart. As usual, in addition to the food, it carried one red rose and both morning newspapers.

Lise settled into the *Daily News* and the day's first cup of coffee; Kurt studied his photograph on the front page of the *Times*. The telephone rang.

The transatlantic call was from Willi Fassmann, who reported the "shocking news" of Nauman's murder. "All of Germany's in an uproar," the fat man said.

"It's on the front page of this morning's newspapers," said Kurt.

"A great man has been lost," Willi intoned. "And though we never got along, of course I feel as if I had lost a brother."

"No doubt," said Kurt, hating the conversation.

"Anything wrong?" Willi asked into the silence that followed.

Kurt was irritated and, for the first time, frightened. Things were happening too fast. "Shôuld there be?"

"Not that I know of," said Fassmann smoothly. "Quite the contrary. That gentleman of much fervor has declared himself in. In *all the way*."

"Any recommendations, Willi?"

"Oh. Sit tight, dear boy, sit tight." His voice was a near-perfect imitation of Josef Haack's.

And the line went dead.

"What's in the *News* today?" Kurt asked Lise.

"Lots of juicy gossip," she reported.

Kurt sighed and returned to an account of the Chancellor's press conference.

"Good God," Lise said, and Kurt lowered the *Times* to look at her. She was staring at him, shock on her face.

"What is it, Lise?"

Silently she handed him the *News*, folded to show Liz Smith's column: *Most glamorous twosome in Manhattan these days is our own jillionairess Diane Abramson and none other than His Honor the Mayor of Berlin, Kurt Hitler. The two were seen at the Russian Tea Room, where their cooing apparently melted the caviar.*

Kurt shook his head. "Lise, you mustn't think—"

"Is it true?"

"Yes, it's true, but not the way it's written. I did meet the lady for a drink but it was strictly business. I'm surprised you'd pay attention to that sort of gossip."

"What kind of business, Kurt?"

"What kind of business? Why, she's planning on locating an international art auction house someplace in Europe. I put in a pitch for Berlin."

"Oh."

"It is my job, you know. I do it all the time. All mayors do!" He felt his voice growing louder. "You don't believe me," he said.

"Oh, Kurt," she said simply.

He got up, took her face in his hands and forced her chin up. "Lise," he begged her. "Please."

"Please what?"

He looked down at her. "Please believe this: I love you."

"No. I don't believe you love anybody. There are bigger things in your life, Kurt. I always had that feeling, but I loved you so much, I thought maybe—never mind what I thought, I was very stupid."

"Whatever my life is, I want you to be a part of it. I need you, Lise. Don't you understand? I *need* you!"

"What for, Kurt? Won't she do?"

"She's nothing, a bitch, a wealthy bitch, one step above a whore!"

"And what am I? A poor one?"

His arms reached down and he pulled her to her feet. "No! You're . . . my God, Lise, you're my chance. My only chance."

"Your chance for what? What are you talking about?"

"About myself," he said softly. "Lise, you must believe me, I've never known love but from you. My parents, well, I didn't have any. The women before you were . . . just women. But with you, tenderness. Someone cared about me, *me*, whatever I was."

"But that's the question, Kurt. What are you?"

His body sagged. "Lise, things happen to a man, things he hasn't asked for or even wanted. Sometimes these things present him with a choice, but it isn't a choice, not really. Life's just going to be a certain way and it's no use to fight it, there's nothing to fight with, so he goes along—he takes the bait and he goes along. After a time it doesn't bother him. He forgets that life was ever different or that there was in fact an alternative. This compromise, it takes its toll. No matter what a man tells himself, he knows. *I* know! All the time I know. And then I found you and I wasn't alone anymore."

"Won't she do, Kurt?"

He tried to smooth her hair, to tuck her head against his chest, but her body was too rigid.

"Did you ever have any intentions of marrying me? Come on, Kurt, you owe me at least the truth. I've given you everything I had to give."

"Lise," he begged her. "Please . . . please . . ."

She slipped out of his arms and walked toward the bedroom.

"What are you doing?" The fear in his voice was unmistakable.

She turned to face him. "I'm going home. I should never have left. I know that now. I guess I really always knew it."

"Please don't leave me," he said. "You haven't understood, goddamnit—you don't know how important you are."

"You lied to me. You're probably lying to her. God only knows how many people you're lying to."

"I love you," he whispered.

"My poor parents," she said as she walked out of the room. "They put so much into a couple of losers."

Yoel Friedman waited for Max in the rear booth of a luncheonette. Max sat opposite him and ordered coffee. The two did not greet each other.

"He'll be along shortly. He's a regular stagehand, a very expensive stagehand. We had to give him six hundred dollars."

"What do we get for it?"

The old man shrugged. "Judge for yourself. The operas are *Cavalleria Rusticana* and *I Pagliacci*."

"Two?"

"Always performed together. Mr. Hitler goes because of the tenor, Placido Domingo; he sings both leading roles. The opera begins at eight sharp. Our friend is the guest of the general manager, which means he will be with him in his box. He is now accompanied by five men; they stay on him like glue."

"Which opera comes first?"

"*Cavalleria Rusticana*. Then there's a thirty-minute intermission while the stage is set up for *Pagliacci*. Both operas are over at eleven. It will be a full house; this is the first time this man Domingo sings both roles."

Max took out a small page of paper, scribbled on it and handed it to Yoel. "I will need some things. A printer who can print this."

"It will be a rush job. But, yes, I can do it."

"A twenty-two pistol with a silencer."

"You will have it."

"And your grandson."

"Oh, God."

"He must wear evening clothes, and he will need a ticket to get into the opera—the seat is unimportant."

"Do you have to use Naftali?"

"And he will need his taxi."

"You'll get him killed. I know it."

"I will call Naftali this evening at seven and tell him what to do."

"Did you hear me, Levy? He's got five bodyguards!"

"I hear you," Max said.

"Then *why*? Against orders, against all odds! Why?"

"For the clowns."

The old man stared at him, uncomprehending. He was about to say something else, but he spotted someone approaching them. "Here's your man," he said.

The man sat down heavily; Yoel Friedman stood and left them.

The man ordered hot tea. "I don't want no trouble," he said.

"Who will be backstage for these operas?" asked Max.

"A pile of people."

"Be precise."

"Eighty-nine stagehands, thirty-three electricians, thirty-five stage carpenters, twenty-one prop men, twenty-eight wardrobe people, five from wig and makeup, and the principals and chorus."

"Tell me about the stagehands."

The man talked in a monotone, as if the lack of expression might somehow absolve him from guilt. "There's the regular stagehands plus the guys from Local One."

"Local One?"

"Union."

Max nodded.

"Stagehands report at seven-thirty to the stage door on Sixty-fourth Street," the man went on. "Then we muster in the lounge, stage left."

Max nodded again. "I need to see something."

"What's that?"

"Placido Domingo's dressing room."

"He always uses 5B. They're funny about things like that."

"I have to see it."

"Tomorrow night. The old man said whatever it is you want to do, and I don't want to know what that is—tomorrow night."

"Yes. But now, too."

"That wasn't part of my deal."

"How much?"

The man stared at his tea. "Another hundred."

Max handed him the money beneath the table. The man shoved it down into his pants pocket and said, "Let's go."

32

Kurt and Liedtke were in Kurt's suite awaiting a telephone call from the Chancellor. Liedtke was unusually quiet —and, Kurt noted, avoiding his eyes.

"I trust she got off all right?" said Kurt.

"She did."

"No scene?"

"None. In fact she said nothing."

"There was nothing to say."

"She's a nice girl," said Liedtke.

"A wonderful girl!" said Kurt, looking at the telephone.

"I wonder what will happen to her?" said Liedtke.

"That's a stupid question, you know. Life will happen to her. Sometimes it will be good and sometimes bad. Sometimes she'll cope and sometimes she'll give up. Years will accumulate and she'll die. And guess what, Liedtke—that pretty well sums up the rest of us, too."

"I suppose so."

"Mr. Liedtke, if you have something on your mind, something to say, which you so obviously do, I really would prefer that you go ahead and say it."

"I liked her."

"Hell, man, I loved her!"

"Well, then—what happened?"

"I met someone."

"That woman I've been reading about?"

"Kindly do not refer to Mrs. Abramson as 'that woman.' Believe me, those words don't do her justice."

"I'm sure they don't."

"You've never known such a woman, Liedtke, and I say that knowing full well that women are your field of specialty."

"Does she love you?"

"Yes."

"The way Lise does?"

"Did."

Liedtke shook his head. "No, that one will always love you."

"Mrs. Abramson is a unique woman. So are her feelings."

"Do I have permission to say something?"

"By all means, Liedtke."

"At such times one must exercise great caution not to confuse one's groin area with one's heart. As wonderful as the groin area can be, it can't sustain a lifetime."

"I am not a child, you know. I assure you, there's much more to it than that—though you would agree that's not exactly a point against her."

"Still . . ."

"Why, Liedtke, I'm afraid that good Jewish blood is rearing its head. Your conversation has suddenly gone Talmudic. How convenient that your long-lost morality should suddenly be found in judgment of someone other than yourself."

"I judge myself, believe me!"

"You do it very quietly, I must say."

"I am a weak man," Liedtke said softly. "You are not."

The telephone rang, and the two men stared at it as if the call was not expected.

"Well?" Kurt said finally.

"One moment," said Liedtke. He handed the telephone receiver to Kurt, who sat on the bed and lit a cigarette.

"Hello, Mr. Chancellor."

"I assume you know about my press conference?"

"I do."

As the old man talked about the need for public confidence and the importance "now more than ever" of the terrorists' trials continuing, Kurt felt good. For the first time in their relationship, the Chancellor needed him. For the first time it was no longer necessary to defer. Kurt liked not deferring. That was not his destiny, and as Josef Haack prattled on he remembered the day when he had learned that destiny.

"Do you know me?" the man with the briefcase had asked him. "Bormann, Martin." The man answered his own question as though filling out a form.

The Chancellor sounded perplexed. "Frankly, Kurt, I would have thought that you would have leapt at the opportunity. Which goes to show you how much we really know each other!"

"I haven't turned you down, Mr. Chancellor, I just said I'd like a little time to consider it." Across the room, Liedtke's face was showing his shock and disbelief. Kurt winked.

"As usual, time is the only thing we don't have . . ."

The man reached out, grabbed his hand and pulled him close as though he might kiss him. "Don't you know?"

"I don't know what you're talking about. And you're hurting my hand!"

"Sit down and listen," the man ordered. "You are the son of Adolf Hitler."

"I don't believe you. I think you're crazy, and if you don't get out of this house I'll shout for help!"

"Would matching fingerprints convince you?" The man opened his briefcase.

"Accepting this position all but assures that you will be my successor," Josef Haack said.

"That job is a killer," said Kurt.

The old man laughed. "It hasn't killed me . . ."

Kurt studied the fingerprints, identified as "Baby Boy Hitler," then his own, which Bormann had just taken. He lowered the magnifying glass slowly. "They match."

"Of course."

"What do you want with me?"

"My boy, it's not what I want. It's what you want. The choice is simple. You can be who you have been: the son of the good Dr. Hauser. Or . . ."

The proud old man was unable to hide the note of desperation in his voice. "If you do not accept, my government will not last a week. I've been at it for a long time—too long, perhaps that's the problem. I had hoped that I would not end my public service being forced from public office."

"None of us wants that, of course . . ."

Bormann was in a hurry. Quickly he sketched a plan involving Kurt Hauser, a group of the richest and most powerful men in Germany, and half a billion dollars. "Well?" he demanded, his face leaning into Kurt's.

"I need time to think about all of this. My God, man, you've just turned my whole world over!"

"Of course. Take time. Take all the time you need."

"I've had a good life as Dr. Hauser's son, you know."

Bormann smiled. Kurt looked into his eyes for a moment, turned away.

Josef Haack was running out of inducements. "I need you, your country needs you. If you do not accept, you are not the man I thought you were."

Kurt smiled. He'd known what was coming. Across the room Liedtke watched in disbelief.

"Well, then, I can hardly refuse, can I?"

"As to the good doctor. He is getting old, dangerously old, and he is not one of us."

"He is . . . he has been my father!"

"But he is not your father. He is a man on the verge of senility. He has earned peace." He held out a tiny blue capsule. "One night, soon, give him peace. In a glass of warm milk or a cup of tea. He will have no peace if he lives until your identity is revealed. The autopsy, which in a man his age would be highly unlikely, will show heart failure."

He studied Kurt closely, a tiny smile at the corner of his lips.

Josef Haack's voice sounded ten years younger: "Then you accept?"

"I do."

"God bless you, dear boy, God bless you!"

Kurt held out his hand for the capsule.

He replaced the telephone in its cradle slowly. Liedtke

looked dazed. "Why did you put him through that?"

"Through what? I'm weary of your questions, Liedtke; save them for another day. Now kindly inform the security men I am meeting Mrs. Abramson downstairs in the Palm Court. Liedtke, do you hear me?"

"Yes, I hear you."

Max and the stagehand took a subway to Lincoln Center and entered the Metropolitan Opera House through a small security office on Amsterdam Avenue opposite Sixty-fourth Street. The office was manned by two uniformed guards and contained a switchboard worked by two operators.

One of the policemen waved in recognition, and they went through a door.

In front of the stars' dressing rooms was a lounge area with chairs and couches where family and a few invited friends could wait.

The stagehand opened the door to 5B; he and Max stepped inside and closed the door behind them. The room contained a Formica-topped dressing table of red birch with a built-in sink and drawers and a completely lighted mirror above it. A full-length triple mirror was mounted on another wall. There was a small side chair at the dressing table, a chaise longue, even a piano for the singer to warm up his vocal chords if he so desired. There was also a small bath with shower.

Max looked into the bathroom, nodded, then closed its door. He went to the windows and turned the handle, and they opened out onto Amsterdam Avenue.

The stagehand watched him intently. "Only windows in the whole opera house that can be opened, these in the singers' dressing rooms and in the general manager's office."

"Why?" asked Max.

"Singers aren't much on air conditioning, they want fresh air."

Max nodded and said, "That's all."

As they left the building, the stagehand said, "Jesus, I

hope I haven't bought myself a pisspot full of trouble."

But he was expressing this sentiment to himself, because Max Levy was gone.

The maître d' at the Palm Court greeted Kurt with a bow and escorted him to Diane's table. She was sipping at a martini.

Kurt leaned down and kissed her. "Somehow you manage to look more beautiful each time I see you."

"How's my Minister?"

"I only just this minute accepted," he said.

Her eyes were wide and innocent. "You make it sound like a big decision!"

"It was. Believe it or not, I'm not eaten up with ambition."

She cupped both hands to her lips and formed a megaphone into which she said, "Bullshit."

"Your language is terrible," he said, cupping the megaphone with his hand.

"Will you discipline me? Will you make me be a good girl?"

He burst out laughing. "Yes, but not in the Palm Court. Oh, isn't that lovely?"

The violinist was playing something Kurt knew but couldn't identify.

" 'Fascination.' "

"I beg your pardon?"

" 'Fascination.' "

"You really are," he said. His hand lay atop hers on the table.

"Is that all I am?"

"No. You're more than that." He squeezed the hand.

"I know it," she said.

"So what's next?"

"I was thinking the same thing myself."

"What would you like?" he asked calmly.

"You."

"You have me."

She shook her head. Her dark hair whispered about her shoulders. "For tonight, for tomorrow. Then you go home. I'm afraid your schedule's highly publicized."

"What about you, Diane? What's your schedule?"

She took a tiny sip of her martini, then put the glass down and felt along its bottom with a long fingernail. "What do you want it to be?"

He signaled for more drinks. "Are you serious?"

"You'd better believe it."

"All right. First I want you to accompany me to the opera."

She frowned. "I hate that crap, loud braying and screeching."

For a moment he thought of Lise, then killed the thought before it could take hold. "You'll learn to love it," he said.

"That sounds like an order."

"That's exactly what it is." He lifted his glass.

"I *am* an American citizen, you know."

"Oh? I could have sworn I heard you call me 'your Minister.' "

"Touché," she said, toasting him.

He covered both her hands with his. "Then I want you to join me. Wait a week or two and let me get settled in my new position."

"I don't think I want to be your mistress."

"I don't think I want you to be my mistress."

She signaled for the maître d'. "Ask the violinist to play 'Dancing in the Dark,' " she said. When the song began she looked at Kurt. "Is that a proposal?"

"That's exactly what it is."

"How unromantic."

"We Germans are a cold lot. Well?" Miraculously, his voice was steady.

"There are a few things I want to know before I give my answer."

"My heart is in excellent condition. Ask away."

"But will you tell the truth?"

"I doubt it," he said, and they both laughed.

The smile on her face vanished. "What after minister?"
"For God's sake, Diane, I haven't even been confirmed!"
"Chancellor?"
"That's the silliest—"
She took her hands from under his and folded them. "Don't play games with me except in bed. Chancellor?"
"It's a possibility." Inside, he was singing.
"Goddamnit, when?"
"He's very old, he won't run again and that leaves—"
"You." She pointed a finger at him like a pistol. "And after?" Her voice was husky, as it was when she was sexually excited.
"There is no after; Chancellor is as high as you can go in Germany."
"To be sure," she said blandly.
Kurt smiled and locked his fingers into hers.

33

Max climbed the dark stairs, exhausted. The day had lasted a lifetime, and he knew that what he sought from her was nothing less than rebirth. He had never sought it from another human being, only from the soil, and he needed it now with a quiet desperation that he had never before allowed to surface.

He stopped at her door, took out the key she had given him and turned the lock. The room was dark, but he could see her outstretched on the bed, lying on her stomach, her face on the pillow away from him. He knew immediately that she was not sleeping.

He sat on the bed and waited for her to speak. He wanted to ask her what was wrong, he wanted to say something, but he couldn't. The wall that was in him blocked his heart and his throat, and he sat like a dumb mute, staring at her form in the shadows.

"I got turned down," she said. When he didn't answer she

sat up and faced him. "Did you hear what I said? I didn't get the part."

He looked at her.

"Don't you have anything to say?"

"I'm sorry."

"You are? Are you really? I don't know about you, I don't know about you at all."

He wanted to tell her how tired he was and that he wasn't certain about what might happen tomorrow. He had made his telephone call to Naftali, had given the boy instructions and been informed that the United States Treasury Department had added five men to Kurt's security detail. How could he tell her that there was more than a possibility that he would die, that he would never return to her and this dingy room?

"I know about me," she said. "This place has given me the message loud and clear. They don't want me, Max. In this whole effing city, no one, not a soul wants Cassie. I'm the man without a country."

"No," he whispered, so softly she wasn't sure she'd even heard him.

"C'mere, Max," she said and held her arms out to him. "Well, don't just sit there, c'mere. I won't bite you. There's something I want to know, you see—hell, *I've got to know*. Here, put that arm around me, now this one, there, that's almost the way they do it in the movies. Come closer, damnit!"

He held her at arm's length, his arms loosely about her.

"Oh, Max," she said, defeated. "Don't *you* even want me?"

His lips moved, trying to form words: his fingers opened on her back in a gesture begging forgiveness.

She ran her hand through his hair, she moved closer and her lips were against his face. She kissed his cheek and his nose and his chin and finally she pushed her mouth against his, wedged her tongue between his sealed lips, removed it and sat back on her haunches.

"What's the matter?" she asked like a child. "How in the world did you get so froze up?"

He shook his head. It was the best he could do.

She sighed. "Do you like me?"

"Yes."

"A lot?"

"Yes."

"Can you do anything about it, Max?"

"I don't know."

"Jesus Christ."

He looked at her steadily. "Want to find out?" she asked him. "If you can't, so you can't. I mean, neither one of us'll make it a big deal."

He didn't answer.

She said, "Nobody wants me." And felt his arms reach out, not holding but holding on. He rubbed his face against hers and she became aware that this strange man was silently weeping.

She drew back her head and looked up at him to see if the expression on his face had changed. It hadn't, it was locked in place and still tears came from his eyes, and she drew him to her like a child and laid his head against her breast, patted and comforted him and said, "Oh, Max, I do love you."

Her words struck him like trip-hammers. The last time he had heard them had been on a train. They had said them together, his mother and father; they had spent the night kissing him and telling him that they loved him.

It was all they had left to give, all they had time to give; the engine was squeezing them to death. They tried to cover him with a blanket of sweetness in the sour stench, and they had encapsulated him, closed him away in a place with no exit.

He had remained in it: love had both protected and frozen him; his sanity had not snapped, but the humanity in him had been shut down.

Now Cassie was kissing the tears from his face and repeating her words of love. He sat up and put a finger to her lips the way one might quiet a child; she kissed the fingers and pressed her lips into his hands. It was as if she were drinking from his cupped palms.

"How much time have you got?" she asked him, her face still down.

"Tomorrow night."

"Holy Jesus! I guess you've got to, huh? Stupid question, I know, but . . . well, are you gonna be okay?"

"I don't know."

"And if you are, I mean if things go all right—well, what'll you do, you know, where'll—"

"Home."

"Oh, sure. Tomorrow night, huh?"

"Yes."

She looked down at her own hands and then she looked at him. "Stand up," she said, and when he did she began to work at his clothes until he was naked and standing like a statue.

"You've got some build," she said, and started undressing herself. When her clothes had dropped to the floor, in a pile atop his, she got under the covers and lay on her side facing him.

"Come to bed, Max," she said.

He joined her under the covers; their bodies were almost touching.

"We don't have much time," she said, "so come close 'cause I don't want to be cold."

Now he was up against her, their breaths mingled, and she reached down with a hand and touched him, gently caressed him until she realized that he wasn't going to respond. She removed her hand and wrapped both arms about him. When their lips touched, he said, "Just you, Cassie."

She smiled, told him with her arms that she understood, and they slept.

Until, to the sound of bass and fife, to the laughter from a thousand throats, the clowns began their performance on the stage of his mind and he cried out in troubled sleep.

She pressed him to her and whispered, "Shhh, I'm with you, I'm with you."

Max Levy slept.

34

Kurt's security detail was now so large that he found it embarrassing. "In our dinner jackets we look like a flock of penguins," he whispered to Diane.

"I love it," she said.

Kurt squeezed her hand. His own excitement was a strange mixture. As in the old days, he looked forward with childlike anticipation to the tenor's triumph, to the heroics and intrigues of a manageable world that in a given time had a beginning, a middle and, with the curtain's fall, an end.

At another level—a level that he would have preferred not to intrude on this evening, one discovered with the entry of Martin Bormann into his life—there was also excitement of a different kind, a different texture. This was the excitement of reality: it had an edge that could and would cut, a depth to be afraid of—and, above all, heights to be gained far exceeding the dreams or imagination of other men.

Kurt and Diane were standing before the Chagalls flanking the Metropolitan Opera House Grand Tier and facing the patterned windows looking out upon Lincoln Center Plaza. He thought of old Zimmer, who would no doubt present a bill for a hundred trillion deutsche marks, the ancient thief! And Willi. Good old Willi. The insurance man would bleat and cry, and who could cry like Willi Fassmann?

"See," said Kurt, pointing to a gypsy in the painting, "he even included Rudolf Bing! Geniuses can also have a sense of humor."

The thought occurred to him: What did the old men really want? Zimmer had more money than anyone he knew—except, he thought, squeezing her hand, Diane. Did Zimmer want more medals? And Willi? Was it possible that Willi could have more government contracts? Everything and everyone in Germany was insured now except the unborn. Perhaps Willi had a plan for that. And General Wahlen. A higher rank? More armies? Tanks? Nuclear bombs? Or Terbach, the labor man. Who *wasn't* organized in Germany? The dead. The unborn and the dead, fertile fields.

And Oestreich, Kurt thought with a shiver, more intrigues? Blood? More blood? An opportunity to use the contents of that ring one more time? And Vieten? What did a man like Amgard Vieten really want? And their new Lybian compatriot? No mystery there. The blood of Jews and everyone else who stood in the way of that mystical dream that made his eyes swim.

They were ascending the red-carpeted Grand Staircase, a sculptured free form molded of concrete, bordered by Italian Cremo marble, capped with hammered bronze handrails. Diane looked at it with a critical eye.

"Well?" asked Kurt, amused.

"Later," she promised, and the thought came to him that people like her *gave* staircases like this one.

God knew there was plenty for everybody, even that unbelievably greedy lot! He hoped they wouldn't make trouble. From now on they would operate exactly—*precisely*—as he ordered.

A fragment of Shakespeare he had not remembered for years came to him: "Thou many-headed monster thing; who would wish to be thy king?"

He almost laughed aloud. It was hard to climb so high, so fast, without picking up delusions along the way.

"Penny for your thoughts?" Diane asked him. "You're grinning like the Cheshire Cat."

"I'm thinking about Placido Domingo, singing one role right after another, and in *this* opera house. The man's got guts, he's proven that, and after I hear him sing I'll tell you what else he's got."

"I can't wait for your verdict," she said with a straight face.

He smiled at her, his eyes complimenting her gold-threaded chiffon gown and sable-trimmed bolero.

Now they were being greeted warmly by the Metropolitan's general manager, to whom Kurt quickly apologized for his "entourage." The manager was gracious and quickly put

Kurt at his ease, whereupon the two men launched into mutual anticipation of Domingo's performance that evening.

Kurt was all questions: Had Domingo ever sung the roles of Turiddu and Canio, "the heavenly twins," in a major house?

"Yes, in San Francisco, in the new Ponnelle production with great success, and in Verona. But the Met, we're a world to ourselves."

"Do you hear that, Diane?" Kurt said.

"Yes."

They would have to do things his way. It was as simple as that, and he hoped they knew it. They were no longer important.

He studied Diane out of the corner of his eye.

She was important, the bitch.

The maniacal sexual excesses. The gutter language. The price to be paid. He thought of Dr. Hauser's thanking him for the warm milk. And Lise . . .

Emptiness in him. Never filled? Goddamnit, *he needed her*! Time. Of course, time. Time would cure . . .

They were on the Parterre level, standing before a door bearing a small gold plaque and the words, EXECUTIVE BOX.

The chief security man said, "Please," opened the door, went in first and then beckoned to them. Embarrassed, Kurt shrugged. The general manager smiled; Diane seemed pleased. "Like a Hitchcock film, wouldn't you say?"

The door leading into the box's anteroom was painted the garnet red of the plush walls and carpets. The mirrored walls set off the cut-crystal lighting fixtures. Four of the security men remained in the anteroom, the other three accompanying Kurt, Diane and the general manager into the box.

As they took their seats, the lights dimmed and the crystal chandeliers suspended from the white dome of the auditorium began their brilliant journey to the ceiling.

Soon the house was in darkness. The conductor made his way into the pit, bowed to the audience and to the orchestra, and began the overture to *Cavalleria Rusticana.*

Kurt sat hypnotized, past and present and future all forgotten as he surrendered his conscious mind to Mascagni's passionate lyricism and to Domingo's dark, brilliant tenor.

To the general manager he whispered, "My God, what a voice!" At the end of the performance he stood with everyone else, applauding maniacally and sending bravos toward the stage. He's like a child, Diane thought, pleased because she knew that *she* was not like a child.

"The question is, can he give that much in *Pagliacci,*" said Kurt. "He didn't hold a thing back!"

"Well, I certainly hope so," said the general manager, delighted by his guest's excitement. The two men laughed, having no doubts: they would hear a Canio equal to that of the late Richard Tucker, who had undertaken the role toward the end of his career.

A private passageway led from the general manager's box to his office suite at the southwest corner of the Parterre level. The general manager had wanted to entertain Kurt in the Eleanor Belmont Room, a proposal instantly vetoed by security. Instead, the distinguished guest and "the world's number-one opera fan" would receive members of the company in the general manager's office.

And what members! Looking about the room, Kurt recognized Montserrat Caballé, Shirley Verrett, Jon Vickers, José van Dam, and conductors James Levine, Karl Böhm, and Richard Woitach.

Kurt whispered to his host, "Do I dare ask for autographs?"

The man laughed and said, "That's exactly what they want of you!"

Kurt was duly introduced to all of them. As the champagne flowed, he said to Diane, "This is the night of my life!"

"That's what you told me night before last," she said.

The lights flickered; it was time to return to the box.

The chandeliers again disappeared into the ceiling, and *I Pagliacci* began.

35

Midway through the performance there came a gentle tap at the anteroom door. A security man sprang to his feet and opened the door to admit a young red-haired man in formal dress with a name tag on his lapel. He handed the security man a small envelope with Kurt's name on it; the security man took it, looked inside the anteroom and ordered one of his colleagues to "get the chief."

In a moment the head of the security detail was in the hall, examining the envelope with a pocket flashlight. It contained a small, folded informal card. On its front was engraved PLACIDO DOMINGO. Inside, in heavy black ink, was a message: "I will be pleased to receive Mayor Hitler in my dressing room immediately following *Pagliacci*." It was signed with the initials, P.D.

"Shit," said the security chief, who wanted to get Kurt out of the opera house and into Diane's limousine as quickly as possible.

With a sigh, he returned to the box and handed Kurt the resealed card. Kurt tore it open with nervous fingers. On the stage the clown stood over the bodies of his victims, his beloved Nedda and her lover, and cried out hoarsely, *"La commedia e finita!"*

The orchestra swelled to the final somber chords of "Vesti la giubba," and 3,900 people went absolutely crazy.

Kurt read the message and flashed a radiant smile to the general manager. "This must be your handiwork!" he said.

The man smiled back, perplexed. "I wish I could take the credit, but no, it's strictly Placido's idea, God bless him!"

"Well, then, let's hurry," said Kurt and left the box, Diane and his guards close by.

Not far from the anteroom they got into an elevator which took them down one flight to the stage level. There they went through the stage door, past the stage manager's desk and across the rear of the enormous stage to the dressing-room lounge.

"Can I come with you?" asked Diane.

Kurt shook his head and smiled, "Perhaps, my dear, someday you'll earn an invitation."

He was about to open the door to 5B when a security man stepped in front of him. "One moment," he cautioned, and rapped on the door.

A voice from within called, "Come in!" The security man opened the door and saw the clown, sitting at his dressing table. He motioned to Kurt, who entered and closed the door behind him, leaving the security team spread out about the lounge area. Diane sat in a chair and tapped her foot, not bothering to hide her impatience.

"I'm honored indeed," Kurt said to the back of Domingo, who sat at the dressing-room table. "Your performance was beyond anything I—"

He stopped as the clown turned, pointing a .22 automatic at his head.

So that was how death looked.

"You're going to kill me," he said.

"Yes."

"The tenor! Where's Domingo?"

The .22 was waved toward the bathroom door. "He is unharmed."

Kurt stepped forward; the .22 prodded him back. "One loud word and you are already dead. Sit."

Kurt sat on the edge of the chaise longue, his legs crossed. The two men were less than three feet apart. Were it not for the gun, they might have been close friends chatting.

Outside they could hear the great sets being moved. It sounded like thunder. Faintly, congratulations were being called to someone, and someone with a deep bass voice laughed. There was the faintest noise from the bathroom, something muffled.

Both men listened intently.

"I hope this doesn't anger you," Kurt began, "but I think

you should know: I've been expecting you. I've been aware of your presence in my life for so many years, I almost feel as though I know you. You were inevitable. May I satisfy one point of curiosity? Why? I mean specifically—*why*? How did my father hurt you? Loved ones? Parents? Little brothers and sisters? In battle? In a camp? In snow? In the desert when the tanks stopped? How did he hurt you? I would like you to tell me and then . . . then I will tell you how he hurt me."

No answer.

"Does it surprise you that I am also his victim? Did you look upon me as some kind of inheritor, the claimant to a will? He left only horror. Only guilt. Only shame. Believe me, there were no claimants, no voluntary ones. Only me, leading a reasonable, normal life until that maniac in Rio dragged me from my bed into hell—and to this moment! So you see, there was a knock on my door, too; I too was transported to a place I did not want to go and to a destiny that I had not sought."

The trapeze artist, Zeevi, squeezing through the train window, all of them watching, a silent audience. The voice of Max's father: "Good luck." Zeevi, grinning: "This one I can do in my sleep." Gone.

"I never knew him—though that doesn't matter, I guess. My God, my God in heaven, what we inherit! To be owned by a life we never knew, misshapen into a sideshow freak by the accident of birth. It would be funny it's so ludicrous. Unless it's yourself, and then it's not funny at all."

No answer.

"A psychiatrist would call it a schizophrenic existence. Being who you are, who you've been raised to be, who you like being, and then suddenly, without warning, becoming someone else, being something that can bring you only pain and torment and not being able to do a damned thing about it. Nothing! Goddamnit, man, I liked Kurt Hauser. He was . . . well, he was a serious-minded young fellow, a bit of a loner, he had his studies, a woman, some music. Being him was a good time, the best time in my life, the last good time in my life. I should have liked it to go on forever. But, well, things didn't work out, did they? I guess they seldom do, and you try not to be bitter about it all, but still, there is this voice that won't be quiet and it does say late in the night, 'It might have been so different . . .' "

Doub Doub, applying ash to his eyes: "Max Levy, I, Doub Doub, now like this thing I was forced to do. If I live it is what I will do. . . ." Gone.

"There is something about you that disturbs me more than that gun. It's your lack of reaction. I should like to think that in the last moments of my life someone is listening, but with you I can't tell. I don't even know if you hear me. It's a small thing, but right now it somehow seems terribly important. You do hear me? You are listening?"

No answer.

Kurt shrugged and smiled, as if bemused. "This Kurt Hitler, now he's quite something else. You see, I really don't know who he is—or what, if anything, he wants. There are people who assume he wants what his father wanted—and they are wrong! The terrible thing, for all parties concerned, for all their dreams of empire, is that if Kurt Hitler could have only one thing, could you possibly guess what it would be?"

He leaned forward. Their faces were inches apart, and Max could smell his breath as he whispered like a lover.

"To be Kurt Hauser! Did you hear me? Come on, man, nod, stop smiling, do something to let me know that you heard that." He shouted. "To be Kurt Hauser!"

The .22 signaled him to speak softly. He sat very still, his arms clasped behind him, his face lifted as though seeking the sun. He brought his head down very slowly until he was staring Max straight in the eyes.

"Baader-Meinhof? Are you a member? I have this need to know who you are, call it a right. A man ought to know who—you're not, are you? Your accent . . . of course, of course! Israeli. Wasn't Eichmann enough? Won't one monster suffice? I'm not even the genuine article. I neither hunt nor fish. I've never knowingly killed anything in my life! So much for your monster. If you stuck me in a glass booth, what could

I tell? I never even knew him. Never! I have visited the camps and I have cried and I have known shame, I have known guilt. Do you believe me? *Do* you believe me? I need to know!"

The commandant: "What? Are the clowns no longer funny?" Gone.

"Dead, I'm an oddity, a footnote in one of those compendiums that keep records of the bizarre, but alive I could do so much good! I *would* do good; I am a good man who would do good things. A man like me, whether you see it or not, could make the earth, the whole bloody earth, better! I am who I am and in me there is good!"

No answer.

Now he was speaking quietly, earnestly. "In a way you could say I'm a Jew. Isn't what's happening to me at this very moment the story of the Jews? Am I not being hounded, murdered, not for what I've done—because I've done nothing —but for who I am? Isn't that the story of the Jewish people? Guilty because you are Jews?"

Clowns vanishing in slime. Gone.

"I would beg forgiveness, but what have I done?"

No answer.

"You fucking, miserable Christ-killer! You hooknosed, inferior, kike swine! You moneylending Shylock, you sheeny motherfucker. Jew-bastard! *He knew*! He knew you well and he almost got you. Oh, but he came close. He's loved for it, did you know that, you Yid cocksucker? They voted for me because *I am his son*! They still love him, they love *me*!"

No answer.

"The world hates you, did you know that? Your money buys you smiles and courtesy, but we hate you! We all hate you! Your blood contaminates mankind! Your nigger skin pollutes civilization!"

And the clown spoke. "Laugh."

Kurt was weeping softly. "What's that?"

"Laugh."

"You're a madman."

"Lachen!"

"Laugh? Why should I laugh? You want to kill me and *I don't want to die*!"

"Lachen!"

"Why?"

"Because I am a clown. Clowns make people laugh."

Kurt had begun to laugh when the sound came: *pffsst*.

The .22 slug was buried between his eyes.

The clown stood and removed his costume. Then he opened the window and crawled through it and got into the back of Naftali's taxi, waiting on Amsterdam Avenue.

"To the airport," said Max Levy.

36

All of Germany was in mourning. The funeral would be held that afternoon in Berlin. Police were prepared for a crowd of half a million.

Josef Haack sat in the Chancellor's bungalow. He did not know what to do next or to whom he might turn. Later he would fly to Berlin for the funeral.

Now he waited for Colonel Klause, who headed the Bundesnachrichtendienst, the Federal Intelligence Service. The colonel had urgently requested a meeting.

Peter Salman ushered in the colonel, who solemnly shook Haack's hand. Colonel Klause was a man known for his composure under all circumstances, but Josef Haack immediately sensed that he was here on this of all days for a very important matter.

The colonel carried a briefcase, which he did not set down. The Chancellor asked him to be seated and then waited patiently for the man to begin.

The colonel glanced at Peter Salman, sitting in his familiar corner. "I'm sorry, Mr. Chancellor, but I would prefer to speak to you in privacy."

The Chancellor nodded to Salman, who left the room. The Chancellor, normally patient, said, "Well?"

Colonel Klause took a key from his pocket and unlocked the briefcase. He removed an envelope, from which he took out a manila file stamped TOP SECRET.

In the name of God, thought the Chancellor. Not today.

Colonel Klause cleared his throat. "Ten minutes after word was received in Germany, I received a telephone call."

Josef Haack thought: I received ten thousand telephone calls.

"The call was from a man who wanted to be an informant."

The Chancellor's ears perked up. "Wanted to be?"

"This man hoped to trade his absolute noninvolvement for details on a plot in which Mayor Hitler was the leading participant."

"A plot, Colonel? What kind of plot?"

The colonel did not answer the question. Instead he said, "I agreed to this man's proposal."

"Shouldn't you have checked with me?"

"The man was adamant that you not be consulted on the matter of his freedom. In fact he gave me exactly sixty seconds to give him my decision. He stipulated that if every shred of information that he gave me, including documents, was not found to be totally accurate and provable, he could be prosecuted and publicly exposed for his offer."

"Then you did the right thing."

"I hoped you would see it that way. Here it is, all in writing, all documented."

He brought the manila folder to the Chancellor and returned to his chair. The Chancellor began to read silently.

Fifteen minutes later he closed the folder. "My God," he said. "Madmen. All madmen."

"Very dangerous madmen."

"One more try. Old men wanting one more opportunity. I suppose I should be able to understand them, but . . ."

"What are your wishes?"

"Arrest the lot of them immediately."

"My men are watching them now; we will move at once."

"More horror. Germany's curse—horror."

"What shall we do about the informant?"

"I have no earthly idea. Men like me will never know how to deal with men like Willi Fassmann."

The Chancellor sat deep in thought, his head down on his chest. He looked up, aware that Colonel Klause was staring at him. "Was there something else, Colonel?"

"Yes, sir."

"Haven't I seen it all?"

"No, sir. I left something out."

The Chancellor was about to explode with rage. Instead, he said calmly, "Tell me, Colonel Klause."

"The plotters were kept informed of your thinking almost every step of the way."

"What?"

"There was an informant on your staff."

Josef Haack's face was rigid. "Yes?"

Colonel Klause spoke softly, and when he was finished the Chancellor gravely thanked him, his face expressionless, and the colonel wondered at the Chancellor's self-control.

"I was thinking," the colonel said.

"Yes?"

"About Fassmann. It's not right that he should go unpunished again. He is a very bad man. That the worst should somehow survive—"

"What is your suggestion?"

"An accident, perhaps. A car out of control . . ."

"I too am tempted, Colonel. But we must be most careful—"

"Of course!"

"—that we too do not become Willi Fassmanns."

"Yes, sir," said the colonel. He bowed and left; Josef Haack returned to his chair, legs crossed, his fingers tracing the bony curvature of his face. He could feel his skeleton. Life had become death. So quickly.

Frau Umbreit came into the room. She was dressed in black, ready to accompany him to Kurt's funeral.

"You look so tired," she said.

He looked at her. "Colonel Klause was here."

"That man. Secrets. So many secrets."

"He has learned that Kurt was the major figure in a plot, a very dangerous plot, another crazy plot by crazy men."

"I don't believe it!"

"I didn't want to, but it was all documented. Even the names of informants."

She stood. "I will get us a cup of hot tea."

"I would like that," he said, and she disappeared into the kitchen. He sat quietly awaiting her return, and in moments she handed him a cup of tea and sat opposite him, stirring her own cup.

They stared at each other and he took a swallow of tea at the same moment she did.

"I do not understand people," he said.

"You? The wisest of men?" she said.

He asked the question very gently. "Why Frau Umbreit? Why you?"

She stared in astonishment. "Don't you know? All of these years and you don't know?"

"Know what?"

"I love you. But you, Josef, did not love me."

"Frau Umbreit . . ."

Her eyes were getting heavy, and she smiled sweetly and stood on wavering legs. "Now give me your arm, Josef, and take me to my bed. I am very tired and I will sleep forever."

He stood to offer her his arm, and like people in a dream they walked out of the silent room.

Epilogue

In the vineyards of Mishmar Elijah Kibbutz, off the road the Israelis call the Road of Courage, midway between Tel Aviv and Jerusalem, Max Levy bent over the grapes in pleasure beneath a blazing noonday sun.

The loose grainy dirt felt good between his fingers; the warmth felt good on the back of his neck.

The vines were in full bloom. He would thin the shoots, tying the best ones to the slender wires.

A voice called, and he stood upright.

"Hey, Max, it's time for lunch!"

He watched her approach. When she was near, he took her hand and he and Cassie held on to each other and crossed the gravel road.